Bad Aunt

2016

A novel

TOBIAS NCHINDO

Bad Aunt

Copyright ©2016 Tobias Nchindo

First edition: December 22, 2016.

ISBN: 9798227014337

CIP catalogue of this book is available from the National Library of Namibia

Table of Contents

TO GOD

My New Home

The first year I began to remember well was 1990. Grandma Tiwe died, after whom my twin sister was named. Soon after, we lost our parents, and my mother's brother took us in. When we arrived in Katima Mulilo town, we moved into a black neighborhood called South Bauleni. Mrs Susiku, my uncle's wife, stood in the doorway. She was short, almost my height, with dark, kinky hair. Her glasses reflected the fading light, making it hard to read her eyes. But I liked her immediately. There was something about the way she carried herself—calm and kind—that made me want to grow up to be just like her: rich and beautiful.

I leaned into Tiwe, nudging her gently. Her bag was still perched on her head, as if she wasn't ready to put down the weight of all that had happened in the village.

"Town girls don't carry bags like that," I whispered to Tiwe, who gave me that look, then slowly lowered the bag.

Uncle's wife smiled as she patted Tiwe's hair. "Look at you two, so, so beautiful."

She showed us to our room. Inside, two neatly made beds were dressed in blue blankets, and a mirror mounted on the wall caught the fading light. The air felt cool, almost too cool, with a soft hum from the ceiling fan above. I glanced up at the window—the town lights slowly pushing away what was left of our first daylight in South Bauleni. The lights flickered like distant stars, reminding me of the evenings back in the village. We would sit around the fire, the soft glow dancing in our grandmother's eyes as she told us stories. But in South Bauleni, there was no fire, no comforting stories—just town lights that felt very different from the life we once knew in my village.

Tears threatened to spill as I fought against the memories of sorrow. It felt unfair—this new life, stripped of our parent's love. First, we lost

Grandmother Tiwe, then our parents. Each loss wore us down, leaving deep wounds that no city lights could ever heal.

I glanced at Tiwe, hoping for a sign that she shared my feelings, but she was busy unpacking her bag. Was she distracting herself or avoiding the thoughts of what we had left behind?

The sounds of the town floated in through the window—soft chatter mingling with the occasional honk of a car. It was so different to our village, where nights were alive with the chirping of crickets and the all-night barking of dogs.

A gentle knock on the door broke my concentration. Aunt entered. "Are you girls getting settled well?"

"Yes, Auntie," Tiwe replied, with her usual drawled tone.

"I know it's a lot to handle, moving to a new place so soon after... everything." Aunt said, "But you're not alone. We're family, and we'll face this together."

I found myself reflecting on the meaning of family. What did it even mean now? Our real family was gone, leaving behind an emptiness Aunt could never fill. Mother had always understood me completely, even when Father seemed distant. And Grandma Tiwe? She wasn't just family—she was my best friend.

"Dinner is ready," Aunt said.

After we saw our room, which was really nice, and finished dinner, we gathered to watch TV. Aunt shared a sofa with Uncle as we watched a quartet perform. I remembered well the gospel song they sang— My God and I.

"Who is older?" Aunt asked, looking at us with her beautiful smile. "Mukenani or Tiwe?"

"Me," I replied. "But all my village people call me Mu."

Just then, a little boy came from his room and plopped down next to Aunt. He looked around six years old, and despite Aunt introducing us, he didn't seem to pay much attention. His name was Samuel, Aunt's only child.

The next morning, I woke up late, slipping into a long, loose nightdress my father had bought for me at the open market years ago. Tiwe was already in the kitchen with Aunt, preparing breakfast. What I liked most that day was Aunt taking us to the shops to buy new clothes. Back in the village, we yearned for Christmas—it was the time Father would bring us second-hand clothes from the open market in South Bauleni. We called them "*Salaula*," a local trade term meaning "pick through a pile," and wore them proudly on Christmas Day.

It was evening as I prepared for bed, unzipping my bag to pull out my nightgown. A photo slipped out, falling silently to the floor. I stared at the picture for a moment before I picked it up. Mother's beautiful smile looked back at me, her eyes warm and full of life. My fingers tightened around the edges, holding on just a little longer before tucking it back into the bag, pressing it between my clothes.

I let my thoughts drift back to the days I wished I could forget but couldn't. Mother's last days lingered in my memory. I loved helping her in the maize field behind our homestead, yet on that particular day, I had no desire to work. The sweltering sun blazed in the sky, its heat pressing down on us relentlessly. My oversized t-shirt clung to me, soaked in sweat—perhaps that was why, Tiwe, ever lazy, feigned a headache to escape the labour.

"When the sun is so hot on a day like this," Mother said, "it means we'll get bad rain."

Mother ran her middle finger over the white patches on her left arm, and my thoughts were consumed by her skin condition. I couldn't help but ask, "Can't a doctor treat them, Mother?"

"We've been everywhere," she replied. "Every native doctor and herbalist."

As we walked home, her arm draped over my shoulders, worry consumed me—about her condition and how the villagers shunned her.

"How did it happen, Mother?" I asked quietly.

She glanced at her hands and then back at me. "It started when I was sixteen," she said softly. "Just a few patches on the backs of my hands. Now, at thirty-three, they've spread—to my arms, my face, even around my eyes."

When we arrived home, Father wasn't around. Tiwe said he had taken four of our fat oxen to the village Induna. The villagers demanded payment for a native doctor they summoned to uncover the mysteries of Mother's skin condition. In our village, the native doctor's word was law.

TOBIAS NCHINDO

I remember that night very well when the villagers condemned Mother. The drums beat all night, keeping the whole village awake. Elders had summoned the sinister Doctor Kufekisa to reveal the mysteries behind Mother's condition. She sat on a traditional mat, wrapped in a black cloth, as he splashed hot water over her. The fire burned all around to keep everyone warm, while drunks roamed, their noise mingling with the pounding drums. Traditional beer flowed freely, and even neighbouring villagers gathered to seek answers from Doctor Kufekisa, who hailed from Zambia. He blew his whistle, and the villagers, especially those intoxicated, cheered in agreement, chanting along as if he were manipulating them diabolically.

"Gather five white roosters for this ritual," he ordered through his whistle, dancing as he spoke. The swift among them quickly fetched the birds from Father's coup. Doctor Kufekisa whispered to his first wife, who communicated his orders to the other co-wives. They swiftly slaughtered the chickens, splashing Mother with their blood.

"They keep saying," the doctor shouted.

"Who are they, Doctor?" a drunken voice called from the darkness, anonymity cloaking the question, for Doctor Kufekisa could not tolerate nonsense and stupid questions.

Silence fell as everyone awaited the verdict.

"She will be buried alive."

A jolt of adrenaline surged through me. At twelve, I was powerless, watching them bury Mother alive. Father was helpless. When we returned home, no one spoke of it. Father lost the will to live and died a month later.

Tiwe and I lost our parents in 1990. It was supposed to be a good year, but here we are, starting a new life in town. New everything—NEW SCHOOL.

New School

In January 1991, Tiwe and I went to register at South Bauleni Community School. Graffiti was scrawled all over the school walls. The windows cracked or missing and the grade 8 classrooms had no doors. Despite its worn-down appearance and lack of resources, South Bauleni held promise for black students in our little town.

I had heard of Riverweed High, the private school near the river. It was said to have sprawling green lawns, modern facilities, and classrooms filled with sunlight streaming through spotless windows. The students there, mostly Boers and others who weren't black, wore neatly pressed uniforms and spoke of school trips to places we could only dream of. Riverweed felt like a different world, one in movies.

Tiwe and I ended up in different classes, which was new to us. We all sat in our classrooms, obeying every strict instruction from our teachers. When we were little, teachers commanded the respect they deserved and had the authority to punish students however they liked. So, we were forced to pay attention even to the most boring teacher of all time.

Our life skills teacher, Miss Margaret O'Hara, was a white woman whom I liked very much. She was not very short, and her black hair was long and flowing. Miss O'Hara walked between the rows as she gave us the classroom rules. I watched her dutifully; it was the first time a white woman was speaking to me.

"Honey," Miss O'Hara said. "Introduce yourself to the class."

I fidgeted with my fingers, thinking of a better way to start my new school life at South Bauleni.

"My name is Mukenani."

"Beautiful name. Who is next?"

"My name is John. John Sibanga," said the boy, standing there, hands in his pockets with his big, big nose.

"Are you related to our headmaster, Mr Damien Sibanga?"

"Yes, Mistress. Mr Damien Sibanga is my biological father, and I love him very much."

"We love him too, honey," said the teacher.

We all laughed...

After we introduced ourselves, Miss O'Hara made me class captain. I had always liked being the class captain, a position I held many times in our village. I remember my mother once said I was a class captain on my first day of school in grade one. So being class captain wasn't a big deal because I had been one even when I didn't remember. When the bell rang for break, which was the sound of something like a railway rail or crankshaft dangling under the camelthorn tree next to the principal's office, I peered through the broken window and saw the principal hitting it, glancing furtively from side to side as though he didn't want us to see him in action. We crowded the school grounds. Tiwe and I sat under the mango tree, eating our food, which we carried in a plastic bag. Usually, it was fat cakes and sugar water, which was a decent meal during our younger years.

There was a dark girl seated all by herself under the mango tree, and she didn't have any food. She was also my classmate, Lisa.

In class, I sat close to her. I noticed her hair and the worn-out school uniform. She was beautiful, dark and tall—I think she was the most beautiful girl in our class, but she was very poor.

"All right, class," Miss O'Hara said. "Now that we are settled, I want to rearrange our seating into a double horseshoe."

Three days into my new school, I was starting to feel more at home. Some of the teachers were really nice, and I had begun to bond with a few classmates. I was lost in my thoughts, going over the day's events, when Miss O'Hara's clear voice interrupted me. "Let's pair up for this activity," she said. Then, looking at me, she continued, "Mukenani and Lisa, pick a topic from the box on my desk. Go ahead."

Surprised but excited, I locked eyes with Lisa, and we shared a small, nervous smile....

Lisa went on to our topic from the box, glancing at it. I thought she would place it on my desk, but she kept it between her Life Skills handbook. Once everyone had their topics, Miss O'Hara instructed us to research in the library. When we were outside our classroom, I leaned against the wall separating our class from the next. Lisa came out and stood next to me.

"Why do Whites and Blacks attend separate schools even after Namibia got its independence?"

I had never seen a white student in any class before, so I didn't know how to answer her question. Why would she even ask such a thing? In our village, the only white people I had ever seen were those in military uniforms carrying big guns.

"Why do Whites and Blacks attend separate schools even after independence? Our topic."

We had yet to learn where the library was. Back then, kids would laugh at you if you asked for directions. Lisa took a few steps towards the teacher and called, "Mistress O'Hara, where is the library?"

Miss O'Hara took our hands and led us to a small, well-organised room. There were only a few books, and our teacher also served as the librarian. She sat down at a desk facing the door.

"There isn't much to research here, children. Most of our materials are poems and history books," the teacher said. "Frankly, there isn't much you'll find in this library."

During that time, our town had no internet, and our school had no computers. Other learners started coming in. Lisa and I looked around the room; our eyes scanned the shelves to find something that could help. Yet, what met our gaze were rows upon rows of kids' books, dictionaries, Bibles, and a displayed, larger-than-life portrait of our new black president. I gazed at the picture of the president and couldn't help but feel a sense of awe and curiosity. It stood there, representing power and authority. Could the answers we were searching for be connected to this leader? Could we find the guidance we needed within his policies, speeches, or personal beliefs?

"We have nothing here," I said.

"Mistress," Lisa said, "why are you the only white woman at this school?"

Miss O'Hara smiled and whispered, "I enjoy being here..."

Miss O'Hara called out my name, KENAANI, in a way that made me feel so special. Back in my village, they would say MU-KE-NA-NI.

"Mistress," I said, "can we talk about something else?"

"I have an idea," she said, "why don't you do your research at Riverweed? My friend Julitta Smit can help you there."

"Riverweed, the White school!" Lisa snapped. "Bad idea, Mistress. The kids there are not friendly."

"You will never know for sure until you meet them. I will call Julitta. How about tomorrow after school, when the other kids have left?"

I stood there, kind of expecting Lisa to push back, but she just stayed quiet, her face giving nothing away. We had both never been to Riverweed before, and the unknown felt really intense between us. What would it be like there? Would we blend in? My mind was racing with questions, and I couldn't help but think that Lisa might be feeling the same way.

"How do they dress at Riverweed, Mistress?" I asked.

The teacher took out a photo and placed it on the table. It was a picture of a white girl in a pink and black dress and shiny shoes. I looked down at my shoes, new, and then at Lisa's worn-out shoes with two little holes that allowed sand in.

"Who is she, Mistress?" I asked.

"My daughter, Sophia. She's in grade 8. She will be joining this school next year."

"This school!" I said, "but things are not right here, Mistress. No books, broken windows, and the buildings are falling apart."

"Yes," Lisa added. "She will be the only one here."

"I want my daughter to know the importance of diversity, to celebrate our differences, not to discriminate against them. Sophia should grow up in a world where she sees everyone as equal. It is my duty as her mother to teach her that."

"Do you enjoy being here, Mistress? You could have chosen to go to Riverweed."

"I like it here..."

"Mistress," Lisa said, "can we think about it? Maybe going to Riverweed isn't a good idea."

Before we could whine further, the bell signalling the next class rang, and while we were in class, waiting for our English teacher, Lisa had written a sentence. I leaned over to read it. *I like it here.* I was curious why she needed to write that. I wanted to ask, but she answered...

"Mistress O'Hara gave us the answer," she said.

"Why do you say that?" I asked, moving my chair closer to hers.

"You ask too many questions."

"Did I say something wrong?"

"Everything you say is wrong."

I knew she was referring to the torn school shoes and the two little holes in them.

Since then, I knew I wanted to become friends with her. Lisa came from a ghetto location. I am grateful to my teacher for pairing me up with her because we became good friends. When we presented our work, our teacher gave us sweet compliments, which caught the attention of other learners. However, before that, we had to make an important decision about going to Riverweed.

"What do you think about Mistress O'Hara's idea? Should we go to Riverweed?" Lisa asked.

I had never been to a White school before, so I was worried about how we would be treated there. I imagined people staring at us, talking about us behind our backs, and even calling us names like stupid monkeys.

"Do you know where the school is?"

"It's located next to the Zambezi River. I've never been there, either," she said as she leaned over to pick up a fallen pencil.

"Oh, here comes our teacher!" someone shouted, rushing back into the classroom.

Our English teacher was a local man, young and fluent in British English. I often watched him closely during lessons because he sounded so cool. Many of us liked him, as he taught us well despite being late for class. He claimed to be the only teacher at South Bauleni with an advanced diploma in education, but whether that was true or not, who cares?

"Good morning, Mr Lubanda," the class rose immediately.

"I apologise for being late," he said while writing the date on the chalkboard. Even though it was already there, Mr Lubanda erased it and wrote it again.

"Excuse me, Teacher," I asked nervously, "can you tell me where Riverweed is?"

He tensed up, narrowing his gaze. "You need to stay away from Riverweed."

"Why is that?"

"Listen," he replied sharply, "Riverweed isn't a place for kids like you."

"But why not?" I pressed, feeling that there was more to his answer.

His tone dropped, becoming low and serious. "Riverweed is for White people."

"But Mistress O'Hara is White, and she's here," I said, my voice shaking a little but still firm enough to stand my ground.

He hesitated, his face tightening as if my words had hit a nerve. Slowly, he moved closer, and the room seemed to grow quieter with each step.

"Listen, child," he said, his voice dripping with condescension, "you're Black. You belong in this rundown school. Your parents should have taught you better when you started to understand things. You are a Black person, and there are limits you shouldn't even think about crossing."

His words created a heavy silence that filled the room. I stared at him, shocked. We all looked at him, our expressions filled with disbelief. What kind of teacher would say something like that?

After school, I sat under the shelter in the backyard with a Kansas City magazine I was reading. Aunt sat down next to me. I started chatting with her about school, the teachers I found strict, and the headmaster who never seemed to respect us. I also brought up Riverweed in our conversation.

"Don't pay attention to that mean teacher," Aunt said. "Riverweed is such a nice place. The kids there are just doing their own thing, not being mean."

"Mistress O'Hara suggested we visit Riverweed for our Life Skills project."

"I can take you and your friend if you like."

I couldn't help but smile as I thought about Mistress O'Hara. She always made me feel special during her classes. She was kind and encouraging to all her learners, even the ones who struggled. Her words were always uplifting, even when you got a question wrong.

The following day, Aunt woke me up to get ready for school. Tiwe was always up early, and Aunt often advised me about the importance of waking up early. She believed it was a valuable trait for a woman. I trusted Aunt's advice – she always had a good head on her shoulders.

"A woman should wake up early and prepare her home," Aunt said.

After Aunt's advice about waking up early, Tiwe and I left to school where I had a conversation with Lisa in class. I discovered a kind and sweet side of her, but I could sense the pain in her voice. She only said a little and avoided many of my questions.

Lisa lived with her mother, *ba*Eliza, and her younger brother, Moses. She said something about her younger sister, Ima, whom I never met because she lived in Zambia with relatives. Her father passed away when she was young. Despite that, Lisa's mother was so cheerful about life.

During break time, Lisa and I sat under the shade behind the school garden, working on solving Math problems from our workbook. Tiwe came and sat next to Lisa, taking the workbook from her.

"Break is for eating," Tiwe said, dropping the book she sat on. "That teacher always sends me on errands."

I knew the teacher Tiwe was referring to; she had sent me on errands a few times. Her name was Miss Cindy, and she died that same year. We sang at her funeral.

"Speaking of Mistress O'Hara's advice," I began, "we should visit Riverweed. Aunt promised to take us there."

"I was thinking the same thing," Lisa said.

"Isn't that a White school?" Tiwe asked.

"Yes, and they say it's beautiful there. You can join us if you want, Tiwe. Aunt promised to take us there."

"No, I can't."

Two Friends, One School

Riverweed, a two-story building, had hedges that were neatly trimmed. The green gate was huge and stood tall. Aunt pulled up the car, and I couldn't help but feel excitement and nervousness. All at once.

"Welcome to Riverweed," Aunt said, tapping her fingers on the steering wheel.

I walked out first, but Lisa remained seated. I understood her reluctance; her school uniform was faded and second-hand. She must have bought it from someone who attended our school.

"We need to go, Lisa," I urged.

"I don't see Miss Smit anywhere," Lisa fretted. "I don't feel right about this, Mu."

"We're already here. We must find her, or Mistress O'Hara will be so mad."

"We don't belong here, and you know it."

"We can't turn back now," I said. "Please, get out of the car."

Aunt remained silent; she was never one to rush into things...

The school was surrounded by tall palm trees, mostly date palms. I remembered how we trekked for hours in the village to collect dates in the wild.

"Do people grow these here?" I asked Aunt. "We have them in the village, but they grow in the forest."

"You can grow any tree wherever you want," Aunt said.

Aunt turned to smile at Lisa, who still showed no sign of leaving the car. She glanced at the school, and we waited for her to decide. She was making me nervous, and I started to doubt my choice. But who could blame her? Riverweed was different from the schools attended by people like us.

"You need to come out right now," I said in a bit of a tone.

She swung the door open and slowly closed it before Aunt hooted and drove away. We stepped on the pavement, which didn't exist at our school.

At South Bauleni, everyone walked on sand and grass, often treading on little thorns.

"Hurry up, please!"

We stood under the date tree to cool off because the sun was too much. I plucked a ripe date and played with it using my fingers. She held her school bag tightly against her chest.

"This school is so beautiful," she said.

While I watched our surroundings, I noticed the condition of my friend's torn school bag. It wasn't the bag that concerned me but how she held it. With that attitude, she would attract bullies.

"You should carry your school bag properly," I said, adjusting the strap on my shoulder.

"Why?"

"They will say we're from the village."

"But we are from the village, Mu."

Lisa was about to show more resistance when a young man dressed in a dark uniform hurried past us.

"Who's that?" Lisa whispered, as if expecting me to tell her who he was.

"You know I don't know him," I replied.

"Do you think he is a gate man?"

"I think so."

He approached an older woman coming from the school and led her to the gate. We found a spot on a bench under a large, withering tree. We watched them as they left the school grounds, and once they were a bit further away, we began discussing the person assigned to the gate. Our school also had a broken gate, but no one was paid to guard it. It remained wide open, yet we still needed permission from our teachers to pass through. I liked that our teachers upheld strict rules and were not up for negotiation.

When the young man in uniform returned, I wanted Lisa to greet him first so I could assess his reaction.

"He has a gun," said Lisa. "He will shoot us in the head."

"Do you speak English?" He shouted at us as if we had told him we were deaf. English is my country's official language, so I can speak and understand even the weirdest accents.

I stared at the gun he had holstered on his waist. I examined his face closely and realized he wasn't White – he was the closest thing to it, mixed – which meant he was Black. He was a black man, so my conscience allowed me to ask.

"Miss Julitta Smit. Do you know where we can find her?"

"Soccer field – Mrs Jacob's granddaughter, right?"

"Who is Mrs Jacob?" Lisa asked.

"The old lady I led out of the gate," he said. "Oh no, Miss Smit will be so angry. She wasn't supposed to leave the gate. That old lady is always on the move. That's not my duty."

We watched him tear down the narrow path leading to the river. Bushes and rocks surrounded the path, but we could see the river and birds.

"Coming here was a very big mistake," Lisa lamented. "I shouldn't have listened to you."

"Even I didn't want to come here," I whispered, gazing at what looked like an eagle soaring high in the sky.

We sat down and hugged our bags. I turned to face Lisa, but she looked away, upset with me. I understood her anxieties. Her shoes were in worse condition than her uniform, adding to her discomfort.

"We don't fit in here," she continued to complain.

The school was so quiet, with no sounds of learners chatting in class. Only a few labourers were seen outside.

"We should come back another day. This can't be normal – kids can't be this quiet," she said.

I stood and walked towards the signboard, which read *Rivierwier sedert 1964*. I remember that we studied Afrikaans in the village before independence. Our Afrikaans teacher was a village man. In Afrikaans lessons, all we did most was shout non-stop the *baboaan, baboaan*, poem, all day long because the boars said so.

"This school is beautiful," I said. "The learners must be learning good stuffs here."

The interior was just as impressive, with paved walkways, lawns, trimmed trees, and flowers. The buildings were painted orange and blue, with cars parked neatly in front. I chuckled at my silly comparisons when I thought about the few old cars at my school – parked haphazardly in every direction.

"This school is beautiful. I don't get it," I said. "Is this a government school?"

Lisa and I stood gazing at the school and its beautiful landscape with giant trees. In South Bauleni, we cut down most of the trees—even digging out the taproots—to keep our surroundings super clean.

"Do black learners attend this school?"

"I don't think so," Lisa replied.

"What kind of white people go here?"

"Boers and others. I see a lot of them in town."

"The kids at this school seem to have everything. I wish I could be different."

"Different? You mean white?"

"Just different. Attend a better school and learn more. Or live in a town with better schools."

"One day, I will graduate and move to the big city of Windhoek. The schools there are much better."

I could see the seriousness etched on her face. Lisa was destined for greatness; she was a brilliant student and always reading her books. Despite facing challenges as a child, she remained dedicated to her studies. Tiwe and I shared the same passion for learning and excelled in school.

We had no idea what time it was since we didn't have watches, and it had been a while since the gatekeeper went to find Miss Smit's grandmother. We could hear the electric bell ringing.

"There are so many nice things here," I said.

"One day, things will be even nicer for us."

"Do you think so?"

"Yes, Mu, I truly believe that."

We paused for a moment, distracted by the faint noise coming from somewhere on the school grounds. Suddenly, the entire premises became crowded with learners in their uniforms. Lisa and I stood somewhere as the learners passed by, some being picked up by their parents, others riding their bicycles, and a few walking to their homes. We humbled ourselves, forcing a smile on our faces as each child passed. None of them seemed to notice us. I couldn't decide what was more embarrassing—being ignored by them or smiling at them like a fool.

"Stop it," Lisa snapped. "You're making me feel uncomfortable."

"Stop what?" I asked innocently.

"Stop that stupid smile."

I immediately wiped it off. I constantly had a smile on my face, even when I was feeling angry.

"You can't smile at everything, Mu; people hate that," she said with a hint of annoyance.

When the gatekeeper returned with Mrs Jacob, he led us to Miss Smit's house in the school yard. The older woman was quite talkative, and I immediately liked her. Mrs Jacob gently brushed Lisa's hair.

"You are a beautiful child."

"Thank you," Lisa replied, glancing at me.

I felt like I was gaining wisdom because ever since meeting Miss O'Hara, my perspective on white people had changed. We had been taught so many bad things about them, especially in our history lessons. However, meeting my teacher and then Mrs Jacob made me realise that some of them were much kinder than my own father.

"My granddaughter will be here soon. Please have a seat," Mrs Jacob said, tapping on a red sofa.

The house was neat, family photos hanging on the walls and a small black-and-white television playing in the background. I smiled at the little dog breed sleeping on the sofa. Where I come from, dogs are not even allowed to stand at the door or sniff the smell from our pots.

Mrs Jacob picked the dog up, and kissed him, and gently placed him back on the sofa. "Poor Minty," she said. "I forgot to turn on the radio."

"He listens to the radio?" Lisa asked. "Can a dog do that?"

"He enjoys music a lot," Mrs Jacob said, kissing the dog over and over. "I'll give you a bath soon, but first, you must eat."

In our village, dogs rarely get fed—they hustle for a meal. I still remember when we were young, Tiwe brought a puppy home. Father told her to return it to its mother, saying that one dog cannot own another dog.

After feeding the dog, Mrs Jacob offered us tea and some buns. The afternoon sun shone through the sheer curtains. I glanced at Lisa and knew what she was thinking. Where we come from, we don't drink tea on such a hot afternoon.

Mrs Jacob sat down next to her dog, gently massaging its back. I took a moment to observe every corner of the house.

"Mrs Jacob," Lisa said, "what time is Miss Smit coming?"

She checked the wall clock. It was almost three o'clock. Just as the door opened, a medium-built white lady entered, carrying two footballs. I knew right away that she was Miss Smit. Based on Miss O'Hara's description, I had imagined her friend to be slim like her. Miss Smit was a bit larger but had a great figure and a beautiful smile, but a little paler than Miss O'Hara's.

"I'm sorry for being late," she said while dropping the balls. "I hope Grandma offered you something to drink."

"Yes, Miss Smit. I'm Mukenani, and this is my friend Lisa."

"I've heard great things about you," Miss Smit said. "Margaret talks about how smart you are."

Lisa and I sat up straight, watching Mrs Jacob go to her room and return with a photo album. I gazed at the photo on the wall above the TV—a girl riding a BMX bike.

"Oh, that's Sophia, Margaret's daughter," the old lady said, noticing my interest. "She'll be here soon. She's a wonderful child. I'm sure the three of you will be great friends."

If Sophia were anything like her mother, being friends with her might not be a bad idea.

"That photo was taken seven years ago, she's grown up now," Mrs Jacob added. "Oh, did I mention she won last year's singing competition? And I was her coach. Would you like to participate in the contest? I'd love to be your coach."

"Come on, Grandma," Miss Smit interrupted. "You're too old for that. Remember how stressed you got when Sophia lost? You nearly had a heart attack."

I remember our teacher talking about the upcoming music competition, but I didn't pay any attention because I'm still a bad singer. However, Lisa was different—she had a good voice. She always stood out in our school choir and was always chosen as the lead singer during school events. Lisa once said she plans to audition for the National Gospel

Contest when she finishes her studies. If she were to win, she would then go on to compete in the African Gospel Contests, where the winner would represent Africa at the World Continental Gospel Contest. Africa has never won that contest, but Lisa believed that she or someone from her generation could change that outcome.

"I hope you didn't go near the river today, Grandma. Last week…"

"I know what happened last week, Julitta. Last week, a crocodile killed someone," she said. "Everyone watched that dreadful incident on TV. Such a tragedy, someone's husband."

"He was just a child, Grandma."

"Yes, but he had his whole life ahead of him."

Around four o'clock, Mrs Jacob dozed off, allowing us to discuss our project with Miss Smit. Lisa took out a notebook from her school bag while I contemplated memorising everything.

"The qualities of a good student include taking notes," Miss Smit said.

"Miss Smit," Lisa asked, "why do white and black learners still attend separate schools even after gaining independence?"

"Pretty much everything remains the same," Mrs Jacob said as she came from her room. "I've been to South Bauleni and wouldn't even recommend it to my worst enemy."

"Please, Grandma, don't say that to the children. And wait a minute, you were snoring just now."

"It's difficult to get fresh air this time of the year," Mrs Jacob said as she sat down and pulled out the Bible from under the table. She sprawled on the sofa and began reading.

"I wasn't sure if saying that blacks are still seen as inferior to whites would be considered racist," Miss Smit said. "But if you look at the state of schools in our society, it seems like all the rundown and broken ones are for black students."

"Our president is black now," I said.

"Yes, dear," she replied. "Let's give him time, things will improve."

"Even after a hundred years, things might not change or could even worsen," Mrs Jacob said.

"Grandma!" Miss Smit exclaimed. "Be selective with your words."

"These kids deserve the truth, Julitta."

"Can't you say it more tactfully?"

We learned a lot from our meeting with her. She expressed hope that one day, black children would attend Riverweed. After we left, she gave us each a magazine and a pen. We couldn't say goodbye to Mrs Jacob because she was coughing and snoring.

"I'm sorry Sophia is not yet home. Say hello to Margaret for me."

Once we left, Aunt was waiting at the school gate with Samuel and Tiwe. We dropped off Lisa and then drove home. It was Samuel's birthday. When we got home, we started preparing everything and even danced around. While dancing in the kitchen, I noticed a shadow at the window. I went to open the door and saw a woman I had met before at church. She was Angela, Aunt's first cousin. She had put on so much lipstick that I couldn't help but stare at her. She liked putting on matching outfits with her fat son.

"Meet my son," she said, pushing the boy towards me. "Jack, meet..."

"Mukenani," I said.

She knelt before her son, her hands roughly fastening his bow tie. The boy, Jack, seemed uncomfortable, his face was so sweaty from the tightness. I couldn't help but notice the dull button struggling to hold his thick neck together. It was as if it had a life of its own, ready to escape at any moment.

"When things go wrong, it's important to learn how to fix them," she said to Jack. "Pretty girls don't like dirty boys."

Who wouldn't smile at such motivating words? Jack was the same age as Samuel, but it felt like his mother was rushing him to start dating girls.

"We're here for the birthday boy," Angela said as I led them to the living room, where the rest of the family was gathered. The room was filled with the sound of laughter and the smell of freshly baked cake. The walls were decorated with balloons and a large banner with Samuel's name hung above the television's stand.

"Oh, just for God's sake, my name is Angela," she said without looking at me. Then, she stopped to face Jack, who was strolling. She grabbed the scruff of his head to urge him to walk faster.

"You need to learn to walk faster. Your velocity is too slow," Angela scolded. She then blew a kiss towards Aunt, who didn't seem pleased with her presence. I sat down next to Tiwe, who was sipping on a Coke.

"Are these the newcomers I missed seeing at church?" Angela asked. "With a little bit of town water and a little bit of decency, they will be so beautiful." She tore open a candy wrapper and gave some to her son. "Which side do they belong to, ours or his?"

"They belong to my husband's family, Angela," Aunt replied. "Can we cut the cake now?"

We all gathered to sing the happy birthday song. Angela's voice was off-key, but she was so busy that it was hard not to smile. Samuel sat there, so happy. Angela then brushed Samuel's hair and started shouting "hip-hip-hip" and such nonsense. She pulled out a mirror from her handbag, touched up her already beautiful face with more powder, and sang a song praising herself—only one pimple.

She then turned to Samuel and said, "You will grow very, very old."

"I don't want to grow old."

"Everyone grows old."

"I don't want to grow old."

"Then you will die young."

Despite Angela's occasional rudeness, I was starting to like her very much. She had a way of saying things that made me smile. I watched her, and I couldn't help but notice that she was beautiful but lacked intelligence. Angela placed a few candies on her son's lap, and he ate them.

"You're such a good boy, Jack," she said, patting his head.

"He is sweating a lot," Tiwe said. "Is he sick?"

"How could a sick person have such a big appetite?" Aunt added. "These formal clothes are too restrictive. Angela, for the love of God, remove his jacket."

"He must learn to wear formal. My son will become a successful businessman, unlike the boys from our village who are all fishermen."

"We don't know what the future holds for our children."

"Yes, but we know what the future should hold for our children."

"Mu," Samuel called, "one day, I will attend school at Riverweed."

Angela looked at him with a laugh, "Your dark forehead will be so shiny from a mile away, and everyone will make fun of it,"

"Leave him alone, Angela," Aunt said. "Not only will my son attend school there, but he will also become the headmaster someday. You know what, Sam? Study hard, and all those white kids will address you as Headmaster Sir."

"Headmaster, Sir!" Angela laughed. "They will also call you 'monkey,' which would make it, Headmaster Monkey Sir."

"I'm not a monkey," Samuel protested.

"I know you're not, but those kids see us as monkeys. All of us are jut monkeys and baboon," Angela chuckled.

"How can a black man teach a white kid in this country?" Uncle said, eating, seemingly uninterested in our conversation.

"If a person of one race can educate someone of another race, then you can do the same," said Aunt. "Remember to put in the effort. Education is a tool that can empower you to conquer any doubts or boundaries you may face. Aim for greatness in your academic endeavours because, through hard work and dedication, anyone can inspire and influence others, regardless of race or ethnicity."

I couldn't find the words to say anything; my mind was filled with thoughts. Aunt made a good point. If a white woman can teach us, a black teacher can teach those white kids, too.

"Dad," Samuel said, "do you have any white friends at work?"

"Quite a few," he said, not looking at Samuel. "And all of them are my bosses."

"They own the shop?" Samuel asked.

"If I were you, son, I would consider Aunt Angela's advice."

Angela smiled, while Aunt couldn't share in her excitement. Based on his tone, Uncle seemed frustrated with his bosses. Despite that, he drove a nice car, and we lived in a good house, so I figured he must have some decent position there.

"You have no idea how much they yell at me each and every day. Sometimes I feel like I'm a kid," he said. "Someday, when you have a job and work for someone, you'll understand. Keeping a job is tough."

"Work for the government," Angela said. "People there don't care. Just look at our community schools; everything is broken."

"Learn to appreciate what you have," Aunt said. "Take on a little more responsibility. Those white kids aren't the ones writing on your walls; you are."

There was a moment of silence as if we were all waiting for Jack to join the conversation. He began scratching his hair, and Angela never liked that.

"Mother, will you read me a bedtime story when I go to sleep?" Jack said out of topic. "I saw it on..."

We all laughed because that was funny.

"Stop comparing TV to real life," Angela said. "Bedtime stories are not for people who came from our village."

"Be more considerate of your child, Angela," Uncle said.

"He needs to stop comparing TV to real life," Angela insisted. "If he wants bedtime stories, he should go to the village and join his cousins around the evening fire to listen to Aunt Dorothy's stories about the clever hare that keeps deceiving baboons."

That was the first time I remember having such a long conversation with my uncle. From that talk, I told myself that people would someday work for me. As I lay in bed that night, I couldn't help but think about Mrs Jacob and Miss Smit. I wondered what kind of person Miss O'Hara's daughter was.

The next morning, Tiwe and I walked through the school gate, flipping through the magazines I got from Miss Smit. I knew Lisa was already in class. Classes hadn't started yet, so learners were arriving, and some were already seated and working on their homework. It had rained the previous night, so the sky was grey and damp. Puddles of rainwater could be seen everywhere, and a few teachers' cars were already parked.

It was the day we had to present our topic to the class. We gathered our points in the first few minutes, and Lisa volunteered to present. I wasn't much of a speaker, so standing in front of a crowd wasn't my big thing. Miss O'Hara's lesson started right after the break.

"Schools that remain divided, even after independence, show how much work we still have to do," Lisa said. "These issues are deep-rooted, but that doesn't mean we should stop trying to fix them."

"Yes, but isn't it just because some people are better?" Lizzy's voice cut through the room, a smirk playing on her lips.

"I wish I were white," Eustace added with a shrug, and we all laughed.

I stood beside Lisa and our teacher, managing a smile as usual. I was starting to feel better about speaking up. Even fools like Eustace were joining in the class.

"We're all just people," I said, my voice a bit stronger than I expected. "In God's eyes, we're equal."

"But that's not how it is, is it?" someone shouted back.

"We've let ourselves believe that." Lisa responded; her tone more reflective now. "It's frustrating, isn't it? After all this time, we're still stuck in this blame game. When do we finally take responsibility for ourselves?"

LATER, after the lunch bell rang, I found myself waiting outside Miss O'Hara's door. The library was open, and our teacher had just returned from the principal's office. Lisa arrived a minute earlier, just before Miss O'Hara invited us inside.

Sitting in our teacher's chair was a scrawny white girl with long hair, enjoying a lollipop. I guessed she was Miss O'Hara's daughter from Riverweed. Her school bag rested on the desk, and her uniform looked crisp, like it hadn't seen a dusty road in its life. Lisa and I stood a few steps from the door, unsure of what to say.

"Honey," Miss O'Hara said to the girl, "I want you to meet my two best learners."

Sophia was slightly shorter than me but had a confidence that made her seem taller. Something about her made me think she wouldn't be nice to us.

"Hi, hello... I'm Sophia," she said, raising a hand casually.

Lisa, closer, shook her hand. "Lisa."

"Nice to meet you, Lisa," Sophia replied, turning to me.

"Mukenani," I said.

"Don't you have an English name?"

Who would want to be called Imelda in the 90s? I was only thirteen years old, and every Imelda I knew in our village was dead.

"No," I replied, my tone sharper than I meant it to be.

Sophia froze, her lollipop mid-air. "Oh. That's... interesting."

Miss O'Hara cleared her throat. "Honey, why don't you tell Lisa and Mukenani a little about yourself?"

Sophia fidgeted in her chair, twirling the lollipop stick. "I'm from Riverweed. I'm just visiting my mum. Guess what? I might transfer here next year."

Lisa and I shared a glance.

"That's... nice," Lisa replied, though her smile didn't quite reach her eyes.

"I guess," Sophia shrugged. "It's a bit... different here." Her gaze swept over the room. "Small and kind of broken."

"Every school has its own charm," Miss O'Hara said, her voice firm. "You'll learn a lot here."

Sophia didn't look convinced. "So, what do you guys do for fun after school?"

Lisa hesitated. "We go home. Sometimes we play netball."

"Netball?" Sophia wrinkled her nose. "Do you even have a real court?"

"We built it ourselves. It's not that hard," I said, my irritation rising.

Sophia leaned back, popping the lollipop back into her mouth. "Huh. Sounds... quaint."

Miss O'Hara clapped her hands together. "Alright, girls. That's enough for today. We'll chat more later, sweetheart."

As we left, Lisa muttered under her breath, "Quaint? Who does she think she is?"

"The queen of Riverweed, I guess."

We walked to meet Tiwe at the gate, our whispers turning into laughter.

A Shared Fate

While bored at home one weekend, I entertained myself by craning over the gate and watching the people walking in my neighbourhood. I stood there, talking to myself. Eventually, I grew bored again. My aunt and the rest of the family were taking their afternoon nap. I always tried to avoid napping in the afternoon because I would wake up feeling as if I was working in my sleep.

I was just about to shut the door when I caught sight of Angela and her little boy strolling into our yard. A warm smile spread across my face. If someone had asked me earlier that day if there would ever be a moment when I would be grateful for Angela's presence to alleviate my boredom, I would have adamantly said no. But that afternoon, I was happy she came. I made way for them to enter.

"I hope cuz isn't sleeping?" Angela began brushing the dirt off Jack's head.

From the first day Angela visited, I knew she was a thorn in Aunt's flesh, but I couldn't help but enjoy Angela's choice of words. I could tell that aunt didn't like Angela very much. It was possible that Angela was aware of a secret Aunt was keeping and leveraged this knowledge to be a parasite in aunt's life.

I flopped onto the sofa, making myself comfortable as I listened and watched Angela.

"You," Angela said to me.

She always called us "You," even though she knew our names. She had trouble telling us apart.

"How are you doing at your new school?"

"I'm the class captain," I said.

"How did that happen?" she asked, playing with her nails. "Well... life is full of mysteries. I've seen many foolish fools become leaders."

Angela's comment hit hard, but I was used to her bluntness. Without her usual sarcasm, she wouldn't really be Angela. I shook off her words and turned my attention to Jack, who was busy chasing a moth by the window.

Angela plopped down on the couch, crossing her legs like she owned the place. "Your aunt is lucky to have me. Without my visits, she'd probably become a total recluse."

I wanted to stick up for Aunt, but arguing with Angela was like trying to catch smoke with your bare hands—totally useless and just made everything worse. Instead, I asked, "Want some tea, Aunt Angela?"

She waved dismissively. "Tea won't fix anything. Let me tell you something, little girl: the quiet ones who seem perfect usually have the messiest closets. Pay attention. It's a skill worth having."

I didn't know what I wanted to say, but thanks to Aunt, who walked in, her face darkening like a brewing storm.

"Angela," Aunt said, her voice flat. "What brings you here?"

Angela flashed a grin, showing her teeth like a predator. "Can't a cousin visit? Plus, Jack needed a little adventure."

Aunt crossed her arms, her lips pressed tightly together, but she didn't say anything.

Jack tugged at Angela's sleeve. "Mum, can I go outside?"

"Of course, sweetheart," Angela replied, giving his head a gentle pat. "Just don't go too far."

As Jack dashed out the door, Aunt spoke, her tone calm. "You've made your rounds. Maybe it's time for you to go home."

Angela leaned back, completely unbothered. "Don't worry, dear Cuz. I'll find my way out. Just think how boring life would be without me."

Angela's smile lingered even after the door clicked shut, as if she hadn't really left at all. For a brief moment, the house was wrapped in an unsettling silence, the kind that makes you aware of your own heartbeat. Her last words hung like a stubborn fog, refusing to dissipate. This moment took me back to another day—a memory that felt just as vivid. Lisa, Tiwe, and I were outside the principal's office during break, gossiping about the new Agriculture teacher who had accidentally broken a classroom window. It was a quick distraction, but once school was over, as usual, Tiwe and I sprawled on our beds before—we we disturbed.

Angela's voice, sharp and demanding, sliced through our living room. Aunt's voice was strained, her words short and clipped. It didn't take long to figure out what was bothering her—Angela was once again asking for money. From my concealed spot, I saw Aunt rubbing her temples, her shoulders tense with stress. Angela continued her relentless chatter, completely unaware of the strain she was causing. Even then, I couldn't help but admire how Aunt managed to stay calm, even though the cracks in her patience were beginning to show.

"Where are they?" Angela asked Aunt. "Can you at least pretend to be happy to see me? Where are those two?"

I began to walk down the stairway; Angela's gaze travelled from my feet to my chest. "A boy is deceiving this community school kid," Angela said.

"No, I don't think so," Aunt said, looking back at me. "I doubt it."

"She is a beautiful young village girl."

"Beautiful, yes, but also naive," Aunt said.

"Beautiful and naive girls are easily misled... be careful."

I went back to join Tiwe in our room. I grabbed a dictionary and searched for the new word I had learned from Aunt.

"What's the word, Mu?" Tiwe asked.

"Naive."

"A person who is super silly?" Tiwe slammed the magazine on the bed. "Wait a minute, Mu, who called you silly, Aunt or Angela?"

While she was talking, I also searched for the word's definition in the dictionary. "Adjective," I began to read, tracing each word with my finger, "describing a person or action that shows a lack of experience, wisdom, or judgment. It's different from being stupid."

"Lack of experience or judgment is the same as being stupid," she said. "Sister, whoever said that thinks you're stupid. Why did they call you stupid?"

"Angela thinks I have a boyfriend, but Aunt thinks I'm naive and beautiful too."

I started to smile, which caused my sister to stand up from the bed and stare at me as if I had gone insane.

"They called you naive, and you are smiling?"

"They called me beautiful too."

In the quiet moments that followed, I rested my head on my aunt's lap as she weaved my hair into braids. After she finished, Tiwe and I made our way to the kitchen, ready to prepare dinner for everyone. As the aroma of our meal filled the air, we gathered around the table, coming together as a family to eat.

"Mukenani," Aunt said, "do you have any new friends from school?"

"Lisa," Tiwe replied, "Only Lisa."

"Invite your friend over sometime."

"I will, Aunt."

On Monday, Lisa was already in the classroom, going through her books. She was the only one there.

"Aunt thinks I should invite you to our place."

Lisa glanced up at me, and I immediately understood my mistake.

"Would you like to come over?" I asked again, attempting to convey more sincerity. "You're my friend, and I would be happy to have you visit."

"I have chores to take care of after school. My mother isn't feeling well. I'm sorry."

I found myself staring into space, hoping she would change her mind. I wanted her to visit; otherwise, Aunt would think we needed help making friends. Lisa dropped her pen into her book and closed it.

"South Bauleni?"

"Yes, South Bauleni."

"It's nice there," she said, sounding uninterested. "People there are different from where I live."

"We're all the same, Lisa."

"Yeah, we're pretty much the same."

What I enjoyed about being friends with Lisa was that she was incredibly organised and disciplined. Even though she came from a poor family, she never let that affect our friendship. I genuinely believed that Lisa had a bright future ahead of her. Knowing that she was thoughtful and organised, I didn't try to convince her any further.

Tiwe and I walked through the corridors after the lunch bell rang, and Lisa caught up with us. She said she could spare an hour to hang out. Once we got home, my aunt was in the living room reading a newspaper.

"Lisa, right? What a lovely name."

"Yes, Mrs Susiku," Lisa replied.

Lisa couldn't stop staring at the house and all its contents. It seemed like she had never been in such a lovely house before. During our meal, she said life had been unfair to her and her family. Her father passed away shortly after her brother Moses was born, making life very difficult. Her mother had to sell small items in front of their house to feed the family and pay school fees. Her younger sister, Ima, still lived in Zambia.

"You have a bright future ahead of you," Aunt said.

Lisa had big dreams and worked hard to achieve them. On the other hand, I had many dreams but couldn't decide. I could pursue a career in law, become a doctor, or even force my way into politics. I knew I wasn't talented in sports or singing, so those weren't my options. It was time for me to focus on one dream and work hard towards it. Inspired by Miss O'Hara, who talked about her psychologist brother in the States, I imagined myself as a psychologist. It sounded intriguing to me.

"When I was younger," Aunt said, "I wanted to be a banker, but now I'm a housewife with a nursing diploma."

"I never knew you studied nursing, Aunt," Tiwe said.

"My husband didn't want me to work. That was long ago; I can barely remember what I learned in nursing school now."

Lisa started visiting us more often, and everyone in our family treated her kindly. I liked her, but some kids at school made fun of her for always wearing the same blue top during study time.

One day, we left the school gate and went to Samuel's school. Samuel was in a fight with another boy. I pulled him away before the caretaker showed up. Later, at home, I told Uncle about the incident during dinner but realised I should have told Aunt first. My uncle slammed the spoon on the table in anger. I knew I had made a mistake.

"No child of mine should be fighting in school," he said sternly.

I wasn't sure what was worse—not telling Aunt earlier or uncle punishing Samuel. Aunt was furious with me. I never expected such a minor issue to become so big and terrible. I learned that it's best to think before speaking and that a little knowledge can be very, very dangerous.

"You should have told me first," Aunt said after Uncle left.

The next day, I stood leaning against the kitchen counter, feeling anxious. Throughout the entire morning, aunt completely ignored me. It wasn't until afternoon, when she finally lay on her bed, that I brought some fruit without her asking. I placed it on the table and humbled myself. Aunt was always kind, so I knew she wouldn't hold that anger for too long.

"I'm sorry, Aunt. I didn't know Uncle would be so angry at Samuel."

"Everything that happens in this house should go through me first. I didn't bring you from the village to tear this family apart," Aunt said, staring at me, making me increasingly nervous.

She rose from the bed, grabbed my hand, and turned it over. "I've seen this illness before," she said, examining my left hand. "Isn't this the same..."

I pulled my arm away, but she pulled it back. I pulled it back again and brought it closer to my eyes. I wondered how I hadn't noticed it myself. Three white patches on my thumb were starting to merge. My thoughts drifted to memories. I started thinking about my mother's skin condition. The villagers buried her alive because the native doctor declared our mother's skin condition a curse.

I didn't know exactly how it started with my mother, but I remembered her saying it began on her fingers. Everything went blank. I knew it was the start of a tough time ahead. I rushed to my room and sat on my bed. Tiwe was working on her science homework. That's when the tears started to flow. She had witnessed my issues with my aunt and thought that was the reason for my current state.

"My life is over."

"Aunt is a good woman. She's just angry, but she'll forgive you," Tiwe said.

Earlier that day, I was upset because aunt wasn't talking to me. Now, I felt sad and scared because I knew my mother's illness was incurable. I knew I would soon be gone.

"I'm dying, Tiwe."

"You're not dying; Aunt is a good person."

Tiwe went back to her homework, leaving me feeling misunderstood. After school, I would eat lunch and retreat to my room to contemplate my life, which felt like it was ending. I was too young to be facing such a terrible condition. In our village, a sickness like mine was seen as a terrible curse.

What would my family, friends, and teachers say? My life and all my hopes and dreams seemed to be over. I had no idea how long this disease would plague me. My mother was killed because of it.

I couldn't find much information online about my skin condition—we didn't have access to such resources back then. I didn't even know what I was dealing with. I scrubbed my skin every time I showered, hoping the condition would disappear, but the patches on my fingers became more pronounced daily, and I began losing my natural skin colour.

While I was taking a bath, Tiwe finished getting ready for school. She sat with her school bag on her lap, waiting for me.

"Do you want to talk about it?" Tiwe asked, looking deeply into my eyes.

I didn't take her question seriously and continued getting ready for school. Whenever I sat down, I would hide my thumbs under my shirt to conceal the patches.

"About Mother's condition?"

I couldn't understand how Tiwe found out about it. I suspected Aunt, but why did it take so long for her to know? I opened my palms and examined them. Tears started to stream down my face.

"It's okay, Mu. Don't be sad."

"How did you find out?"

Tiwe had known about my condition the same day I noticed the patches with Aunt. She explained that she had been waiting for me to confide in her but realised I was dealing with all the emotions alone.

"It wasn't Aunt. I told Aunt about it that day."

Every night, I would wake up thinking it was all just a terrible nightmare. I feared that my face would lose its colour, too. When I was little, the first thing my village people would notice when they met me was my pretty face and my big chest. Even though my face was dirty, many people said Tiwe, and I would become beautiful ladies. I worried that my lovely face would change into something ugly and mean kids, especially at school, would make fun of me.

Hope and Healing

The third semester began, and as I stood in front of the mirror, I wondered what scared me the most: the thought of death, how others would gossip, or what I will do to them.

"God is so cruel," I muttered. "God is wicked."

Tiwe sat down with her school bag, noticing my tears. She held my hand, gently touching the patches on it, and said, "God is never cruel. God is good."

"Why me, Tiwe?"

"We all face challenges in life differently. None of us are completely okay, Mu. Every single one of us."

"I wish I could just die."

Even if the circumstances were different, I would still have said the same thing to Tiwe. Unfortunately, I could hear her words but never truly believed them.

"Now, let's go to school."

Thankfully, my school shirt concealed the patches, sparing me from worrying about being noticed. Once in class, our teacher assigned us work to do in pairs. I always partnered with Lisa because she knew the answers to most questions.

"You can write," I told her, handing her a pen. "Your handwriting is better than mine."

Lisa didn't look at me. She took the pen and began writing. I stared down at my hands, hoping for some miracle.

"I've read about your skin condition," Lisa said.

She took the paper to Miss O'Hara, who stood by the door due to the lack of chairs. Our crowded classrooms forced teachers to stand or sit if a student was absent. Absences were rare; our principal ensured this by assigning tasks like tree digging or rubbish hole digging. It was in our best interest never to be absent or broke school rules. Miss O'Hara was kind, yet she gave harsh advice when needed. She never resorted to corporal punishment, but her words were punishment on their own.

When Lisa returned from handing in our work, my mind raced. I had not disclosed my condition to her, and I thought I was doing a very good job hiding it beneath my uniform.

"I've read about it somewhere, but I can't remember where," Lisa said. "It's not a real illness, Mu."

I was in denial, though surprised she knew about it.

"You knew about my condition?"

"You're my friend, Mu," she said. "You should talk to Miss O'Hara. She's from a big country; she might have heard of it. If I were you, I'd learn to accept my condition."

"Have you accepted yours?"

"I will finish my studies and get a good job."

At home, I checked the mirror before lunch. Tiwe called me over with Angela and Jack present. Samuel moved his plate closer because Angela had a bad habit of taking meat from others' plates.

"You," Angela said, taking a piece of meat from my plate and giving it to her son. "Learn to share. Eating alone is bad for you. It makes you fat, and then you die. Look at my son, Jack; he looks so good."

I couldn't help but chuckle to that joke despite my efforts not to. Tiwe glanced at me and then at Jack who resembled a little hippo coming out of the lake. Jack wiped his sweat and chewed with so much commitment. Angela watched, and Tiwe nudged me, knowing Angela was about to teach her son table manners.

"I told you never to wipe your sweat with your hands. Where is your handkerchief?"

"You used it for your shoes, Mum."

"Why did you give it to me? That's your personal property," she yelled. "And look at me when I'm talking to you."

After we finished eating, I thought Angela would ask about Aunt. She grabbed her bag and left with her son. When Aunt came downstairs from her room, I served her some juice before she took me to her room. She said it was time for us to talk. I could see in her eyes that she wanted to discuss my skin condition, which was becoming more noticeable on my hands.

"Child," Aunt said as she placed her hands on mine. I was glad that Aunt wanted to talk to me like a mother would to her child.

I couldn't bring myself to tell Aunt that she was the first one to notice my condition. I remember that day well; Aunt was still upset with me. She expressed her desire for me to confide in her like a daughter should to a mother. She was understanding and wanted to give me time to face my situation. I appreciated her wisdom, but I truly wanted her to be there for me right from the beginning to help me navigate my struggles. If only she knew how many times, I contemplated ending my life... taking a knife to my throat, but I lacked the strength to do so.

"What should I do now? I don't want to die."

She held my hands tightly. "You will live a long life and see your children and grandchildren grow."

"What should I do, Aunt?"

"We have an appointment with Doctor Charles this Saturday."

"I don't want to see a doctor."

Aunt gently touched my chin and ran her fingers through my hair, which was starting to resemble hers.

"A doctor is never an enemy. We need them in our lives. Don't worry, you'll like Doctor Charles. He's kind, and he tells funny jokes."

I was about to say something when a loud voice grew closer, and the door burst open. Angela was still yelling into the phone. I was surprised to see her; she had just left with her son a few minutes ago. Angela stood with her hands on her hips, wearing clothes so tight that I could see the outline of her protruding belly button. She had a nice athletic body, and a pretty face, but she spoiled it with too much makeup.

"Today is my birthday, and I want you to help me celebrate it," Angela said to Aunt.

I glanced at Aunt and saw in her eyes that she wanted me to leave. I stood in the corner by the door and listened to their argument.

"One of these days, I'll kill you," Aunt growled "You're becoming a real pest. Don't you fear God?"

"I've already sinned against God because of you. You begged me to take you to Doctor Kufekisa for that juju that your husband ate with his food."

"It was your idea, Angela. My husband loved me even before your silly juju idea. I was happy, and I was already expecting his child."

"Enough with these silly confessions. We both look foolish doing this. Now, will you help me celebrate my birthday or not?" Angela demanded.

I started to understand a few things. I couldn't tell Tiwe about it; Tiwe was terrible at keeping secrets. I watched them drive away from the yard. Angela was even driving Uncle's car.

The next day at school, I was in the library with Lisa while Miss O'Hara taught in Tiwe's class. We searched for information about my situation in books, magazines, or newspapers but found nothing.

"Maybe Riverweed knows something about you," Lisa said. "Ask Miss O'Hara."

My mind was filled with so many thoughts, and I didn't want to read anything about my condition. I feared what I might discover. The books would describe it as a curse, just like the villagers had told my mother. While I was lost in my thoughts, Lisa was browsing through the shelves in our small, empty library.

"Can we just leave Lisa?" I said, lacking interest.

When we walked out of the library, we saw Miss O'Hara coming from her class. I turned to Lisa and demanded that she should never mention anything to our teacher.

"Mistress O'Hara," said Lisa.

Our teacher gestured for us to follow her without stopping.

"You too, Mukenani; I need to talk to both of you."

"Why do you want to talk to her?" I asked Lisa.

"It's not about you, Mu," she said thoughtfully. "I will be taking my brother to the clinic tomorrow, so I won't come to school."

I sat next to Tiwe while Lisa stood there, tapping her finger on the teacher's book. Miss O'Hara tidied up the books behind her chair and then turned to Lisa.

"You have managed to make everyone love you. The teachers are pleased with your commitment to your studies. I like to reward my learners for a job well done."

She took out a mathematical instrument and handed it to Lisa. I started feeling jealous. I deserved some recognition from my teacher too.

"You have to keep up the good work, Lisa," Miss O'Hara said.

"I will, Mistress O'Hara," Lisa replied. "Thank you, Mistress."

Miss O'Hara turned to us and said, "You two are also doing well, but you need to do more. What did you want to talk to me about, Lisa?"

"My younger brother has been sick for a while now. I will be taking him to the clinic. He's not well, Mistress."

Lisa took on a huge responsibility at such a young age. My sister and I were there, feeling her pain as well. I had momentarily forgotten about my troubles.

"Do you want to leave now, child?" asked Miss O'Hara.

"We still have a Physical Science test to write."

Miss O'Hara reached into her purse and handed her a few coins. Back then, a few coins could go a long way. Tiwe walked over to Lisa and put her arms around her shoulders.

"Your brother will be okay," Tiwe said.

After the test, I walked her to the gate and wished her brother a speedy recovery.

Two days passed, and Lisa still had not returned to school. After classes, I was in the library, saying goodbye to my teacher. We talked about Lisa, which was probably why I was there.

"Do you know where she lives?" asked Miss O'Hara.

"Yes, Miss O'Hara," I said. "But I'm not sure of the exact house. The last time Aunt and I dropped her off near the Sabbath church."

"Let's hope she's back at school tomorrow," the teacher said.

"I hope so, Mistress O'Hara," I said, turning around to see my sister coming.

Tiwe and I went home after that, but we stopped by Samuel's school to pick him up. Samuel was playing with some other kids near the school gate. Jack was sitting under the mango tree by the borehole, clutching his schoolbag. His lips were so dry and cracked like he hadn't eaten. Samuel said Jack always finished his food during break, even when Angela had told him to save some for lunch. I held my schoolbag in my left hand and watched Jack, who had become my favourite clown, even though he didn't say much. It was the way his clothes hung on his chubby frame. His bow tie looked like it was choking him.

We were preparing to leave the school grounds when Angela suddenly appeared. She had just acquired an old black VW Golf, and, as usual, she was impeccably dressed. We hopped into the back seat while Jack comfortably sank into the front passenger seat.

"I've told you never to sit without your seatbelt," said Angela.

Angela began singing her favourite reggae song, but it was horrible. Tiwe, sitting next to me, started tickling my leg every time Angela spoiled a good high note.

"Girls, just because I'm in my late twenties doesn't mean I have given up on my childhood dream of being a reggae star. Don't you agree, girls?"

We didn't have a chance to respond because Angela never gave us one. "Anyway, your opinions don't matter," she declared, continued singing, belting out the lyrics, "ONE LOVE." She then proudly claimed, "I met Bob Marley in 1988."

"But he died in 1981," Tiwe said.

"He's dead?"

"Maybe you met his son," said Tiwe.

"How do you know he's dead?" Angela asked.

"Aren't his birth and death dates hanging on your mirror?" Tiwe pointed at the picture of him, *Bob Marley, 6 February 1945–11 May 1981.*

"Maybe you met him in 1971," I said with a smile.

"I met him," she said louder but didn't sing.

When we arrived home, Aunt shared the shade with our cat, who curled beside her. We decided to have lunch on the kitchen counter; it was easier to peek through the window at Angela and Aunt, but we couldn't hear a word they said. After Angela had left, Aunt told me about the doctor's afternoon appointment. When we got there, I was nervous. Doctors always deliver terrible news. I had never been to a doctor before. All I knew in the village were herbalists.

"Her condition is called Vitiligo," said Doctor Charles.

I felt relieved that it wasn't some kind of curse or disease like Doctor Kufekisa had warned the villagers about when my mother had the same illness. If it's just a regular disease, people won't fear me or avoid me.

"Your melanocytes stop producing skin pigment, causing lighter spots to appear on your skin," explained Doctor Charles.

I didn't have to ask about curses; Aunt was there to ask all the questions. Even though the doctor's words sounded foreign to me, I understood.

"Is there a cure for it, doctor?" Aunt asked.

"Not at the moment," he replied. "I'll prescribe a cream for her daily to help with the colour. She can still use makeup."

I remembered seeing Angela apply a lot of makeup and knew she would help me with this. Later, when I told my sister about it at home, she remained silent. She went to the living room, where Aunt, Uncle, and Samuel played cards. Tiwe came to tell me that Uncle wanted to speak with me.

"Ever since your mother, my sister, passed away," Uncle said. "I've learned a lot about this condition. It's not a curse. You are still beautiful, and science has made great advancements."

I blinked hard, holding back the tears.

"I've been in touch with a specialist. There are new treatments that might improve your skin if you're interested. But it's completely up to you. You're amazing just the way you are."

Treatments? What kind of treatments? I wanted to ask, but I hesitated.

That night, as I lay in bed, Uncle's words kept repeating in my head. Was I ready for this? Did I even want it? I looked out the window, where the moonlight poured into our room. Somewhere out there, I felt Mother's spirit, and for the very first time, I quietly asked the darkness,

"Mother, what would you do?"

The question lingered like an echo as I drifted into an uneasy sleep. The next day at school, it had been six days since Lisa had been absent. I spoke to my teacher about it, and Miss O'Hara and I visited Lisa's neighbourhood after school. The houses all looked the same—a dull shade of cream. We saw Lisa carrying firewood behind the church. I offered to help her with the firewood.

"He's gone, Mu," she cried. "My brother died."

I had never comforted someone in such a situation before, so I held her hands to show her I was there for her. She then rested her head on Miss O'Hara's shoulder.

"It was dysentery, Mistress, and he died from it."

We listened to her cry for a while. Even our teacher was at a loss for words. I held her hands tightly.

"When is the funeral?"

"We've already buried him. The church gave a coffin."

Our teacher remained silent. I could tell she was too emotional to speak. Lisa's mother was resting on a mat under the mango tree in front of their shack. A man and a woman around her age came out of the house. Lisa said that the woman was her mother's younger sister, *ba*Christina, famously known as *bana*Monde in her village, and her husband, *basha*Monde.

"I'm thinking of moving back to the village," Lisa's mother said. "But the schools in town are better. I want a brighter future for my daughter."

"My sister and her kids have been through a lot," *bana*Monde said. "After her husband passed away, things became tough. I've often urged her to come to the village and work on the land our parents used to farm when we were young. She always says maybe by the end of the year."

Lisa and I grabbed some water buckets and went to a public borehole. We joined the line with other residents to collect water. It wasn't too far of a walk, and as we finished, we balanced the buckets on our heads. Along the way, we talked about school, with Lisa constantly asking me for updates.

"We had two tests. In maths. Our teacher was looking for you and said you should see him as soon as you get to school."

"Two tests in just six days!"

"You know our maths teacher; he keeps giving us work."

The weight of the pail on my head started to become noticeable. It had been a while since I carried water like this. Living in the city was making me lazy.

"We can rest here," Lisa said.

Despite Lisa's pain from losing her brother, I could see she was trying to move on. She pushed her pain aside and avoided answering my questions about what happened.

"And your sister? Ima, right?"

"She was here with our uncle, but she left yesterday."

"I wish I could meet her."

"Ima," Lisa smiled, "you will like her. She is so kind."

After some time had passed, Tiwe and I went to town to buy some stationery. Lisa joined us as we crossed the road from the bookshop near the government buildings. On the other side, Miss O'Hara's daughter, Sophia, and her friend Raven were enjoying ice cream. I admired their style, especially Raven, who was dressed in a way our village elders would disapprove of. They wore shorts and tops that exposed their shoulders. I liked it, but Aunt would never let us dress like that; our community doesn't approve of such style.

"Kiernan, right?" Sophia asked. "I'm Miss O'Hara's daughter; we met at your school. Remember me!"

"Did she just call you Kiernan?" Tiwe whispered in Subia language. "White people and their ignorance of African names."

"She's just a silly girl; ignore her," Lisa said.

"Why is it so hard for them to say our names correctly?" Tiwe complained. "We pronounce theirs right, but they can't do the same for us. It's disrespectful."

"It's not just white people, Tiwe," I said. "There are plenty of African names that we struggle to pronounce too."

Sophia and Raven looked at us intently. Sophia had never seen my sister before, so I understood her confusion.

"Which one of you is Kiernan?" Sophia asked, blowing a bubble with her gum.

"Mukenani," Tiwe said. "It's Mukenani, not Kiernan."

"MUKANANA," Sophia repeated.

"Do you have an English name?" Raven, the other white girl, asked. "All black people have English names."

"How about we call you Tina?" said Sophia.

"Do you like Tina?" Raven shouted as if I was deaf.

"She is Mukenani, not Tina," Tiwe said. "What's so difficult about that?"

"Tina," I said with a smile. "I like Tina."

"Tina sounds amazing," Sophia said. "You know what? How about the two of us becoming friends with the three of you? Don't you like that?"

Who wouldn't want to be friends with Sophia and Raven? They could show us their ways, and we could share ours. Having such friendships during our younger years was a dream come true. Who wouldn't want to be friends with two beautiful white kids?

"I would love to be your friend."

I looked at Lisa, and she pulled me aside.

"They can't be our friends," Lisa said.

"They're good people, Lisa," I said, as if I had known them forever.

"They're bad people. They'll use you," Tiwe added. "We don't need them, and you don't know them."

"She is Sophia," I said. "Our teacher's daughter."

"Yes," Tiwe acknowledged, "but I don't like the other one. She talks too much, and she's full of herself."

"I like them, and I want to be friends with them."

I walked back to stand before my new friends.

"Where do you live?" Raven asked.

"South Bauleni, and you?"

"Riverweed."

I recalled a day when I was in Riverweed with Aunt. The trees and houses there were stunning, large, and well-maintained. However, I noticed many peculiar-looking dogs in the yards.

"I like it there," I said. "Only white people live there."

"You know what?" said Raven. "Maybe one day you can visit."

"Maybe I will."

Before we said our goodbyes, we hugged each other repeatedly. It made me think about how back in the village, and even at my current school, we only shake hands as a greeting. Shaking and shaking all day long.

Crossing Cultural Differences

While window shopping, I saw Sophia and Raven leaving the restaurant near the T-junction. I rushed over to catch up. Raven looked so cool in her pink sash, branded MISS BEAUTIFUL 1991. The two girls displayed a sense of coolness that my friend Lisa lacked. In fact, there was no comparison.

Our meeting that pleasant day marked either our second or third encounter, and it was clear that good things were happening all at once. They taught me the ways of femininity—how to strut, dress, and even adopt a classy accent. How lucky was a girl like me to have such friends? My new friends truly cherished me, fitting in seamlessly despite our differing skin colours.

Since befriending Sophia and Raven, I had distanced myself from Lisa and given her full-time to Tiwe. While I cared for my friends from Riverweed, Tiwe held a special place in my heart. But Raven and Sophia where cool—Not only did they share their hand-me-downs, but they also offered helpful guidance, urging me to stay true to myself by emulating them. Despite our close bond, Raven set the rules and sought input from Sophia. I dutifully followed every directive with unwavering loyalty. In my younger years in the village, I used to be the one making decisions for my friends. Now the tables had turned. It was cool though.

My visits to Riverweed gave me a glimpse into a different way of life as I began to adopt the habits of my more relaxed peers. I swiftly picked up on urban trends, such as mirroring their fashion choices and mastering the art of nail painting. It was an exciting period of rapid growth for me.

The next time my new friends and I visited shops; it happened to be Friday. We spent the rest of the afternoon shopping for Raven's birthday party. She bought a yellow dress for me—the dress that reached just below my knees, and she insisted that I wear it for her birth party, which was taking place, later that afternoon at her father's place. I hadn't met Raven's parents before, so I was worried they wouldn't accept me. I remember that same day at school, I asked Tiwe to accompany me, but she happily declined. I couldn't ask Lisa because we weren't on speaking terms then.

At four o'clock in the afternoon, everyone started arriving for the party, which was held in the backyard of Raven's family home in Riverweed. The house was twice the size of ours (although I wouldn't call it a mansion) and was next to the tar road. On the other side of the road were two big trees providing shade for two trucks that belonged to Raven's parents. Raven led us to the backyard, where a large swimming pool sparkled, surrounded by a well-maintained lawn. A black gardener named Mr Bauchi, who had been working there for a long time, was busy trimming the grass. The area was adorned with natural and artificial plants and colourful balloons. A black maid was working to make everything look beautiful. A white lady was in charge, ensuring everything was in order. She was Mrs Williams, Raven's mother. She spread her arms wide, and Raven rushed into them, embracing her tightly.

"Raven Williams," the woman said. "Happy birthday, honey."

"Thank you, Mum," Raven said, breaking free from the hug.

Mrs Williams was petite, with long blonde hair. She then smiled at Sophia, who threw herself into her arms, and for a while, they hugged. When she was done, I knew it was my turn. I walked a few steps closer and stopped. She didn't open her arms for me to throw myself into like my two friends did.

"I see you brought someone," she said to Raven.

"My friend Tina."

"Nice to meet you, Tina." She gave me a handshake, and that was more than enough; it meant I was welcome.

"Thank you very much, Mrs Williams," I said with a bit of an accent I had learned from my two friends. I was beginning to get attention for my new English-speaking style at school.

"Which school do you attend, sweetheart?" she said while holding my hand.

"South Bauleni, and I'm in grade 8."

"I have heard of it," she said. "It is good that you are in school and sound so intelligent. When I was younger, I had a soft spot for clever people. Do you think I married my husband for his looks?" she chortled.

Coming from the other side of the house was a bearded man who needed to lose weight. Mr Williams held a glass of something he was drinking. He wore a white golf shirt tucked into tight black shorts and no shoes. Like his wife, Mr Williams was so friendly to me. On my first day in their home, I felt welcome, and we went to help with the decoration. The housekeeper was also chatty with me, and Raven seemed to like and respect her a lot.

"You must go and change, sweetheart," the housekeeper said to Raven. "Your friends will be arriving soon."

"Thank you, Nanny," said Raven, and we ran to her room together.

Learners at Riverweed all wore yellow, but I stood out in black. I was the only black girl there, but no one mistreated me. I was friends with Raven, who had just been crowned Miss Beautiful at Riverweed High, so I earned their respect. Raven and Sophia chose me out of our town's black girls.

Raven was the only child of Mr and Mrs Williams. Some people called her a spoiled brat behind her back, but only the brave ones said it to her face.

In Raven's room, I sat on her bed. I gently touched the smooth duvet and began glancing around her room, exposing the village girl in me, as I had never seen such a beautiful room with so many things hanging on the wall. I noticed the photos of her family. Among these family memories, there was another beautiful poster of a woman on stage, and I really liked that one. She held a microphone high, striking a dance pose. Her wild mane of hair and stylish outfit exposed her long, toned legs. With her arms raised, she showed passion. The audience in the poster looked overjoyed, reaching out as if trying to touch the magic of the performance.

"I like the picture."

"You can have it," Raven said.

"Are you sure?"

"100%."

"Who is she?"

"Tina," Sophia answered. "Tina Turner."

"You named me after her?"

"She's beautiful, right? And she's an amazing singer. They call her the queen of Rock 'n' Roll."

"What's your favourite song by her?" I gazed at a stack of cassettes sitting next to a blue and black Jensen cassette player.

"I have a lot of favourites, but I'll just choose the best," Raven said.

Raven started the music, and I watched as she and Sophia clumsily danced to the rhythm. Their steps were not smooth, but somehow, they captured the lively vibe of the song, filling the room with a funny energy. I loved that about my friends from Riverweed because they didn't care.

After the music ended, I asked, "Can I borrow it. I mean, can I borrow Tina's music?"

"You can have it," Raven said. "And keep the poster too."

"Thank you."

"I was thinking," Raven said, "how about you become an emcee?"

"I've never been one before. I don't think I can do it."

"You'll be great, Tina," Raven reassured me.

Sophia wore red underwear and a white bra while I stood behind Raven in my traditional gown. Earlier, Sophia had criticised my choice of clothing and said that she would understand if it were a different occasion.

"It's a party, Tina," she said. "Not a cultural festival. How are you going to swim in that?"

"Swim? Are we swimming?" I asked as I followed Sophia and Raven out of the room.

"It's a party, Tina. People swim," Sophia said. "Wear your new dress."

In my village, we had many water ponds, and during the rainy season, we would enjoy afternoon swims with the other villagers. I had learned to swim there, so I wasn't afraid of water.

"Can I swim in my dress?" I asked as we approached the housekeeper next to Mr Bauchi, the gardener.

I started to ponder and ponder even harder, realising that if I wanted to fit in, I should go with the flow of time. The housekeeper and the gardener were standing there, but I could sense they were lost in their thoughts.

"Tina, you have such a nice figure," said Sophia.

I dropped my gown to reveal my new yellow dress. I looked beautiful in it, and before anyone could say something, we heard voices coming from the main door. We hurried to see if others had arrived. Raven's grandparents, an elderly couple, were already there. Soon, more learners started to come, all dressed in yellow. We gathered in the backyard and finished singing the happy birthday song when Raven's grandmother smiled at her, holding a pink-wrapped box.

"Oh, my dear child, you're even more beautiful than your mother," said her grandmother. "I have a special birthday present for you. I know you'll love it."

I turned to face Raven's mother to see if she would be offended by her mother's comment. She didn't care.

"Thank you, Grandma. I'll open it later," Raven said, clutching the present.

"No, darling, tear it open now," insisted her grandmother.

"If it'll make you happy, Grandma, I'll open it now."

She tore it open and fell silent. Some children had already jumped into the pool, while others remained with us.

"Don't you like your present, sweetheart?" her grandmother asked.

I had known enough about Raven; she often said incredibly unpleasant things. I quickly grabbed the gift, turned to my left, where her grandfather was standing with his present.

"Here's a lovely gift from her grandmother. Now it's time for her to open the gift from her grandfather."

Everyone appreciated my presence and energy. I moved around as if it were my party, saying things I never would have imagined myself speaking. It was amazing, my sudden transition from being shy to being the host.

"Oh, Grandpa! Are you for real?" Raven said. "Is that all?"

"Even you, Mum? What were you thinking?"

Raven's gifts piled high next to her, neatly wrapped. She turned her gaze on me, clearly waiting for me to produce a gift of my own. I glanced down at my empty hands and then back at her, giving her a weak smile. I forgot to tell her that where I come from, we don't give birthdays invitations: you show up, eat enough, and later talk about how poor the event was.

Thanks to Mr Williams who kept asking her why she didn't like her expensive gifts. "Honey, it's the most expensive gift ever."

"Come on, Dad, not everything expensive is beautiful," she rolled her eyes before throwing herself into the pool.

"What do you want, honey?" Mr Williams asked.

"A pink teddy, Father, a teddy!"

Mr and Mrs Williams exchanged glances, sharing a silent understanding. I froze on a spot as I watched them leave. Moments later, they returned with the stuffed animal they had just bought. Raven took it, but instead of hugging the teddy, she flung it into the pool and hurried off to her room. Reluctantly, I followed her, panting behind her mother and Sophia.

"Mum, why do you hate me?" Her voice trembled with hurt, but I could see she was faking it.

"We love you; you are the best things that ever happened to your father and me."

"I just don't like the teddy, Mum."

Mrs Williams slumped her shoulders and let out a tired sigh.

"Raven, you can't keep behaving like a child. It's not really about the teddy bear, is it?"

"Why does everything have to mean something, Mum? I just didn't like it."

Sophia rolled her eyes, clearly losing her patience. "Seriously, Raven? You practically begged for it!"

"Stay out of this, Sophia! You don't get it!"

"I don't get what?" Sophia said "That you throw a tantrum every time you don't feel special? Grow up, Raven!"

Raven stormed off to her room, slamming the door so hard....

"I'm sorry you had to see that," said her mother. "She's... just going through a phase."

A New Home for Lisa

The end of the year was approaching at South Bauleni Community School, marking the completion of my first year there. Throughout the year, I made a few good friends, including Lisa and my two fabulous friends from Riverweed. However, my absolute favourite was my kind-hearted teacher, Miss Margaret O'Hara, whom I had grown to adore.

It was during break, Miss O'Hara called Lisa and me for a special meeting. She had a proposition for Lisa—she asked if Lisa could come and live with her. It was common for teachers to extend such humanitarian gestures during our younger years. I always admired this about some teachers, perhaps because life was simpler back then. We relied on our gardens and farms for food, and our parents didn't have to worry about expenses like DSTV, airtime, gambling, clothing, or expensive fuel and electricity. We worked hard, and alcohol wasn't abused like it is nowadays. Life was much more affordable.

Miss O'Hara lived in a two-bedroom house provided by the school. I was genuinely happy for my friend because she wouldn't have to walk long distances to get to school.

"Your mother talked about the possibility of relocating to the village," Miss O'Hara said to Lisa. "You can stay in Sophia's room. It will bring you closer to school, giving you more time to focus on your studies."

I had a few questions of my own that I was thinking. Is it really a good idea to live with Miss O'Hara? We come from diverse cultures, so there's a chance it might not work out. Will Lisa feel comfortable in her house? It wasn't my decision to make.

"Can I think about it, Mistress?" Lisa said. "Maybe I should talk to my mother."

"Oh, I forgot to mention," Miss O'Hara said, "Sophia will attend school here next year, so you'll have a friend. You'll have a sister."

I liked Sophia, but I liked Raven even more. Sophia was always so cautious about everything. Raven, on the other hand, didn't overthink. I nudged Lisa's elbow, hoping she would accept our mistress's offer.

"I'll discuss it with my mother; thank you, Mistress O'Hara."

We walked back to class after that, with me lagging behind Lisa, trying to figure out why she hesitated. Why didn't she jump at the chance? Miss O'Hara wasn't just any teacher—she had this way of making everyone feel comfortable just by being there. If it were me, I would have said yes in a heartbeat. I could totally see Miss O'Hara as a fantastic mother, the type who listens.

When we got to our desks, I couldn't keep quiet anymore. "Are you going to move in with our teacher?"

Lisa took a moment to respond. She played with her pencil, spinning it around like it had the answer. "Do you think I should?" she finally asked, looking at me with a doubt that didn't seem like her at all.

"If I were in your shoes, I wouldn't hesitate for a second."

The next day, we found ourselves outside Miss O'Hara's office, waiting for her to let us in. The door creaked open, and she was already at her desk, glasses resting on her nose as she jotted something down in her planner. She looked up, and her warm smile made the room feel so much more inviting.

"The school year is almost over," Miss O'Hara said, her eyes on Lisa. "What do you think about moving in next year?"

It was the beginning of my second year at South Bauleni. Miss O'Hara, helped by the three of us, was tidying up her house because Lisa was moving in. As we entered Sophia's room, I was captivated by photographs all over the walls. The pictures of Sophia and her mother, laughing.

"Where is her father?" I asked myself...

The sight of these images triggered a flood of memories, reminding me of Miss O'Hara's previous mention that Sophia would also be attending South Bauleni. At that moment, Lisa's face betrayed a hint of worry. It was evident that she was worried whether Sophia would welcome her into her room or if she would be relegated to staying in Miss O'Hara's house instead. I couldn't help but empathise with Lisa's concerns, as I, too, shared the same worry. While we had established a strong bond of friendship with Sophia and her family, the prospect of living under the same roof was entirely different. It was a leap into the unknown, a venture that held the potential to either strengthen our relationships or unravel the delicate threads that bound us together.

"Before anything else," Miss O'Hara said, placing her arm around Lisa's shoulders before pulling out a red bag from under the bed, "I have new dresses for you."

"Thank you, Mistress O'Hara," Lisa said as she pulled them out, "I like all of them."

We could hear raised voices as the front door swung open. Sophia and Raven had arrived, lugging in many bags we assisted with. We stood there while Miss O'Hara, Sophia, and Raven sat on the bed.

"Honey," Miss O'Hara said to Sophia, "you still remember Lisa, right?"

"I remember her mum, and having a sister is so much fun!" Sophia said. "You and I are going to be great sisters."

Lisa let out a breath, unsure if she was just dreaming. Sophia shared her mother's love with a stranger and her space. This made me admire little skinny Sophia even more. She wasn't just a pretty face—she had a kind heart, too.

"I'm coming to South BATULENI, too!" Raven blurted out as if she had bumped into a stray rand. "I'm going to love it here!"

"Yes, Mum," Sophia said. "Her parents were difficult at first, but they eventually agreed."

Why would anyone leave a school like Riverweed for South Bauleni? If I were Sophia or Raven, I wouldn't even think about it.

On the second day of school, we all gathered for assembly in the open space that faced the Grade 12 classrooms. We lined up in straight rows, with the younger students shifting nervously while the older ones shared knowing glances. Normally, assembly took place on Mondays, but on that day, it was happening on a Thursday. Mr Damien Sibanga, our headmaster, walked onto the stage with a confidence that made me think he practised his entrance each day he was ready for assembly. He wore a baggy grey suit, and he resembled a military officer more than a teacher. His big afro didn't quite match the dark grey of his suit. We all knew him as strict and serious, with a sharp tongue that could cut through anything.

He stepped up and cleared his throat, a sound that could easily be mistaken for thunder. "Good morning, students," he started. The teachers stood quietly. "Welcome back to another year at South Bauleni. As you all know, assembly and devotion are compulsory," he stressed the word like it was a sacred rule. "And by compulsory, I mean whether you like it or not."

A few nervous laughs spread through the audience, quickly quieted by Mr Sibanga's intense stare. Our headmaster had this way of making us feel like he could see right into our hearts.

"Now," he said, placing his hands behind his back and walking across the stage like he was inspecting a line of soldiers, "we have some new students this year—two in particular that I'm sure you've all heard about." He paused, to let the suspense build as he normal did. "Raven and Sophia, please come forward."

Raven and Sophia, the first white students ever to join South Bauleni, stepped out from the crowd of uniforms.

Mr Sibanga gestured for them to stand next to him.

"I want everyone to show Raven and Sophia the respect they deserve," he declared, his voice taking on a playful seriousness that made it hard to tell if he was joking or being serious. "Just because they look different from us doesn't mean they're really different from us."

I blinked, trying to make sense of his words. Around me, I could feel the same confusion settling in with the other students. Mr Sibanga had a talent for making statements that left you wondering if you should laugh or agree.

The headmaster's eyes scanned the crowd, daring anyone to speak out. But of course, no one did. At South Bauleni, standing out from the crowd is the fastest way to receive embarrassment of a lifetime. It was safer to stay silent, to blend in, and to let the moment pass.

After a long, uncomfortable pause, Mr Sibanga removed his eyeglasses, lifted them to the sun, turned them in and out before he spit on them, wiped them with his handkerchief and paced them back, and continue.

"This is how you should dress," he barked, gesturing to Raven and Sophia, who were both dressed impeccably in our school uniform. "Everything should be in place—neat and clean. There's no excuse for sloppiness in this school."

I hadn't been a fan of our school uniform before, with its stiff collars and itchy fabric, but seeing Raven and Sophia wearing it somehow made it look... better. They carried it with so much confidence as if they'd been wearing it all their lives. I caught myself straightening my collar, hoping to emulate a fraction of their poise.

"I am Headmaster Sibanga," he declared, pausing dramatically as if expecting applause. "EXODUS!"

The word erupted from his mouth with such force that it startled even those of us who knew it was coming. It was his signature move, a bizarre way of signalling the end of assembly and the beginning of our march to the classrooms. The first time I'd heard it; I thought he was trying to tell us a story from the Bible.

With that, we began to disperse, a murmur of voices rising as we shuffled toward our classrooms.

Sophia, Lisa, and I were all settled in our classroom, ready to take on the day's lessons.

"I still can't believe you agreed to study here," I said to Sophia. "Wheels are not turning as they should here."

"But they are turning, aren't they?" Sophia asked.

"They are, but so slowly."

"What are you doing about it?" she asked. "At my old school, we demanded how we wanted things to turn."

"How?"

"Maybe we could start by painting the school, fixing the broken windows and chairs."

"That's not possible," Lisa said. "We don't have money."

"There are so many ways to raise the funds."

"Painting our school and fixing all the broken windows is like building a new school."

Tiwe, Lisa, Sophia, Raven, and I gathered in Miss O'Hara's office during our break. We chose to enjoy our food in the library while sharing funny jokes. Our teacher was also there and seemed to enjoy our conversation, mainly when we discussed Sophia's project.

"This school is in bad shape," Raven said. "But don't worry, we'll fix it so fast that it'll look like a proper school again."

"We need a lot of money," said Lisa.

"Since it's a community school, the community should help us out," Raven said. "Let's start by seeking the headmaster's approval. We need his blessing for this project."

After our last lesson, we went to meet the principal in his office. Raven and Sophia seemed to catch his attention more. Lisa, Tiwe, and I stood while our two friends sat down. Mr Sibanga's office was not completely empty; there was a 1992 calendar with some dates circled in green. Before we started our conversation, he took a moment to circle January 9, 1992, which happened to be a Thursday.

"I hope you both bring great ideas from Riverweed," he said.

"We're really excited to be here, headmaster," Raven replied.

"And we also have some good ideas," Sophia added.

"Headmaster," Raven spoke up. "The five of us came up with an idea to raise funds for renovating our school. If we start this project now, hopefully, in two years, you'll have a nice, spacious office that matches your status."

The principal smiled smugly as if he found the news he had just received mocking himself and his office.

"There are a lot of things that are wrong in this school," Sophia said.

"Hold on, young ladies," he said, "there are also many things that are right at South Bauleni."

"Sir," Tiwe hesitantly raised her hand, but the principal ignored her.

"How do you plan on raising the funds?" he asked.

Raven pulled a letter from an envelope and handed it to the principal. After reading it, he remained silent for a moment before chuckling.

"We attempted this endeavour in 1982 when I was the Head of the Department, and it failed. We tried again in 1988. The people here are unwilling to give their money, and many are poor. Nevertheless, I will support you." He glanced at the letter once more as if he had forgotten something. "You must include a timeline in your request. An open donation request does not work well in our country."

"We will also need a school stamp and many copies," Sophia said.

I forgot to tell my friends that we do not have a photocopier machine at South Bauleni. Sometimes, when we needed copies, Miss O'Hara would go to Riverweed.

"Write plenty of those," he instructed, "I can sign them tomorrow."

"We can make copies at Riverweed," Raven said.

Principal Sibanga's eyes remained fixed on Sophia and Raven, as if he pitied them for leaving Riverweed for South Bauleni. He let out a deep sigh before signing the document.

As we exited the principal's office, our minds swirled with unanswered questions. Breaking the silence, Tiwe's voice quivered with hesitation. "What's our next move?"

"We're going to Riverweed," Raven said, "and from there, we'll distribute these letters to every shop."

The next day after school, we walked to Riverweed. Lisa had a new uniform. Raven, being the oldest, led the way. The gatekeeper was there. We stood behind Raven and Sophia, who looked great in our uniform. Raven's mother, a seamstress, had altered our uniform to Riverweed's standards.

I glanced at Tiwe's skirt, which was long and loose like mine, almost like a dress.

"Have you seen Coach Julitta?" Sophia asked the gatekeeper.

"Soccer field," he said. "The girls are preparing for a friendly match."

"Girls play soccer?" I asked. "Girls are supposed to play netball."

"Girls can play anything, Tina," Raven said. "I played soccer and was the school team captain, playing defence."

I looked at her, full of questions. Our fathers in the village would never approve of us playing a boy's game.

"You really play soccer?" I asked.

"Yes, Tina," Sophia confirmed. "I play centre forward, and I love it."

As we made our way to the soccer field, the usual path was closed off for maintenance, so we took the one that went by the fish pond. The first thing that caught my attention was the soccer field at Riverweed. It was well maintained, with neatly trimmed lawns and pavilions where learners lounged. Every student was clad in blue and black tracksuits, creating a uniform look. It was Wednesday, a day dedicated to sports that rarely happened at South Bauleni. While we also had sports day, it often turned into manual labour.

Excitedly, Raven pointed out Miss Smit as the whistle blew. She was dressed in a white tracksuit and a blue cap; she oversaw a match between the male and female soccer teams. Miss Smit greeted Sophia with compliments on her uniform, drawing attention from everyone. Even Raven received a warm hug and praise.

Just as Miss Smit began to address us, a commotion from a foul in the game interrupted her. We found a spot on the pavilion, and we were the only black kids there. It was strange because nobody seemed to care or even notice us. While there, I saw two talented players from the girls' team, number 9 and number 7. Later, I found out that number 9 was Liv De Waal, the new captain of the Riverweed soccer team, and number 7 was Gloria Bekker. After the game, we went to Miss Smit's house, where we met Mrs Jacobs. I followed behind Raven because I wanted to ask her something.

"You don't like her very much, do you??" I asked Raven.

"I guess you're talking about Liv. She's mean. She wants everything I have."

"Is she the reason you moved from Riverweed to South Bauleni?"

Raven looked at me, her face serious. "I can't stand her, but she's not the reason. Not completely."

"What do you mean by that?"

"Liv and I were close friends. We shared everything, but then she started to see me as competition—grades, sports, even our friends. It wasn't just about being better; she wanted to take everything I had. It got toxic, but that's not why I left Riverweed. I left because I craved something new, something real. Riverweed felt like a cage. Everyone was so obsessed with being perfect, but it was all a facade. I wanted to escape and find out what life was like beyond that school."

At that moment, Sophia, who had been walking ahead of us, stopped and joined the conversation. "I didn't really want to leave Riverweed," she said softly. "Mom made the choice for me. She thought it would be good for me to try something new and escape the stress of Riverweed. At first, I was really upset, but then Raven talked to me about it, and... I guess I started to realize that maybe it wasn't all that bad. Maybe I need it."

"I think I managed to convince you, Sophie," Raven added with a slight laugh.

Miss Smit showed us around the school, including her office. There were lots of trophies displayed on the shelves and many pictures. She was specifically hired for sports, which didn't exist at South Bauleni.

After making some copies, we said our goodbyes and went into town.

From Letters to Soccer Match

Our first stop was a livestock medicine shop where the owner showed interest after reading our letter. As daylight waned, we reached the last supermarket where the owner donated white paint. Though paint was all we got that day; it was indeed a learning experience.

"What's our next move?" Tiwe asked.

"We wait till Friday, then revisit the shops," Raven suggested.

On Friday, each shop expressed interest in seeing our school's progress, but many said they wanted to know how much the school has raised. We had nothing. We informed our principal to at least give us a start-up capital, so they take us seriously. He said the usual thing, the school had no money."

"Why not organize events like a non-uniform day? Learners can donate, say five cents, to wear casual clothes."

In those days, finding even one cent was challenging; I wished it were still 1989 when my father had plenty of two-cent coins. During break, we called for an assembly led by the headmaster. Raven delivered a speech to the students, impressing me with her courage.

"Don't you think it's time for better classrooms?" she challenged the students, met with an initial silence that didn't bode well.

"We all deserve a better school," Sophia agreed. "But first, let's learn to stand on our own feet and work together. If we unite, we can raise the funds to rebuild our school."

"The future is in your hands," said the headmaster "One day, you'll look back and proudly say, 'I made South Bauleni."

He also announced the start of the project with a non-uniform day, beginning the next Friday.

Early that Friday, students came dressed in their own clothes, while we did the same, collecting 5-rand, equivalent to nearly 30 Namibian dollars today. Teachers, including the principal, contributed one rand each, bringing our total to 42 rand.

"What's our next step?" Lisa asked. "Should we revisit the shops?"

"No," Raven replied decisively. "We'll hold a cake sale. With the money, we can buy sweets and other goods."

After school, we bought everything needed for our venture. That night at Miss O'Hara's house, we baked the cakes. On the first day of sales, we sold out. Learners at South Bauleni donated various items, and by week's end, we had raised 500-rand, equivalent to 3,000 rand today. We needed approximately 27,000 rand, as estimated by the construction company.

"It's time to approach local businesses," Raven declared. "With 500 rand, they'd better take us seriously."

During our visits, a businessman who owned a construction company said to us that Riverweed had also asked for a donation for a science lab.

"I have requests from two schools," he explained. "I'll help, but only to the winner of the soccer match, South Bauleni verses Riverweed."

"Our boys are ready," said Tiwe.

He chuckled, "I meant the girls."

"We don't have a girls' soccer team," Lisa said.

"Then start forming one."

Just then, Miss Smit, Liv, and Gloria entered. Sophia offered Miss Smit her seat.

"Now that we're all here," he began, "I have a new idea. I'll donate services worth 100,000 rand to the winning team. How about organizing a girls' match between the two schools?"

Liv smiled confidently, clearly dismissing the competition. South Bauleni had never fielded a girls' team, and Riverweed knew it. The sponsor suggested each school contribute 20,000 rand, with the winner receiving 140,000 rand.

After much discussion, we agreed to proceed, facing two challenges. First, we needed a skilled coach, and second, we had to raise the funds.

"I have someone in mind," Miss O'Hara said. "My cousin on holiday loves soccer."

We couldn't contain our excitement about meeting our new coach. A few days later, Mr Sibanga announced her during assembly. Her name was Peace, a young white woman with many tattoos. Looking at her, I could tell we had finally found a coach who knew what she was doing. We went from class to class, but none of the girls signed up, not even me. Only Raven and Sophia took the initiative, forcing our names onto the list.

"This won't make a team," Miss Peace said. "We need more girls. Every girl should be on the soccer field, and classes should compete against each other. From there, we can select our team."

Right after the break, the headmaster suspended classes and gather everyone at the soccer field near the bushes that led to the open market. Surprisingly, some of the girls played well. Tiwe and I, along with Sophia, Raven, and other girls, were chosen to be on the team. Lisa, because of her height, became the goalkeeper. We went for training day after day, and in the beginning, I would get so tired. We practised whenever we could. When we were finally ready, Miss Peace gave us a nice uniform. I still remember it clearly because I have a team photo. We wore black shorts and green tops with our names on them, while Lisa wore all red.

The sun climbed in the sky that Saturday morning. Riverweed sports field was well packed. The atmosphere created an undeniable sense of excitement. The pavilion was divided into two sections and filled with learners, some of their parents, and locals. Their passion for the game was evident in every chant and cheer that echoed through the air. Across the field, our own learners sat quietly, with no parents.

"Tiwe," said our coach, "make sure you don't kick the ball straight up. The ball should move forward, not upwards."

I knew my own limitations. My kicks lacked the stamina and accuracy to make a real impact. Even though I had speed, I struggled to find my place on the field, always overshadowed by Tebuho, who seemed to excel where I fell short. I stood next to our coach on the sideline, watching as our girls marched onto the field—shoulders slumped, and the usual lively chatter and noise we all made at South Bauleni were noticeably absent on our side. It was evident to any observer that team spirit was at an all-time low. The Bauleni Girls moved slowly, their eyes lacking the usual fire. Instead of a solid team prepared for the game of a lifetime, the Bauleni Girls were more like a collection of individuals going for slaughter.

Our coach followed behind with a troubled expression. Her attempts to rally the team seemed empty, even to herself. The once promising team spirit had vanished, replaced by a feeling of impending doom.

The game began. Liv, the captain of the Riverweed team, immediately showed her skills to put us to shame. She was fast, nimble, and smart, manoeuvring through our defence like my all-time favourite footballer, Mr Sadio Mané. In just a few minutes, Liv scored the first goal, causing a wave of excitement among Riverweed students.

Liv's teammates rallied around her, riding each like a bunch of playful puppies. The scoreboard displayed our early setback, setting a tough tone for the rest of the game. Despite our efforts, Riverweed's momentum continued to grow. Their teamwork was flawless and before we could regroup and came back to reality, Liv scored again. This time, her shot was unstoppable, slipping past our goalkeeper effortlessly. The crowd erupted once more as the ball found the net. With a score of 2-0, the reality of our situation sank in. We needed to wake up from our slumber.

The pressure was on, but we couldn't give up. Our coach encouraged us to start fighting. We knew we had to disrupt their flow, challenge their dominance, and create our own opportunities.

When the second half began, my heart raced as I realised this was my moment to shine. I prepared myself to step onto the field, ready to seize whatever chance awaited me. I looked at our fans, who were losing faith in the face of adversity, and a surge of resolve washed over me. With each step I took onto the field, I carried the weight of their expectations on my shoulders, silently promising to fight until the very end.

When the referee's whistle blew, Tiwe's pass found me, and I sprinted forward with all my might, my eyes fixed on the goalpost. However, the tough defender, Gloria, proved to be a formidable opponent, effortlessly taking the ball away from me, just like taking a candy from a baby. I didn't let it discourage me. I steadied myself, knowing that setbacks were a normal part of the game.

Moments later, as Liv manoeuvred past Tiwe, thanks to Raven's well-timed intervention, the ball was at my feet, presenting a golden opportunity near the goal. Even with Gloria chasing after me, I summoned all my strength and kicked the ball with great force. As it soared through the air, I held my breath, watching the white ball as it found its place in the back of the net.

The crowd's excitement peaked, with our supporters jumping and cheering. I glanced at my coach and saw her nod of approval.

Our focus sharpened with the game's clock counting down the final moments. Each passing second reminded us of the limited time to change the game's outcome. With only 15 minutes left and Riverweed still in the lead, every move on the field became crucial, every decision vital to our success. On the sidelines, our coach's words of encouragement motivated us like a battle cry, urging us to give our best despite our challenges. Her unwavering faith in our abilities fuelled our determination, pushing us to exceed our limits.

In the heat of the match, something happened as Liv, Riverweed's star player, charged towards our goal, but before she could take a shot, Raven, our strong defender, sprang to stop her. A collision occurred, causing Liv to fall to the ground. The referee's whistle blew, and it was a foul, awarding a penalty to Riverweed.

At that moment, it felt like our hopes of winning were slipping so far away. As luck would have it, our goalkeeper, Lisa, miraculously saved the penalty.

The game reached its climax, and the pressure mounted.

Tiwe passed me the ball, our last chance to change the course of the game, but before I could react, an opponent tackled me aggressively, causing me to fall to the ground. Clutching my ankle, I lay there in pain. Miss Peace hurried onto the field.

"It's painful," I confessed, "but let me finish the game."

At that moment, there was no time for doubt, only a determined resolve to see the game through, regardless of the consequences. Amid the thunderous cheers from our fans, Tiwe's successful penalty kick gave us hope. We fought back from the brink of defeat, levelling the score and defying the odds with every passing moment. With the final whistle marking the end of regular time, we prepared ourselves for the ultimate challenge in overtime.

Despite our best efforts, neither team could break the deadlock, the tension building with each missed opportunity. The game turned into a nail-biting penalty shoot-out, a test of nerves and skill to determine the winner.

In a moment of pure brilliance, Lisa emerged as our saviour. Her reflexes denied our opponents two penalties while our team flawlessly executed each penalty kick. With every successful shot, our spirits soared, the promise of victory calling out to us.

The final whistle blew, announcing us as the winner of the match. Our fans erupted in joy, their cheers filling the whole sports field. We embraced each other tightly, tears of happiness running down our cheeks. Lisa was hoisted onto Tiwe's shoulders, our champion of the day. Victory belonged to us — South Bauleni.

The businessman, and two ladies came up to us with a big grin. "Well done, girls. You played well." And he left without giving us our price and no one asked.

As the initial thrill faded, something good happened. The Riverweed team, led by their coach, came to us. Despite their disappointment, their faces showed respect and true sportsmanship.

"You girls played well," Miss Smit said. "It's clear you've worked hard, and it paid off. Well done." She then turned to Lisa, who had been the star of our victory. "You were great."

"Thank you, Miss Smit," she replied softly.

The gesture from the Riverweed team didn't stop there. They invited us to join them for a small gathering after the match. It was their tradition to host a friendly get-together, win or lose, to celebrate the spirit of the game. At the gathering, we shared stories, laughter, and snacks. The initial competition gave way to friendship as we mingled and got to know each other better. But Liv and Gloria, clearly were mad at us.

As the sun went down and we went our separate ways, a strong connection had formed between South Bauleni and Riverweed. We understood that even though we were opponents on the field, we could also be allies and friends off the field.

On Monday, the vibe at South Bauleni was amazing. Everyone gathered at assembly. Our principal, Mr Damien Sibanga, stood at the front, a big smile on his face as he got ready to speak to us. It was the first time we had seen him so happy.

"Today, we're not just celebrating a soccer game," he said. "We're celebrating teamwork, perseverance, and the South Bauleni spirit. These girls have shown us what we can do when we work together."

The applause was deafening. The girls' soccer team, including me, stood in a line, feeling proud and appreciated.

"This win is not just for us," Raven said, her words echoing through the crowd. "It's for all those who supported us, believed in us, and stood by our side. This is only the start. Together, we will make our school better."

The students erupted in cheers... our teachers too. Miss Peace stood next to the principal. "We achieved this together," Our coach said. "From bake sales to practice sessions, every contribution mattered. This victory proves our potential for greatness."

The businessman who had challenged us surprised us by joining the assembly. "I am truly impressed by your determination and teamwork. As promised, my company will be donating 100,000 rand towards the rebuilding of South Bauleni. You all deserve it."

It was like a dream coming true. Not only did we win the match, but we also get money needed to renovate our school.

In the days that followed, it was unbelievable to see the construction starting. The old, run-down classrooms were being demolished to make room for new ones. The whole school was filled with excitement. The principal's words kept resonating in our heads: "The future is in your hands. One day, you'll look back and proudly say, I MADE SOUTH BAULENI."

And we would. We were certain of that now. Together, we could achieve anything.

Student Exchange Program

Another incident that I remember well happened after school. Raven, Sophia, Lisa, Tiwe, and I were at the soccer field. The boys played against the local Madala team at our field, and our team won. The crowd cheered, but my attention was drawn to Lisa, who sat between Sophia and Raven, appearing somewhat dreamy.

"Riverweed is beautiful," Lisa said. "I want to attend a school like that, or even better."

"What if you could go to Riverweed right now?" Sophia asked without even looking at Lisa.

"Right now? What do you mean?" Lisa asked, her face scrunched up.

"You and Tina could go there for two weeks!" Raven leaned closer and whispered as if sharing a secret. "They have this exchange program. Last year, Liv and I visited Windhoek High for one week."

"Is that for real? I thought it was just something people talked about."

"You and Tina would get to experience what Riverweed is like."

"I'm not sure…" Lisa hesitated. "It sounds like a very bad idea."

"I understand it's a bit scary," Raven said, placing a comforting hand on Lisa's shoulder. "But trust me, it's a good opportunity. You'd get to explore a whole new place and learn a lot. It's not just about Riverweed; it's about seeing things differently."

"That's the best part," Sophia added. "You'll have the chance to bring back something new. Plus, it's only two weeks! You'll be back before you know it. Just think of all the cool stories you'll have to tell!"

"All right let's do it. I'm willing to give it a shot," said Lisa.

"I guess it could be fun. But how do we even start this? Who do we talk to?" I asked.

After school, Tiwe and I hurried to our room to change out of our uniforms. The day had dragged on endlessly, and our conversation with

Raven and Sophia replayed in my mind. Tiwe flopped onto her bed with a sigh as I slipped my dress.

"That idea Raven and Sophia suggested I think it's a terrible one."

"I want to go," I said.

"Don't say I didn't warn you."

The delicious smell of Aunt's cooking wafted through the house. When we entered the kitchen, Aunt was busy serving. Angela and her dear son had just arrived...

"Hello, fam!" Angela shouted.

As we settled at the table, Tiwe said, "Mu, tell Aunt about the exchange program."

"What's that?" Angela asked.

"I think it's when students go to another school for some days," Tiwe explained. "Mu wants to go to Riverweed for the exchange program."

"That sounds like a horrible idea to me," Angela burst out laughing.

"I think it's a terrific idea," Aunt said. "It's a chance to try something new."

"I think it's a bad idea," Angela countered sharply. "You have no idea what you're getting into. Riverweed might not be as great as it looks."

Tiwe glanced back and forth between Aunt and Angela...

"If Mukenani is determined to do this," Aunt said, "then we'll support her."

The following day, we found ourselves outside Miss O'Hara's office. She was busy sorting through papers when we walked in.

"Miss O'Hara, we have an idea we'd like to share with you," said Raven.

"We were thinking," Raven continued, "about starting a student exchange program here at South Bauleni. Liv and I took part in one last year, and it was an amazing experience."

"A student exchange program?" Miss O'Hara asked. "That sounds interesting. How do you see it working?"

"Lisa and Tina can be the first ones to participate. They could spend two weeks at Riverweed, getting a first hand look at education there. It would give them a new perspective and allow them to bring back valuable insights."

"I think it's a good idea," Miss O'Hara leaned back in her chair, pondering the suggestion. "But you know how Mr Sibanga can be... particular about these things. It might be a hard sell."

"We get that, but we think it's worth a shot, Mom," Sophia said.

"Okay. Let's put together a proposal and present it to Mr Sibanga. We'll highlight the educational benefits and the positive effects it could have."

A few days later, we found ourselves in Mr Sibanga's office. Miss O'Hara had prepared a proposal detailing the advantages of the exchange program. Raven, Sophia, Lisa, Tiwe, and I stood by.

Mr Sibanga, clad in his usual oversized grey suit, sat behind his messy desk. His serious expression didn't change much as Miss O'Hara presented the proposal.

"Mr Sibanga, we believe that starting a student exchange program could greatly benefit our students. It allows them to experience different educational settings."

"And you think this will work?" he asked, his gaze steady. "You know, Miss O'Hara, I'm not really into sentimental programs. I prefer things to be clear-cut and practical."

"Sir, principal" Sophia said. "We truly believe this program could be very practical. It's an investment in the student's future. They'll come back with new skills and knowledge that could help the whole school."

"Alright," he grumbled at last. "But if this turns into just another one of those feel-good projects that don't produce real results, you'll hear from me."

The news about the exchange program spread quickly throughout the school. As our departure date approached, the excitement and nerves were through the roof. Finally, the day we were supposed to leave for Riverweed arrived. Lisa, Sophia, and Raven showed up with Miss O'Hara and Lisa. Aunt, usually so calm, was now a whirlwind of last-minute tips and advice.

Aunt stood next to the car, hands on her hips, giving us one last set of instructions. "Just remember to keep your room clean and treat your room-mates well. Hostel life can be tough."

"You'll be just fine, Tina," Sophia said. "It's going to be an exciting journey."

"Exactly," Raven added. "Just stay open-minded and remember that Riverweed is a different place. You're going to gain so much experience."

"I can't believe this is happening," Tiwe said.

"Mukenani and Lisa," Miss O'Hara said, placing a comforting hand on our shoulders. "Just be yourself and embrace everything."

The journey to Riverweed lay ahead, and the skyline of South Bauleni slowly disappeared. As we drove, the comforting presence of Aunt, Sophia, Raven, and Miss O'Hara wrapped around me like a warm blanket, their supportive words mixing with my swirling thoughts about the adventure ahead. Aunt finally stopped the car right in front of Riverweed's big gate. The engine fell silent...

"Here we are," Aunt said. "Remember what I told you. Stay strong, be respectful, and no fighting."

"You both are going to do amazing. Just be yourselves and enjoy the experience," Miss O'Hara added.

The gateman opened the gate with a nod, greeting us with a polite formality that made Lisa and me feel more welcome. After a final round of hugs and promises, Aunt waved goodbye and drove off, leaving us at the entrance of our new school.

The gate man led us to the principal's office. Mr Pieter, welcomed us with a warm smile, his tall figure and commanding presence softened by the kindness in his eyes.

"Welcome to Riverweed," Mr Pieter said, reaching out his hand. After a quick introduction and some details about our stay, Mr Pieter turned to the gateman. "Please take them to Miss Van Der Merwe, the matron. She'll help them settle into the dorm."

The gateman showed us the way to the dormitory. When we reached her office, Miss Van Der Merwe was so nice to us.

"You must be Lisa and Mukenani," she said, shaking our hands. "I'm Miss Van Der Merwe, and I'll be in charge of making sure your stay here goes smoothly."

She led us to our room, Room 12, and gently knocked before opening the door. The room was bright and tidy, and two girls stood up to greet us.

"Hey, I'm Elsie," one of them said cheerfully. "And this is Marinda."

"Welcome to our room," Marinda added, her eyes friendly. "If you need anything or have questions, just ask us. We want to make sure you feel at home."

Elsie and Marinda were so welcoming in everything they did. They took us on a tour of the dormitory, explaining the shared bathroom, the study area, and their favourite hangout spots. Their kindness helped ease the overwhelming feelings we had about this big change.

As evening fell, we all gathered in the common area, chatting and getting to know one another. The initial nerves started to fade as we began to view our exchange program as an exciting journey filled with new friendships and experiences.

The next morning, the reality of living in the dorm at Riverweed started to hit us. We all shuffled out of our room and went to the communal showers. Sharing such a personal space with everyone felt a bit awkward. The bathroom had several shower stalls lined up against one wall, each separated by nothing. It was clean and organized, with a light, fresh scent of soap and shampoo. When we walked in, I spotted the other girls moving around naked. Their laid-back attitude made the whole place feel more chill. They were chatting and laughing while getting ready for their showers, taking off their clothes with a casualness that felt strange to us.

Lisa and I exchanged nervous glances. We had never been in a situation like this before. Seeing everyone so comfortably naked, without a trace of embarrassment, was new for us.

"I'm not sure I can do this," I whispered to Lisa.

"Let's wait until everyone else is done. It might feel less weird."

We lingered at the entrance of the bathroom, observing the others as they went through their routines. Elsie and Marinda, laughing and chatting while rinsing off, made it all seem normal. Their confidence helped ease some of our nerves, but we still felt a bit anxious.

After a little while, as the bathroom started to empty, we decided it was our turn. We quickly took off our clothes, our movements a bit rushed and awkward. We stepped into the shower area in our undies, trying to copy the relaxed vibe of the other girls.

As the warm water flowed over us, the initial awkwardness slowly faded into a feeling of relief. The tension melted away, and we began to enjoy the straightforwardness of the communal shower experience. It was different from what we were used to, but it was also part of this new journey we were on.

By the time we were done, we stepped out of the shower, wrapped ourselves in towels, and exchanged a small, relieved smile. It was another step toward fitting in at Riverweed, and even though it had been a strange experience, it was one we could look back on with pride.

Once we were all dressed, Elsie, Marinda, Lisa, and I made our way to our first classes. We walked past countless classrooms, each door labelled with neat signs. Everything felt so modern and spotless, a big change from what I was used to. When we finally arrived at our classroom, the scene was both thrilling and a bit intimidating. Mr Janse van Rensburg, our English teacher, was at the front, organizing papers on his desk and getting ready for the day's lessons.

As soon as we walked in, I caught Liv's eye. She narrowed her gaze slightly before sharing a look with Gloria. They both erupted into laughter. I could feel my cheeks heat up with embarrassment as their giggles filled the room. It felt like we were the punchline of a joke we didn't understand.

Mr Janse van Rensburg quickly noticed the commotion and stepped in. With a steady yet firm voice, he said to Liv and Gloria. "That's enough, girls." He then turned to us with a friendly smile. "Class, I'd like you to meet Lisa and Mukenani, who are visiting from South Bauleni for the next two weeks as part of our student exchange program. Let's give them a warm welcome."

The room quieted down, and the laughter faded. Liv and Gloria, still grinning but quieter now, tried to pull themselves together as he continued with the introductions. Lisa and I exchanged anxious looks, trying to adapt to our new environment while handling the unexpected attention from Liv and Gloria.

Even with the awkward beginning, the teacher's introduction helped lighten the mood. The students began to calm down, and as we took our seats, we focused on the lessons ahead, ready to dive into the Riverweed experience, no matter how tough it might be.

During break time, the four of us—Lisa, Elsie, Marinda, and I—ended up in the dining hall. The delicious aroma of freshly baked bread and tea filled the air. At South Bauleni, we never had anything like this. Here in Riverweed, the dining hall was something special. Students were moving around, laughing with friends, and their plates were stacked high with food.

We found a table in the corner and sat down. As we started eating, Elsie and Marinda shared tips on how to enjoy the dining experience to the fullest. As the break came to an end and students began to return to their classes, I asked, "Aren't Liv and Gloria in the hostel?"

"Oh, Liv and Gloria?" Elsie replied. "No, they're day students. They live close by and go home after classes."

Right after leaving the dining hall, we ran into Liv and Gloria, who were loitering in the hallway like a couple of hungry wolves. They blocked our path...

Liv, with her perfectly styled blonde hair and polished look, sneered at us. "Oh, look who decided to show up," she said mockingly. "Did you two escaped from some zoo? You don't belong here. This place is for people who actually matter."

"Seriously," Gloria added, her dark eyes shining with malice. "Maybe you should go back to where you came from and let the real students focus on their education."

Elsie and Marinda stood by, silent as if this was just another day. Their lack of response felt like a betrayal, making Liv and Gloria's harsh words sting even more.

On the second day, as we entered our new classroom, Mr Janse was already at his desk, getting ready for the lesson. Liv and Gloria were at the back, their eyes on us like hawks. As we settled into our seats, Liv's loud whisper sliced through the room. "Just watch them struggle through the lesson. They probably don't even know how to use a ruler."

"I bet they think this is some kind of adventure," Gloria made a silly chortle. "They're just here to take up space."

After school, we went into the library, and a while later, Gloria crept up behind us and, with a playful smirk, dropped a stack of books onto the table. "Oops, my bad," she said, her voice dripping with sarcasm. "Didn't realize you two were here. Not like you're doing anything that matters."

Liv chuckled and then knocked a pile of books off the table, sending them crashing to the floor around us. "Maybe you should just go back to where you belong. This library is too sophisticated for you."

We hurried to gather the scattered books, aware of the stares from other students.

The breaking point came during gym class. We were told to run laps around the track, which was already tough enough. As we struggled to keep pace, Liv jogged alongside us, hurling a constant stream of insults. "Is this your best effort? I've seen snails move faster." She then turned to her friend, "Gloria darling, snails do they move or walk?"

"I think it's the same thing," she said, "what matters is that they are super slow."

"Well, I think you two are just here to fill space and add some diversity, right? Just give up already and go back home."

By the end of class, both Lisa and I were drained, not just from the physical activity but from the emotional weight of their bullying.

"Next time Liv and Gloria try to mess with us," Lisa declared, "they'll see the village side of me. I refuse to let them walk all over us."

Our conversation was cut short when Liv and Gloria approached, strutting toward us. They didn't need to say much; their disdainful glares said it all.

"Go back to your filthy school,' said Liv.

"I think you have said enough," Lisa said brushing her off with her shoulders.

Liv didn't like that at all and went on to slap Lisa. Lisa didn't like that either and went on to return the slap even harder. The sound rang out across the gym hall. Other students who disliked Liv seemed to revel in the moment.

Gloria rushed to help Liv, lifting her while glaring at Lisa with pure rage. "You'll regret that," Gloria hissed.

Later that day, we found ourselves in the principal's office, where Liv's parents were already waiting. Liv's mother was pacing, clearly agitated.

"This is unacceptable!" she yelled as soon as we walked in. "How dare you touch my daughter? I demand that you be sent back to your school right now. You don't belong here!"

"Veronica," Liv's dad said firmly. "Just take a breath." "Our daughter brought this on herself. Liv and Gloria have been picking on those girls, and it was only a matter of time before someone fought back."

"We need to handle this calmly," Mr Jensen said. "These two are here on an exchange program, and we have to sort this out without making it worse."

"These girls think they can come here and stir up trouble. They should be sent back right away," Liv's mom said angrily.

"The other girl didn't fight," said Liv's father. "I think she should be allowed to finish her program."

"Well, then," said the principal. "That other one can stay."

"Excuse me, sir," I said. "Maybe I should also go."

Liv's mom looked pleased, while her dad's disapproval was clear. Once the decision was made, we said our goodbyes to Elsie and Miranda. Our two-week trip had been cut down to just three days, and we felt a mix of relief and sadness. Elsie and Miranda were nice and wished us the best, but it was hard to ignore the feeling of disappointment.

"I'm sorry things didn't go as we hoped," Elsie said, giving us a warm hug. "Maybe next time will be better."

"We're going to miss you," Miranda said.

Lisa and I managed to smile, even though we felt a bit bitter inside. We thanked them for their kindness and walked toward the gate where Aunt, Tiwe, and Samuel were waiting for us.

Tiwe burst into a loud laugh when she saw us. "That was quite the experience!" she exclaimed. "You made history as the first Black students at Riverweed!"

"I'm just happy you're coming home," Aunt said. "It's been a rough few days, but I'm proud of you for hanging in there."

"Looks like we didn't really fit in," Lisa said.

With one last look at Riverweed, we got into the car, ready to go back to South Bauleni. As we drove away, Tiwe continued laughing, reminding us that even when things get tough, there's always space for some humour. We laughed too.

"Well, good things don't last forever," I said.

The next day at school, Miss O'Hara, Sophia, Raven, and I met with Mr Sibanga. He leaned back in his chair; his face hard to read at first. But as we stood there, his expression sharpened, and a frown appeared. He crossed his arms and let out a long, frustrated sigh.

"So, you're back," he said. "Three days at Riverweed, and you're already back. What happened?"

"Mr Sibanga, it wasn't their fault," Miss O'Hara said. "Some students were awful to them."

"Well," he said, "it was Lisa who fought and got expelled from Riverweed. Mukenani didn't, and she should go back and complete the program."

"Alone?" Miss O'Hara asked.

"Yes. Alone, Miss O'Hara."

The Final Question

I was standing in front of Mr Sibanga's desk, my heart racing. How could he expect me to go back to Riverweed all by myself? I shot a glance at Miss O'Hara, searching for some kind of support, but her face was impossible to read.

"Well, Mukenani," Mr Sibanga said, his tone was calm yet authoritative, "the decision has been made. You will be returning to Riverweed. The headmaster there has confirmed that your spot is still open. Do you understand, young lady?"

"Yes, Headmaster Sibanga," I said, even though I was angry at him.

When I arrived back at Riverweed, Aunt was with me as we walked through the gates. Mr Pieter, the principal, welcomed us in his office.

"Welcome back, Mukenani," Mr Pieter said with a comforting smile. "I know this has been tough, but I believe you have what it takes to get through it."

As we made our way to the dormitory, Aunt pulled me into a tight hug. "Remember what I told you. Stay strong, be respectful, and let your mind be your greatest weapon."

The dormitory was quiet when I walked inside. Elsie and Marinda acted like they were busy with their books. There was no friendly greeting, just an uncomfortable silence. I dropped my bag on the bed and took a deep breath, preparing myself for what was to come.

"Hey, girls," I said, trying to break the ice.

Elsie glanced up for a moment.

"I thought you were gone for good," she replied.

"Did I do something wrong? I thought we were friends."

The girls didn't respond. Their silence hit harder than I imagined. I let out a sigh and curled up on my bed.

The next morning, I walked into class alone. The teacher looked up from his desk, his eyes acknowledged my return, but Liv, Gloria, and their group whispered among themselves, their laughter piercing through the air like daggers. Each snicker felt like a weight on my shoulders, pulling me down. I couldn't take it anymore. I dashed out of the classroom and found a bench beneath a sprawling oak tree, where I let the tears spill freely.

"Sweetie," a warm voice broke through my thoughts.

I looked up, blinking back the tears.

"Mrs. Jacob!"

"I remember you! How's your friend... Lisa, was it?"

"She got sent back... she had a fight with Liv."

Mrs Jacob nodded, showing she understood. "No. Your friend stood up to Liv. It's tough to be in a place where you feel out of place."

"It really is," I said. "I don't know how much longer I can handle this."

Mrs Jacob took my hand and squeezed it softly.

"Listen, dear. You're intelligent and strong, and you have something special—your intelligence. Use it. Your mind is your greatest asset. Don't let them get to you. Find a way to turn this situation around."

"But how? How can I stand up for myself?"

"Challenge them. Show them you're not just here to take up space. Prove that you're someone to be taken seriously."

The idea sparked in my mind. I would challenge Liv to a quiz competition. It was time to stand up for myself in a way that would show who I was.

The following day, I saw Liv before classes began. She was surrounded by her friends, laughing as if nothing bothered her. I took a deep breath and went to meet her.

"Liv," I called out, even though I was so scared.

She turned; her smile was quickly replaced by a sneer.

"What do you want, black girl?"

"I'm here to challenge you," I said, holding her gaze. "A quiz competition. You'll represent Riverweed, and I'll represent South Bauleni."

"A quiz competition? Why would I waste my time on that?"

"It's a chance to show who's the smartest," I said. "Unless you're scared of losing, of course."

Liv's face turned red with anger, but she quickly regained her composure. "Alright. You're on. Just don't kill yourself when I crush you."

"We'll see about that."

"One more thing," Liv added with a smirk. "I'll pick the topic—how about literature?"

"I love literature," I said even though I hated it.

The news about the quiz spread quickly. It was set for the last day of the exchange program. Mr Janse van Rensburg, our English teacher, handed us a hefty booklet.

"This has 500 pages of literature events from 1991," he said. "The quiz will include everything in this book. Make sure to study hard."

The challenge was on. Later that evening, Elsie and Marinda approached me in my room, their expressions tinged with regret.

"We're sorry," Elsie said softly, her eyes cast down. "Liv made us keep our distance."

"I understand," I replied gently, hoping to ease the tension. "What changed?"

"The matron had a word with us," Marinda said, glancing at Elsie.

They both settled down beside me, and Elsie pulled out some notes, ready to quiz me. As we went through the questions, I stumbled over most of the answers.

"Maybe you need a tutor," Marinda suggested, a thoughtful look crossing her face.

A name popped into my mind. Without hesitation, we made our way to Miss Smit's house. When we arrived, Mrs Jacob was outside, feeding her dog.

"Sweetie! How are you getting ready for the quiz?" she asked, looking up with a warm smile.

"Mrs Jacob, could you help me? I really need a tutor," I said.

"Of course! I'm so bored now that Sophie's off at school in South Bauleni," she chuckled, her eyes sparkling with excitement.

Day after day, Mrs Jacob helped me, and Elsie and Marinda coached me in the dorm. Gradually, everything started to click. I even began to enjoy literature.

As the competition day drew near, I asked if students from South Bauleni could attend. Mr Pieter agreed. Plans were set for a group of students and teachers to come to Riverweed for the event.

Finally, the day of the competition arrived. Mrs Jacob's encouraging words rang in my ears, giving me the motivation, I needed. Riverweed Hall was filled with students, teachers, and the South Bauleni visitors.

I stood on the stage in my South Bauleni uniform. Liv stood next to me in her uniform too. She was slender, beautiful, and clearly from a rich family. Mr Janse van Rensburg took his position as the quiz master...

"Welcome, everyone," he announced. "Today's competition features Riverweed's Liv against South Bauleni's Mukenani. The subject is literature, and only on events that took place in the year 1991. For the first round, please choose a number between 1 and 20 for your question."

The quiz kicked off, and the questions came at us quickly. Liv answered confidently, and as for me, I was really having a hard time. The audience was captivated as we battled it out...

As the competition continued, the second round, I realized I was keeping up well. Liv's earlier confidence started to wane as I answered question after question correctly. The tension in the room intensified with every moment that passed.

At last, we reached the final question because of a tie. The quizmaster glanced at both of us, a slight grin on his face.

"This is the last question," he said. "It will decide the winner."

My tutors—Mrs Jacob, Elsie, and Marinda—were in the audience, giving me the thumbs up for encouragement. I inhaled quietly, remembering all the lessons with my teachers, and everything I had prepared.

"What was the most important literary event of 1991 in South Africa, and why does it matter? Liv will go first," said the quizmaster.

Liv gave the wrong answer confidently.

"That is incorrect Liv," said the quizmaster who called me to the microphone. "If you get this question right," the quizmaster looked at me. "You will be the champion."

The room went quiet. I sauntered up to the microphone, and then a small grin played at the corner of my mouth because Mrs Jacob had asked me the same question. I knew the correct answer.

"The most important literary event of 1991 was when Nadine Gordimer received the Nobel Prize in Literature, a well-deserved recognition of African literature worldwide, making her the first South African to win this honour. She wrote about the struggles for black people in SA during apartheid."

"That is correct," said the quizmaster.

Applause erupted from the crowd. Liv ran off the stage into her mother's arms, crying like a spoiled brat she was. As for me, a wave of pride and relief washed over me as I stood tall, knowing I had made my school proud. I saw Miss O'Hara, Tiwe, Lisa, Sophia, Raven, and Aunt, all clapping for me.

"The winner of today's quiz is Mukenani, representing South Bauleni. Congratulations!" He said to the microphone.

There were hugs and cheers in the school hall. The last hug came from Liv, who looked at me with sincere regret and said, "I'm sorry."

I smiled back, feeling a sense of closure. "Thank you, Liv."

"Let's go back to South Bauleni, Mu," Tiwe said, wrapping her arm around my shoulders.

From Soccer Fields to College Dreams

Enough time has passed since giving Liv an embarrassment of a lifetime, and everyone has stopped talking about it. I was in grade 11 when my aunt passed away after a brief battle with some illness, and her death marked the beginning of a downturn in our once peaceful home. Angela came to live with us, but she wasn't nurturing towards my sister and me. Despite this, playing soccer provided a sense of solace.

One night, I had a dream. In it, I felt a warm hand on my face — my aunt wiping away my tears.

"You are beautiful," she whispered, tracing the patches on my chin with her finger. Her touch conveyed a sense of solidarity as she gently applied cream to my face. Tears streamed down my cheeks as I watched myself in the mirror.

"These are your beautiful tattoos," she said.

When I woke up, I applied the cream, hoping it would magically erase the patches. I remained in bed, refusing breakfast even when Tiwe urged me to face the world. Frustrated, I yelled at Tiwe, who persisted in encouraging me not to give up.

It had been four days since I last attended school, knowing Miss O'Hara would be looking for me. I was in my room when Tiwe informed me that Miss O'Hara was waiting in the living room. When I was there, I found her sharing a laugh with Samuel. I took a seat next to her. She pulled out six magazines from her bag.

"In my country, many people live positively with vitiligo."

Angela entered, dismissing the condition with a callous comment. "Just cover those nonsense with makeup. Even the dead wear makeup these days. Just look at me."

I chuckled inwardly, seeing the irony in her comparison. She was obviously comparing herself to a corpse.

"Meet my niece, Agatha," Angela said. "She's in Grade 11 at my village school."

"Nice to meet you, Agatha," I said as I walked Miss O'Hara to her car.

"You must be yourself, Mukenani," Miss O'Hara repeated. "If you hide behind makeup, you'll never be truly free."

After she left, I read the magazines she had given me. The stories of women embracing their skin conditions lifted my spirits. I pulled out Tina Turner's poster, hanging it proudly on my wall. I smiled as I removed the makeup from my pretty face.

"These marks are my special tattoos, a gift from God," I smiled.

The next day at school, I decided not to wear makeup. As I faced all my classmates, I found solace in their smiles. It dawned on me that people had never made my condition an issue to my face, except for Angela, a bully I didn't take seriously.

In 1995, during my final year of secondary school, Miss O'Hara conducted a career guidance session. Everyone in our class began shouting university courses and career aspirations. Like many others, I expressed my desire to become a lawyer.

"What about you, Lisa?" Miss O'Hara asked.

"I want to be a teacher," Lisa replied. "I heard it's free to study at the teacher's college."

"That's a great choice," Miss O'Hara said. "We can all achieve our dreams, study anywhere, even here in our country."

"Mistress O'Hara," I said, "I want to study at the University of Pretoria."

"Where's that?" John asked.

"It's in South Africa," said Sophia.

"A white university?!" Lisa said. "It might be expensive."

"If you pass very well, you can apply for a scholarship," Miss O'Hara said.

"I think I'll stick to college," Lisa said. "I still want to be a teacher."

"I'm going to study in South Africa. My uncle said if Tiwe and I pass, we can choose any university in the SADC region."

"I wish you all the best," Miss O'Hara said. "As for me, I have some exciting news. I will be relocating to Windhoek for my promotion as principal."

A lot has happened since secondary school. Sophia had joined Raven in the US. Lisa had been accepted into the teachers' college, and Angela had found solace in her shebeen business back in the village. Miss O'Hara had earned a promotion as the headmistress at Sunpride Primary School, a private school in Windhoek. Tiwe and I had been admitted to study law at the University of Pretoria. Uncle had remarried.

At the brink of everything, I found myself amazed by how life had pushed us along, sending us down various roads while still connecting us through our common beginnings. We were all pursuing something—whether it was our dreams, achievements, or just a sense of belonging. As for me, I was starting to believe in the journey, realizing that the most exciting chapters were yet to come.

PART II

Lisa is now in Windhoek

The year was 1999, and Lisa, now all grown up, had left South Bauleni to the city of Windhoek after finishing teacher's college. She walked down the bus stairs, her dark skin and height giving her the confidence of someone who had lived in the city all her life. Her attention was caught by the bright sign of a barbershop across the street. She adjusted her puffed-up hair and crossed over.

"I want it cut really short," she said to the barber.

After the haircut, she sat on the service station bench, watching the city and its busy streets. A chubby man rolled down the window of a taxi. At 03:43, Lisa checked her phone and instinctively clutched her handbag, because of the rumours about criminals posing as taxi drivers. Like many others, she chose to spend the night at the service station, curling up on the bench and securing her red jacket, but she didn't get much sleep.

In the morning, Lisa used the public shower at the service station. Once dressed, she took a taxi to Sunpride. A big sign at the entrance read, SUNPRIDE PRIMARY SCHOOL.

"The city's best school," said the taxi driver.

"It's beautiful," Lisa said, uninterested because the taxi man was talking a lot.

A week earlier, Sanana and his mother, Agatha, had left South Bauleni for Windhoek too. Sanana had won a scholarship to continue his primary education at Sunpride. The two were seated at the back of a black and blue double-decker bus, driving along the Trans-Caprivi highway. Agatha, Angela's niece and Lisa's college friend, sat quietly, her long black hair flowing in the breeze from the slightly open window. She wore a loose white dress painted with flowers, gazing out at the herds of cattle, shepherds, lanes, and fields passing by.

The boy kept counting the cattle grazing on the plains. He wore worn-out clothes and slippers that had seen better days. He munched on a piece of bread, and despite his age, Sanana had the height of a toddler and wore eyeglasses to improve his vision.

When they arrived in the capital, the bus conductor shouted in a colonial accent, "Welcome to Windhuk!"

Agatha checked her pocket watch—it was morning again.

A week had passed since their arrival. Agatha had left early that day, leaving Sanana alone at home. The room, furnished only with a single mattress, two bags, a broken plastic chair, and the wood-burning stove they had brought from the village.

As the first raindrop fell, Sanana hurried to the door, trying to block the water seeping in through the door by wedging shingles into the frame. He sat on the chair, staring out at the drizzle, his thoughts drifting to the peaceful days spent by the Zambezi River with his best friend Henry. They would fish, play soccer, and watch the fishermen. On Sundays, they attended church together. There was always enough food, and he had many beautiful memories. When thunder rumbled in the distance, Sanana went on to lay on the mattress. He drifted to sleep, the rain pounding on the zinc roof. When he woke up, streetlights brightened the neighbourhood. Agatha entered, smiling at her son, who was trying to stifle a yawn, as she tossed her handbag onto the mattress

"The people in this city are wicked. I went from one mall to another, hearing the same thing over and over: 'You're overqualified.' It was exhausting. But guess what? I finally got a job—only after I hid my qualifications."

"Is it a good job, Mum?"

"It's in a nice location, every house there is like a mansion. They call the neighbourhood Whiteville."

"Are you working as a maid?"

"Just to make sure we have food. We don't have any family here, so I need to take any job I can to pay the rent. The money Aunt Angela gave us helped with the deposit."

"But you're a graduate, Mum. You shouldn't have to work as a maid."

"We all must start somewhere. Not everyone you see on the street is a dropout. Many have degrees, but life has led them to hustle. Our time will come. We will leave this place someday."

"I don't like it here. I don't have any friends."

"You'll start school tomorrow and make plenty of good friends."

"What happened to our school in the village, Mum?"

"Its a great opportunity, honey. You're lucky to have that scholarship—Sunpride is an incredible school! You'll learn so much there and grow in ways you never imagined."

"I miss Henry and my dog. I miss the river and the fishermen."

"Once I get my teaching job, we'll visit during every school break."

"Mum, is my dog still alive?"

"Aunt Angela will take care of him. Crocodile will be fine."

"He's not Crocodile, Mum; his name is Lizard," the boy said, beginning to sniff the air. "That smells good! But I didn't cook."

"Oh yes, there was a party at my new boss's house, and she gave me leftovers."

"Can leftovers smell good?"

"They're rich, sweetheart. Very wealthy. They have a son your age."

"I'm hungry, Mum."

"Eat as much as you want but remember to save some for tomorrow. Tonight, we'll have a good meal. The chicken smells good, and I was tempted to taste it, but my king must eat first. It's tradition, right?"

"Thank you, Mum."

"Tomorrow is a new day. Now eat," Agatha said with a smile.

The morning came quickly, and it was still early when Sanana held Agatha's hand as they arrived at the bus stop. He wore a new black T-shirt and his old black shorts. Schoolchildren in grey and white stood in groups. Maids too.

"Mum, you have to buy me a school uniform."

"They will give you one at school. It's part of your scholarship."

They passed a group of schoolgirls sitting on a cinder block bench. One of them, Renate, snickered at Sanana. "He's tiny," she said, and they all laughed.

"Ignore them, honey. They're just kids."

Children aged eight to twelve marched to the school bus, marked Sunpride. The driver, old, descended the bus stairs and stroked Sanana's hair. The boy glanced at the others, who looked down at him.

Agatha knelt before him. "Now that you're with other kids, I shouldn't go with you. Besides, I need to be at work before seven."

As the bus left, Agatha stood at the bench where other domestic workers gossiped about their employers. The sun rose, breaking through the clouds, as the bus made its final turn toward Sunpride.

Miss Margaret O'Hara, the principal of the school, was sitting at her desk. When she saw Lisa, her kind eyes sparkled with recognition. Lisa smiled gently from across the desk, and it felt as if all the years they had been apart disappeared in the comfort of their shared smiles.

"Your school is beautiful, Miss O'Hara," Lisa remarked.

"Our school," Miss O'Hara said. "We are colleagues, now."

"Thank you, Miss O'Hara, but you will always be my teacher."

"Before I forget, how is your friend, Mukenani, and the others?"

"She hasn't finished her law degree yet."

"She'll make a great lawyer."

"And what about Sophia, your daughter, Miss O'Hara?"

"She's in the States now, with her own television show. I haven't seen her in over six months." Miss O'Hara glanced at the clock. "There's another teacher starting today. She should be here soon. I hope you two will get along."

A young woman entered, introducing herself as Mary.

"You two will be responsible for the seventh-grade classes," Miss O'Hara said. "Remember, we must work as a team."

The trio left the office, strolling through the hallways. Mary was shown to her class first, followed by Lisa. As the principal was about to return to her office, the Old Driver arrived with Sanana.

"I was expecting this student. Please take him to the seventh-grade class. There's a new teacher, but first, take him to the tailor for his uniform measurements."

Lisa faced a quiet class of students, all admiring her elegant appearance, particularly her shaved head. Sanana took a seat behind Renate...

"It seems we have two new faces," the teacher said. "Me and my young friend here. What's your name?"

"Sanana Neo," he replied, standing up.

"I'm delighted to be here," the teacher continued. "My number one rule is friendship. We are all friends here, and friends share everything."

The bell rang for break, and students crowded the hallways. Sanana wandered towards the back of the school, reaching the parking area where Renate and Nadia were laughing.

Renate blocked his path. "What exactly are you?"

"Yes, are you a kid or an adult?" Nadia added with a sneer.

Sanana tried to move past, but Nadia grabbed his arm.

"Please, leave me alone," he muttered.

Renate smirked. "How did someone like you get into Sunpride?"

Sanana's face flushed as he lowered his head, sweat forming on his brow. But just then, the bell rang...

Inside the classroom, the students settled down. Sanana, having missed breakfast, sat quietly, his stomach growling. Before the lesson could begin, Principal O'Hara appeared at the door. "Let's meet in the staffroom after class," she said.

After the bell rang for the next lesson, Nadia, who was the class captain at the time, led the teacher to the staffroom. Along the way, she couldn't stop praising Lisa's beauty.

"Thank you," said Lisa, "but you're the one who's truly beautiful."

Nadia kept swinging her arm through Lisa's. "So, your father owns this school?"

"Yes, and we live in Blackville."

"That's where all the wealthy people live! You're so lucky."

Nadia gestured toward an open door. "The staffroom's on your left, teacher."

Lisa entered and took a seat among the teachers. Principal O'Hara stood with Miss April, the deputy principal, while Mrs Hausiku, the former acting principal, sat in the back corner. Tension everywhere....

Principal O'Hara glanced at an empty seat. "Where's the geography teacher?"

"It's Monday. You should know," Mrs Hausiku replied, her voice dripping with sarcasm.

Lisa smiled, remembering a professor at college who had a habit of missing classes, especially on Mondays.

"Colleagues," Principal O'Hara said, "this year's results have dropped by seven percent. The only subject still at the top is geography. Let's give a a round of applause to the geography teacher in absentia."

The room applauded, except Mrs Hausiku, who remained silent.

"Thank you, everyone," Principal O'Hara continued. "Miss Lisa, please stand."

A few older women at the back whispered. "She's so dark."

"Welcome. And this is Miss Mary, our new science teacher."

"She's so short!" Mrs Hausiku added.

"Alright, you're dismissed," Miss O'Hara said, cutting the tension.

As the teachers left, Lisa dialled her mother's number.

"I like it here, Mother. The school's big and clean."

"Be careful. Windhoek's not like our little town."

"I understand, Mother. But there's this old witch—she said I'm too dark. I'll handle it."

"Just stay out of trouble."

Lisa ended the call and turned to see Mary standing nearby, her smile forced.

"Can you believe she said I'm too short?" Mary asked.

Lisa shrugged. "Why should I care?"

Mary muttered a curse and hurried off.

Later, in Slumsville, Sanana and his mother shared a plate of rice.

"How was your first day at your new school?" Agatha asked.

"The school's nice, but I don't like it there," Sanana replied.

"Everything will be okay. One step at a time."

From Slumsville to Sunpride

Another new day in Slumsville, and mother and son were ready to leave their small room.

"Grey shorts and a white shirt, huh?" Agatha pushed the curtain aside and walked past Sanana towards the fridge. "So handsome."

"I like this uniform, Mum. It's cool. It's my first uniform in this city."

"No, it's our first uniform in this city."

Agatha wore a uniform: a long-sleeved white dress with a black collar and a small black belt. She attached her round name tag to her chest, which read *Agatha Neo.*

"It's cool, Mum. You look beautiful in it," Sanana pouted his lips and swung his school bag over his shoulder, turning towards the door. "Everyone keeps saying I look like a little fat dog," he sighed, dropping his bag. "And I'm starting to believe them."

Agatha knelt, her touch gentle as she ran her fingers through his short black hair and softened her tone, "You're my son, and I love you."

"I hate them all," Sanana muttered.

Agatha pushed her hair back, noticing the pain in his eyes. She remembered how he used to wake up for school in their village.

"God has wonderful plans for you. Remember Jeremiah 29."

"For I know the plans I have for you," Sanana began to recite, "plans to prosper you and not to harm you, plans to give you hope and a future."

"So, keep your faith in God."

She picked up his school bag, and they left their house for the bus stop. Sanana trailed behind, glancing around at the children who stared at him every day. He pulled his mother to a stop, and said, "Everyone is looking at me, Mum."

Agatha wiped her face with her hand, locking eyes with him as she struggled to find comforting words. She gripped her phone tightly, her eyes staring off into the distance. "The bus is here."

Sanana, halfway up the bus steps, was shoved by another learner, who seemed much older than his peers. They called him Benjamin. Laughter echoed from the windows as Sanana sat, blood dripping from his elbow. Agatha stood there.

"Come on, my young friend, grab my hand." The Old Driver helped him to his seat.

The children began singing a nursery rhyme, *Five Little Monkeys Jumping on the Bed*.

"I enjoy music," the Old Driver said. "When I was a young boy, around your age, many years ago, we sang this song all the time. It reminds me of my childhood, of simpler times." The Old Driver stroked Sanana's hair, glad to have brought a smile to the boy's face.

"What's your name, sir?" Sanana asked.

"Jeremy, but everyone calls me The Old Driver."

Despite the traffic caused by roadworks, they arrived at school in time for the first lesson. The children made their way to their classrooms. Sanana walked alone behind the geography teacher, passing classrooms painted with children's artwork and cartoons. He overheard children talking about the geography teacher.

"Look, there he is!" a girl shouted, pointing at the teacher. "Our geography teacher is back!"

The learners exchanged smiles as their teacher, Mr Maswahu, swaggered into the room like he owned the school. His worn black suit, red tie, and grey shoes were the epitome of confidence—though "fashion-forward" might not have been the right term. It was as if his wardrobe was still trying to figure out what year it was. He looked like he could be his own grandpa, yet somehow managed to be the cream of the school—but the gentleman was so disorganized.

"Good morning, Mr Maswahu! Welcome back!" the learners shouted.

"A simple good morning is just fine. Please take a seat," Mr Maswahu said as he wrote "geography" on the chalkboard. Before anyone could settle, his phone rang, and he quickly excused himself, rushing to the principal's office

"Mr Maswahu," Miss O'Hara said, "you're the best teacher I have, but there's been talk, and I can't defend you anymore. I'm sorry, but you need to find another job. Try a government school; they are more tolerant. This decision comes from the chairman. I apologize, but we no longer need your services."

"It's all right, Principal O'Hara. I was considering quitting myself. I'm wasting my potential here, and the salary is meagre. Please don't hinder my future endeavours."

"You're a good man, Mr Maswahu. If it were up to me, I would keep you. As for your future, all I can offer is my word."

In the classroom, Mr Maswahu leaned momentarily against the door frame, and the learners fell silent. He turned to face them.

"You have all been wonderful learners, and I wish you the best in your studies. I have four words for each of you: You are all amazing." He began packing up his belongings...

"We don't understand, teacher," Little Sue, who was particularly fond of him, spoke up.

"This is my last day at this school. I have received an offer elsewhere."

Sue's mouth dropped open; she couldn't believe her favourite teacher was leaving Sunpride.

"Can't you stay?" she pleaded.

"Someone even better is on their way. You will never be lacking in anything."

"But we want you."

"Goodbye, kids." He opened his arms wide, and one after another, he received hugs. They watched him leave...

"He's gone," said Sue. "Our geography teacher is gone."

In another classroom, the learners filed in individually, greeting the teacher as they took their seats. Lisa then left the class to answer a phone call, asking Nadia to check on the learners' uniforms.

Nadia stared at Sanana's missing socks and large feet, making a comment that drew laughter from the other learners.

"Why are you so mean?" Erica asked Nadia.

"She's the class captain; she can do what she wants," Renate said.

"That's not fair," Erica replied.

"He doesn't have any socks?" Renate smirked.

That sparked a burst of laughter from the other kids. Even when the teacher entered the class, the children were still giggling. Sanana stood barefoot...

"Teacher, he doesn't have socks," Nadia said.

"Go put on your shoes, sweetheart," Lisa leaned towards Nadia and gave her a stern look. "That's not how you should treat someone."

"I'm sorry, Teacher. I was just doing my job," Nadia said.

"You don't have to be mean to fulfil your duties. How would you feel if I treated you that way? Would you like it?"

"No, Teacher."

"You need to apologise to Sanana."

"I'm sorry," Nadia mumbled, avoiding eye contact.

Sanana remained silent. Although it made him feel better, it was the first time Nadia had apologised to him.

"You too, Renate."

"But I didn't do anything, Teacher."

"I know, Renate... apologise now," the teacher demanded.

"I'm sorry," Renate hesitated.

The teacher picked up a book from her desk and walked down the row. The last book they had read was less than a hundred pages, but the one she held seemed as thick as an Oxford dictionary. The learners fell silent when the teacher dropped the book on Heidi's desk.

"Okay, let's get started," she said as she turned towards Renate and Nadia. "Take out those books from the box and distribute them."

"Do we have to read this, Teacher?" Heidi asked.

"Yes..."

"Teacher, this book is huge. Our last teacher—"

"I am not your last teacher," Lisa interrupted, standing up from her chair. "This is grade 7. You need to start reading more challenging books. In other parts of the world, children your age and even younger read books of this size in their primary schools. There's nothing wrong with it... I trust and believe in all of you. You are all intelligent learners, and I know you can finish reading this book."

"But Teacher," Nadia said, "this book is huge. It will take us years to finish."

"I finished this book in one week."

"Four hundred and twenty-something pages in one week?" Heidi exclaimed, flipping through the pages.

"You can do it. All of you can do it."

"But," Heidi persisted.

"That's enough!" the teacher shouted. "Keep quiet already."

She pursed her lips, smiled, and continued writing on the chalkboard, LITERARY FICTION. "The first thing you do when you enter a library or go to buy a book is read the title and blurb."

"What's a blurb?" Heidi asked.

"Sanana, why don't you tell little Heidi what a blurb is?" she said, giving Sanana a warm smile.

Sanana hesitated, but the teacher's encouragement gave him the confidence to speak up.

"I think it is the short information at the back of the book that tells you what the book is all about."

"Exactly."

"Wow!" said Heidi, "Where is he getting all these answers? Either he's so smart, or I'm so stupid."

"Reading a book is like watching a movie. Which one do you prefer, children?"

"TV," a boy in the back shouted.

"We all enjoy watching TV," Nadia added.

"And what about you, Sanana?"

"We don't have a television."

Children began laughing...

"Not even a small TV," Nadia laughed.

"You will study hard. One day, you will live in one of the nicest parts of the city. You will live in Blackville," the teacher said.

"Blackville!" Renate said, "In your dreams."

"There's nothing wrong with dreaming," Sanana said.

"Well said," the teacher said. "Now, let's delve deeper into our topic for today. Literary fiction, a character-driven novel?"

The lesson continued for what felt like forever until the sound of the bell signalled a much-needed break. One by one, the learners left Lisa's classroom. Just as Sanana was about to make his exit, the teacher said...

"You're intelligent."

"Thank you, Teacher," Sanana said.

"Who do you live with?"

"My mother."

"What's your mother's name, sweetheart?"

"Agatha Neo."

"Agatha Neo!" Lisa muttered under her breath, her lips tightening as she glared at him. "You can go now."

Sanana couldn't help but wonder if the teacher somehow knew his mother.

In Slumsville, Sanana strolled back home, enjoying the sound of music blaring from the shebeen. The streets teemed with people, amidst chaos as dogs and ducks skirmished over scraps. Rubbish and rainwater littered every corner. Sanana turned the final corner and pushed open the rusty gate. He went where his mother hid the keys and pushed open the creaky door. He fetched a large jar, filling it with water from a bucket next to the door, and made sugar water. On the wooden table, he found two fat cakes his mother had left for him. After lunch, he took out his novel from his school bag and began reading, eventually dozing off.

Sunlight streamed through the door and the holes in the zinc roof, bringing light into the house. Later in the day, Sanana watched other children playing soccer on the dusty street until the sun began to set. He switched on the lights; he curled up on a mattress. When his mother arrived, she gave him a goodnight kiss.

The following day, morning, Sanana frowned at the two cakes and the sugar water on the plates.

"This is what the Lord has provided," Agatha said.

"I understand, Mum."

He ate his breakfast in silence while his mother finished her chores.

"Mum," he called.

Agatha ran her fingers through his hair. "Do you want more?"

"One day, I'll be the one taking care of you."

"I know, and I bless you."

"Thank you, Mum. I bless you, too."

Agatha hugged her son tightly. "The bus will be here soon."

The school bus disappeared into the morning. Raindrops drummed against the windshield. Sanana blew warm air into his hands. The Old Driver turned on the heater and some music, filling the bus with a peaceful atmosphere.

In the classroom, children settled into their seats one by one, waiting for instructions from their teacher, who was wasting time with her phone.

"Jimmy," Lisa said, "say a prayer for us."

Jimmy, the pastor's son, wanted to change the strategy, "I'll read John 3:16 before I pray," he said.

"Just give us the prayer, boy, and stop your Johnny nonsense."

The class erupted in laughter, prompting the teacher to regain control, and let Jimmy say a short prayer.

"Erica," the teacher continued, "since your mother is a musician, lead us in a song now."

Erica started the song, which was the only part of Lisa's class that she enjoyed.

"Now, learners, please keep yourself busy and make no noise."

A knock on the classroom window caught Lisa's attention. Mary motioned for Lisa to come outside. Lisa gestured back, but her colleague shouted, "Staff briefing now!"

Mary and Lisa were the same age, but Mary declared herself short and hot. It had been two months since the two new teachers started working together, yet they hadn't formed any bond.

"Good morning, colleagues," the principal began. "I have received a complaint from parents about the unprofessional behaviour of some staff members."

"Excuse me, Principal O'Hara... but what constitutes unprofessional behaviour?" Mrs Hausiku said.

The staff members knew Mrs Hausiku was always eager to voice her opinions and argue during staff gatherings. She always made sure to have the first and last say, causing her colleagues to lose faith in her intelligence.

"Empty vessels make the loudest noise," Lisa whispered to herself, but Mrs Hausiku had been attentive enough to overhear her remark...

"You've only been here briefly and already causing trouble. Next time, close that dirty lid, darkie."

"At least I have a lid."

"Everyone," Miss Mwiya spoke. "Can't we have a civilized meeting?"

"Thank you, Miss Mwiya," Principal O'Hara said. "Sunpride is a private school. Parents pay a significant amount of money for their children's education, and in return, they expect good education to happen at this school. Let's team up and bring out the best in each other."

Principal O'Hara was known for her kindness, and despite her vulnerability, she was not afraid to fulfil her duties as required. When school ended, at the bus stop, the kids scattered to their homes. Before Sanana got off the school bus, the Old Driver said, "I'll walk you home, my young friend."

The two friends trudged through the rainwater in Slumsville. The Old Driver managed to squeeze through the gate as he followed the boy into the house. He glanced around and noticed that the room was empty. His fingers brushed against the only picture on the wall.

"Is this your mother?" the Old Driver asked.

"She works late... you won't get to meet her."

"And what does she do?"

"A lot."

"What do you do after school?"

"Homework."

"What else do you do?"

"I wait for my mother."

What Colour is God?

It was Friday, the day for Bible study at school. Nadia handed out the Bibles, Jimmy opened with a heartfelt prayer, and Erica led the class in a song. The kids loved it, especially since they got to sing their favourite Christian songs.

"What colour was Mary?" asked the teacher.

"Which Mary?" Heidi shouted.

"The mother of Christ," said someone.

"Oh, that one," the boy at the back said, his voice tinged with curiosity. "Mary was a white woman."

"What colour is God in heaven?" the teacher asked again.

"White!" they all shouted.

"We've never seen God, so why do you say 'white'?"

"We watched Jesus on TV, and he's supper white," said Jimmy, who loved Fridays because of his love for God.

"And what colour are you?"

"Black!" they all shouted.

"If God is white and you're black, where do you come from?"

"Lucifer," a boy at the back shouted.

"But teacher," Renate said, "I'm not black. I'm brown. And Nadia is yellow."

"Yes, teacher, you're so black," Erica added.

Lisa looked down at her hands, and Erica fell silent. She was saved by Principal O'Hara, who walked in, and the learners stood up to greet her.

"Children," the teacher said, "God is not black or white. God is not one race or one colour. God is like a chameleon; he always changes colour. When he's with Whites, he becomes white. With Blacks, he becomes black. When he's with you, he becomes you. Do you understand now?"

"What is a chameleon?" Heidi asked.

"Some changing colour lizards," said someone.

"But mistress," Jimmy said, "I watched Jesus in a movie, and he was white."

"God is like a chameleon," she shouted but then noticed the principal seated. She softened her tone. "God is like a chameleon."

"But mistress," Jimmy persisted, "Jesus is white. Jesus is white, not black."

Lisa walked over to Jimmy, leaned on his desk, and forced a smile. "When I'm talking about God, don't bring up Jesus."

"Jimmy is right," Erica said. "Jesus is a white man; there are no black people in the Bible."

"The Bible doesn't mention any specific colour," Nadia said, thinking she was partially white because of her skin colour.

Principal O'Hara gestured for the teacher to follow her as she left the classroom. Lisa bumped into Mary. The two new teachers had formed a strong bond over the past few days.

"Principal O'Hara seems upset," Mary said. "I hope you're prepared."

"Who cares? She's just a foreigner; she should return to America," Lisa said.

"Don't let her intimidate you – this is our country."

In her office, Principal O'Hara sat across from her deputy, Miss April. She twirled her pen while the deputy tapped her fingers on the table.

"This new teacher is bringing a lot of trouble here," said Miss April.

"I'm more concerned about the other teacher," said Principal O'Hara.

"Do you mean Mary?"

"Yes. Mary is revealing only what we expect to see. She's quite crafty."

Lisa walked in and stood beside the deputy.

"I'm sorry for interrupting your lessons. I made a surprise visit to your classroom. I wasn't pleased with your lesson during the religious studies class," Principal O'Hara said. "What concerned me the most was the lack of content in your teaching."

"Excuse me, Principal O'Hara, but that comment might be taken as an insult."

"I apologize, Miss Lisa," Principal O'Hara said gently, then turned to Miss April. "What colour is God, Miss April?"

Miss April said without much thought, "God is a white man. I can't imagine a black God."

"I don't understand why I'm here," said Lisa.

"You mentioned that God is like a chameleon, correct?"

"Yes, Principal O'Hara."

"We need to be careful about our words when discussing God with the children," Principal O'Hara faced her deputy and asked, "Miss April, why do you think God is white?"

"That's the only thing that popped into my head, Principal. Can you imagine a black God? Who would love him? These children will never believe us. Let's tell them what they want to hear. Children like happy endings."

"A black God is a bad ending?" Principal O'Hara asked.

"I grew up knowing Jesus is a white man. To be honest, I like him white," Miss April admitted.

"Let's tell them the right things, Miss April," the principal insisted.

Later that evening, Jimmy sat alone in the living room, the soft glow of the television flickering across his face. The room was dimly lit, and he kept the volume low so as not to disturb his sleeping parents. Usually, Jimmy was only allowed to watch religious films, but lately, he had developed a newfound interest in horror movies. He would watch them without his parents' knowledge. This evening, his uncle, Mr Maswahu, known for his drinking habits and recently fired from Sunpride, woke up feeling thirsty in the middle of the night. With a can of beer, he stood behind him, opened it, and let out a loud burp.

"What happened to God, boy?" his uncle asked.

Jimmy leaned forward. His uncle plopped down next to him and pulled him into a tight hug, which made Jimmy squirm out of it. "You smell of alcohol, uncle."

"It's the scent of freedom, son," his uncle said, grinning at the screen as he sipped his beer. "You're growing up, huh? I'll be even prouder of you when you start three things: alcohol and fights. That's when you'll become a man."

"Do you think so, uncle? Alcohol and fights?"

"Alcohol and fights, and it doesn't matter if you win or lose."

"Alcohol and fights," Jimmy repeated, nodding. "Wait a minute, uncle. You said three things."

"Girls and women."

"Girls and women, uncle?" Jimmy asked, puzzled. "Now they are four?"

"You girls, me women."

Before his uncle could impart more of life's wisdom to him, Jimmy's mother called out from the door, "Time for bed, Jimmy." She then shot a disapproving look at his uncle. "You're a bad influence on my son. When are you going back to the village?"

"I'm teaching your son the harsh realities of life, and you want to send me away? All this boy knows is church, church, and church. At his age, he's never even had a fight with anyone."

"And you, what have you accomplished so far? All you do is come home with new scars every weekend."

"Let me help you, sister. Your son needs me. His father is always busy preaching at crusades week after week."

"Look at yourself; you've wasted twice your pension. Every day, you're fired like a confused goat. Why do people still employ you in their schools?"

"Is it my fault that I'm good in geography?" he said, stumbling into his room, leaving the door open.

The next day in Slumsville, Sanana was enjoying his breakfast when he heard a knock on the door. The Old Driver stood there, holding a kitten in his arms. The kitten was wide awake and safe in his grasp. Sanana didn't pay much attention to it because he never liked cats.

"I brought a new friend," the Old Driver said. "For company and to catch mice."

"Do you mean rats?" Agatha interrupted, poking her head out the door and pulling Sanana aside. "And who said we have rats in this house?"

The Old Driver stroked the kitten's fur, struggling to find the right words to say to Agatha.

"My name is Jeremy, and I—"

"I know who you are, sir. Aren't you the bus driver?" Agatha asked. She inspected the Old Driver and then turned her attention to the kitten. "Does that thing eat?"

"A little."

"How many times a day?"

"Three to four."

"Sir, we only eat twice a day here. Take your stupid cat and leave."

"I have something else for you," the Old Driver gestured to two boys by a pick-up truck. They began to carry a box towards him.

"Is this for us?" Sanana asked, offering to help with the lifting.

"For you and your mother."

"Go back inside," Agatha ordered.

Sanana slammed the door shut, then fell onto the mattress. Having a TV for the first time meant the world to him, and his mum was ruining it.

"Who said we don't have a TV?"

"Your son is smart and should have something to entertain himself while you're away."

"I'll save up and buy a TV for us alone."

"I just wanted to help."

"I appreciate your offer, but we will manage on our own. Thank you for your kindness."

Noise and Worship

In Blackville, the chairman rose from his seat at the sound of the knock. The Old Driver stood tinkering with the bus keys. He knew he didn't visit often unless he was seeking favours.

"It's about Nadia, brother. She needs a motherly figure in her life," said the Old Driver.

The chairman sighed, running his hand through his greying hair. "I know, I know," he admitted, the exhaustion of being a single parent evident in his eyes. "But finding a good woman out there is not easy."

The Old Driver nodded and let out a deep sigh. "Any news on Jessica?"

"She's considered dead in this house, and you're aware of that," the chairman replied bluntly, with a hint of frustration.

"Nadia is the only one who believes that lie. What if she were to come back from wherever she went?"

There was silence for a while before the Old Driver spoke again. "I found your son. He's quite an interesting young boy."

"I know."

The Old Driver began tapping his fingers on the table. He glanced at his younger brother, a mix of surprise and confusion in his eyes.

"Why didn't you tell me?" he asked, sounding a bit hurt. "Why did you let him struggle like that?"

The chairman smiled kindly, placing a comforting hand on the Old Driver's arm.

"I gave him the scholarship," he replied calmly. "And very soon, I will bring him back home."

Just then, the chairman's phone rang on the table. He picked it up and listened as Principal O'Hara's urgent message came through. His expression changed, and his shoulders slumped. The news seemed to drain the colour from his face.

"I'm coming there right away."

Later, the chairman entered Principal O'Hara's office, wearing a sleek black suit and holding a shiny golden walking stick. Principal O'Hara greeted him with a respectful nod.

"Mr Lingani, thank you for coming," she began.

The door creaked open before she could delve into the details, and Nadia burst into the room. The chairman's stern gaze softened as he turned to his daughter.

"Let me talk to your principal," he said, reaching into his silver briefcase and pulling out a box of chocolates. "Here, take these." He then turned back to Principal O'Hara. "Now, tell me, did you hear that from a parent?"

Principal O'Hara shook her head, meeting his gaze with solemn intensity. "No, Mr Lingani, I heard that from many parents."

"Gather everyone for a meeting."

Meanwhile, in Lisa's classroom, she rested her legs on the desk while reading a fashion magazine. Many learners rested their heads on the table out of boredom and a lack of work. The school intercom blared, announcing the chairman's arrival. Lisa left the room, eager to greet the chairman. She greeted him, shaking his hand and almost embracing him, but Principal O'Hara pulled her away. Before the meeting could begin, Lisa offered to lead a prayer, which she did with a smile that seemed to never fade in the presence of the chairman.

"I would like the following teachers to stand," the chairman said. "Miss Lisa, Mrs Hausiku, and Miss Mary."

His gaze lingered on Mrs Hausiku as he was familiar with her.

"Colleagues, please rise," Principal O'Hara said.

The three teachers complied without any resistance, a rare occurrence.

"This is a private school, and I will not hesitate to terminate the employment of anyone who fails to uphold the standards we strive to maintain," the chairman said. "To the three teachers, you will receive warning letters."

"I don't understand," Mrs Hausiku asked. "What have we done?"

"Your letters will explain everything," the principal said.

"Mrs Hausiku," the chairman said, "these new teachers need your guidance."

"These student teachers lack respect," Mrs Hausiku said.

"Please, we are not student teachers," Lisa said.

"Let's all return to our classes," said Principal O'Hara.

Mary whispered to Lisa with a silly grin. "I can see the way you're looking at the chairman. Do you have plans for him?"

"Do you think I intend to remain a class teacher forever?" Lisa smiled.

"I already like your plans. I wouldn't mind being your deputy."

"Mary, you're going to be there! Come on, let's head over to our classes and fill up those empty containers."

In Whiteville, Agatha was busy with her chores. The room was filled with toys, and the TV played animated videos for children. Agatha sat down on the bed, lost in her thoughts.

Meanwhile, at school that same day, Sanana shared a bus seat with the Old Driver. Through the window, he watched Nadia getting into a black sedan that disappeared down the school's streets.

The school bus continued its route, dropping off children one by one. Sanana waved goodbye to the Old Driver. He adjusted his black school bag on his shoulders and listened to the sound of the bus fading away as it travelled over the concrete stones. He trudged along a rough street towards his home, leaving wet footprints behind him. Finally, he reached the last corner and leapt over a waterlogged gate that led to his house. He reached under a stone to get his key.

"Honey, Agatha called."

Sanana walked past his mother and turned around, fixing his gaze on the ground. Agatha took her son's hand; she felt him pull away and rush into the house. A smile formed on his lips as he spotted a small black TV on a white wooden table.

"Promise me you'll do your homework first?"

"I promise. You're the best mum ever."

On Sunday morning, Agatha woke up to the noise of the TV that Sanana was watching. She went outside to fetch water from their shared communal tap. After filling all three containers, breakfast was served.

"It's time to eat breakfast; we're going to church now," Agatha said, placing a bowl before her son.

It was already half past eight when Agatha and her son finally went to the house of God to give thanks. Since they had arrived in the city, they hadn't attended church before. Sanana wore black shorts and a white T-shirt with patches and two small holes on the shoulders. His mother wore a long white dress embellished with colourful flowers. Her slippers made a rhythmic *slap-slap* sound with each step. Sanana counted "one-two, one-two" to the rhythm of his mother's slippers.

In the background, music from different shebeens echoed, like any other day. Behind those shebeens was a small tent where a few people gathered to worship the Lord. Mother and son hurried inside as the drunkards began to shower Agatha with compliments. A man in a suit, a lady, a young boy, and a little girl were seated on a church pew. Agatha stood by the entrance, watching everyone, reminiscing about her small village back home, where even a population of less than a hundred could fill a church. She pondered why city people seemed to dislike going to church.

"I'm Mrs James, and this is my husband, Pastor James. Our son Teddy and our daughter Renate."

If only Sanana had the charm to make himself vanish... he would have done it the moment he laid eyes on Renate. She was always unkind to him despite being the pastor's daughter. Sanana shuffled his feet and hesitated before his mother moved aside, allowing the boy to take the lead to the pew.

"This is my son, Sanana. You can call me Agatha."

"Are you new to this area?" asked the pastor's wife.

"My son and I arrived here a few weeks back."

"My family and I have been here for over two years now, but, sister, people here seem to dislike church."

Agatha glanced around the church again, noticing its small and empty interior. The music coming from the shebeen seems to distract little Teddy, who was dancing with his legs seated.

"How do you handle the noise from these shebeens?" Agatha asked.

"The ear hears what it wants to hear."

"But it's so loud."

As the sermon started, two or three older ladies walked into the church and sat together on the front bench. After the church service, Sanana and Teddy skipped outside, following behind Renate. The two boys went to play behind the shebeen, dancing to the music. Despite being only seven years old, Teddy was taller than Sanana.

"Teddy, come back here!" Renate shouted.

The two friends kept dancing, grooving to a Kwaito tune...

"Stay away from him!" Renate said reaching for Sanana's hand.

Sanana kept on dancing. His elbow swung recklessly, colliding with Renate's left eye. She began to cry. The pastor's wife and Agatha rushed out of the church.

"What happened?" the pastor's wife asked.

"Sanana... his elbow..."

"I didn't mean to, Mum," Sanana said.

Renate's mother knelt before the boy. "Don't feel bad about it."

Lisa's Ambition

They hurried to catch the bus the next day because Sanana was having trouble waking up. At school, Lisa left her class, leaving the vice-captain in charge. The class fell silent, with everyone seated except for Sanana and Renate. Renate, still upset with Sanana, made sure to supervise him closely. She even took the measuring tape and instructed Sanana to remove his shoes, which he did without protest.

"Do you ever grow?" said Renate.

Principal O'Hara peeked through the classroom window and overheard Renate's question to Sanana. She immediately summoned Lisa to her office.

"Your behaviour is unacceptable, Miss Lisa. The way you allow some learners to mistreat that boy is disappointing. This is your final warning," Principal O'Hara said.

Lisa remained silent, but her expression hinted at a possible outburst if the lecture continued.

"This is your last chance."

"I don't understand," Lisa said.

"You need to address the bullying in your class. Now, go back to your classroom and take care of it."

When the lunch bell rang, Nadia was about to exit the classroom when Lisa smiled at her with so much love.

"Is your dad at home?" Lisa asked.

"My dad is always home," Nadia said.

"What about your mother?"

"My mother died when I was born."

"What if I go with you to Blackville and get the chance to meet your father on a personal level?"

Nadia smiled and said, "I can introduce you to my dad's new dog. He's ugly and lazy, but I like him."

They drove through the most beautiful part of Blackville. The houses were big, and there was hardly any litter in sight. Despite their unique designs, the mansions were remarkably similar, as if they were all crafted from the same blueprint of wealth.

"This whole neighbourhood screams wealth. I'll live in this city area one day," Lisa said.

A large gate swung open. It was quite a distance from the main gate to the house's front door. The chairman sat in a thatched shelter away from the main entrance.

"I told you he's always home. There he is, too, next to Dad."

A menacing brown pit bull glared at her; its mouth covered in drool. Nadia bounded into the house with excitement after saying hello to her father. She dropped her school bag onto the sofa before going to the fridge. She surveyed the contents inside, grabbed a can of fruit juice, and turned on the TV. She opened the curtains and closed them again.

Lisa was sipping from a wine glass.

"Are you my daughter's teacher?" the chairman asked.

"Yes, Mr Lingani," she said.

"Now, tell me, how is she doing in class?"

"She needs a motherly figure to help her with a few screws."

"You two are very close, I see?"

"I make it a point to communicate with all my learners on a personal level; it helps with the bonding."

"Do you have any children of your own?"

"Hopefully, someday."

"You have your whole life ahead of you."

Lisa shot a sharp look, and Sneaky, the dog, began licking her right toe. She wore a forced smile and started massaging Sneaky's head.

"You're good with dogs too?"

"I adore dogs, especially beautiful and well-fed ones like this guy here."

"I bought him for seven thousand from a friend who breeds dogs."

"In my village, we have dogs too, but they're not very attractive. Do you happen to know what breed they are, sir?"

"Let's say I understand the type of dog you're talking about. I used to own one, but he grew old and died last month."

Lisa glanced at her wristwatch, adjusted her skirt to cover her knees, and grabbed her handbag.

"It was great meeting you, Mr Lingani, but I have many books to mark. You know how we teachers are: we work around the clock, even during holidays."

"Being a teacher is tough, I understand. I used to be a teacher myself."

"Actually, it's not hard work at all, sir. I love being a teacher. The children bring me so much joy."

"Well, if that's the case, you have a promising future in education. And one more thing," he added, "the door to this yard is wide open for you."

"Thank you, Mr Lingani," Lisa said, gently massaging Sneaky's back. She glanced back and saw Nadia waving from the doorway.

A little while later, Nadia threw herself onto her father's lap.

"I like her too, Dad. I can't wait to see her after the long weekend."

The week rolled on, and by Tuesday after the long weekend, life at school had settled into its usual rhythm. Principal O'Hara walked past Lisa's classroom, and all the learners stood up to greet her. Lisa's phone was on the desk, and she was playing with a pencil.

"Sanana," called Principal O'Hara. "You're going to Miss Mwiya's class. Come with me."

Sanana gathered his things. Lisa was still fiddling with her pencil, unfazed.

"You'll do great in Miss Mwiya's class," Principal O'Hara said.

Once they left, Lisa called Mary to update her on the situation.

"So, the boy is out of your class, but why do you sound so down?"

"I have issues with his mother, not him. Plus, he's smart and cute."

"What did the principal say about moving him out of your class?"

"She didn't say anything to me. I was prepared to listen and respond this time."

"I'm starting to become a big fan. How's our bright future looking?"

"I prefer to keep my plans to myself."

"Fair enough. I'll keep you in my prayers."

After they hung up the phone, Lisa reached the door, peeked her head into the hallway. Sanana followed Principal O'Hara through three blocks and entered the second classroom in Block 4. The schoolchildren and their teacher stood up to welcome them.

"Please take a seat right behind John."

"Thank you, Miss Mwiya," Principal O'Hara said before leaving the classroom.

"It's my responsibility, Principal O'Hara. Thank you for bringing the boy to my class," Miss Mwiya turned towards her learners and asked them, "In my class, we are all...?"

"Equal!" the children shouted in unison, except for Sanana.

While all this was happening, Sanana looked around the entire classroom.

"Now, children, who can recite Jeremiah 29:11?"

Except for Sanana, the learners eagerly raised their hands.

"Sanana, recite Jeremiah 29:11, my child." Miss Mwiya winked at him, and the whole class fell silent.

Sanana stood up from his chair, glanced behind him, and formed a slight smile at the corner of his mouth as he remembered that Jeremiah 29:11 was his mother's favourite Bible verse. He began confidently, "For I know the plans I have for you," declares the Lord, "plans to prosper you and not to harm you, plans to give you hope and a future."

"Now, let's all recite Psalm 23."

"The Lord is my Shepherd; I shall not want. He makes me lie down in green pastures. He leads me beside still waters. He restores my soul. He leads me in paths of righteousness for his name's sake. Even though I walk through the valley of the shadow of death, I will fear no evil, for you are with me; your rod and your staff, they comfort me. You prepare a table before me in the presence of my enemies; you anoint my head with oil; my cup overflows. Surely goodness and mercy shall follow me all the days of my life, and I shall dwell in the house of the LORD forever."

"Now, kids, let's sing 'Rock of Ages.'"

A Plan to seduce the Chairman

Lisa appeared stunning, dressed to make an impression, with the sole intention of seducing the chairman. Nadia had extended the invitation, and Lisa was grateful for the opportunity. It was still early morning when Nadia opened the door and embraced her teacher.

"Teacher," Nadia said.

"How about you call me mother?" Lisa whispered in a seductive tone.

"I love that, Teacher."

Nadia called out for her father's attention as he descended the stairs. "Dad, do you remember my teacher? She's so beautiful, isn't she, dad?" She held onto her father's hand and swung on it. "What do you think, dad?"

"Please have a seat, Miss..." her father began.

"Miss Lisa," she interrupted. "But I prefer just Lisa."

Nadia rushed to the fridge to offer her teacher a drink.

"My daughter seems to have taken a liking to you."

"I enjoy being in the company of children."

Lisa knew that her appearance and charm were her greatest weapons, and she intended to use them to her advantage. As the conversation flowed, Lisa steered it towards her accomplishments and expertise in teaching. She spoke about her innovative teaching methods and the positive impact on her learners. She could see the chairman becoming more intrigued and impressed with every word. When it was time to leave, she rose, thanking the chairman for his time and hospitality.

The next day, teachers gathered in the staffroom, waiting for Principal O'Hara's staff briefing. Lisa and Mary sat together, determined to express dissatisfaction with the principal's habit of delaying the morning briefing.

"I have no idea how to get to America," Lisa remarked.

"But someone knows the way to Namibia," Mary whispered back.

"Get a passport; it's a free world," Miss April said.

"Listen to who's talking, the principal's puppet," Mary retorted.

"Who are you calling a puppet?" Miss April stepped closer, invading her colleague's personal space. "I'm doing my best to fulfil my duties. Do you have a problem with that?"

"Yes, you're a traitor," Mary yelled.

"You're lazy and making excuses. Focus on your work instead of finding faults in our management."

"Is this what you call management? It's more like a circus," Mary scoffed.

"You're right, it is a circus," Lisa added, pointing her five red nails at Miss Mwiya. "One day, I'll be in charge of this school, and you better hope I don't."

"Lead this school? With your silly diploma," Mrs Hausiku, who had been silent all along, squealed.

Principal O'Hara entered the staffroom, accompanied by a young man in his twenties. He wore dreadlocks.

"I'm so happy to announce to you all that our school radio station is complete and ready for air. Allow me to introduce Mr Mwilima," Principal O'Hara said. "He will be the station manager and responsible for selecting presenters. Let's encourage our learners to sign up."

"Thank you, Principal O'Hara," Mr Mwilima said. "The school radio is an integral part of education. It provides a platform for learners to develop their communication skills, build confidence, and engage in meaningful debates."

"Excuse me, sir," called Lisa, "who are the hosts?"

"We are going to use our school learners."

"Can't teachers handle that? I mean, can we use someone with more experience? Someone with more style. Someone like me?" said Mary.

"This is a school event, and the learners themselves will be the best choice."

"I don't mind, I can do it. My grandmother worked in radio. It runs in the family," Mary said.

"Let's begin with teachers and then move down to learners," said Lisa.

"Who will want to listen to that annoying voice? Don't you have any self-respect?" said Mrs Hausiku.

"I will ignore that insult, thank you very much," said Lisa.

"Can we please start our tour of the studio?" said Mr Mwilima.

Teachers took a tour of their radio station, and some, like Lisa, Mary, and Mrs Hausiku, who never had anything positive to say, continued to make insensitive remarks.

"This project was meant to be grand. We received a huge donation from our sponsor," said Mrs Hausiku.

"The equipment is costly, madam. We were fortunate to get a big discount."

"We appreciate your hard work, sir," said Miss Mwiya. "This is a wonderful accomplishment."

After the tour, children gathered before their teachers and lined up according to their classes. Mr Mwilima stepped up to the microphone and addressed the learners.

"Our school studio is now complete," he announced. "For all the boys and girls who aspire to be presenters, please write your names on a piece of paper, and drop it in the box in front of the studio. This is a wonderful opportunity to enhance your communication skills."

The learners responded with soft applause, and one by one, they made their way back to their respective classrooms. Sanana stood with a smile on his face as Mr Mwilima approached him.

"What is your name?"

"My name is Sanana," he said, running off to join his class.

In Lisa's class, Nadia sat on her lap. The teacher's phone rang, interrupting their conversation. After a lengthy discussion with the chairman, the lunch bell rang, announcing the end of the school day. Nadia and Lisa walked through the corridors while Sanana strolled, taking the final turn before leaving the hallway. He saw a poster that caught his attention. It read, *Registration for school presenters needed.*

"You have a lovely voice," the Old Driver said.

"No, they wouldn't choose me. Everyone dislikes me," Sanana said.

"They don't hate you."

"They hate me... all of them. They won't choose me."

When it was Friday, Sanana held a tiny piece of paper. He watched from afar as learners left the registration box one by one. Jimmy was the final learner to leave. Sanana glanced around, almost scratching the box.

Laughter echoed from Nadia, Renate, and the other kids. Sanana concealed the paper in his pocket and hurried to the other side, where he wept.

It was 13:30, and the Chairman was lounging outside his beautiful house, reading the newspaper called THE NAMIBIAN. His loyal Pitbull, Sneaky, was curled beside him, wide awake. Lisa said she remembered to thank the chairman for giving her a job. Nadia went to the living room to watch her favourite show. She couldn't help but steal glances at her father and teacher through the window.

"Now, tell me about yourself," the chairman said.

"There's nothing to say except that I'll graduate this August. I have a sister named Ima, who is in her second year at the teacher's college in Zambia. Mother is well in the village. I lost my younger brother during my secondary school days, and my father died when I was little. I have a stubborn aunt named *bana*Monde and her humble husband, *basha*Monde. And other relatives live far away. But enough about me, sir. Did you ever get married?"

"As you can see, it's me and my daughter."

"I admire the love you have for your daughter. It makes me miss the love my mother has for me."

"We can't compare a mother's love to anything."

"Many amazing fathers are out there, including you, sir."

"One day, you'll make a great mum."

Lisa's Ascension to Principal

Learners filled the school hall, their voices buzzing as teachers tried to maintain order. The Old Driver sat next to Sanana, his face unreadable. The principal tapped the microphone twice before speaking, her voice cutting through the chatter

"Dear children, today we have two learners who will take on the role of radio presenters. We had a total of two hundred and seventy-five candidates. Their term will last for one year." The principal paused, scanning the silent crowd.

"Now, I would like to invite Mr Mwilima, who will guide us through this. Please give him a round of applause."

The audience erupted into applause as Mr Mwilima commanded the microphone with his words. "Thank you, Principal O'Hara. Now, I need a volunteer to come up on stage."

Renate strode to the stage, her presence commanding every eye in the hall. Renate didn't care.

"What is your name, young lady?" Mr Mwilima asked.

"Renate."

"Alright, Renate, please pick a name from each box."

He shuffled the names in the blue box labelled "girls", and Renate plunged her hand in. Mr Mwilima then handed her the microphone, and she read the name. "Nadia Lingani!"

Lisa burst onto the stage as if it were her name, dragging Nadia along. The entire hall rose in excitement.

"Congratulations!" Mr Mwilima said. "Renate, please do us the honour once again."

After dipping her arm into the box, Renate pulled out a name, her smile fading slightly.

"The name, young lady," Mr Mwilima prompted.

"Sanana Neo," she said.

A specific group of learners cheered from Miss Mwiya's class. Sanana couldn't believe it was his name. He glanced up at the Old Driver.

"I did it for you, and I'm not sorry if you ask me."

"But why?"

"I believe in you. Now go on."

Sanana's legs felt like jelly as he stumbled toward the stage, his palms slick with sweat. Hesitant claps grew into scattered cheers, and someone chanted his name. His heart pounded louder with each heavy step.

"Congratulations. Please sit over there," said Mr Mwilima.

Sanana and Nadia sat next to Principal O'Hara, Sanana's nerves evident as he shifted uncomfortably in his seat, glancing at Nadia, who sat at ease beside him. The principal's calm presence did little to steady his racing hear.

"Thank you very much, Mr Mwilima, and thank you very much to our two presenters," said Principal O'Hara.

Somewhere in the crowd, Mary leaned toward Lisa, her voice barely a whisper. "This kid you hate... seems to have a good guardian angel." She glanced at Sanana, a smirk tugging at her lips.

Lisa's eyes narrowed, her grip tightening on the edge of her seat. "Very soon, that guardian angel will get tired, and it will abandon him, and then I will come in and ruin his life. I promise you he will not last a semester at this school."

"Who offended you, the boy or his mother?"

"You want to know a lot of things at the same time, and I don't like it. People who ask lots of questions ruin plans."

"This plan of yours might be a solid one. Your confidence is amazing."

"Wait and see, Mary. I'm running this school soon, and who knows, I might consider you, my deputy."

Time passed, and Mr Mwilima coached the two presenters. On Monday, during break, the school hummed with anticipation, everyone waiting to hear Sanana's voice for the first time.

"It's a beautiful morning," Sanana's voice echoed through the speakers. "We are still in the first semester, and the exams are approaching. Let's make sure we prepare well. My co-presenter, Nadia Lingani, will teach you how to prepare for the exams tomorrow morning. Lastly, our principal has requested that all teachers meet after the break, but before I go, I'll leave you with one of my favourite nursery rhymes, *Old McDonald*. Enjoy!"

"This is not kindergarten," Lisa, seated on her chair, cursed.

Sanana felt the excitement as he walked out of the studio. The voices hit him at once, cheers crashing around him. Little girls shouted his name, their adoration a chaotic chorus. The boy waved to his new fans. Once in class, Sanana also received congratulations from his classmates and class teacher.

"That was beautiful," Miss Mwiya said.

"Thank you, Teacher."

"Joe, please make sure everyone remains quiet. I need to attend this meeting," said the teacher.

While the teachers gathered in the staffroom waiting for Principal O'Hara, officials from the regional office held her up. When she arrived ten minutes later, Lisa had already left.

"Miss Lisa!" Principal O'Hara called out. "Can we have our meeting now?"

Lisa stomped down the hallway to her classroom, her fists clenched with anger. Principal O'Hara's repeated disregard for their time had pushed her to the edge—this wasn't the first time they'd been kept waiting for staff briefings.

"Every single time, she treats us like we're her employees," Lisa muttered. "They can have the briefing without me."

Lisa's phone rang. "Hello?"

"Hello, Miss Lisa," the chairman's calm voice greeted. "I heard about what happened. I'd like to invite you to dinner tonight to discuss it further."

"Dinner? Um, okay. That sounds... good."

"Excellent. I will send you the details."

After the call ended, silence filled the room as her thoughts swirled. The dinner ahead could either end her aspirations or open a new path filled with unexpected possibilities. Minutes later, Mary walked into Lisa's classroom, a grin tugging at her lips as she sat on Lisa's desk. Lisa smiled back, but her eyes held something unspoken..

"You seem unusually cheerful today," Mary said.

"I'm about to say goodbye to being a class teacher."

"Are you resigning?"

She shook her head, with a very big smile. "Nope, I'm climbing the ladder right here and doing it quickly."

"I still don't understand."

"Ask me another time, Mary. Tonight, I have an important dinner date with the man who will one day be the father of my children."

"What is his name?"

Lisa gave her a pointed look, her tone tinged with gentle scolding. "Mary, focus on improving your own life. You spend too much time meddling in other people's affairs."

"I think I must leave," said Mary, her expression unreadable.

As soon as she was out of sight, Mary cursed under her breath, "Do you think I don't know about your schemes for the chairman's money?"

Lisa felt the evening drag, but it finally arrived. The chairman sat at the finest restaurant in town, dressed in his black suit, glancing at his wristwatch. Two pink candles lit the table, with a bottle of wine and two sparkling glasses set for the occasion. The sound of high heels on the wooden floor drew everyone's attention. He stood to pull out Lisa's chair. After she apologized for being late, she placed her handbag on the table. As she took her seat, the chairman knelt, surveying the room. Every eye was on him in suspense. Just as he prepared to speak, Lisa stood, her voice breaking the silence, clear and determined. "Yes. Yes. I will marry you." She took the ring and slipped it onto her finger. "When is the wedding?"

"How about five months from now? I was thinking we could have a traditional ceremony," said the chairman.

"Marriage is marriage, whether traditional or civil. The important thing is that I'm marrying an amazing man like you, but I think next week is better."

"Next week seems too soon," the chairman said.

"With your influence, we could even get married today," Lisa assured him with a smile.

After a three-day honeymoon, Lisa glided through the crowded hallways of the school, her steps light and purposeful. The sparkle of her wedding ring caught her attention, and she couldn't help but steal glances at it, a tangible reminder of her new status as Mrs Lingani. She strode into principal O'Hara's office and banged in...

"Call for a staff meeting," she demanded, standing with her hands on her hips.

"Please take a seat, Miss Lisa," Principal O'Hara said.

"Mrs Lingani—and you know it."

"I am the headteacher here."

"That was then—this is my office now."

"You only have a diploma; you can't become principal."

"A diploma and my maiden name... LINGANI."

Principal O'Hara's phone rang, and after the phone dialogue, she started packing her belongings.

"Now, introduce me to the teachers."

"You have changed a lot, sweet child," Principal O'Hara said. "What happened to you?"

"This is life, Miss O'Hara; you have what I want," said Lisa. "Don't worry, your salary will remain the same. I'm doing this because of your kindness and what you have done for me in South Bauleni."

The teachers gathered without speaking to each other; Mary kept smiling as if she knew something that many didn't. Principal O'Hara and Lisa followed each other, Mary's grin widened, and Mrs Hausiku stared at her.

"Let's make this quick; our first lesson is about to begin," Principal O'Hara said. "I received a call..."

"I know what you're trying to say, O'Hara," Mrs Hausiku said. "The gold-digger did it. First, she married him, and now she's in charge. These kids nowadays are shameless. The way they dress, the way they behave, and the way they act. The way they—"

"Quiet, old lady," Lisa snapped at Mrs Hausiku and turned to face Principal O'Hara. "Now, make the announcement and get to the point."

"I'm stepping down as principal. Mrs Lingani will take over from me."

"I'm not surprised," Mrs Hausiku said. "I saw it coming from a mile away."

"You have nothing to worry about, Mrs Hausiku," Lisa said. "I won't fire you. I'll keep you here for one reason: to drive you in all directions.

Now, go to class and wait for further instructions. Mary, come to my office now."

When Mary walked in, Lisa was on a phone call in her new office, her legs spread wide on the table.

"Do you still remember that promise? I think about it every day," Mary said.

"Yes, Mary, you're my deputy," Lisa said.

"Thank you so much, Principal Lingani."

"Now, tell Nadia to announce the assembly."

The principal and other teachers stood in front of the students, and the chatter slowly died down as the assembly began. Miss O'Hara stepped up to the podium, her expression composed yet hiding a swirl of emotions. She cleared her throat, ready to make an announcement.

"Students," Miss O'Hara began, her voice steady, "I am honoured to introduce our new principal, Mrs Lingani Lisa."

A ripple of surprise went through the crowd. Lisa had taken this position by force, her marriage to the chairman securing her the job. However, none of the students knew the story behind her sudden rise to power. Despite her reluctance, Miss O'Hara delivered the speech with poise, the words crafted by Lisa herself. Not a single student realized that the sentiments Miss O'Hara conveyed weren't her own but those of the new principal standing beside her.

Lisa stepped forward as Miss O'Hara finished. She surveyed the sea of young faces.

"Thank you, Miss O'Hara," Lisa said, her voice firm and authoritative. "I look forward to working with all of you to create a bright future." She paused, letting her words sink in before continuing. "Go back to class."

After the assembly, in Mrs Mwiya's class, Lisa asked Sanana to come to her office. She placed an envelope on the table. "You should give this letter to your mother. Keep it safe."

Sanana carefully slipped the letter into his pocket and returned to his classroom. Once he arrived home, he gently laid the letter on the wooden table. However, his mother was still busy with work and wasn't home yet.

As part of her usual morning routine, Agatha prepared Sanana for school the following day. Just as they were leaving, Sanana handed his mother the letter. Agatha placed it back on the table before they hurriedly approached the bus stop. That day, there was a new driver instead of their usual Old Driver who had reported sick. Lisa was in her office when she saw Sanana walking past her windows. She slammed her pencil down on the table and got up to chase after the boy.

Lisa entered the classroom and stood in front of Sanana.

"Did you give the letter to your mother?" Lisa asked sternly.

"Yes, principal... yesterday," Sanana said.

"Go back home now and tell your mother to read the letter."

"But can I go after school?"

"Go home, now."

"But the bus only leaves after school, and I don't have money for a taxi."

Mr Lawrence, the head of the cleaning staff at the school, happened to be passing by. Lisa ordered him to go with Sanana to the school gate. Every learner knew Mr Lawrence, and they disliked him. The only thing Mr Lawrence disliked more was when learners littered. He escorted Sanana to the school gate. They waited for a few minutes until a taxi finally pulled over. He broke the silence and spoke to the boy for the first time, "Don't worry, son. Get in the car."

He handed some money to the taxi driver, and Sanana sat in the back. "Bus stop, Slumsville," Sanana said to the driver.

As the sun grew stronger, the streets became crowded with locals who seemed to have lost hope in life. Sanana walked alone through the narrow path that led to his house. He picked up a letter from the table and started reading it.

Your child's scholarship has been officially terminated as of today. The school is undergoing significant changes. I suggest enrolling your child in a government school that offers free education. Mopane Community School down town is a good option. Many children like him are studying there.

Principal Lingani Lisa.

When Agatha returned from work that night, it was already dark. Sanana was preparing supper.

"Something smells delicious," Agatha said as she placed her handbag on the chair. "How was school?"

Sanana walked across the room and returned, holding the letter.

"You were supposed to read the letter, mum."

After reading it, Agatha said, "You will return to school. There are plenty of good schools in our city."

"But I want to go back to the village."

"We will remain in this city; you and I will succeed."

The following day, Lisa stood behind the table, chatting with her mother on the phone. She made funny faces as the conversation dragged on longer than expected. Occasionally, she glanced at Agatha, who had already taken her seat. Once the call ended, Lisa closed the door and plopped down on a chair.

"Lisa! Is this you?" asked Agatha.

"Life is great when you have everything you need."

"Can I talk to the principal?"

"Who says I'm not the principal?"

"But we finished school a few months ago; we haven't even graduated yet!"

"What do you want?"

Agatha pulled out a letter from her bag. She noticed that the principal's name was Lisa.

"I got this letter. Can you explain what it says?"

"Come on, Agatha, it's all written in plain English."

"I don't understand why my son's scholarship got cancelled!"

"Do you want me to explain it with violence?"

"He's just a kid, Lisa. He doesn't deserve this."

"I cared for your son like I care for all the kids in my school. He's bright, even if he's a bit different. He's smart. By the way, I never knew you had a child."

"John and I were just friends..."

"You were my closest friend, Agatha. You betrayed me. I loved you like a sister, but you betrayed me. John was my first love; do you know what that means?"

"You have to trust me."

"You're a traitor, and your son won't be returning to my school."

Agatha got up from her chair, and for a moment, she didn't say anything. "All I have is my word, Lisa."

Later that day, Lisa got another visitor.

"John!" she exclaimed, "When did you come back from SA?"

"Yesterday, and I heard you work here."

"I don't work here; I'm the administrator here."

The diamond ring on her finger piqued his interest.

"Oh, I'm married. He is a great man."

"Remember what I told you before I left for my studies two years ago? You promised to wait for me."

"I remember, John, but things have changed... I'm married now, and I love my husband."

At that moment, Nadia entered, dropping her school bag on the table with a soft thud, pausing the conversation.

"Sweetheart, give me a moment." Lisa turned to her visitor and said, "We can catch up again, John."

A week passed, and the Old Driver had recovered from his malaria. Upon hearing the news, he visited Sanana. The boy was washing dishes near the door. Agatha sat next to him, reading a sports magazine.

"I heard about what happened, but everything will be okay," the Old Driver said.

"Who exactly are you, sir?" asked Agatha.

The Old Driver took out a photo from his pocket. "Do you know the pregnant woman?"

The photo showed a man and a pregnant woman. Agatha turned it over and read the writing on the back. *His name is Sanana. My great-grandfather's name.*

"This is my mother, and who is he?"

"He's my younger brother," said The Old Driver. "Is Sanana your son?"

"Are you implying he's not my son?"

"Your son will return to school."

It was night in Blackville when Lisa came out of the shower, water dripping from her slender body. She reached for her phone and saw a message from John—his response to her heartfelt message about their shared past. Little did she know, the chairman had already read it. Lisa dropped the phone on the bedroom bench and leaned down to kiss her husband goodnight, but he turned away.

"You've been talking to a man!" he said, his voice low.

Lisa tried to explain, but her words only fuelled the argument. She watched her husband clutch his chest in pain. Her screams woke Nadia, who rushed to their side.

The chairman was rushed to the hospital in an ambulance, the sirens blaring through the dark night. When they arrived, friends and family flooded the waiting room...

By the following evening, the chairman's condition had worsened. His body lay motionless, pale against the stark white sheets, each breath shallow and laboured. With a weak gesture, he beckoned his lawyer, who leaned in, straining to hear his faint words.

The Last Will

The chairman died in the early hours after three days in the hospital. A month after his death, the Lingani family gathered in the living room. The Old Driver was concerned about the promptness of the will reading, but Lisa insisted on it being done as soon as possible. As he sensed the tension in the room, the lawyer cleared his throat to break the silence.

"Before I start reading the will, I have a video recording of Mr Lingani," he declared solemnly, hitting play. The room fell into hushed anticipation as the chairman's voice echoed from the recording...

"I have a son," he said.

Lisa's body tensed, her anger threatening to erupt. Yet she managed to quell it, realising it was just the beginning of the recording.

"He must be present when my will is read," The chairman's voice persisted, cutting through the room's silence.

Lisa was hit by a wave of emotions, a mixture of shock and disbelief coursing through her veins.

"He lives with his sister. My brother Jeremy knows where they are. Please bring him back before my will is read."

After the recording, there was silence for a while before Lisa shouted. "Who is this boy? You must read the will now."

"Do you know where we can find your brother's son?" the lawyer asked the Old Driver.

"Yes, and he is already in his father's house," the Old Driver replied.

"What do you mean he is already in his father's house, and how did you know he should be here?" Lisa rose.

"He was my brother, and he told me."

The Old Driver hurried to the door to let Agatha and her son inside.

"I can't believe this is happening in my lifetime," Lisa turned to face the other side.

"I will replay the video," the lawyer said.

After the recording, Agatha said, "When my mother passed away, I raised my brother as my son. I didn't want him to grow up without the love of both a mother and a father."

"Sanana is my brother?" Nadia asked.

"He is not your brother," Lisa shouted.

"He is your older brother," the Old Driver said.

"I will read the will now…"

I, Mr Lingani Justin Paul of Blackville, now declare that my will shall be governed by the law of Namibia and by the country's legal requirements. I now designate Agatha Neo, my son's older sister, as the executor and trustee of my will. If she cannot fulfil her responsibilities or passes away, I appoint SUNPRIDE management to assume the role of Executor and Trustee.

I have made the following decisions regarding the distribution of my assets:

I bequeath the sum of eighty million Namibian dollars (N$ 80,000,000), free of tax, to my daughter Nadia Lingani.

My only brother, Jeremy Lingani, passionate about driving, will inherit all five of my cars and the garage in Soweto. He will also receive seventy million Namibian dollars (N$70,000,000).

My son, Sanana Neo, will inherit the family house in the village of Mamiyeto and eighty million Namibian dollars (N$80,000,000). He will also be granted eighty per cent (80%) ownership of SUNPRIDE school, while his sister Nadia Lingani will receive the remaining twenty per cent (20%). The family house in Blackville, erf 474, is to be inherited by my two children and must not be sold under any circumstances.

I want to express my love and gratitude to my wife, Lisa Lingani. She can keep all her jewellery and wigs if she wants. This is my final will.

Lisa stomped her left foot on the tiles, her hands clasped together as she massaged them. She couldn't help but bite her bottom lip in frustration, her eyes almost swallowed by their orbits. The rest of the family avoided looking at her.

"I inherit my stupid wigs. My pieces of jewellery?" Lisa exclaimed, her foot drumming on the floor with even more intensity. She began pacing around Sanana, her little finger tapping against her incisors. "This left-handed dwarf can't be my husband's heir. There's no resemblance at all."

"Show some respect," said Agatha.

Lisa took her seat but continued to direct her fury towards the Old Driver. "Your brother can't be that heartless, can he? And how did you know the boy would be in the will?"

Lawyer Albert picked up his briefcase and headed for the door, but Lisa stepped into his path, her shoulders blocking the way.

"According to the law, I'm entitled to inherit half of whatever he owned," Lisa stated.

"With all due respect, Mrs Lingani, the will is legally binding. Please consider giving peace a chance."

Lisa sank into her seat, her fingers tracing the edge of the table. Across from her, Sanana and Nadia sat stiffly, facing each other but avoiding eye contact.

"Can I show you around the house?" Nadia asked, without looking at Sanana. Sanana turned to Agatha, silently seeking permission.

"This is now your father's house," Agatha said.

Nadia moved up the stairs, her footsteps steady and sure. Sanana followed, his hand brushing the banister as he kept his focus on the steps ahead.

Agatha, the Old Driver, and Lisa sat silently for a moment. Lisa removed her husband's picture from the wall and stared at it. "I can't believe this is happening in my lifetime. I dedicated one month of my life to this man." With a deep breath, she dialled Mary's number.

Meanwhile, Mary, having a glass of wine, twirled through her school-owned apartment, already lost in celebration, certain her friend was about to become wealthy. When the phone rang, she snatched it up, still moving to the music. "I'm on my way... we're going to party all night!"

"Something is wrong, Mary. Can you lower the music?" Lisa's voice sounded strained.

"Why are you so angry? Hello, hello, are you still there?"

"Just come, Mary."

A while later, Mary stood before the gate, bouncing on her feet. She cradled a small white Havanese and glanced at her phone. It had been half an hour since her last conversation with Lisa, who was now waiting at the door. Mary stepped back, gasping, as she saw Sneaky the Pitbull lounging beside Lisa, drool dripping from his intimidating face.

"Just come, Mary," Lisa said. "This lazy dog doesn't even bark at strangers."

"Then why do you keep him?" Mary asked.

"He was here before me, but I'll get rid of him soon."

Lisa took a few steps and turned to face Mary, noticing what she was carrying. "What kind of dog is that, and where did you get it?"

"You mean Mr Smith?" Mary stroked her pet's curly fur.

"Smith? You call that thing Mr Smith?"

"I got a dog to match my new title as deputy."

Lisa and Mary spent the whole day in the bedroom. Mary couldn't help but laugh. As a gold digger, she was curious about the nature of Lisa's marriage, the reason behind her friend's misfortune, and how Sanana came into the picture. Mary had become the deputy principal. What would happen if Lisa got demoted? Neither Mary nor Lisa were qualified for their positions, which gave Mary more reason to encourage her friend to contest the will.

The next day, Lisa and Mary met Lawyer Tom, who owned one of the largest law firms in Windhoek. Lawyer Tom told Lisa that he had handled many cases like hers before and that she should trust him completely. Their meeting took place near the dam.

"How long were you married to your late husband?" the lawyer asked.

"One month and something like two weeks?"

"You are a rightful widow, and you are entitled to your share. I will do my best, but your husband was powerful."

"Are you doubting yourself?" Mary asked. "You must win. My friend was a good wife. How could that man be so cruel and wicked even in death?"

Lisa stood and observed the tranquillity of the dam. "I still don't get it," Lisa said. "When will they receive their inheritance?"

"It's clear that you're not included in the will. Unless you have some magical Cinderella wigs hidden away in your closet," Lawyer Tom said, realising his attempt at humour fell flat.

"Do you think this is a joke?" Mary shouted. "This is my best friend, and I love her."

"How long?" Lisa asked again.

"First, we need to take inventory of the decease's documents and assets and determine their values. Then, settle the final bills and ongoing administration expenses. After that, we file the necessary tax returns and pay the applicable taxes. Finally, the beneficiaries receive their share," explained Lawyer Tom.

"For how long?" Lisa repeated.

"It depends. Six months to three years."

"My friend and her late husband had a customary marriage. How can we challenge the will?"

"Do you have any marriage certificates?"

"We never went to any official court. It was a simple ceremony in my uncle's living room."

"Who officiated the marriage?"

"It was my late father's younger brother, Uncle Malumo."

"According to Article 66 of the Constitution of the Republic of Namibia, common law and customary law that were in effect at the time of independence are still valid as long as they don't conflict with the constitution or any other statutory law," Lawyer Tom explained.

"But a customary marriage is still valid, right?" Mary asked.

"Yes...even though it was a union between two families in the middle of your living room, it was under the customs of your community. You're married. Customary unions follow ancestral systems. You're legally married to your husband; he paid lobola, which is recognised as legal in our country. He paid lobola, right?"

"Yes, he did, but he complained about it until his death."

"Was the lobola too expensive?" Mary asked.

"Fifty cattle."

That caused Lawyer Tom to choke on his saliva. He looked around, trying to distract himself. "I understand," he said, "they weren't merciful to me either."

"You got married through the village?" Mary asked. "When it's my turn, I'll never go down that path. I'll have a white wedding and stand before a fat old judge. And it will be a marriage in community of property, and he must have money."

Lisa looked down, silently suggesting to Mary that she should sometimes be more discerning.

"We have to travel to the village the day after tomorrow to meet your relatives," the lawyer said.

"That's exactly what I was thinking," said Mary. "We'll fight this together, tooth and nail, and we'll come out victorious. Have faith, my dear friend. Can I hug you?"

"Stop with the theatrics, Mary," said Lisa. "I can't stand people who exaggerate."

"I'm a good friend, and you're accusing me of being fake?"

"I didn't mean it that way... You're my best friend, and I appreciate your support. Can I have that hug?"

"I don't like it when people think I'm a serpent that betrayed Eve or Goliath that deceived Samson."

"I don't read the Bible that often, but wasn't it supposed to be Delilah who had an issue with Sam?" the lawyer asked.

"Delilah or Goliath, who cares? My motto in life is to be loyal to my friends. You have hurt my feelings, Lisa, and it will take time for me to trust you again." Mary grabbed her handbag and was about to leave when Lisa grabbed her arm.

"Please, Mary. You know these are difficult times for me. I appreciate you, and I need you."

Lisa held Mary's arm for a moment. Mary shrugged her off and took her seat.

"I will call you if anything comes up," said the lawyer.

When the lawyer had left, Mary picked up a few sticks that she kept breaking to express her unhappiness. Lisa kept herself busy observing the dam and the birds that enjoyed its rich ecosystem.

"How about I take you out for lunch?" said Lisa.

"I could have said yes, but I'm getting fat."

"How about we visit your favourite tavern?"

"I could have said yes, but my belly is getting bigger."

"How about I take you shopping?"

"I could have said..."

"Stop with your nonsense, Mary. How many times do you want me to apologise? I'll wait for you in the car."

When Mary threw the sticks she held, she took a few steps and shouted, "I'll accept all your offers. Where do we start?"

"I could have said no, but you're my friend," said Lisa as she got into her car.

Meanwhile, on the Slumsville footpath, the Old Driver and Agatha walked in silence, Agatha leading the way. The only sound was the distant barking of dogs.

"The last time I was here, it was too noisy," the Old Driver said.

The door noise alerted the landlord, who was waiting for Agatha. He wore blue shorts, a white vest, and oversized slippers. Two of his front teeth were missing.

"My child," the landlord began, "I understand times are tough. You haven't paid your rent. I need to pay for water and other expenses."

"Excuse me, landlord," the Old Driver said. "How much does she owe?"

"One thousand, five hundred."

"That's quite a sum," the Old Driver said, glancing between Agatha's room and the landlord.

"This is Windhoek, sir. Things are pricey here. Focus on the utility, not the cost," the landlord said.

The Old Driver handed the landlord some cash from his wallet and provided the address for the remaining payment later that evening.

"They are moving out today," said the Old Driver.

The Old Driver sat waiting for Agatha, who was collecting a few items. She came out with two bags, feeling so reluctant.

"I don't think it's wise to move in right now. The will was read today. Something doesn't feel right," Agatha said.

"This is a chance for you and your brother to have a better life. That boy is the son of my late brother, and he deserves a good life. It was his father's dying wish; we shouldn't deny him that."

"Lisa will not be pleased. Do you think she will welcome us with open arms?"

"What other choice does she have?"

"I need to inform my bosses in Whiteville."

In Whiteville, the Indian boy led Agatha and the Old Driver into the living room, where the couple settled in to watch TV together. The room felt snug, with the gentle sound of the television and the aroma of tea lingering in the air. Once Agatha finished sharing her story, the woman said, "I'm glad your younger brother got to meet his father."

"Thank you for all your help since I arrived in this town, ma'am. You've been so kind." She reached out to pat the boy's dark hair gently and left.

Lisa and Mary arrived at the Lingani mansion carrying many shopping bags. As they were about to head upstairs, Lisa turned back to see Sanana watching TV with Nadia. Sanana got up to greet her.

"Where's Agatha?" Lisa asked Sanana.

"She went out with Uncle Jeremy," Sanana said.

Lisa and Mary made their way to Lisa's bedroom. Mary stared out the window at the orchard and the beautiful Lingani yard.

"This place is too gorgeous to leave behind. I wouldn't if I were you. I adore this house and all its furniture," Mary said.

"Stop it, Mary."

"Let's talk about your parents," Mary said, "you need them during times like this."

"My father died a long time ago, but I have faith in my mum and my aunt. Especially my aunt."

"Any men in your family?"

"I trust my uncles. Everything will work out. After all, he was my husband."

"They sound like my uncles. I already like them and can't wait to meet them."

Mary grabbed her handbag, hugged Lisa, and said, "Rest up for now," before leaving.

Lisa curled into bed for her afternoon nap. When she woke, the sun had set, and the streetlights lit up Blackville. Agatha was cooking dinner and didn't notice Lisa entering the kitchen.

"Whoa!" Lisa said, adjusting her earring, "You're here cooking dinner. What a landslide."

Agatha shut the pot lid and was ready to leave. Lisa blocked her way with her usual shoulder.

"I don't need your drama, Lisa."

"Oh, so you still remember my name?"

"Believe it or not, I still care about you."

"I saw the look on your face when that dumb lawyer read the will; you were enjoying it," said Lisa.

Agatha pushed past Lisa, took a few steps, and turned to face her, "Our friendship meant a lot to me. I had nothing to do with John." Agatha left the door open as she walked over to the Old Driver, who was watching TV with the kids.

"How many rooms are in this house?" Agatha asked, sitting down next to Nadia.

"Six," Nadia said, "Sanana can have the room next to mine."

There was a knock on the door; the Old Driver rushed to answer it. The landlord, who had come for his rent, stood there smoking a pipe, looking tidy in formal pants and a shirt. After he got his money, the Old Driver escorted him to the gate.

Nadia showed Agatha and Sanana to their rooms. Sanana placed a photo of Agatha on the dressing table and went to bed. In the other room, Agatha sat on the bed and took out an old photo from her bag, which she placed on the headboard.

"We met him, Mother," she whispered, "But we met him too late. Your son is in his father's house."

A Visit to the Village

The chairman was born and raised in Mamiyeto. Lawyer Tom accompanied Lisa and Mary, driving through the night. The chairman's only living relatives were Jeremy, known as The Old Driver, Uncle Liam, a village pastor, and Aunt Dorothy, a schoolteacher. When Lisa arrived at the village, she met Aunt Dorothy at a nearby shebeen. Lisa stopped the car, rolled down the window, and greeted, "Good morning, *ba*Dorothy."

From Aunt Dorothy's piercing stare, Lisa could tell that if she continued with her persistent greetings, Aunt Dorothy might respond with her usual anger. She had never liked Lisa because she disapproved of her marriage to the chairman. She was never afraid to voice her opposition to anyone who cared to listen, and she didn't mind saying it to Lisa's face. In Aunt Dorothy's eyes, Lisa was seen as a gold digger and too young to marry a man in his sixties. Lisa herself would be turning twenty-two in September of that same year.

"*Ba*Dorothy, I have something for you."

Aunt Dorothy turned to the other side and let out a curse before sitting at a table with Angela, the owner of the shebeen.

"Is she just bitter or drunk?" Mary asked from the front seat of the black Ford Everest SUV.

"I don't like her either," Lisa said.

As they drove away, Aunt Dorothy grabbed her phone and started dialling. "Hello, Jeremy. Did you know this useless girl is here?" Aunt Dorothy said. "Do you know why she's here?"

"I didn't know but I think it's about the will," The Old Driver said. "My brother left her a little something."

After the call, Aunt Dorothy peeped at Lisa and her friends through the shebeen reeds. Lisa was carrying goods from the city into Uncle Liam's thatched house. Uncle Liam was there with two elderly men after milking the cows. After exchanging pleasantries, Lisa and her friends met Uncle Liam, who was sipping on boiled milk.

"Where's Dorothy?" Uncle Liam asked Kamwi, Aunt Dorothy's son.

"She went to *ba*Angela's shebeen," the boy said, bowing before his uncle.

"This morning? Your mother is losing touch with reality. How can she have beers for breakfast?" Uncle Liam said.

"Uncle Liam," Lisa said, "we should give *ba*Dorothy a break today."

"My sister wasn't like this... she's getting worse every day," Uncle Liam said.

While that was happening, Lawyer Tom examined the hut and the old-fashioned, carved furniture inside. He stared at the Omega FM VHF radio, held together with rubber, playing FM.

"Could you please turn off the radio?" Uncle Liam asked Lisa. "Yes, that button right there."

Lisa observed the button to success.

"Let's say a prayer," Uncle Liam said.

After a lengthy prayer in his native Subia language, Uncle Liam took a long sip, allowing Lisa to introduce her friends.

"Uncle, these are my friends: Mary and Lawyer Tom," Lisa said. "This is Uncle Liam, my late husband's uncle. The lady we met earlier is *ba*Dorothy, the youngest in this family. My late husband's aunt. She's a teacher at the local school here." Lisa glanced at the picture frame on the wall—a woman in her graduation gown.

"Yes, that's my sister from back in the day," Uncle Liam said. "After her husband and child died in a car accident, my sister turned to alcohol."

"Have you ever considered rehabilitation?" Lawyer Tom asked.

"What exactly do they do there?"

The silence among them indicated that no one had an answer to that question.

"Mr Liam," Lawyer Tom said, "do you know about Mr Lingani's son?"

"Yes, that was twelve years ago, and the mother passed away shortly after giving birth."

"Do you happen to know which village the woman came from?" Lisa asked.

"She's from this village; did you see one of the two elders who greeted you? The fair one, *ba*George."

"Uncle Liam," Lisa said, "my husband's will was read a few days ago, and he didn't leave anything to me." Lisa wiped away a tear that seemed as if she had manipulated.

"I'm sorry to hear that," he said.

Lisa then glanced at the lawyer, who started speaking in the local language.

"You can speak in English, sir," Uncle Liam interjected. "I used to work at the mine with Viljoen."

The lawyer smiled upon hearing this, as he had forgotten his native language due to living in the city and education.

"He only left his estate to his daughter and Mr Jeremy, and one little boy he claims is his son," said Mary.

"I'm happy he remembered his lost son," Uncle Liam said.

"Uncle, sir," Lisa said, "my husband and I got married according to the customs of this community, and I want the laws of my people to determine the inheritance of my late husband's properties."

"Yes, Mr Liam," the lawyer agreed. "My client is unhappy with the will, and anyone in her position would feel the same. That's why we have come to you as the head of this family so we can proceed from here."

Mary kept massaging her hand with utmost compassion.

"Please allow me to meet the elders from both families," Uncle Liam said.

In the morning, Lisa woke up bright and early. She begged Mary to go with her into the woods. While half-asleep, Mary rambled on about things that made no sense to Lisa. Despite this, Lisa felt a sense of urgency and discomfort in her stomach, so she redirected herself towards Aunt Dorothy's house. After a single knock, Aunt Dorothy shouted, "Do you want to break down my door this early morning?"

"It's me, *ba*Dorothy. Lisa."

"What do you want? Go away."

"I need to go to the woods, and I was hoping for some company."

"You mean you want an escort?"

"Something like that."

"Stop eating so much..."

"Please, *ba*Dorothy."

"Just go away."

Aunt Dorothy lit a candle and got out of bed. Next to the door, she had a makeshift toilet made from a plastic bottle for when she needed to use the bathroom. When she noticed the bottle was filthy full, she went to the back of the house to empty it after relieving herself. Lisa was returning from the woods when she waved at Aunt Dorothy.

"Good morning, *ba*Dorothy."

"Morning."

"I'm sorry about the death of your husband and son."

Aunt Dorothy stared down at Lisa's bunny slippers and shook her head in disapproval.

"What kind of shoes are those?"

"They're carpet slippers, quite trendy nowadays. You can have them if you want."

"No," Aunt Dorothy said with a slam of the door.

Lisa returned to bed, only to find Mary wide awake and looking for company in the woods. The two friends went into the woods together, where they ran into Aunt Dorothy, who had come to ease herself too. Mary was carrying Mr Smith.

After handling their morning tasks, they trailed behind Aunt Dorothy, chatting away, but Aunt Dorothy could hear every word they said. The conversation was in her favour, as she couldn't help but smile. The compliments were overwhelming, causing her to stop in her tracks.

"Good morning, *ba*Dorothy," Mary said. "Do you know where we can grab some beers after lunch?"

"Come over to my place, but not after lunch. I'll take you there now," Aunt Dorothy said.

"This time, the beer tastes so bitter."

"Who drinks alcohol for the taste? We drink it for the action."

Back in the city, Sanana made his way to the kitchen, his sleepiness evident from his yawning. Inside the kitchen, Agatha was preparing breakfast. He was about to sit down when the Old Driver walked in. The boy rushed over to him, giving him a warm hug, and guiding him into the kitchen. A little while later, Nadia joined them, still half-asleep.

The family of four gathered around the table and enjoyed breakfast together.

"My children," said the Old Driver. "We will be going to the village today. Dorothy called."

"Why, uncle?" asked Nadia.

"Finish your food. I will come and pick you up later."

"It's a holiday..." Sanana blurted out.

The Old Driver went to his car, with Agatha following behind.

"What's happening, Uncle Jeremy? Why this sudden trip to the village?"

"My late brother's wife is currently in the village. She called for the elders to discuss her situation."

"Do you think it's fair what your brother did to his wife?"

"I can't judge my brother now because he is not here to tell us his side of the story."

"I know Lisa can be stubborn at times, but deep down, she's a good person. She just had a difficult childhood."

"You sound like you know her."

"We were best friends in college, but it's a long story."

The Old Driver, lost in his thoughts, tapped the car's steering wheel. "Who is John? Last time, I overheard you and her arguing about John."

"John was Lisa's boyfriend in college. She believes that I had something to do with him."

"Please get the children ready, we are leaving to the village."

Meanwhile, Lisa made breakfast for Uncle Liam, who had returned from his usual walk around the church. Lawyer Tom and Mary were enjoying the sun in the courtyard, chatting away.

"Are you interested in my friend?" Mary asked the lawyer. "The way you look at her, the way you come with us to the village, the way you eat her food, and the way you-"

"I'm married, and I love my wife and kids."

"I thought you were going to say happily married?"

"There's no such thing as happily married."

"How long have you been married?"

"Seven years."

"Do you have kids?"

"A daughter. And you?"

"No, I'm still young and just starting my career. A child would slow me down, and I'm not married."

Lisa came out and sat with them, followed by Uncle Liam.

"Uncle," Lisa said, "I need to visit my mother."

"I will also meet with some elders," Uncle Liam said.

"I have some paperwork to do, so I'll stay here," Lawyer Tom said.

"We promised *ba*Dorothy some beers," Mary whispered.

"I'm going to see my mother; *ba*Dorothy can wait. Let's go now."

"Is it far?"

"About an hour if we walk fast."

Lisa and Mary took the path through the dense forest, making Mary uneasy. Mr Smith, who was in her arms, would bark, adding to her restlessness. The sight of snake tracks crossing the path from whatever directions silenced them.

"What's the name of your village?" Mary asked.

"Come on, Mary, is that necessary? We're already here."

"It's a village name, Lisa... I'm your best friend."

Lisa pointed towards her mother, sitting under the shade of a large camelthorn tree in front of their thatched hut. Lisa's mother, *ba*Eliza, shared a traditional mat with her sister, *bana*Monde, and they were enjoying some groundnuts from a conventional basket. There were a few huts and families scattered around.

"My feet are killing me," Mary flopped down on the mat next to Lisa, who had arrived a few seconds earlier. The village dogs noticed Mr Smith and started barking. Mr Smith hid behind Mary. *Bana*Monde stared at Mary's dog, her mouth hanging open. "What happened to your cat?" *Bana*Monde asked.

"It's a dog," Mary said, panting as she lay on the mat.

"What kind of dog is that?"

"A friend of mine from Cuba gave it to me."

*Bana*Monde glanced over her shoulder, still hearing the barks of two local dogs who seemed very hungry.

"Well, yours looks beautiful and well-behaved."

"Aunt," Lisa said to *bana*Monde, "where is uncle?"

"He travelled to Mamiyeto; Pastor Liam called him. Is there a problem with your in-laws?"

"A big one, Aunt. My late husband left me with nothing."

"Never!" *bana*Monde shouted.

Mary was about to fall asleep when she saw Lisa's aunt standing before her. She recalled that her friend had warned her about her aunt being quite strict and not tolerating any nonsense. *Ba*Eliza kept munching on groundnuts.

"Child," said *bana*Monde, "your late husband was such a joker, you'll inherit everything."

"Not everything, Aunt. My late husband had a son and a daughter."

"Who cares?" *bana*Monde scoffed. "They're just kids; the boy had been abandoned long ago."

"Do you know the boy, Aunt?" asked Mary.

"He's the son of a nobody," *bana*Monde answered.

"My child," *ba*Eliza said, "what did you get from the will?"

"Nothing, Mother. He left me nothing."

"Just wigs and jewellery," Mary said.

"So, he gave you something already yours?" *bana*Monde asked.

On the other side of the compound, a teenage boy in tattered clothing approached with a machete and some ropes. He hung the tools on a tree and knelt before his masters to offer greetings. As he was leaving for his hut, *ba*Eliza called him back.

"Kill that white rooster, the one attacking the others."

The young boy started chasing the rooster and began preparing it. As the sun set, the village grew darker, and everyone gathered around the evening fire. *Bana*Monde's husband, *basha*Monde, arrived.

"My daughter," *basha*Monde said, "you married into the wrong family. You need to be strong."

"What did they say?" *ba*Eliza asked.

"The men are fine, but the women..."

"Dorothy needs to stop smoking marijuana. She's causing chaos in this situation," *bana*Monde said.

"We're meeting the day after tomorrow."

"She married that old fool, and he's leaving her with nothing."

"Please, Aunt, don't insult my husband."

"Shut up... he's a fool. And you're defending him. How could he do such a thing? People will talk and laugh at you and our family."

"But Aunt—"

*Bana*Monde turned to her husband and said, "Your soft tone makes you seem weak. This is a battle."

"Sometimes you need to choose your words carefully; you're too toxic," the husband said.

"People are afraid of me."

Mary couldn't take her eyes off *bana*Monde, who had become her favourite clown since the afternoon.

"I was the spokesperson of the 1982 demonstration against apartheid," *bana*Monde stated, pointing at her husband. "I was also—"

"Yes, yes," her husband interrupted. "You were also the leader of the National Youth League in 1984 and 1985 and the beginning of 1986. And you almost went to parliament."

Mary couldn't help but chuckle at the exchange.

"Why do my past successes seem to bother you and sting your wicked soul?" *bana*Monde said.

"They don't bother me; they bore me," the husband said before leaving for his hut. The wife followed, and they all retired for the night.

The following morning, Lisa and Mary bid farewell to everyone. The boy accompanied them back to Mamiyeto, carrying his Omega radio, which played beautiful music, and his two hunting dogs, Silver, and Billy. Lisa and Mary passed by Aunt Dorothy's house, and she was busy with her morning chores.

"Morning, *ba*Dorothy," said Lisa. "About yesterday—"

"Who cares about yesterday."

"What's the deal with you and that old woman?" Mary asked.

"That woman is not my problem right now; I don't like her either. Who cares? She's an old drunkard who was lucky enough to get a degree.

"Let me take a bath, and then we can visit your aunt's favourite place. I need a beer. Are they cold?"

Angela Enjoys Life in the Village

Angela, the owner of a shebeen, sat across from Aunt Dorothy and two other customers. She hadn't changed much, her love for makeup still boldly evident. One regular leaned forward and requested some music to liven the atmosphere. Angela whipped her head around, her earrings swaying with the motion, and barked at her worker, "Belinda! Turn on the music—and learn to think beyond the box!"

Aunt Dorothy started her typical small talk, which bored other drunkards like her. All she ever talked about was teaching and her love for her job. Lisa and her friends arrived, and Angela went to greet them. They all sat facing Aunt Dorothy.

"*Ba*Dorothy," Mary said, "when your husband died untimely, may his soul and that of your son rest in peace."

Aunt Dorothy kicked the bottle into the sand and knocked the chair over. "You listen here," she grumbled. "Don't talk about my son and husband." She stumbled and cursed as she walked away.

"She's upset about yesterday," said Mary.

"No, she's not angry; she's frustrated, Mary."

"About what?"

"About her life. Do you think someone who drinks that much alcohol enjoys it?"

Angela sat down after serving her special guests, giving them undivided attention.

"I know you," said Lisa to Angela. "I used to see you somewhere on campus."

Angela chuckled lightly and shrugged. "I used to go to campus once in a while."

Lisa and her friend bought Angela beers, and she was enjoying every moment of it. She began talking about property ownership in customary marriages in Mamiyeto, explaining how the laws seemed to shift depending on the individuals involved and the bribes given to local authorities. Customary laws in their land were unwritten and flexible depending on the circumstances. Sometimes, the property was owned by the husband and wife, while other times, the woman received household items from the traditional authority. Men owned cars, farm equipment, and all domestic animals.

Angela took a sip from her bottle, her eyes wide with interest.

"Keep going," urged Lawyer Tom.

"Do you know who owns the children?" Angela asked.

"Who?" asked Mary.

"Children are considered the property of the father." Angela took another drink, leaving them in suspense. "Do you know who owns the wife?"

"Who?" Mary asked again.

"Come closer," Angela said, pulling Lawyer Tom to the centre of the table. "The husband and her family."

"What do you mean by that?" Lisa asked.

"In your situation, since your husband is dead and buried deep down below sea level, you must marry his brother."

"What do you mean I must marry my late husband's brother?"

"You will marry Jeremy. You know Jeremy, right?"

"The Old Driver?" Mary asked.

"Who is the Old Driver?" Angela asked, unaware of that nickname.

"Mr Jeremy."

"You must be strong, or else you will leave empty-handed. Look at me! I married my husband when I moved to this village from South Bauleni, and he drowned while fishing. I didn't kill him... he couldn't swim. Whose fault is that?"

"Not yours," said the lawyer.

"I wish I had died first... then they wouldn't have accused me of anything."

Lisa gazed at her friend, her eyes lingering on the straw she was using to sip her beer. Angela doesn't sell those.

"Come on, Mary, did you bring that from the city? A straw?" Lisa said.

"What is a straw?" Angela asked. "Oh, the tube!"

"Haven't you heard of contagious diseases?"

Lisa glanced at two friends sitting nearby who were sharing a bottle.

"People in the village have no shame and aren't afraid of diseases. They are drinking from that bottle one after another, and it's unhealthy."

The shebeen started to fill up, which made Angela so damn happy. She kept saying welcome and welcome. The final surprise was a personalised LINGANI car. The black Toyota bakkie was reversing. Vehicles like that were good for her business and very rare in the community. Even though her vision was blurry, Angela shouted at the top of her lungs as she ran to hug Agatha.

"You're here. Are you...?" Angela began.

"It's me, Aunt," Agatha said. "It's me, your sister's daughter. I came with my brother, too."

"And who is this little girl?"

"Nadia, Mr Lingani's late daughter."

"Jessica's daughter?"

"Who is Jessica, Aunt?"

"Jessica is her mother." Angela stroked Nadia's hair. "You're growing up so fast. City food must be very nutritious. I last saw you when you came with your father for Christmas six years ago."

Nadia smiled.

"Now, where is my king?" Angela said.

The Old Driver and Sanana came from the other side of the car.

"Come here and give your aunt a hug."

Sanana never enjoyed Angela's hugs. They were always too tight.

"Aunt Angela where is Jack?" asked Sanana.

"He went fishing."

"And my dog?"

"He went with Jack. He loves the river."

"Do you feed him?"

"Feed him? This is the village; dogs hustle for their meal here." Angela turned to the Old Driver. "Jeremy, you're getting so grey."

"Aunt, do you still have the keys to mum's house?" Agatha asked.

"I'll send some kids to clean it for you. We'll meet up later."

The people at the bar, especially Lisa and Mary, stopped talking. Lisa never expected Agatha to be from that village.

"You should have known," said Mary. "Weren't you best friends in college?"

"We never discussed that," Lisa said. "I'm so annoyed with that little boy."

"You mean Sanana?"

"He can't be my husband's heir."

After Agatha and the Old Driver left, Angela ordered Belinda to be extra kind to the customers. The rest were indoors when Sanana brought the final bag from the car. He was about to enter the yard when Jack called to get his attention. Jack had two small fish in his hands, with a puppy trotting ahead of him. Sanana hurried over to meet his dog. He had grown and was looking quite good for a village dog. Jack had now become a grown young man, but he had also become so poor and chubby. The last time Jack lived in town with his mother, he dressed well. Life in the village had taken a toll on him, and he had become a fisherman. Fate had gone against his mother's wish.

Jack stood there, stroking his bearded chin.

"Thank you, Jack, for looking after my dog," Sanana said. "I have something for you."

The three of them made their way to the courtyard made of reeds. The small, thatched house was in terrible condition. Angela, Agatha, and the Old Driver were inside. Sanana reached into his bag, pulled out a wristwatch, and gave it to Jack. Agatha smiled at Sanana, Jack, and the dog.

"I haven't seen my brother this happy in a long time," Agatha said.

"I should go back to the shebeen. Customers feel more comfortable when I'm there."

"Well, I need to talk to Uncle Liam," the Old Driver said.

"Drop me off at the shebeen first," Angela said.

"But before that, let's go meet Uncle Liam. This concerns you too, Angela," came the reply.

They made their way to Uncle Liam's house, where he had just returned from church, accompanied by two elders. They all gathered in his sitting room...

"We will gather at Uncle Malumo's house on Wednesday," he said. "This situation is quite difficult, as it involves conflicting laws—customary and traditional. We must approach this matter with caution."

"I am pleased that my nephew has connected with his father's relatives," Angela said. "I know civil law takes precedence over customary law?"

"Are you sure, Angela?" Aunt Dorothy asked.

"I'm not sure, but I believe so."

"This won't be simple," Uncle Liam reiterated. "I know that family, and they will go to great lengths to ensure victory in this case."

"I am confident that we have determination on our side," the Old Driver said, "but we must also respect our traditions."

"If we address this matter traditionally and reach a mutual understanding, the will can be altered," Uncle Liam suggested.

"That won't happen," Aunt Dorothy snarled. "There's no reason to change the will, as it benefits us."

"Dorothy is correct," said the Old Driver. "My brother had his reasons. We must abide by his wishes."

"Agreed," Uncle Liam concluded. "We must all speak with one voice on that day."

At Angela's shebeen, Mary massaged Lisa's tense shoulders, showing her empathy. Lawyer Tom remained motionless...

"We should go back home," Mary suggested.

"You're right, Mary," said the lawyer.

As they were preparing to leave, Angela returned. She was about to walk past them when Lisa blocked her path.

"You should have told us that the boy is your sister's child."

"How was I supposed to know? I never even knew who his father was," Angela said. "Please excuse me; I need to attend to my shop. Oh one more thing, we are meeting tomorrow. Just memorise your lines very well."

Widow Seeks Justice

"My husband died," said Lisa during the family meeting.

"We know that already," said Aunt Dorothy.

"Let's give her a chance to speak; remember, we have an Induna in our midst," Uncle Malumo intervened. "Please continue, my child."

"Thank you, Uncle Malumo. My late husband and I had a traditional marriage right here in this very room. According to customary law, I should receive a share of his properties. The will that was presented goes against our customs in Mamiyeto. Our traditions dictate that a wife should inherit from her husband. Thank you, wise elders."

"Something must have happened to make him do this," said Aunt Dorothy.

"Or he didn't do it?" *Bana*Monde said.

"My daughter loved her husband," said *ba*Eliza.

"Please investigate my case, my elders. I married him traditionally, so tradition should guide us in resolving this issue."

*Bana*Monde was about to speak, but a look from her husband made her think twice. She hesitated before finally saying, "Someone altered the will; the brother-in-law I know wouldn't do something so wicked."

An elderly man stood up from his seat. However, Uncle Malumo insisted that he remain seated while speaking.

"I have a few questions that I would like to ask," he said, referring to the statement made by the grieving widow. "She should inform us about what she received from the will. Secondly, are we challenging the will's validity, or are we here as a family to agree? And thirdly, what is the stance of the family on this matter?" The old man was well-respected in the village due to his wisdom and previous role as a retired school principal. Whenever he spoke, everyone paid attention.

"Can I say something?" asked *bana*Monde.

"Before that," said Uncle Malumo, "let me introduce the two families present. I will begin with myself, Malumo. I am the older brother of her late father. The woman over there is her mother, *ba*Eliza. The lady next to *ba*Eliza is her elder sister, *bana*Monde. The gentleman over there is her husband, *basha*Monde, and the man next to me is my cousin, Stevo."

After Malumo, Liam started introducing her family members.

"I am Liam; the late man was my nephew. His father was my older brother, and the woman over there is my sister, Dorothy. The man wearing shades in the shade is Jeremy, the older brother. He is the only one remaining out of the two. We also have *ba*George, who is Sanana's maternal uncle. Sanana is the little boy seated next to his sister, Agatha. And next to Sanana is Nadia, the late's only daughter."

"Can I speak now?" *Bana*Monde asked.

"Your turn will come; can you relax for now?" her husband said.

"Thank you for coming," Uncle Malumo said, adjusting his big bifocal glasses.

The whole house fell silent. *Bana*Monde grabbed everyone's attention with a loud hand clap as tradition demanded. "Can I speak now?"

"Can you be patient? What are you so eager to say?" her husband asked again.

*Bana*Monde ignored him. She clapped again, and the others followed suit.

"I need to say this before I forget," *bana*Monde began. "My sister's daughter got married this year, and her husband died. It was sudden; he was never ill. How did he find the time to write such a useless will? He left his inheritance to his two children, which is fine with me; they are his kids. He was a good man for doing that, but what I find disturbing is that he left almost half to his older brother. Something doesn't add up. A man as kind as him wouldn't be so cruel as to leave his wife with just shoes and jewellery."

The Old Driver raised one eyebrow and smirked, then started shaking his legs to calm himself down.

"Some of us who never went to school might not understand this," someone behind the Old Driver said. "I've been listening to everything said so far, and I'm disappointed with how things are in this country. This so-called will is a selfish act that shouldn't be accepted anywhere. When a husband and wife get married, they become one. We read that in the Bible. You can't leave your spouse with nothing after you're gone. I don't support this will. If it were up to me, we should traditionally solve this so the wife can receive what is rightfully hers." The old man's speech seemed to amuse Lisa and Mary.

"How could a husband be so heartless? Leaving his wife with nothing," *bana*Monde said.

"Nothing!" Aunt Dorothy said, her eyes bloodshot. "She received shoes and jewellery. Isn't that enough?"

"Dorothy," *bana*Monde said, "you're a woman; you know this isn't right."

"*Bana*Monde," Aunt Dorothy said, "there must be a reason her husband did what he did. Don't you think so? These young girls of this generation only care about money and a luxurious life. They don't believe in love or know what it means."

"Blame it on the older generation. Why are they preying on the younger generation? As soon as those old fools receive their pensions, they start chasing young girls from the streets and schools." *Bana*Monde quickly looked at her husband, whom she still hadn't completely forgiven after six years. He almost left her for a younger woman who nearly put him in a wheelchair.

*Basha*Monde glanced up, his lips turning inward, but his wife didn't pay much attention.

"Now he's back, with a scar. Its men like him who corrupt our children," she said.

*Bana*Monde's nostrils flared like a buffalo's, especially when the conversation turned to her past with her husband.

"The past is in the past," *basha*Monde said. "Let's focus on why we're here."

"Exactly," Aunt Dorothy toaid. "There's a reason he didn't include her in the will. Only uneducated people think they can challenge tradition with the will. A will is more important than traditional laws. He had his reasons, and we should respect that."

"Can any reason justify oppressing your wife and humiliating her?" *Bana*Monde asked.

*Basha*Monde gave his wife a stern look. "Sometimes it's best to listen and not react to everything," he said.

"Leave me alone; this concerns my niece's future. I know you don't care about this family. Go back to that Matilda who wasted your retirement money," she retorted.

Mary whispered to Lisa, "This is starting to sound like a lover's quarrel."

"You're out of topic, woman. Can you pick a better time?" the husband snapped.

"Yes," Aunt Dorothy agreed. "It's simple; your daughter wasn't a good wife."

"What are you implying, Dorothy? Are you trying to say that my daughter wasn't a good wife?" *ba*Eliza asked.

"I said it, so what?" Aunt Dorothy responded, almost singing it.

"Are you suggesting that I killed my husband?"

"You said it, little girl, not me."

It was almost noon, and the meeting had not progressed. The arguments were petty, especially between Aunt Dorothy, who had come to the meeting under the influence of alcohol at such an early hour, and *bana*Monde, who was naturally drunk.

The owner of the shebeen, Angela, joined the gathering. She sat next to Aunt Dorothy, and they shook hands.

"Any progress?" Angela whispered.

"With this old witch barking like a wolf, progress will never be achieved," Aunt Dorothy whispered back.

Lisa and her friend sat, listening to the entire proceeding. Uncle Malumo maintained that Lisa deserved half of whatever her husband owned, but that suggestion caused *ba*George to shout, "Never!"

Aunt Dorothy supported *ba*George, stating that the marriage between Mr Lingani and Lisa lasted only one month. She used her career in education as an example, saying that their marriage was still on probation and her husband had died before her probation was over. So, she did not qualify for any inheritance.

"One year," Aunt Dorothy shouted, "they should have been married for a whole year, not one month. It takes a year to earn the title of a wife."

"That's nonsense," *bana*Monde snapped. "Once you're proclaimed husband and wife, you are a wife. Where are you learning these ridiculous ideas? Is that what you're teaching our children at school?"

"Children? Your useless granddaughter who never answers any of my questions in class. She inherited your stupidity."

"Stop insulting me, Dorothy. I'm older than your mother."

"I'm not insulting you. I'm giving you an academic report about your useless granddaughter. You never even attend parent meetings."

"Can we please stay on topic?" Uncle Malumo said.

"Isn't it the same thing?" Aunt Dorothy argued. "One month is not enough to claim anything. It shows that you married him for money and then killed him."

*Ba*Richard, *ba*George's cousin, supported this idea, saying that Mr Lingani had worked hard his whole life for his wealth before Lisa came into the picture. He should be able to leave it to whomever he deems fit.

"He made it clear in his will. Let's respect the dead."

"There is one man who hasn't said a word," Uncle Malumo said, turning to *ba*Stevo. "Do you have anything to say?"

Uncle Stevo removed his glasses, wiped them clean, and returned them to his face. The room fell silent, waiting for him to speak.

"If we can't resolve this transitionally, then we will do it spiritually," he said.

This statement made *ba*George chuckle because the old man believed he was more advanced in witchcraft. "You talk too much nonsense, Stevo. You're better off staying quiet as you usually do. You know you will still lose if we go down that path."

"I will crush you," Uncle Stevo said, rising from his seat.

"Only a foolish cat challenges a lion because of some little resemblances."

"We're all part of the same family, so let's find a peaceful solution," said Uncle Liam.

"Lisa deserves her fair shares, end of story," *bana*Monde argued. "Why do we always have to follow Western customs? Do they follow ours? Wills and all that legal stuff have no place in our community. We handle things the traditional way, like our ancestors."

"Change can be a positive thing," Aunt Dorothy said.

"What nonsense are you talking about?" *Bana*Monde snapped back. "Dorothy needs to choose her words carefully. Let's have a sensible discussion about important matters with a sober mind."

"*Bana*Monde, I'm not your husband whom you can control like a puppet. Be careful before I remind you of your flaws," Aunt Dorothy said.

"Women like money," said Stevo. "She married him because he was rich."

"Not all women love money," said someone who hadn't said anything. "Some love more money while some love just money but many of them will go to any length to get money and if you're lucky, they will love you and your money."

"Are we not saying the same thing?"

"Say it with more diplomacy."

"Well," someone suggested, "perhaps we should take this matter to a traditional court. As it stands now, resolving it as a family seems impossible."

Drinks and Disputes

Lisa and Mary, still in their nightgowns, peered through the reeds that made up the courtyard fence. Aunt Dorothy was walking down the footpath towards Angela's shebeen, carrying a black container and singing her favourite Christian song, *"Church in the Wildwood."*

"Your favourite in-law enjoys travelling that road," Mary chuckled.

"It's the same road that will be her downfall," Lisa added.

At the shebeen, Aunt Dorothy stood banging on the front door, shouting, "It's me, Dorothy... open it now."

"Give me five minutes," said Angela.

"Open the door; five minutes is too much. Make it two," she continued, singing the song's first chorus.

Vaino, Mwaka, and Otis arrived and joined in the singing. Angela welcomed them from inside with her not-so-great soprano voice.

"Mistress, you love that song," Mwaka said to Aunt Dorothy.

"Stop calling me Mistress, you sound as if I stole your husband."

Angela finally opened the door, and Aunt Dorothy redirected her anger towards her. "It's like you're rich, huh?"

"Sorry, my good customer. I closed late last night."

"It doesn't matter..."

Aunt Dorothy sat across from Otis, Mwaka, and Vaino. Mwaka wore a grey top that accentuated her large breasts, with her arms wrapped around them. A sealed beer bottle sat in front of her, and she stared at it. Vaino and Otis were dressed in new clothes, spending their salary from the school construction project.

"*BaAngela*," Vasco said, "Two bottles for my brother's teacher."

Aunt Dorothy didn't bother to say thank you, but they knew she was so happy. Angela brought the beers over, and Aunt Dorothy opened one with a single bite, taking a long sip. She was about to place the bottle on the table but took another sip. It was already half gone...

"*Ba*Angela, take two for yourself, you're a good woman," Otis said just as Lisa and her friends arrived. Aunt Dorothy frowned, but three beers from the lawyer lifted her spirit.

"How are the learners doing at your school?" Lawyer Tom asked.

"Some are improving," she said without making eye contact.

"Teaching is a special calling. I don't think I can cope," Lawyer Tom added.

"Every profession is a calling."

"True, but teaching is a unique calling."

After a while, one of the regulars, an elderly man in a long black coat, arrived. Vaino started praising him before he even took his seat.

"He's the only retired prosecutor in Mamiyeto," Vaino announced.

"Only God in heaven we give the glory," the old man replied joyfully. "Now, my young friends, tell me what happened last night."

"*Ba*Angela, please get our old man something to drink," Vaino instructed.

"*Ba*Angela," Lisa said, "I'll cover the old man's bill. Bring him five and put them on our table."

Angela leaned into whisper to Lisa. "Are you sure you want him to join you? He's a terrible noisemaker and a liar too."

"Noise is what we need right now."

The old man kindly agreed to join them, greeting everyone twice.

"I'm Lisa, the late Mr Lingani's wife."

"He's been such a good friend since primary school," the old man reminisced.

"As a retired prosecutor and the senior citizen of this community, could you tell us more about the different types of marriages common in our country?"

The old man took a sip and began sharing his knowledge...

"Traditional marriages, also known as customary marriages, can occur in various locations. The ceremony can take place under a tree, in the middle of your living room, or in traditional courts. If the wedding is held under a tree, it happens at the bride's house—the bride and groom exchange vows based on their community's customs without a marriage officer. Often, traditional marriages do not involve a formal registration process. If the ceremony takes place under traditional authority, a marriage certificate may be issued, although it is not officially documented except in the local Khuta. When the wedding is conducted at home, the unwritten customary laws do not require registration and can vary from one community to another.

In Namibia, we are of both patrilineal and matrilineal descent. Within the Mamiyeto community, we follow a matrilineal system with some influence from patrilineal traditions. In my experiences at university and as a prosecutor in the local court, I have observed that different communities have unique perspectives. Some families or tribes place great importance on children from the mother's side, but the children still carry the father's surname. In certain families, children are considered to belong to both sides, but in our culture, children are associated with the father's lineage.

Regarding inheritance, the child has no right to claim land from the mother's side. That's the aspect I find most intriguing." The elderly man burped before taking a long sip of his beer. "Now, levirate marriage."

"What's that?" Mary asked.

"Widow inheritance," said the lawyer.

"Does that still happen?" Lisa asked.

"Well, yes and no," Angela said. "But you have a choice to make."

"You have to marry your brother-in-law," the old man said.

"What if I refuse?" Lisa asked.

"Then be prepared to lose everything."

"That won't happen," Lisa declared. "I won't accept losing, no matter what."

"Be prepared to marry Jeremy," Angela said.

"I can't marry that old fool," Lisa protested.

"Jeremy is a small price to pay. Marry him, and you can be the queen of your castle," Mary said.

Lisa stared off into space but snapped back to reality. "Alright, Uncle Bill," Lisa said. "Now tell me, who resolves cases in customary law?"

"Cases can be resolved by either the husband and wife's kin groups or traditional courts if they can't agree."

"Traditional courts?" Mary asked.

"Yes, we use traditional courts to settle disputes according to customary law," Uncle Bill said. "You know what I'm thinking. Marrying Jeremy might not be such a bad idea. He still looks good."

"But they haven't said I have to marry him," Lisa said.

"Tomorrow, you're meeting at the traditional court. I know they will bring it up."

The words of the old man were left to linger overnight. The next morning, Lisa and Mary were all dressed up. Cattle headers went to milk them, women swept their yards, chickens scratched the earth, and dogs began their hustle.

Lisa wore a yellow top that exposed her shoulders and a quarter of her chest. She wore tight white trousers that accentuated her figure. Her friend wore jeans and had long hair extensions.

"How does my hair look, Lisa?"

"It's a wig, Mary, and you look great in it."

Lisa's phone started ringing.

"Where are you?"

"We're almost there, Mother. We're waiting for Tom."

"You're almost here, and you're still waiting for Tom. If you're going to talk like that today, you'll lose. Do you know what that means?"

"It means they will win."

"Do you know what that means?"

"Society will laugh at us," Lisa glanced over her shoulder. "Mother, I have to hang up now. Tom is finally ready."

The traditional court was a short distance from the Lingani house, next to the water well. The three walked along the narrow path that curved to the right. Men and women watched the city girls closely, paying attention to their attire.

"The city is corrupting our children," an elderly woman said to Lisa's mother.

Lisa's mother paced back bad forth, agitated as she waited for her daughter. When Lisa was there, she looked into her daughter's eyes to see if there was still some shame left.

"Can you explain today's schedule to me, Mom?"

"Yes, I'll take you to the back of this court," she pulled her daughter behind the traditional house. "Have you forgotten your manners? This isn't the city. You can't dress like this."

"People in church dress like this nowadays."

"This isn't church, this is tradition... you wait here and don't move."

*Ba*Eliza walked over to the other side of the court, where *bana*Monde was arguing with her husband.

"Come with me now," said *ba*Eliza to *bana*Monde. "It's true what you said. These children are naked."

Lisa stood examining her outfit.

"Look," *ba*Eliza pointed at her daughter.

"You can't enter the court dressed like that. Cover yourself," said *bana*Monde.

"Aunt, this style is so popular these days," Lisa protested.

"Yes, but it's not popular here," *bana*Monde said. "This is not the city where you can dress however you want. You know our customs and traditions."

"And you smell horrible," *ba*Eliza added, pinching her nose.

"Mother, this is expensive cologne," Lisa said.

"Be quiet, child," *bana*Monde said.

Mary approached, and in the eyes of the two older women, Lisa was better dressed than her friend.

"See," *ba*Eliza pointed out, "you can't dress like that here."

"Why, Aunt?" Mary asked.

She took out two *chitenge* from her handbag. Lisa wrapped one around her waist, but her mother insisted she cover her shoulders.

"They are waiting for us," Mary said.

They all knelt and clapped their hands before entering the court, as was customary. The elderly sat on benches while the women sat on traditional mats. The two Indunas took their seats at the high table, and Secretary Jani on the far left. Sanana sat on Aunt Dorothy's lap, with her sister Agatha beside them. The Old Driver sat across from them, sharing a bench with *ba*George and *ba*Richard. In the centre of the room was a mat where the defendants and their complainants sat.

"Mrs Lingani and Sanana," Secretary Jani said, "please come and sit on the prepared mat."

Lisa made her way to the mat. Before Sanana could join her, *ba*George started clapping.

"This is not a case between Sanana and my late cousin's wife. The boy has nothing to do with this," *baGeorge* said.

"I agree with *ba*George," *ba*Richard added. "This is a matter between Mrs Lingani and the will."

"Yes, but Sanana should sit with his stepmother," Secretary Jani insisted.

"There's no need for that," the second Induna said. "He can stay with his aunt or even go home."

The second Induna glanced at the first Induna, who nodded in agreement.

"You can let the boy go home," the first Induna confirmed.

"Now that the boy is gone," Secretary Jani began, "allow me to read the statement given to the court about the grievances presented by the late Mr Lingani's wife. Mrs Lingani married her late husband, Mr Lingani, in March of this year, right here in our village, at *ba*Malumo's house. The marriage was witnessed by *ba*Malumo, Mrs Lingani's uncle from her father's side, and *ba*Stevo from her mother's. Her mother, *ba*Eliza, *basha*, and *bana*Monde were also present. On the groom's side, who is now the late Mr Lingani, *ba*Dorothy and Pastor Liam were in attendance. We are aware that his older brother, Jeremy, was not present at that time. The groom's family paid a lobola of fifty herds of cattle to the bride's family. The payment of lobola, as we all know, is governed by customary law. Therefore, Mr Lingani passed away shortly after his marriage, leaving behind his wife, daughter Nadia, and son Sanana, along with all his wealth. Mrs Lingani, the legal wife, only received her wigs and jewellery."

When Secretary Jani reviewed Lisa's statement, the entire court fell silent.

"Mrs Lingani, is there anything I missed or added?"

"Nothing, Secretary Jani," said Lisa.

"If anyone else has something to add, please speak now," the secretary said as he took out his pen to write. "The floor is open to anyone with a contribution."

"Thank you," *bana*Monde began. "She was married, lobola was paid, and she lived with her husband until his death. What he did was cruel to his wife. It's not right."

"Yes," agreed someone. "She should have control over all her late husband's property. It's her right as his wife."

"My brother left a will. We must respect that," said the Old Driver.

"What will?" *bana*Monde said. "Leaving everything to that thing?"

"He is not a thing. We paid lobola, and it wasn't cheap," said Dorothy.

"What do you mean by 'expensive'?" *bana*Monde asked. "When you married my late brother seventeen years ago, we paid a hefty lobola, regardless of your age. You remember that."

"Yes, I remember because I was a graduate. Have you forgotten that?" said Aunt Dorothy rolling her bloodshot eyes.

"I'm older than you, and I was a prominent figure in the anti-apartheid movement," *bana*Monde boasted. "I led the National Youth League in the mid-80s and almost entered parliament."

When *bana*Monde shared her local portfolios, her husband mouthed along with her.

"Forget about your local portfolio," Aunt Dorothy snapped. "Do you even realise what you did to me?"

*Bana*Monde pondered, gazing at the thatched roof.

"You claimed you bought me when my husband died. Remember that? You accused me of killing him. Remember?"

"Where are you coming up with these lies? You're too old to be spreading lies," *bana*Monde said.

"It's not a lie."

"So, what if I said it?"

The Indunas murmured to each other as *bana*Monde and Aunt Dorothy hurled abuses.

"We have encountered similar cases before, common in our community," the first Induna stated. "We all know that lobola is a traditional obstacle to women's property rights. We believe that paying lobola gives the husband and his family authority over the wife and her economic contributions. Namibian law recognises customary practices, but we have a dilemma here. This marriage is customary, and we must address it accordingly. They received lobola, but does that mean the husband is the buyer? No...it does not. It's a gesture of appreciation, part of our culture and tradition. Mrs Lingani belongs to her husband's family. She has a claim to her husband's belongings with one condition. She must marry someone from the same family."

The Old Driver's smile quieted the room, but it faded when Agatha glared at him. Lisa stayed seated on the mat, her intense eyes locked on the first Induna, whom she believed was spouting nonsense.

Meanwhile, far from the tension of the meeting, Sanana sat on a fallen log, snapping and tossing sticks into the Zambezi River. It was peaceful, with birds gliding overhead and fishermen in their canoes. His dog splashed in the water, coming over to nuzzle Sanana's feet before darting back to the river. Jack plopped down next to him, and the two watched the setting sun.

"My mother and I used to live in South Bauleni, in town," Jack began. "My friend Samuel and his father... they died in a car accident two years ago. Tell me," he paused, looking at Sanana, "I've never been to the capital. Is it far?"

Sanana grinned, never expecting to be the one describing Windhoek to someone.

"It's beautiful, with lights everywhere at night. And there are so many cars."

"What about your school?"

Sanana's thoughts raced, unsure of what to say. He continued to toss the remaining sticks. "It's a nice school, but I prefer it here."

"I attended South Bauleni primary school when I lived with my mother in town," Jack said. "We had a good life there until we returned to the village. I left school and learned how to fish."

"Would you like to go back to school?"

"It's too late now. I can't be in the same class as the kids."

"They say it's never too late to start learning."

Jack stretched his legs and looked out at the water. "Well, we'll see what tomorrow brings." He gave Sanana a small smile before standing up to leave. Sanana nodded, watching Jack walk away...

The next morning, Lisa had gone to say goodbye to her people. Mary sat next *bana*Monde, and Mr Smith rested next to Mary, who faced *basha*Monde. Each person was lost in their thoughts. A sudden breeze blew through, causing *ba*Eliza to return to reality from the chill.

"What should we do next? My daughter can't return empty-handed; our enemies will laugh at us," *ba*Eliza said.

"It won't happen," *bana*Monde said. "We will emerge victorious in this battle."

"This isn't a war, woman," her husband said. "Our daughter must marry that man." *Basha*Monde turned to Lisa, "You will marry Jeremy."

"He's too old," Lisa said.

"You married another older man before, just two years younger. You will marry him," *basha*Monde insisted.

"I agree with your uncle," *bana*Monde added. "Marry Jeremy, and then we stop this nonsense."

"We are going back tomorrow, but I will think about it," Lisa said.

Making Friends

In Blackville, a day had passed since Sanana brought his puppy from the village, and they were in the orchard, climbing mango trees. Sanana's little dog was wrestling with Sneaky, lounging under the guava tree and biting his tail, but Sneaky didn't seem to mind.

"Sneaky has a new friend now. He won't be bored anymore," said Nadia to Sanana.

Lisa was still in her sleeping gown as she stared petulantly out the window, watching at the children. Their giggles drifted softly through the warn morning, but soon her attention turned to the sound of footsteps growing closer and closer. She opened the door, and there stood the Old Driver, his hands buried deep in his pockets. His fake smile was something else. He said nothing...

"I don't like that smile," Lisa said, buttoning up her blouse. "Stop smiling and tell me what you want."

"Let's have a family meeting," he said, still smiling.

During the meeting, Agatha and the Old Driver insisted on sending Sanana back to school.

"Do whatever you want," Lisa said, then left as if she never wanted to argue with anyone.

Meanwhile, Sanana was unaware of the conversation inside as he continued playing outside. When Agatha came with the good news, it was difficult to read his mind. Maybe he didn't want to go back to the same school where he had been bullied, or perhaps he was too happy to return as the owner.

"Big brother, can you do me a favour?" Nadia pleaded. "You know about the morning devotion at our school?"

"I'm new there," Sanana replied.

"It's my turn to lead the assembly. Can you do it for me?"

"I can't."

"Please, you're smart and good at English," Nadia persisted.

"You can do it, honey," said Agatha. "Remember how well you did with the school radio? They loved you."

Sanana's initial reluctance wavered under Agatha's reassurance and Nadia's earnest request. With a nod, he agreed to take on the responsibility.

The school reopened on Monday for the second semester. The day before, the Old Driver, Agatha, and the children went shopping for school supplies. Early in the morning, as the children waved goodbye to Agatha standing at the door, Lisa left the house. She wore a stylish beige dress and high white heels, her earrings sparkling in the morning sun. Agatha watched her closely, but there was no response to her greetings. Just as she was about to turn and head back inside, a blue BMW sedan pulled up. She greeted the lawyer and offered him something to drink as they settled in for a conversation.

"You're the executor of the late Mr Lingani's estate," said Lawyer Albert.

"Yes, but we follow tradition," Agatha replied. "If she marries Uncle Jeremy, we have to follow tradition."

"Mr Lingani left a will…"

"I didn't even know the man; besides, tradition has decided. Mr Lingani and Lisa had a customary marriage recognised by our community. The exclusion of Lisa from inheriting any assets in Mr Lingani's will is quite puzzling."

"I understand your concerns, but following the legal procedures is is important," Lawyer Albert said. "Despite the cultural aspects involved, we must adhere to the formalities of the legal system. From my research into your people's customary law, widows typically have rights over their deceased spouse's estate, even without a will explicitly stating so. Mrs Lingani has statutory or customary rights to inherit a portion of her late husband's estate, irrespective of the will's contents. These rights may include a share of her late husband's property, assets, or wealth to ensure her well-being after his passing. I'm aware of the complexities in this situation. In your community, property generally goes to the children, but since Mrs Lingani has no children with the deceased, there is a solution. She can marry one of Mr Lingani's living relatives, who will inherit at least 30 per cent of the late husband's property. Mr Jeremy is already part of the will, so Mrs Lingani's only option is to marry him."

"What should I do?" Agatha queried.

"It is our duty, you and me, to execute the will."

Meanwhile, Sanana and Nadia arrived at school in a sleek black SUV, turning heads as they walked through the busy school grounds. The sun bathed the green lawn as they made their way to the administration block, where they ran into Renate. Renate couldn't help but ask, "Are you friends now?" Her eyes shifted between Sanana and Nadia.

"He's my brother," Nadia said.

"From where?"

"From my father."

The bell for morning devotion interrupted further conversation. Nadia took the lead at the assembly, a tradition at the start of each semester. "Good morning," Nadia began. "I'd like to introduce my brother, Sanana."

Sanana confidently made his way to the podium while Nadia stepped back.

"Go ahead, brother," she whispered.

"Good morning," Sanana said. "School is the foundation for our future. We should begin each semester with inspiration. Welcome back, everyone. Today is a gift, and I thank God for it. While not everyone enjoys school or getting up early, the thought of seeing friends and learning from our favourite teachers should motivate us."

Sanana paused, observing the attentive audience.

"It's good to see everyone here for the morning assembly after the break. Let's kick off the second semester of 1999 with high hopes and dreams. Even if we face limitations, let's strive to reach our goals. To those who struggled last semester, keep pushing forward. Welcome back to Sunpride. Now, let's all recite 1 Peter 5:6-7."

Humble yourselves under the mighty hand of God, that He may exalt you in due time: Casting all your care upon Him; for He cares for you.

Sanana and his classmates made their way to their class. In Miss Mwiya's class, the children made noise. Some were chatting, while others threw objects. Sanana watched Joseph, who was busy drawing a tree on the chalkboard. Fat Immanuel enjoyed a snack. Darci and Hannah sang a tune, and restless Maggie couldn't stay in one place. Maggie saw Miss Mwiya first and she shouted from the door. "Teacher is coming!"

A hushed silence filled the room as the learners behaved their best, standing up to greet their teacher.

"Maggie, please lead us in prayer," instructed Miss Mwiya.

The children remained seated, listening to Maggie recite her memorised prayer.

After singing a hymn, Miss Mwiya said, "As we all know, Mr Lingani, the school's owner, passed away last semester. We also know that our principal, Mrs Lingani, is his widow, and Nadia is his daughter. We didn't know that Mr Lingani had a son. Sanana, please rise."

"Teacher!" Maggie exclaimed. "Sanana is Nadia's brother?"

"Yes, and young lady, you should behave yourself."

"Teacher," Darci raised her hand. "Is Sanana more important now?"

"In this class, we are all important."

At the same time, Mary sat in Lisa's office...

"Have you thought about it?" Mary asked

"I can't marry that old ignoramus," Lisa replied.

"If I were you, I'd seriously consider it," she said before walking out.

As soon as Mary left, the Old Driver entered, jiggling his wristwatch. Lisa hissed softly, her eyes locking with his.

"You know, you're a beautiful woman," the Old Driver said, throwing himself into a seat.

"What do you want, Uncle Jeremy?"

"I just came to say hello and see if you need anything."

Just then, her phone rang.

"I think I will just go; maybe we can talk at home."

After he left, Lisa glanced at her phone, uninterested. "What do you want, Mary?" she asked.

"I saw him come in," Mary's voice came through the phone.

"This old man has changed. You should see how he dresses now."

"Girl, read between the lines. He's trying to look young."

"Well, he looks funny, not young."

"Listen, this is about business, not love. Do you want to end up on the streets? Marry the old fool and watch him die in two to three years."

"Marry him yourself."

"If I were in your shoes, I would've married him in the village."

"I can't marry him; he's old."

"Your late husband was old too, but you married him."

"Enough, Mary. Your advice is terrible."

At home, Lisa shared a glass of wine with her visitor. The Old Driver entered; his once wild beard now neatly groomed. He sat down on the sofa in front of Lisa's visitor, eyeing John with traces of jealousy and anger.

"Where do you know my brother's wife from?" he asked John.

Before John could answer, Lisa said. "He's my cousin from my mom's side, but he lives in Opuwo."

"Cousin?"

"Yes, Uncle Jeremy. We haven't seen each other in a while," said Lisa, playing with a rose she had received from John.

The Old Driver's stare shifted to the rose...

"I'm not an expert on love, but I've heard that a rose symbolises love. Is it appropriate to give that to a cousin?"

"I picked it up, sir," John chuckled, though not with joy.

"And you picked it and decided to give it to someone's wife. That's very considerate of you, young man."

"I suppose I chose the wrong flower, sir."

"I need to take my car for a wash, young man. Make yourself at home," the Old Driver left...

Once he left, John drew closer to Lisa and held her hand.

"Did I sense jealousy in that old man's voice?"

"I'm his brother's widow; it's natural for him to be concerned. Your pants were trembling," Lisa covered her mouth to muffle a giggle.

"That old man doesn't intimidate me."

Nadia came from the back of the house, about to enter, when she stopped to watch John and Lisa kissing. She remembered the man visiting his stepmother at school, the same day her father was rushed to the hospital.

A Love Built on Secrets

Lisa walked into the living room, having just said goodbye to John. Nadia stared at her intensely....

"Why are you looking at me like I owe you?" Lisa asked as she took her usual spot and changed the TV channel. "And you," she pointed the remote at Sanana, "get that annoying dog out of my living room."

Lisa and John continued to meet at his small but luxurious apartment in the heart of Windhoek. John had a taste for the finer things in life. With his charm and eloquence, he could easily manipulate wealthy women. During a visit to John's apartment, Lisa's phone rang. Mary complained about Lisa's poor decision-making. After the phone call ended, John got out of bed, struggling to put on his Bermuda shorts. Lisa, already awake, slipped into a high-waisted brief before coming up behind him and giving him a tight hug.

"I have to marry Uncle Jeremy," Lisa said, breaking the silence.

John made no reply...just a quite nod.

"Aren't you worried?" she asked, searching for any sign of emotion in his eyes.

"Go ahead and marry him."

Lisa turned away; her gaze on the mirror. "Do you love me?" she asked, scanning John's face for any sign of sincerity.

"I love you, but we need money to secure our happiness. Marry him."

At that moment, Lisa realised their relationship was built on something more sinister than love. She gazed into John's eyes, wondering what other secrets lurked beneath their fractured love.

"I'll think about it," her words barely audible. "I must leave now."

The dishes from dinner were almost cleared away. The evening air had calmed, and the city lights shone over Blackville. Blackville was always so quiet, almost as if no one lived there. There was no loud music, no street vendors.

The Old Driver glanced around, searching for Lisa. He had been restless since arriving and finally decided to ask, "Where is your stepmother?" Nadia took her plate to the sink, and the Old Driver's gaze followed her. "What's wrong with her?" he peered into Sanana's eyes.

Sanana had finished eating and was now preparing leftovers for the dogs. The Old Driver was about to ask again, but Sanana left to tend to his dogs.

"What's wrong with these children? Why are they avoiding my question?"

The Old Driver caught sight of Lisa parking outside. Agatha was coming down from her room into the kitchen, where she found the Old Driver smiling at the sight of Lisa. Agatha let out a loud sigh before tapping his back. "Why are you looking at her like that?" she asked. "You marry her, you betray your brother."

Not long after, Lisa entered the kitchen wearing a revealing nightdress. She sat at the table and adjusted her gown slightly. Agatha stood, observing every move that the Old Driver and Lisa made. Lisa picked up two apples and stood very close.

"Russetted or yellow?" she asked, holding an apple in each hand.

"I prefer green or red," the Old Driver returned the grin.

"I like the colour green," she said, placing the two apples back and choosing the green one. "You know what, Uncle Jeremy, you are so kind."

The Old Driver glanced at Agatha, who had her head resting in her hands. His forehead glistened with sweat, which Lisa wiped away with a cloth. He fluttered his eyelids, resembling a young boy experiencing his first crush.

"You know what, Uncle Jeremy?" Lisa said to the amused old man, "The door to my room is wide open."

She swayed her hips and took small steps as she left. Once she was gone, Agatha slammed the cloth onto the kitchen counter and hurried to her room. And that gave the Old Driver something to keep him awake the entire night. The following day at school, he sat facing Lisa in her office, sipping from her teacup. He looked around, fidgeting with his wristwatch, a recent habit of his.

"Get straight to the point, Uncle Jeremy," Lisa said.

"Do you know about my late brother's first wife? They never got divorced."

An upright crease formed between her eyebrows, and she gulped but maintained her direct gaze at the Old Driver.

"Where is she?"

"She vanished years ago."

"How?"

"She had an Asian lover she eloped with. My late brother claimed he was Chinese, but he was Japanese."

"So, she abandoned Nadia when she was just a baby. What kind of mother does that?"

"But she won't be returning, right?" asked Mary, poking her head into the office.

There was no need to fill her in on the topic of their conversation; she had been eavesdropping since the Old Driver entered.

"I doubt it."

Mary finally entered, plopping down beside the Old Driver.

"To my next topic, madam principal," the Old Driver said, "Are you familiar with that restaurant near the dam?"

"The one with all the geese and swans," Mary said, as if she was obligated to answer the question.

"Exactly. How about dinner tonight?"

Mary blinked twice at her friend as a sign to accept the offer.

"What's the occasion, Uncle Jeremy?" asked Lisa.

"That's not important, she'll be there," Mary said.

After the Old Driver left, Mary hurried to close the door behind him. She returned to her seat and spoke confidently. "Whatever you say, just say 'yes.'"

"I hope this plan works in our favour."

"Trust me, I've competed in many leagues of this calibre, from primary school leagues to community school and even college leagues."

"No wonder you're so sharp."

Jessica's Return

The Old Driver lived in a suburb for middle-income earners. His three-bedroom house was a gift from his brother on his 40th birthday. He wore a dark, solid suit. The waiter led him to his reserved table. Soft music played, creating a peaceful atmosphere in the room. Lisa placed her small black handbag on the table.

"I hope I'm not late. This place is beautiful," Lisa said, looking around at the lovely surroundings.

"You're even more beautiful," the Old Driver said.

Lisa laughed at the compliment, knowing the direction his nonsense was heading.

"When are we leaving for the village for lobola?" Lisa asked, her purple lips well-polished as she licked them.

"Saturday morning," he said. "That should give us ample time to make all the necessary arrangements and ensure everything is in order."

Lisa nodded, but her eyes betrayed a different emotion than her enthusiastic facade suggested. The reality of the impending marriage settled in; a sense of uncertainty washed over her. She couldn't shake the feeling that this was not her desired path.

"S-Saturday, I can't wait," she stuttered, her voice faltering as she forced a smile, trying to convince herself more than anyone else. Deep down, she knew that this journey would mark the beginning of a new chapter filled with lies and deceit. With a friend like Mary, Lisa chose to bury her fears and focus on her mission.

The two families gathered in Uncle Malumo's village living room. It was a cold Sunday, and the Old Driver was about to get married for the first time in his sixties. He hoped it would be his first and last marriage.

"As culture demands," said Elder Nyambe, the chairperson. "The visitors are expected to pay four thousand Namibian dollars, with two thousand to start the discussion and two thousand to close it."

*Ba*George placed the money in a palm leaf plate at the centre, and Mary, the youngest in Lisa's group, counted it. She clapped her hands to signal that the money was complete.

"You're welcome once again," Uncle Nyambe said. "Now that the money is complete, we want to know why you are here."

*Ba*George said, "We are after the beautiful heifer from your kraal."

Laughter erupted among the elders, breaking the tension.

"In our kraal, we have different breeds of cows like Hereford, Jersey, Afrikaners, and Sanga. Which breed are you interested in?"

"Sanga. Pure breed and quite indigenous," *ba*George answered.

Lisa's family chatted among themselves. Mary exited the room and returned with Lisa. The *chitenge* covered her lower body, and without makeup, she still looked stunning. She wore a traditional black hat.

"Is this the Sanga you seek?"

*Ba*George and the others nodded.

"Now it's your turn to present the ox to us."

"Ox?" *Ba*Dorothy, the agriculture teacher, asked. "An ox is castrated and used for pulling carts and ploughs. Jeremy is a bull."

"A bull?" *Bana*Monde chortled.

"Yes, a bull. Our Jeremy is a bull used for breeding and nothing else."

"Jeremy doesn't have any children," *bana*Monde said. "That makes him an ox."

"Well," someone said, "bring your bull over."

When the bull arrived, they snorted as *ba*Richard said, "This is our bull, and it's a little Brahman... pure breed."

*Bana*Monde looked down and whispered to *ba*Eliza next to her, "Not even close to a steer."

"A steer?" *Ba*Eliza whispered back.

"Castrated and used for beef."

After the Old Driver's grand entrance, they asked the two couples to share the mat in the centre. The groom appeared humble and old, having shaved off all his grey hair.

"Our bull and our cow," Uncle Nyambe said, "I will ask the parents, *ba*Eliza, the mother of our cow, and Pastor Liam, the head of the Lingani clan, to leave us now."

Once they had left, the real story began...

"Lisa," Uncle Nyambe called, "do you know this man?"

"Yes," Lisa said, tilting her head down, hands clasped together on her stretched legs.

"How do you know him?"

"He's the man I want to marry."

"Out of all the men in Namibia and beyond, you decided he's the one, no one else."

"Yes. I chose him."

"You know him very well and believe he's the man of your dreams."

"Yes."

Uncle Nyambe turned towards his guests and said, "I don't want to ask your Brahman, but we need to hear from him. *Ba*Richard, you can ask him before continuing the lobola negotiation."

After a loud applause from all the families present, *ba*Richard leaned forward and said, "*Ba*Jeremy, take a good look at this young lady. She doesn't have any scars, and she is in great health."

The Old Driver forced a smile. His forehead dripping sweat like he was weeding.

"Are we not going to hear stories about violence in your home?"

"No, I'm not a violent person."

"You chose her out of all the women?"

"Yes and I love her very much."

"Thank you," he said, allowing the chairperson to continue.

"I will ask the two couples to leave us," Uncle Nyambe said.

The Old Driver stumbled through one door while Lisa used the back door.

"This is the most difficult part, but I believe we will unite these two peacefully," the chairperson said. "*Ba*Stevo, you have a way with words. You can deliver painful news to sound like a church benediction. It's time for the lobola amount."

"Thank you very much. The lobola amount is thirty-six thousand," he said, and then he went mute.

There was a sudden silence, and the visitors frowned.

"*Ba*Dorothy, our damage," *ba*George said.

*Ba*Dorothy was sweating a lot, and it was paparazzi. She cleared her throat and said, "We accept."

The intense gaze from *ba*George and all her relatives caused her to change her statement.

"Our in-laws, this isn't the first time we're marrying into your family. We're still family, you know. We ask some leniency, and besides, our brother has never been married before, while yours is a second-hand marriage," said *ba*Dorothy. "And we know why she is marrying him."

The look *ba*Dorothy received from *bana*Monde meant that the circus was about to begin. *Basha*Monde gently shook his head at his wife.

Uncle Nyambe observed each group member, but his chuckle was directed more towards Mary.

"I'll lower it to thirty-five," Mary said.

"Thank you, Miss Mary," *ba*Richard said, "but we are still on our knees."

"If we had asked for one cow as lobola, you would have insisted on giving us a goat. If we had asked for a goat, you would have begged for a pigeon," *bana*Monde said. "Our daughter is young, educated, and childless. We considered that during our meeting last night. I won't lower it any further."

The look she received from her husband made her change her statement. "It's thirty-five. I'll lower it to thirty-three."

"Our dear in-laws," *ba*George said, "please consider lowering it more."

"How many times must we lower it? Why can't you tell us how much you want to pay?" *Bana*Monde said.

"*Bana*Monde, you talk too much," *ba*Dorothy said.

"You also drink too much."

"Ladies, we're still family. Let's unite these two in marriage," someone said. "Thirty thousand dollars."

"Our dear in-laws, we're still begging."

"You people," said *bana*Monde, "it's Namibian dollars, not US dollars."

"Fuck you, woman," said her husband.

"Fuck you too, man," said the wife, and everyone laughed. "Do you think I don't know how to speak American."

"I'll lower it to twenty-two," Uncle Nyambe declared, "and this is final. We need ten thousand in cash and twelve cows."

The groom's family understood that further pleading would be considered an insult once the chairperson lowered the amount. They whispered amongst themselves.

"We accept," *ba*George said, "but we'll provide a deposit of four thousand. If you allow us."

He placed the money in a bowl. Mary tallied the cash and confirmed it with a hand clap.

"Thank you, but before that, when can we expect the full payment?" asked Uncle Nyambe as he took out a diary book.

"In three months."

"*Ba*George and *ba*Richard, please sign this agreement."

He gave the book to Mary, who then passed it to the two elders. Once the two elders had signed, they ushered in the couple.

"You are now husband and wife. No kissing."

"Bring some refreshments, let's celebrate," said Uncle Stevo.

A Lifetime of Longing

After paying lobola, the Old Driver and Lisa arrived back in Blackville. Agatha was perched on the swing alongside Nadia, her face revealing no emotions as she watched their approach.

"Angela sent her regards," said the Old Driver to Agatha. "And she also gave me dried corn and some other farm supplies."

Agatha continued to swing back and forth, without a single word. Lisa went straight to her room without exchanging greetings with anyone. The dogs trotted over from the orchard and played around the Old Driver.

"I have something for you," the Old Driver said to Sanana. He took out a red plastic wristwatch from his pocket. "I bought it from the supermarket thirty minutes ago."

"Thank you, Uncle," Sanana said.

"Do you know how to read time?"

"My teacher in the village taught us."

Nadia stood behind her brother. Agatha kept swinging, her mind racing, feeling like she had nothing to say to the Old Driver. She felt he had betrayed his brother and had chosen to marry a young girl who would only cause harm.

"Young lady," the Old Driver said to Nadia, "I have something for you too."

He pulled out four rainbow polymer clay bracelets from his pocket and dangled them in front of Nadia, who grabbed them from the air. It had been a while since she had received a gift from anyone. The last gift she remembered receiving was a box of chocolates from her late father.

"Thank you, Uncle Jeremy. I love them; they're so beautiful."

"Now go with your brother and bring the rest of the items from the car."

The Old Driver sat next to Agatha, and for a while, no one spoke. He kept rubbing Sneaky, who lay next to the pole.

"You'll meet someone and fall in love one day, and then you'll understand," he said.

Agatha stopped swinging as if she had heard the most ridiculous thing ever. "Your brother would be turning in his grave."

"It's tradition. I couldn't have gone against it, and besides, I love her so much."

"Did you even stop for a moment to wonder why your late brother didn't include her in his will?"

"That doesn't matter. What matters is that I love her, and she loves me."

Agatha chuckled at such a foolish statement. She never realised how ignorance comes with age.

"She married you because of the condition the elders imposed on her. She wants to continue enjoying your late brother's wealth. She doesn't love you; deep down, you know it."

"I can see it in her eyes. She loves me; she told me so. Please, from the bottom of my heart, let me enjoy my marriage. I never knew marriage could be so sweet."

"You've only been married for three days and already concluded that marriage is sweet. Uncle Jeremy, when we had nothing in this city, you were like a father and a mother to us. I'm looking out for you because you're a good man. Something tells me that Lisa will ruin you."

"She was your friend, but you never took the time to know her. She's an incredible person, and I hope the two of you can rekindle your friendship."

"I hope I'm mistaken, and I wish I am."

The Old Driver left to his wife's room. The door was ajar, so he peeked inside and saw his wife scrolling on her phone, on the bed with only half of her clothes on.

"Why are you in my room? You can only see my nakedness six months after my late husband's passing," said Lisa.

"I came to say goodbye. I'll see you tomorrow or later in the afternoon. Is there anything you need before I leave?"

"Uncle Jeremy. I'll be fine," Lisa said.

"I should be your husband, not your uncle," he mumbled as he closed the door. "Rest well, my dear wife."

On the way home, he kept shaking himself that it wasn't a dream. Once he arrived home, he hesitated to call her, so he texted instead. Lisa deleted the message without even reading it.

Agatha was still sitting on her swing chair when a sedan honked at the gate. She knew it was Lawyer Albert's car. She got up to open the gate. The lawyer didn't come out of his car. Agatha got in...

"It was Mr Lingani's last will, naming you the Executor of his will. The first part of the will says: *I appoint Agatha Neo to be the Executor and trustee of this will, and in case the aforesaid shall die in my lifetime or shall refuse or be unable to act in the office of Executor and the trustee, I appoint Sunpride Management to fill the vacancy in the office of Executor and Trustee hereof.*

As the late Mr Lingani's lawyer, I must fulfil his last wish. They will mention two executors, Agatha Neo, and Sunpride Management. My client left his inheritance in the terms of a will. By the Republic of Namibia law, any person who makes a will can leave properties to anyone or any organisation. A spouse has no duty to leave any part of their estate to the surviving spouse or the children of the marriage."

"What do I have to do?"

"We will apply for a grant of Probate. We notify banks and ensure that all assets, such as property, are not yet sold. Once you, as an executor, get permission to look after the assets, we pay any outstanding debts and bills and distribute assets."

After the lawyer left, Agatha called for a family meeting with the Old Driver, his wife, and the children. Before that, she had a private conversation with Lisa and Mary. Mary seemed to understand it better after Agatha's explanation, and when they were alone, she made sure Lisa understood it all.

The family met after the 8 o'clock news. Agatha's shoulders slumped as she began the meeting.

"Now that we have followed the traditions, it can't change the will, but it does help in this situation. Should we proceed with executing the will?" Agatha asked.

Lisa let out a sigh. "I am still not happy. I am so upset with him. Why did he have to embarrass me like that? What I can't understand is why. He was a good man; something tells me my late husband didn't do this. There's something off about this will." She took a hopeful breath and gave Agatha a sharp look.

"Look at it this way," Agatha explained. "Your new husband's inheritance is N$70,000,000, including cars and the biggest garage in town, which is now yours too. You still have this house; it's a family home, and you can stay here if you wish."

"Agatha is correct," the Old Driver said. "What's mine is yours."

"Should I call the lawyer to join us?" Agatha asked.

"I was his wife," Lisa fluttered her eyelashes.

The following day, Lisa was on a phone call with her lawyer, who supported the idea. After finishing the call, she had a conversation with Mary.

"Should I come over and be your witness?" Mary asked through the phone. "In a situation like this, you shouldn't be alone."

"I can handle it, Mary," Lisa said.

"You know what they say, the last minutes can be very dangerous. I should be there to support you. My presence has a strange way of making things right. I'm doing this for you, Lisa."

"Later, Mary."

The following day, the family met the lawyers....

"As the legal representative of the late Mr Lingani, my only role is to carry out his final will. We are here to inform you that all the necessary legal steps have been completed. As stated in the will, the Executor, Agatha Neo, will now distribute the assets to the beneficiaries. There are three options for the beneficiaries to receive their inheritance: they can inherit it all at once, in stages, or through a discretionary life trust."

Lisa leaned forward, but there was a loud knock at the door. Agatha went to answer it. Standing there was a well-dressed woman in her late forties, holding two travel bags. She was tall, slender, and had a coloured complexion. Next to her was a man in a formal black suit, holding a silver briefcase.

"Don't tell me you're the woman who married my husband for his money," she scanned Agatha before pushing her aside and walking towards the group.

The lady adjusted her wig, moving it away from her forehead and securing it behind her ear. She glanced at everyone in the room, but her gaze lingered on Mr Lingani and Lisa's picture on the wall. She then turned her attention to Lisa, who lay against the Old Driver's chest.

"Oh," the lady exclaimed, "so you're the woman." She plopped down in a chair across from Nadia. "You must be the lovely Nadia."

"Jessica!" the Old Driver said.

"Nadia's mother?" Lisa asked.

Nadia's expression softened as emotions played across her face. The smile that appeared on her lips was a mix of feelings. Was it joy, finally meeting the mother she had only heard stories about, or was it a distant smile tinged with confusion as she grappled with the sudden appearance of this stranger claiming to be her mother? Memories of her father's stories about her mother's untimely passing flooded her mind.

Jessica bent down; her touch gentle as she reached to caress Nadia's hair. "I'm your mother." She then clasped her daughter's hands, but Nadia pulled away from the embrace of this stranger who claimed to hold such a significant place in her life.

"You are not my mother," Nadia's voice trembled with raw emotion as she struggled to make sense of the whirlwind of feelings raging inside her. She then turned away and stomped to her room.

"I must attend to my daughter," said Jessica to Lawyer Ken.

"Your daughter can wait," her lawyer declared, his tone dripping with disdain. "I have more important matters to attend to."

Jessica's heart sank, overwhelmed by Nadia's action and her lawyer's stone-cold attitude.

"What kind of lawyer are you, sir?" the Old Driver's voice broke the tension.

"I am a lawyer who wins many cases," he replied. "Please sit down so we can do this and call it a day."

Agatha nudged Sanana and whispered, "Attend to your sister. Go now."

Mr Ken placed his briefcase next to the sofa where he sat, straightened his collar, and removed a black cloth from his breast pocket to polish his shiny black shoes. "I prefer being direct," he stated. "According to the civil law of the Republic of Namibia, Mrs Jessica Lingani is still the legal wife of the late Mr Lingani."

He placed the marriage certificate on the table. Lawyer Albert reviewed it before passing it to Agatha, who then handed it to Lisa. Lisa gave it to the Old Driver, who placed it on the table as he couldn't read or write.

"My client will challenge the will," Mr Ken declared.

"Probate has already been granted," Lawyer Albert said.

"This document is the caveat regarding Mr Lingani's estate," he said.

Lawyer Albert skimmed through it. He then passed it to Lisa, who attempted to pass it to the Old Driver, but he didn't receive it. Lisa returned it to the lawyer.

"I'm sorry, Miss Agatha," Lawyer Albert said, "but the caveat has been granted, so we must wait for now."

"What exactly is a caveat?" Agatha asked.

"A caveat is a formal notice that advises against distributing the properties to the beneficiaries," Lawyer Ken said.

"She abandoned her child twelve years ago, and they were separated from my brother," the Old Driver said.

"Separation is not the same as divorce," Lawyer Ken said. "My client holds a 'caveable interest'... a marriage certificate under the civil law of our country."

"This woman is nothing but a fugitive," the Old Driver said. "She left this house twelve years ago."

"Don't call me a fugitive. This is my house, and I'm here to stay. Look at you; you have no shame. All this time, you were lusting after your brother's wife. Can't you see what she's planning? She's going to ruin you."

"What does that even mean, old lady?" Lisa snapped.

"I mean, you're only after money, and you're fake," Jessica said.

Lisa stood up, but her husband pulled her back down.

"Between the two of us, who's the real gold-digger? You abandoned your husband and daughter, and now you're back. You're a disgrace to women everywhere. If I were you, I'd go back to Asia and die there."

"Excuse me," Lawyer Ken said, "I have another important meeting to attend." He grabbed his briefcase, put on his sunglasses, shook hands with his client and colleague, and left without looking back.

In Nadia's room, Sanana sat.

"My father left me even before I was born," Sanana said. "I met him this year, but he was already dead, and my mother died shortly after I was born. But now, your mother is here. She's come back to you."

"She only came back because of the money Dad left behind," Nadia said.

"But she's here now and she is still your mother."

"Should I forgive her?"

"She is your mother. With Dad gone, you need her now more than ever."

"Do you think so?"

"She loves you. No matter where she was, she was always thinking of you."

Nadia stood by the window, torn between the pain of the past and the hope of a future with her mother... torn between forgiveness and fear of being hurt.

That evening, Nadia stood before her mother, her heart pounding with emotions. Tears filled her eyes as she finally found the courage to speak.

"I don't understand why you left."

"I was foolish, but I never stopped loving you."

Sanana entered the room and stood next to Nadia.

"Are you truly my mother?"

"Yes, sweetheart. I carried you in my womb for nine months."

"So does this mean you won't leave me again?"

"I promise." She then threw her arms around her daughter, and they embraced. Jessica then gestured for Sanana to join them.

"Thank you," Jessica said to Sanana. "Now, could you please help me unpack my belongings? We'll be sharing this room for now, sweetie. I hope that's all right with you."

The children marched downstairs, holding hands, and started moving Jessica's bags to Nadia's room. The Old Driver and Agatha watched the children.

"I can't trust that woman," said the Old Driver. "She's giving her daughter false hope, and then she'll leave again. I've never liked her for my brother right from the beginning. She's like a squirrel in the backyard, always moving around."

"How long were they married before she disappeared?" Agatha asked.

"Three years, and I always knew she didn't love him, just his money," the Old Driver said.

"Why did she leave if he was rich?"

"She stole from him."

Agatha couldn't say anything else or ask any more questions. Lisa came downstairs, dressed up, planted a rushed kiss on her husband's shiny bald head, and went towards the main door.

"Do you know where she's going, Uncle Jeremy?" Agatha asked.

"I don't appreciate you monitoring me or my wife's every move," said the Old Driver as he left for his car.

Agatha had to shift her attention to the newest visitor in the Lingani mansion. Jessica was sitting between the children, showing them her photo album. She showed her wedding pictures and those of Nadia when she was a few days old.

Meanwhile, in John's apartment, Lisa stood facing the wall. John sat on the bed, his chin resting on his hands. The silence seemed endless until Mary burst in.

"So, we have another big problem?" Mary said as she dropped Mr Smith onto the carpet, causing the poor dog to let out a painful cry. On a good day, Mary would feel that pain, too.

"Is it true that the witch is back? Hello, can someone talk to me?"

Lisa's phone started ringing, interrupting their conversation. They all rushed out to meet Lawyer Tom. Lisa was upset about Jessica's return, but Lawyer Tom assured her he would do everything he could to help.

"But now that the first wife is back, it seems like we're back to square one," said Mary.

"She has a solid case," Lawyer Tom said. "But don't worry, I've dealt with similar situations before, and I've only lost four out of the many cases I've handled."

"So, how many have you won?" Mary asked.

"Well," Lawyer Tom said, "I've won four."

"That means it's a tie," Mary said.

"You need to win this case so that your losses don't outnumber your wins," said John.

"By the way, who is the lawyer representing Jessica?" asked the lawyer.

"Lawyer Ken or something," said Lisa.

"We have a serious problem," Lawyer Tom said, worried. "That man has no shame. He will do anything to win his cases."

"Are you scared of him?" Mary asked.

"Yes, Mary," Lawyer Tom admitted. "I don't enjoy going up against him. It makes me very uncomfortable."

"So, are you going to drop this case?"

"No," Lawyer Tom said. "I didn't say that."

It was another day. When Lisa returned home from school, Jessica laid on Lisa's bed, painting her nails.

"There are so many other rooms in this house," Jessica said. "I have reclaimed my matrimonial room."

The commotion in the bedroom caught the attention of the Old Driver, who had come back from picking up the kids from school. He tossed his car keys on the table before hurrying upstairs. The Old Driver tried to mediate the situation, but it seemed that the conflict between Lisa and Jessica had just started.

As the night went on, Lisa found herself in her new room, sitting on the bed.

"Don't pay attention to her," the Old Driver said. "My house may not be as big as this one, but it's decent enough for us. Once I receive my inheritance, we can move to any place you want."

"You know our customs," Lisa said. "You can't see my nakedness until the mourning period is over. It's a six-month wait, but after that, I'll go with you wherever you want."

The next day, Jessica stood in front the big buildings with walls made of glass. The law firm, next to a retail shop, was where Lawyer Ken had his office. Inside, he scolded his secretary for missing an important phone call during her break. Lawyer Ken sipped his tea before diverting his full attention to his client.

"My wife and I discussed your case," the lawyer began.

"Your wife?" Jessica asked.

"Yes, Mrs Lingani. She is also a partner in this law firm. And do you know what that means?"

"What does it mean?"

"It means that you have a lot of advantages in this case. She is also a woman, so she understands your difficulties. She has been in your shoes before."

"Does that mean she was married before?"

"Yes, and her ex-husband left a will as well."

Lawyer Ken reached for his landline phone, but the sound of the door opening caused him to put it back down. A woman in her late thirties entered and sat next to Jessica. She was Zulu and had a petite stature, like her husband. Her hair was styled into twisted, long Mohawk dreadlocks that formed a ponytail.

"This is my wife, Amahle, and this is Mrs Jessica Lingani."

"I've heard so much about you, Mrs Lingani," Amahle said, extending her hand for a handshake.

Jessica understood it would be impolite to stare at the woman for such a long time, especially at her hairstyle, which she secretly admired. She returned to her seat and glanced around the office. The walls were adorned with many certificates of merit, but her attention was drawn to Lawyer Ken's dual qualification, MBA-LLM.

"We should abandon contesting the will. Look at it this way: your daughter will inherit almost half of the property, and as her biological mother, it will be your responsibility to manage it. That other Mrs Lingani will receive nothing and must leave the house. Case closed."

"It's like leaving with nothing. I married him; I deserve something."

"You won't be leaving with nothing, madam," Amahle reassured her. "Your daughter will be wealthy, and it will be your duty to manage her assets."

"But that's my daughter's inheritance, not mine. Can't we find another solution?"

"This is the best option for you, madam. Contesting the will would be costly, and there are no guarantees of winning the case. Besides, your hands are not entirely clean. You duped your late husband out of a lot of money."

Jessica rubbed her chin, realising her chances of winning were slim, and prison too. "Alright, you have a valid point."

"Well then," Lawyer Ken concluded, "our fees remain the same. Have a nice day, Mrs Lingani."

As soon as she left the room, Amahle leaned forward, gripping her husband's wrist.

"This woman is greedy," she said, pulling out a grey envelope. "Is this his will? He was incredibly wealthy."

Amahle closed the envelope and stared into her husband's eyes. "I don't believe that old man wrote this will. It seems like there's a lot of fraud involved. How can someone be so generous towards his brother, leaving him and his children an equal inheritance while being unkind to their wife?"

"You think someone tampered with the will?"

"Yes, and I want to meet this Lisa woman."

"Our interests align unless she provides written consent."

"I am not Jessica's lawyer."

"But you are associated with this firm, Amahle, and you know it goes against the client-lawyer relationship."

"We need to make more money from this case. I will visit Lawyer Albert and try to gather information from his eyes. But don't inform your client until after the meeting so we can charge them as a new case."

"That man is corrupt and has ties to the government."

"You sound like you know him."

"We attended university together."

In Blackville, Jessica tossed her purse onto her bed. Nadia plopped down on her mother's lap, starting to tickle her. Lisa was in her room getting ready. She had gotten a call from Mary earlier and agreed to meet at the dam. Mary sipped a beer in the empty restaurant as the late afternoon sun streamed in. Lisa walked in and took a seat across from her. A young waitress came over, but Lisa shooed her away.

"Now tell me, how did it go?" said Mary.

"He gave me a choice: accept the will, live happily ever after with my new husband's share, and remain part of the Lingani dynasty."

"That's it," Mary exclaimed. "Think about it: your husband inherited a fleet of cars and that huge garage in town—he's wealthy. Marry him in community of property and wait for him to die. Then you can marry John."

"I'm not a killer, you know that," Lisa said.

"Yes, but this is survival. In a few months, you'll forget all about it."

"Jeremy is a good man; he doesn't deserve that."

"Jeremy is old. Jeremy is standing in the way of your happiness. Jeremy is a senior citizen, and most of his peers are already gone. Jeremy is your key to riches. Be smart, my dear friend. This world is a jungle, and only the strong survive."

"I never knew you were so cruel," Lisa said.

"I admired you from the moment I met you. I wanted to be your friend. I may not know much about your past, but I see a strong woman capable of great things. You achieved so much in one semester—married him, became his widow, and took charge of that prestigious school. And here I am, Mary, your right-hand woman. No one accomplishes that much quickly unless they are me and you."

Lisa Faces Backlash

Lisa sat on the sofa next to her husband. On the opposite side, Jessica busied herself with the children. The arrival of Lawyer Tom completed the puzzle, as he joined his colleagues, Lawyers Ken and Albert, their heads huddled together in a quiet discussion.

Then, Lawyer Albert's voice pierced through the silence, capturing everyone's attention. "As the lawyer representing the late Mr Lingani," he began, his tone composed and respectful, "I would like to express my deepest gratitude to the entire Lingani family for maintaining a sense of calmness during this difficult period. Now that all matters have been resolved, we can proceed with the distribution of assets."

"My late brother was a peaceful man," the Old Driver said. "I am grateful that we have fulfilled his final wishes as stated in his will. Thank you very much. The two heirs to my late brother's fortune are his children, who are still minors. I hope that Agatha and Jessica will always prioritise their best interests."

"She is my daughter, and it is my God-given duty to ensure her well-being," Jessica said.

"Thank you, Jessica," the Old Driver said. "We all know that Agatha is a college graduate and needs something to keep her busy." The Old Driver glanced at his wife. "You are still the school's principal; find something for Agatha."

"Principal?" Jessica snapped. "This gold-digger? Principal of my school? What happened to Principal Buhari?"

"Who is Buhari?" Lisa asked.

"He was the principal before O'Hara," the Old Driver said. "Buhari died in 1995 or '96. He had been sick for a very long time and suffered greatly."

"You married my husband, killed him, and took over the school. You have no shame," Jessica said.

"My husband died of a heart attack."

"My job here is done," Lawyer Ken said as he grabbed his briefcase and took a few steps before turning to face Jessica. He pushed aside the fleeting thought about his fees and said, "I will take my leave now."

The next day at school, during the staff morning briefing, Lisa took a deep breath. Jessica and Agatha stood beside her. Those who disliked Lisa and favoured Jessica knew that the real Lingani had returned.

"Allow me to introduce Mrs Lingani Jessica," Lisa said. "And Miss Agatha Neo, our new geography teacher. We can all now return to our classes."

"Wait a second," Jessica said, "hold on for a moment." She walked to the centre of the room, removed her black and white scarf, and placed it on her left arm and handbag. The rest of the staff, especially those who never liked Lisa, began hoping things were changing.

"For years, this school has been at the top of the country until recently. The results from last semester are a major concern, and we must address this. My question is, what happened to Principal O'Hara?"

"We are still the top in this country," Lisa said.

"The results from last semester are not good because of you and your lack of leadership skills. Who is Miss O'Hara?"

O'Hara sat quietly, feeling a surge of excitement at the mention of her name. She hoped that the situation might be turning in her favour. Everyone knew that she was the rightful headteacher at Sunpride. She remembered the few weeks when Lisa ruined the school with her poor and self-centred leadership style.

"Let me tell you what happened," Jessica began. "They invited her for interviews, she met the requirements, and she got the job... It's permanent unless stated otherwise. Now, she's a classroom teacher because someone took her position without following proper procedures. I researched and discovered that this person is set to graduate this September. Tell me, what are the requirements to run this school?"

"Bachelor's degree, five years of teaching experience, and a year of school management," Mrs Hausiku stated.

"But our principal has a letter stating that she completed her pre-primary diploma. Does this qualify her to run the school?"

"No, it does not," Mrs Hausiku responded with evident satisfaction. She never concealed her dislike for Lisa and had no qualms about showing it.

"Qualifications in education do not matter," Lisa said. "Let me tell you something you didn't know. Miss O'Hara only has a diploma in education, nothing more."

"So?" Mrs Hausiku shouted, rising from her seat. "You mean to say that it's just a diploma? Someone with a diploma is leading me, despite my master's in education from UNISA. How is that possible?"

"We do not care about your master," Lisa said. "A master's degree in education means nothing. You will remain a class teacher with your stupid master."

"That's why I no longer pursue further studies," someone said. "It's a waste of time and money."

"The way things are in education in our country, it's better to study something where qualifications matter," Mrs Hausiku said. "Look at our poor sister here, Doctor April. What a shame."

"Is that a compliment or an insult?" Miss April said.

"I'm insulting you," she said.

"Agatha," Jessica said, "we must do what's best for this school. Your brother's legacy is at risk."

"I don't know much about Miss O'Hara and her work ethic. Why don't we let the teachers vote?"

"Lisa has no teaching experience. There's nothing to vote for. She can't handle this school," said Mrs Hausiku.

Mary's fingers danced across her phone keyboard, tapping out a text message that she sent to Jessica. Jessica's lips curled into a gentle smile as she read it. She then turned to the teachers and announced, "If we're all happy with Lisa leading, let's allow her to continue."

"Why? She is a horrible leader," Mrs Hausiku asked.

"You can all go to your classes."

In the school cafeteria, Sanana and Nadia shared a peaceful moment while enjoying their breakfast, laughing, and sharing stories. Before long, Erica, Renate, and Jimmy came over to join them.

"I'm sorry for what happened last semester," Renate said to Sanana.

"It's okay," Sanana said.

"We're playing football after school. Do you want to join us?" Jimmy asked.

"I love football… what time?"

"Right after school," Jimmy said.

"Thanks, Jimmy."

Sanana made new friends, played football with them, and even joined the school team. He also regained his position as a school radio presenter. Jimmy became a school preacher who led devotions during assemblies.

That same afternoon, Lisa was in her room, her face buried in the pillow when her phone rang. She picked it up, glanced at the caller ID before tossing it back onto the bed. It continued to ring until she finally picked it up.

"Are you avoiding the phone or are you far away from it?" Mary asked.

"I have so much on my mind right now. I don't know what to do, Mary," Lisa said.

"Do you want me to come over? I'm bored out of my mind in this awful apartment."

Mary fiddled with her hair; her legs stretched out on the bed. She watched a television playing some local songs. A large portrait of herself hung on the wall, displaying her dark lipstick and long hair. The picture was a reminder of her early college years, and she always carried it with her whenever she moved.

"Lisa, are you still there?"

"Yes, Mary. You can come over."

Mary tossed her phone onto the bed and got dressed. Lisa had been waiting at the gate when Mary arrived in a taxi. She led her to her room. Lisa rolled up the curtains, allowing the sounds of birds and insects from the orchard…

"I'm tired of all the noise in this house. That old woman is a menace," Lisa complained.

"Do you want my advice?" Mary asked.

"I already know what you're going to say," Lisa said.

"I want to say that you should move out of this house. Your husband is very wealthy, so ask him to buy a house in this neighbourhood or Whitesville."

"But you never wanted me to leave this house before. Why the sudden change of heart?"

"Things change, Lisa. It's time for you to buy a house somewhere."

"Do you think moving in with that old man is a good idea?"

"I'm your best friend, Lisa. I wouldn't lie to you."

Meanwhile, Sanana quietly walked across the room. He was feeling hungry and went to look for Agatha, already picturing the delicious food. As he entered the living room, he hoped to find Agatha busy in the kitchen, but all he saw was Jessica painting Nadia's nails.

"Aunt Jessica, have you seen my sister?" Sanana asked.

Jessica gestured for him to sit down. "No, I haven't."

By the afternoon, Agatha still hadn't returned home, worrying her brother even more. Jessica and everyone else kept calling Agatha's phone, but there was no answer. Sanana sat between Nadia and the Old Driver, his eyes on the front door. A loud knock caused him to jump from the sofa. He made eye contact with the men in police uniforms and led them to where the others were sitting.

"Is this the residence of..." Detective Vosloo began, reading from an ID card he had taken from Agatha's handbag. He was in his late forties and appeared confident, as if he knew something the rest of the city didn't.

"That bag belongs to my sister; where did you find it?" Sanana asked, almost reaching out to grab the bag.

"Your sister is Agatha Neo?" the first officer asked.

"Where is she?" Sanana demanded.

The silent expressions on the faces of the two police officers filled him with apprehension. He rubbed his chest, trying to calm himself as he sat back down. His mind raced with worry, knowing that Agatha had no friends in the city and couldn't be gone for the entire day.

"We suspect she was kidnapped," Detective Vosloo said.

"Well, this is a common occurrence in our city. If it's a ransom situation, they will make contact. But don't worry, ma'am, in sixty per cent of cases like this, the culprits are apprehended," one officer said.

"Sixty per cent chance of resolution? So, a forty per cent chance she's no longer with us?" the Old Driver asked.

"We will give our best effort. If you have faith in God, now is the time to seek divine intervention."

"Last time I heard of such a case, we ended up burying an empty coffin," Lisa said, showing no remorse as she sat with her legs folded on the sofa arm.

"Lisa, show some respect—we're discussing a family member here," Jessica scolded.

"Let's not leave out other possibilities. Considering how unpredictable this city can be, she may have met an unfortunate fate. Ignorance is a dangerous thing," said Lisa.

"Child, I understand you weren't raised properly by your parents, but please refrain from speaking if you have nothing wise to contribute," Jessica rebuked.

"I won't argue with you today."

"Your sister will return," said Jessica. "Now, go with your sister to your bedroom."

Once Sanana and Nadia left, the two police officers faced the rest of the group.

"Please, take a seat," the Old Driver said.

"Does she have any enemies?" Detective Vosloo asked.

"Not to my knowledge," the Old Driver answered.

"She rarely ventured beyond the walls of this house. She was a peaceful woman," Jessica added.

"Do you think it's necessary to have enemies for a person to be kidnapped?" Lisa asked. "Agatha was in the wrong place at the wrong time, don't you think?"

"Stop with the silly jokes," Jessica said. "You're such a cynic, Lisa."

"Officer," the Old Driver said, "Agatha was named the executor. Do you think this could be connected to the crime?"

"And who might you be, sir?" asked the officer.

"Apologies for my lack of introduction," the Old Driver said. "I'm Jeremy, the older brother of the late Mr Lingani. Is this a homicide investigation, detective?"

"No, not exactly. But we have reasons to believe that Agatha was kidnapped. Rest assured; my team is searching throughout the city."

The Old Driver led them to the front door. Jessica and Lisa exchanged silent glances. Could one of them be the kidnapper?

"Are you involved in this at all?" Jessica asked Lisa.

"If you're joking, it's not funny. And, between the two of us, you're the one who looks suspicious. Why can't you accept that your time is up? You're jealous of my natural beauty and youth."

"Natural beauty..."

"Yes, natural beauty. Not like your old face caked in makeup, looking like an adopted snub-nosed monkey."

Lisa rushed to her room, changed into jeans, walked out the main door, and went to her car. After seeing the police out, the Old Driver entered Sanana's room to find him curled up on the bed. He sat down next to him.

"Your sister is a good girl," he said. "God protects people like her."

"Do you think so, uncle?" Sanana asked.

"We should all pray for her; now go and join your sister in the orchard."

Jessica was on the phone in her room, smiling. When she finished her call, she went to answer the door, where she met the police. It hadn't been an hour since they received the news about Agatha, and now the police were back.

"I have some bad news," Detective Vosloo announced. "She's in critical condition. Whoever did this to her wanted her dead."

"Will she be okay, detective?" Jessica asked.

"Her condition is serious."

"Where is she?"

Lisa and Mary arrived and went to the bedroom. Lisa entered first, and Mary peeked into the empty hallway before shutting the door and turning to face her friend.

"What's the good news I've been hearing?"

"I already told you, Mary. Agatha has been kidnapped," said Lisa.

"You don't sound happy," said Mary.

"Why should I be happy? Even if she's dead, I can't do anything about that little boy's inheritance."

Mary peered through the window and frowned at Sanana, Nadia, and the dogs in the orchard. Nadia sat on a swing made from old tyres, reading a magazine. Sanana sat on the other swing. Mary sighed, closed the curtain, and picked up her handbag.

"Let's go downstairs." Mary said.

"Why?"

"I'm hungry, Lisa. I need to eat good food. I'm tired of having rice and chicken."

Lisa looked out the window at the children. Mary stood behind her, and no one said anything before walking to the kitchen.

"I never thought I'd step foot in such a big and beautiful house. That's the beauty of having a friend like you, Lisa. Even in my very next-"

"Stop it, Mary."

"Well, I'll eat in peace then, but be careful and smart."

"Now you understand that all my effort is going to waste. I can't leave this house, Mary."

"You're leaving this house, but you're going to build a better one. Keep playing your cards, especially since you're beautiful and old Jeremy is really into you. Go with him and leave him with nothing."

"Is this going to be my fate, Mary? Becoming a widow and getting married again. I know I'm greedy, but I'm not a murderer."

"You're not a murderer, but let's deal with anyone who stands in our way together."

The two detectives stood outside Mr Lingani's office.

"Detectives," called out the Old Driver. "Please come inside."

Mr Lingani's office was huge and painted a creamy colour. The floor was covered with old linoleum. The walls were adorned with pictures of Nadia, alone or with her father. The most enormous portrait, positioned behind the main chair, was of Mr Lingani. The Old Driver led them to their seats.

"Before all this happened, it seems like the deceased lived alone?" Detective Mark asked.

"Nadia, his daughter," the Old Driver said. "My brother lived with his daughter for over eleven years. He got married a few months ago but unfortunately died a month later due to a heart attack or stroke. I can't differentiate between the two."

"When did he bring Sanana into his house?" Detective Vosloo asked.

"After his death," the Old Driver replied.

"Please call your wife," Detective Vosloo said to the Old Driver.

The Mystery of Agatha's Assault

Lisa stood next to her husband. Jessica was having a conversation with the two officers before they joined others.

"Detective, what happened to her?" Lisa asked.

"A Good Samaritan found her," the detective said.

"Will she survive? Where is she?" Lisa asked again.

"We need to ensure her safety. Even her family cannot know where she is being treated," he responded, taking a notebook from his jacket. "I assume she is not married. Does she have any friends?"

"Are you referring to a male friend, like a lover?" Jessica asked.

"Yes, Mrs Lingani," the detective confirmed.

"Agatha rarely left the house. I have never seen anyone visit her," the Old Driver said.

"She always kept her thoughts to herself," Lisa added. "But you never know; many deceitful people are out there."

"Tell us more about Agatha."

"Agatha is a peaceful woman. She dedicates herself to taking care of her brother," Lisa explained. "Who could have such a grudge against her? No one is safe in this city."

"How well did you know her?" Detective Mark asked Lisa.

"I knew her a little," Lisa said.

"How little, Mrs Lingani?"

"On a scale of one to ten, I would say not even three."

"Didn't you both attend university together?"

"College, not university. Seriously, detective, do you know everyone you trained with at the police academy or everyone you attend church with?"

"Yes, if that person happens to be my best friend."

"Are you accusing me of something, detective?"

Detective Vosloo pondered deeply. Agatha didn't have any known enemies. Based on the situation, the Old Driver, Lisa, and Jessica were all suspects—anyone could be the culprit. Who among the three had the strongest motive and resentment and was capable enough to want to kill her?

"What do you know about Agatha's past?"

"Like I said, detective," Lisa said, "I don't know much about her. She was the type of person who kept everyone at a distance. Why don't you direct those questions to her brother? She used to be his mother."

Detective Mark jotted down Lisa's words, noting "was and built" in his notebook. He then waited for Lisa to provide more information.

"Am I a suspect, detectives?"

"That will be enough for now."

After they left, Lisa and Jessica continued to argue, but the Old Driver remained silent.

"How can you be certain they wanted her dead? Maybe they just wanted to teach her a little lesson," Lisa said.

"I'm starting to suspect you. Tell us the truth," Jessica demanded.

They descended the stairs. Jessica led the way, occasionally confronting Lisa and the Old Driver.

"You heard him, Jeremy," Jessica said. "We all heard them. They're accusing all of us, and I don't appreciate it. I can't even harm a fly, let alone a person."

"Why are you so scared?" Lisa asked as she walked towards her car, where Mary was waiting. "Are you hiding something?"

Lisa drove off and parked her car outside Mary's apartment. They sat at the table, where a bowl of fresh fruit was placed.

"Oh no, did you, do it?" Mary asked.

Lisa dropped the orange onto the silver tray. The orange rolled off the table, bouncing on the floor and ending up under the chairs. She then grabbed her handbag and started walking towards the exit. Mary grabbed her arm.

"Please forgive me. My financial problems are causing me to say things I don't mean. I can't even eat a decent meal," Mary pleaded.

"This isn't about you, Mary," Lisa said. "We all have problems."

"Mine are a lot."

"You're just greedy. You receive a salary every month."

"This isn't a salary; it's just some measly tips. I'm sorry for suspecting you had something to do with Agatha."

"Tell me, Mary, do I look like a murderer to you?"

"Please, let's go back inside. Guess what? I have a surprise for you. I cooked potatoes and eggs. I know you'll love it," Mary said, trying to change the subject.

"You always cook potatoes and eggs. How can that be a surprise?"

"Don't tell me you think I don't eat a balanced diet in this apartment. I know times are tough, but I always eat decent meals. Do you think I could look this good if I didn't watch what I eat?" Mary said, turning around to check her appearance.

"I need to go back home. Tomorrow is a school day."

"Do you forgive me?"

"I'll think about it, Mary."

On Monday morning, lessons had yet to start. Lisa was having a phone call with her mother and aunt in the village in her office. She began to share her sadness about her current situation with them. Despite all the plans she and her friend Mary had made, everything seemed to be falling apart.

"Life is life," said *bana*Monde. "Always remember you are a fighter."

"Aunt, she was a close friend of mine in college, but now she has taken everything."

"You mean the girl in the village with that little boy, Angela's niece?"

"Yes, Aunt. She was kidnapped, and now the police think it's me. Do you think I should be worried?"

"Did you do it?"

"I'm not a criminal, Aunt. Besides, Agatha is a good girl. I love her, and she did much for me in college."

"You mean she wrote assignments for you?"

"Come on, Aunt. Are there any difficult assignments at our silly institutions in this country? Everything is basic—even fools graduate there. People fail grade 12 and pass universities with flying colours."

Mary peeked in first before walking over to an empty chair. She was dressed nicely but always complained about money. Lisa sat holding the landline as Mary approached. She gazed into the distance, trying to look unbothered.

"Are you still upset? Can we talk? All I wanted was to confirm it."

"Why do you keep saying you're sorry, Mary?"

"I'm sorry. You're my best friend. You must forgive me."

"I forgive you. Can I go back to my work now?"

Mary dashed from her seat around the table where Lisa was seated. She threw a hug at her but asked first. Lisa returned the hug, and the friends shared a hearty laugh again.

Right after school, Renate and Nadia stood beneath the tree. Just as they were there, Erica walked by on her way to the school bus. She stopped to ask about Sanana, who had been absent that day. Not long after, they heard the school bus horn. Renate and Erica rushed to secure their seats, leaving Nadia behind as she waited for her uncle.

When Nadia returned from school, she found Sanana sitting on a daybed in the corner of the living room. She joined him, pulling out some handouts from her schoolbag and placing them on the table.

"I brought some for you," Nadia said. "Percy gave them to me."

Jessica walked the stairs, looking all dressed up. She stood to face the children. Sanana looked around the room as if nothing else mattered anymore.

"Convince your brother to eat something. I've prepared something delicious for both of you."

Nadia hurried to the kitchen, and came back with a tray of food, which she placed before her brother.

"Let's eat together," Nadia said.

While they were still at the lunch table, Lisa arrived home from school. The Old Driver hurried to his wife's room. The door was slightly open, so he poked his head inside.

"Can we talk?"

"Wait outside; I need to change," Lisa said.

"I'm supposed to be your husband."

"I don't love you, and you know it," she said before slamming the door.

The Old Driver hit the wall with his open hand before rushing out, ignoring the children. When the Old Driver had left, Nadia went to receive the door. Angela stood there. She had brought a pumpkin from the village, which Sanana helped carry to the kitchen, while Nadia took the bag.

"Get me some cold water to drink," Angela said. "This house is a castle."

"Aunt Angela," Sanana said, "how did you find your way here?"

"I lived in South Bauleni even before you were born. I'm a city girl, and your mother would have agreed. Now, I'm hungry." Angela pulled out her phone and waited for a few rings before speaking. "How was business yesterday and today? I hope you're taking care of my customers. Don't give alcohol on credit without asking me first."

She paused for a moment before dialling the Old Driver's number. "Jeremy, I've arrived and need to see you now."

Lisa was coming out of her room when she rushed back inside. She called her friend to let her know about the villager's arrival.

"I can already smell trouble," Mary said. "Who showed them the way to our city? Who exactly is here?"

"That Blabbermouth Angela," said Lisa.

"Do you want me to come over? I can do it now. You know what they say? Two heads are better than one." Mary chuckled on the phone. "Should I come now?"

"Let's wait and see why she came. I'll fill you in on all the details later."

The Old Driver walked in. Angela turned her fury on him, "What happened to my niece, Jeremy?"

"Agatha will be alright, Angela," the Old Driver said.

"Where is she?"

The Old Driver knew that Angela would ask that question. He didn't know where the police were keeping Agatha for her treatment.

"Where is she?" Angela asked.

"The police said no one can see her," Sanana explained.

"What kind of police force do you have in this city?"

"It's for her safety. They're still investigating," the Old Driver said.

"What did they say happened to her?"

"The police said she was kidnapped, assaulted, and left for dead. Luckily, someone found her."

The kids, especially Sanana, acted like they didn't care, but he was paying attention to the conversation.

"The person who did that wanted to kill her. I knew my niece was not safe."

"What are you trying to say, Angela?"

"Oh, come on, Jeremy, don't be so clueless. Wild dogs and snakes are all over my niece. Who can be safe?"

The Old Driver never imagined a moment like this would come. He thought the elders would ask him to go to the village, not send someone, especially Angela.

"Jeremy, we've known each other since we were kids. We grew up together, and I always saw you as an older brother. Doesn't that mean anything to you?"

"Who do you think is behind this?" asked the Old Driver.

"Money, Jeremy, read between the lines. Jesus died because of money. Remember Judas from Sunday school?"

"You think it's about money?"

"Money and everyone in this house, even you."

The Old Driver grabbed his car keys from the table and went towards the exit.

"I can see right through you," she shouted.

Lisa overheard the conversation between the Old Driver and Angela near the stairs. Angela came from the village with her suspicions. It seemed like a village matter. She and her relatives had their suspicions, and she came to confront them. Could she and the villager's instincts be pointing in the right direction?

The family gathered for the eight o'clock news. Sanana rested on Angela's lap. Jessica shared a seat with her daughter. Lisa sat alone on a sofa facing the television.

"Jessica," Angela said. "Is that businessman you ran off with years ago still alive?"

"I'm not interested in your drama," Jessica said. "This is my house; return to the village."

"This is my nephew's house. Remember the will?"

"And this is my daughter's house. Why don't you direct your anger towards someone who shouldn't be here."

Lisa remained silent, but she managed to decipher the target of Jessica's insults.

"Did you marry him?" Angela asked.

"What do you want to know?" Jessica yelled.

"My sister suffered; she died a miserable death. You know that you ruined her life?"

"Is it my fault that he left her for me? Besides, your sister died while giving birth."

"You left him for that man, and now you are showing up. Let me guess, it's harvest time."

Angela's phone rang.

"Yes, Dorothy, I will keep you updated on the search for the criminals."

"As soon as I find some time, I will join you. I don't trust Lisa," Dorothy said.

"Do you know who's back? The one and only, Jessica."

"Jessica is still alive?"

While that was happening, Miss O'Hara arrived at the Lingani mansion and asked to speak to Lisa, who took her to the shade. Miss O'Hara had come to share a bad dream she had about Lisa. Lisa sat playing with her nails, taking occasional sips from her Pepsi can. Miss O'Hara sat across from her, their eyes meeting in conversation.

"It was horrible," she said.

"You're getting old, Miss O'Hara," Lisa said.

"My dreams always come true. They're like visions," Miss O'Hara said.

"You know, Miss O'Hara, I truly love and appreciate you. I'll never forget how you took me in when I was still at South Bauleni. Whatever happened, it has nothing to do with our relationship. I may have taken your position, but your salary remained the same. That's how much I owe you," Lisa said.

"I know you're a good girl, be very careful. The police seemed so real in my dream."

"No one will arrest me because I haven't done anything wrong."

Miss O'Hara stood up and faced two police officers who had entered the gate. She knew it had something to do with her dream. She looked at

Lisa, who was still engrossed in cleaning her nails, unaware of the officers' presence.

"Mrs Lingani," Detective Vosloo said, "you are under arrest…"

Three Women Share a Cell

Lisa jolted from her seat as two policemen stood facing her. "I don't understand," she said.

"You'll understand once we get to the station."

At the police station, Detective Vosloo presented Lisa with her phone records. They had also accessed the phone records of the other three suspects, including call logs and text messages. The text messages exchanged between Lisa and Mary were particularly incriminating.

LISA: If she dies, as per the will, I will be the executor and the school chairman, and you, Mary, become the principal.

MARY: I can't do it. Agatha is such a nice girl. Please stop whatever you're planning.

The news of Lisa's arrest spread across the country, and everyone had an opinion. A few days later, a new inmate arrived while Lisa was in her cell. Veronica, a young woman, entered. Lisa tried to initiate a conversation, but she ignored her, directing her stare on the two beds to her left.

"You can choose any bed," Lisa offered. "I'm all alone here and bored. I'm glad you're here."

"She's glad I'm here!" Veronica scoffed. "Silly girl!"

A little while later, another inmate joined them, carrying a Bible. She introduced herself as Farrah. She was plus-sized and started reading Bible verses.

"Be quiet!" Veronica shouted, wiping away her tears and getting up from the bed. "What do you know about God? Wait a minute, you're the new pastor for that church, and you're here illegally. I remember seeing you on TV."

"Yes, sister, I remember you too," Farrah said. "I'm sorry about your son."

"Enough with your meaningless condolences," Veronica snapped.

As the lights went out that night, everyone in the cell, including the preacher, found it hard to sleep. At 3 a.m.,Veronica and Farrah woke up because Lisa was shouting in her sleep, pleading her innocence.

"The witches and wizards are up to something," Veronica whispered.

"The devil is a liar!" Farrah declared, rushing to wake Lisa, who clung to her, trembling, and scanning the room with suspicion.

"It was just a stupid dream," Veronica said.

It was pitch black in the cell as the three of them started opening up to each other after Farrah emphasised the importance of sisterhood, especially in places like prisons.

"We can't go through this alone," she said. "We need to stick together to survive."

"I'm not usually like this," Veronica admitted. "I've made a mess of my own life."

Veronica had a six-year-old son whom she accidentally suffocated during her sleep because she was always high.

"I'm sorry about your son," Lisa said.

The next day, during recreation time, Lisa and her new friends were in the laundry room. Afterwards, they went to the commissary to buy toiletries. Farrah reminded them that they needed to catch up on time for lunch. By the time they reached the hall, lunch was long over. Disappointed, they returned to their cell hungry. Despite the long day, supper arrived—a slice of bread and a cup of watery goat milk. Two women who seemed to be prison leaders sat at the table behind them as they sat down. The prison rule was that newcomers couldn't eat supper for their first three days. Lisa knew the rule and brought her meal to the leader, surrounded by six other women. When she returned to her friends, Veronica and Farrah were puzzled.

"Wait, we can't eat for the next three days?" Farrah asked.

"That's ridiculous!" Veronica exclaimed, taking a sip of her milk.

One of the gang's errand women slapped Veronica on the top of her head and took the cup from her. She then did the same to Farrah, who remained silent. Veronica couldn't contain her anger and annoyance, saying, "You terrible monster! Don't you have any sense?"

"Stop, Veronica," Lisa said. "We need to leave now."

It was at this moment that the mystery began to unfold. The entire cell was filled with sorrow. Despite being a spiritual woman, Farrah struggled to hide her anger and frustration, which was evident from her expression. She lay on her worn-out bed face down while Veronica paced restlessly in the room, blaming her friends for leaving her alone to fight for their food. She couldn't stop fussing about what they could have done as grown women to get back their food.

"Their days are numbered," Veronica muttered before finally mustering the courage to go to sleep.

"Let us thank the Lord for this day," Farrah said, picking up the Bible and kneeling. Lisa followed suit.

"You and your prayers?" Veronica remarked.

"Let us pray, my sister," Farrah insisted. "It was the will of God."

"Go ahead, I'm listening," Veronica said without meaning it.

The sun shone brightly, but the dawn did not bring an immediate meal for prisoners, as breakfast was not served in jail. Instead, they had to wait for lunch, feeling irritated. Soon, a guard summoned the trio. They were driven to an unfinished house, the superintendent's house. Their task was manual labour.

"What are we supposed to do here?" Veronica asked.

"Move the sand from there to there."

"We're not builders."

"Get to work, or you'll miss out on lunch."

They laboured grudgingly, finishing just in time for lunch. After eating, Veronica was transferred to another facility, while Farrah was released days later.

After school, Jessica was still preparing lunch when she heard voices coming from the sitting room. *Ba*Eliza and *bana*Monde had come from the village with a lot of anger. Angela went downstairs to greet them, but they didn't respond. The two old ladies met Nadia, who also came to see them. Jessica then joined them.

"And who are you?" asked *bana*Monde.

"Jessica. My name is Jessica," she said.

The Old Driver walked in, and the women directed their anger to him.

"What did you do with my daughter, Jeremy?" *ba*Eliza snapped.

"You better come up with a better explanation," *bana*Monde said before turning to Jessica, "Bring cold water, shoo-shoo," she gestured rhythmically.

After Jessica brought the water, she returned to the kitchen to continue cooking. The children went outside to play.

"One more thing, Jeremy," *ba*Eliza said, "who is she?"

"That's Jessica, my late brother's first wife."

"Now I get it," *bana*Monde said, "my niece was surrounded by her enemies. You will take us to her first thing tomorrow."

"No," Lisa's mother said. "You are taking us there now."

In jail, Lisa tried to hide her bruises, but her leaping gave her away. She was dressed in a dull grey prison uniform, which made the old ladies burst into tears.

"They are also hurting you," *bana*Monde said.

"Aunt, you're embarrassing me."

"I'm trying to support you, and now I'm embarrassing you."

"I didn't do it."

Despite the warder's warning to control her emotions, *bana*Monde continued to cry. Lisa turned to her mother and said, "Mother, you weren't supposed to come. This is a mistake."

"Prison can't be a mistake."

"I didn't do it, mother."

*Ba*Eliza looked uncertain. It was as if Lisa could hear her mother's inner doubts. "Do you think I did it, mother?"

"No," her mother admitted. "I'm scared. What will happen if the judge finds you guilty and sentences you to years in prison?"

"I'm innocent, and I will prove it. I have faith in my God."

When the warder announced the end of the visit, Lisa was escorted back to her cell. *Bana*Monde sadly said, "My niece's life is over."

"Don't say that," *ba*Eliza said. "If she's innocent, God will defend her."

"I'm scared. What will happen if they do sentence her?"

"Let's not think about that. My daughter will not go to prison. She's innocent."

"How many innocent people are in prison? Sometimes, you think like a child. You're saying something that you don't even believe."

After they left, Mary paid a visit to her friend. She went there to assure Lisa that she did not know who wrote those messages, and she swore on the graves of all her departed family members.

"I still don't understand," Lisa said. "Who sent those messages?"

"Even I don't know. I swear on my grandmother's grave," Mary said.

"I always have my phone with me wherever I go. Someone is definitely behind this."

"I know you're innocent, and I never responded to any of those messages."

It was finally time for another villager to join the family. The door swung open, and *ba*Dorothy entered with a red bag, a giant watermelon, and an umbrella. After saying hello to children, she sat next to Nadia and Sanana. The two elderly ladies sat in silence.

"How is Agatha?" *ba*Dorothy asked.

"She's recovering. At least that's what they told us a few days ago," Angela said.

"They can't prevent us from seeing her. That's against the law. Take me to the police station."

Before Angela could respond to her educated friend, Jessica descended the stairs. "Agatha has been discharged. Jeremy is bringing her home."

The Old Driver entered first, followed by Agatha. Despite the bruises on her face, arms, and knees, she could walk independently. Sanana rushed to embrace his sister.

"Wait a minute," *ba*Eliza said. "Now that she's not dead, what will happen to my daughter?"

*Ba*Eliza knelt before Agatha, but Angela led Agatha to her seat. Jessica sat, busy on trimming her nails, but kept an eye on the situation and seemed entertained.

"Please, my daughter," *bana*Monde said.

"Leave her alone," *ba*Dorothy said. "Can't you see she's still recovering? How selfish can you be?"

Agatha rested on Angela's lap. Later that day, Sanana shared a bed with his sister. Agatha took a photo from the drawer and gave it to her brother. "Keep it; that's our mother."

"She was beautiful."

"You know, she's out there somewhere, watching over us."

"Sister," the boy said, "how did she die?"

"She didn't suffer. Her last smile was for you." Agatha gave a novel to her brother and said, "It was Mother's favourite book. Take it, it's yours now."

In the morning, the two elderly ladies came into Agatha's room after some hesitation. After exchanging morning greetings, they sat on the bed. Jessica, passing by Agatha's door on her way to her daughter's room, overheard the two ladies pleading with Agatha to drop the charges. She went to Angela and *ba*Dorothy's room to inform them about the commotion caused by the villagers so early in the morning.

"My daughter's future is in your hands," *ba*Eliza said. "She's a good girl."

"Your daughter is a criminal. Look at what she did to me, all for money."

"If you release her, I will take her back to the village and never to return."

"She needs to face the consequences of her actions. Your daughter is wicked."

Angela and *ba*Dorothy came into the room.

"Let her rest," Angela said.

"Angela, you're a mother; you shouldn't be so harsh," *ba*Eliza said.

"Jack would never do something like this."

Just then, the Old Driver arrived with Mary to take the two villagers to see Lisa. She was counting down the hours until her sentencing. But before that, Mary and the villagers needed to make the Old Driver feel like the worst husband in the world.

"Yes, Uncle Jeremy, Agatha values your opinion," Mary said.

"What kind of husband are you?" *bana*Monde said. "Step up and do something."

"I'm trying my best," the Old Driver said. "Agatha is hurting; we need to give her time."

"We're running out of time, Uncle Jeremy," Mary said. "The sentencing is tomorrow."

*Ba*Eliza sat holding her daughter's hand while *bana*Monde stood next to her. Lisa remained still as if nothing else mattered.

"Did you do it, my child?" *bana*Monde asked.

Lisa rose from her seat, her gaze locking with Agatha's, who stood by the door. At that moment, with the room in heavy silence, Lisa's resolve surged.

"I swear," she declared, her voice trembling fervently, "I didn't do it."

Lisa moved towards Agatha, and urgency infused every word she spoke. "I didn't do it. Even if it means facing imprisonment, I implore you to do something for me. Find out who tried to harm you. Please, say something."

Agatha remained unmoved, her gaze flitting to the old villagers in the room before she limped out, leaving Lisa standing there.

"How are they treating you in this place?" The Old Driver asked Lisa, who didn't respond to such a question. Instead, she demanded the warder take her back to her cell.

"Do something," *bana*Monde urged the Old Driver as they left the room.

Agatha was in her room when The Old Driver asked to speak with her. Angela and *ba*Dorothy leaned against the wall nearby. The Old Driver began talking about forgiveness and that vengeance is for the Lord, but Angela and *ba*Dorothy saw it as justice.

"I can't do what you're asking," Agatha said. "She will end up in prison and die there."

Two elderly villagers entered, begging and sobbing. Lisa's mother began narrating how poverty had caused her to lose her husband and son, and how she wished her daughter hadn't taken that path...

"I can't bear to lose another child," she said. "It will destroy me before my time."

"OK." Agatha said to *ba*Eliza. "But I'm doing this for you"

Agatha called Detective Vosloo, who informed her that taxpayers' money had funded all the investigations, so the new law didn't allow charges to be dropped. They had gathered enough physical and testimonial evidence to prove that a crime had been committed.

"Legally, we can't ignore that, and the victim did not file the charges," he said. "The sentence is tomorrow. You have to attend because nothing can be done."

When morning finally came, the villagers and everyone had settled well in the courtroom, hearing the judge's verdict. Lisa couldn't believe it—her life was over.

"Eight years!"

*Ba*Eliza woke up in the hospital, disoriented and in a state of disbelief. The events leading up to this moment played like a haunting movie in her mind. The judge's harsh sentence of eight years had shattered her world, leaving her feeling helpless. When she regained her senses, the hospital room came into focus. The sound of beeping machines and the scent of antiseptic filled everywhere, reminding *ba*Eliza of the harsh reality her daughter now faced.

WHO WILL TAKE OVER AS PRINCIPAL?

From Teacher to Principal

Jessica called for a staff meeting to announce Principal Lingani's situation, though the main agenda was to appoint Mary as the new principal.

"I've also chosen Miss O'Hara as the deputy principal," Jessica said.

"Excuse me, Mrs Lingani. This practice of randomly assigning staff positions is confusing in our school," Miss April challenged, her voice laced with defiance. "I suggest we follow the government's procedures for applying and attending interviews."

"This isn't a government school," Jessica retorted. "It's my school."

"There are many qualified teachers," Miss Mwiya said, "even among our male colleagues."

"Qualifications shouldn't be confused with capabilities," Mary added.

"Exactly," Jessica agreed. "Now, can we all please proceed to our classes?"

In Mary's office, she was on a call with her mother, propping her feet on the table and swinging them back and forth.

"Mother, did you notice the number I used?" Mary giggled, twirling the phone cord around her fingers. "It's a landline right here in my office. I'm now the new principal of this school. I'm in charge, and they all love me."

"So soon?" her mother asked.

"I have to go, Mother."

"But why so soon?"

"Mother, I'm hanging up now. Some lazy teachers need my attention to get them settled in their classes. I'm determined to make Sunpride great again. I'll run it with an iron fist, the language these uninspired teachers understand."

She then went from class to class, ensuring all teachers were present in their classrooms. In one class, she interrupted the History teacher who was discussing soil erosion.

"I may not know much about History, but that doesn't sound like a history lesson. Please consult your syllabus."

It had been two weeks since Lisa was sentenced to years in prison. Lisa's mother and sister were on their way back to the village. Angela and *ba*Dorothy sat together, enjoying tea and a plate full of bread slices. The Old Driver carried their bag to the car, and they watched as the two women left. Jessica joined Angela and *ba*Dorothy for breakfast.

"Jessica," *ba*Dorothy called, "we will also be leaving today. No one will do my work for me when I'm not at school."

"My niece is doing well now," said Angela. "Please take care of her for me."

"I will treat Agatha and Sanana like my own children. Feel free to visit anytime you want."

"We can still send you traditional food," said Angela.

"I love ripe pickled cucumbers and some spiny African horned cucumbers," said Jessica.

"You mean hedgehog gourd?" asked *ba*Dorothy.

"Yes, I love that a lot."

Jessica drove them to the bus stop, where they met the two elderly villagers in time to catch the bus.

Meanwhile, Amahle, Lawyer Ken's wife, was in her office when her husband walked in. She couldn't wait to share her discoveries.

"We need to take action," Amahle said. "I have all the evidence that proves the will was a fraud. First, I need Albert's address. Then, I will go to prison and engage this woman. We are going to close this case once and for all. Trust me on this. I didn't study abroad for nothing."

Lawyer Albert was in her office. Amahle was led to his office by a guard. When she settled in, she and Lawyer Albert talked about the latest news in town, giving him the impression that she was a good person before she dropped the bombshell.

"I'll get straight to the point," she said. "I've noticed something fishy about Mr Lingani's will."

"The will is valid, and it was my legal duty to ensure that my client, Mr Lingani's final wishes, were carried out," Mr Albert said.

"The will never truly reflected the deceased's final wishes, so my husband and I question its validity. Tell me, Mr Albert, was the will revised or completely rewritten?"

"What are you trying to imply, Mrs..." he trailed off.

"Amahle."

"Amahle, Mr Lingani was the kindest man I've ever known. He was good to me; whatever I presented to the family was his wish."

"Are you avoiding my question, Mr Albert? Was the will rewritten or revised?"

"Before he passed away, he made changes to his will. It's something everyone does."

"Perhaps the final version of the will was altered under pressure or when he wasn't in the right mind? I can understand if the widow wasn't a good wife, but his brother benefiting so much seems excessive. Can we see the previous version of the will?"

"Please leave my office."

"I have every legal right to request it. Let's not forget your ethical responsibility."

"Alright," he sighed. "Come back next week."

Once she had left, Albert immediately called the Old Driver...

Meanwhile, Amahle waited for Lisa in prison. Once Lisa arrived, the lawyer introduced herself and handed over the old will to *Lisa*.

Firstly, I bequeath to my daughter, Nadia Lingani, the sum of one hundred and fifteen million Namibian dollars (N\$ 115,000,000), absolutely and free of any tax. Next, I bestow upon my son, Sanana Neo, the family house in the village of Mamiyeto, along with one hundred and fifteen million Namibian dollars (N\$ 115,000,000). I also leave him all five of my cars and the garage in Soweto. Furthermore, I grant him eighty per cent (80%) of the shares of Sunpride School, while the remaining twenty per cent (20%) goes to his sister, Nadia Lingani. Regarding the family house in Blackville, ERF 474, I leave it to both of my children, stipulating that it should never be sold under any circumstances. This document represents my final will.

"My late husband never included me in his will," said Lisa.

"Not exactly, Mrs Lingani," said Amahle. "The will you see before you was created before your marriage to your husband. If you examine it closely, you'll notice that his brother, Jeremy, is not mentioned in this will. However, in the new will, he suddenly appears and receives a significant portion."

"Do you think there might be another will?"

"Yes, Mrs Lingani, I have the original will right here."

"And how did you get it?"

"Don't worry, Mrs Lingani, and please keep this between us. Your husband didn't leave you with nothing."

I leave my daughter Nadia Lingani N$ 80,000,000. I leave all my cars and the garage to my son Sanana Lingani, the family house, N$ 80,000,000, and 80% shares in Sunpride School. The remaining 20% goes to his sister, Nadia Lingani. The city house goes to my children and must not be sold. My wife, Lisa Lingani, gets N$ 70,000,000, and from her share, she should donate 50% to a charity of her choice. This is my final will.

"Mrs Lingani," Amahle said, "your husband didn't leave you empty-handed, but why is he compelling you to give so much to charity?"

"My husband had his reasons," Lisa said. "What's 50% of N$ 70,000,000?"

"I'm not good at math, but that to me looks like half of it. Do you want me to represent you, Mrs Lingani?"

"What about my situation? Can you assist me as well?"

"I'll try my best."

After Amahle left, she went to her husband's office to discuss how nervous Lawyer Albert was.

"You don't believe me, do you?" she asked.

"Lying makes us great lawyers," he said.

Lawyer Ken poured himself and his wife some wine, but she declined, saying she needed to stay sober and focus on her new case.

"Tomorrow, one of those two criminals will have to confess," she said.

"How do you plan on making that happen?"

"I will make him an offer. I must go back there now."

"Why?"

"It's obvious his partner in crime is there now."

The Old Driver stormed into Lawyer Albert's office in a foul mood. He plopped down on the chair, causing his wristwatch to jingle.

"Do you think we should be worried about her?" the Old Driver asked.

"She seems dangerous to me," Lawyer Albert said.

Amahle walked in and stood behind the Old Driver, exuding confidence as if she had already won the case.

"Well, gentlemen," Amahle said, "I'm here. Now, tell me where the original will is?"

"Is this the woman?" the Old Driver asked, leaning back in his chair.

"Yes, Mr Lingani," he said.

The tension had built up as Amahle settled into her seat, smoothing her skirt. "This must be Mr Jeremy Lingani," she said, extending her hand for a handshake, which he declined.

"How may I help, Ama-?" Lawyer Albert began.

"Amahle," she corrected him. "You know why I'm here, but I'll say it. The will you presented is not the original, and I have proof. How is it that Mr Lingani is now a beneficiary when he was never mentioned in the old will?"

"People can change their will however they want. Maybe he felt it wasn't fair and decided to include his brother," Albert said.

"You're not taking me seriously. The final will doesn't mention Mr Jeremy Lingani at all. Let me quote the last paragraph directly:

'My wife, Lisa Lingani, gets N\$ 70,000,000, but 50% goes to the charity of her choice. This is my last will.'

"How did you know that? It was supposed to be a secret," the Old Driver said.

Amahle giggled, and Lawyer Albert stared at the Old Driver, who had unknowingly confessed to a crime.

"I have the valid will right here with me, and please, don't ask me how I got it."

"What do you want?" Lawyer Albert asked.

"You know what I want, my dear learned friend, but I'll make it easy for you. I want my share from this fraud, 25 per cent."

The Old Driver rose from his seat and protested, "That's too much!"

"My offer is final, and either way, I'll still get my percentage when both of you go to prison." Amahle grabbed her briefcase and walked out, leaving her business card on the table.

When she had left, Lawyer Albert directed his frustration towards the Old Driver.

"You're such an old weakling," he said. "You spilled everything to her, you foolish old man."

"I never wanted to do this. Give her what she wants; I'm not ready to go to jail."

Amahle listened at the door before bursting in, and she remained standing. Lawyer Albert and the Old Driver had no choice but to agree to her terms. From there, she went to prison, where she met Lisa. When she informed her about the offer she received from Lawyer Albert and the Old Driver, Lisa was shocked by the Old Driver's unexpected behaviour, as she had always considered him the kindest man she knew.

"Those two will be taking your place soon," Amahle said to Lisa. "Once I receive my share from them, our case will be a piece of cake."

"What about my case?" Lisa asked.

"We'll appeal; I'm confident you'll be out soon."

Agatha found a letter from prison and, after reading it, dropped it on the bedroom bench. Sanana was rummaging through some things in his sister's room when he found the letter and stuffed it into his school bag. During break time, he sat on a bench near the school hall. Erica joined him and snatched the letter before he could hide it, quickly reading aloud, *Meet Lawyer Amahle; she'll be able to explain everything to you. I didn't do it. From Lisa.*

"That's private," Sanana protested.

Erica made her way to a nearby tree, her heart racing as she finished reading the final line of the letter. She plopped down next to him, unable to contain her laughter.

"Do you trust Principal Lisa? Do you think she's innocent?" Erica asked.

"You know what's going on?" Sanana replied nervously, glancing around.

"Everyone at school is talking about it. Do you believe her?"

"She's so mean," Sanana whispered. "But I don't think she did it. What do you think, Erica?"

"I believe her," Erica said without hesitation.

Sanana pondered Erica's response momentarily, tapping his finger on the ground. "Why?"

"I don't know," Erica admitted, her voice softer this time. "But I have an idea. Why don't we visit her lawyer?"

"Why?"

"I don't know."

After their lessons ended, Sanana and Erica left the school. Sanana double-checked the address on a piece of paper he held: *Tom & Associates*. They entered the office just in time to see Lawyer Tom sitting in an armchair, with the rest of the office adorned with books on a wooden bookshelf.

"Yes," Lawyer Tom said, looking up from his papers. "Ah, there it is." He picked up a floppy disk from the tiled floor and faced his visitors. "I remember you, Sanana, right?"

His handshake was firm, which made the children feel a bit more at ease. Sanana took out the letter and gave it to Lawyer Tom, who read it silently.

"Aunt Lisa didn't do it," Sanana said.

"Do you have any evidence?" asked Lawyer Tom.

"No, sir," Sanana replied.

"What about you, young lady?" Lawyer Tom asked, turning to Erica.

"No but she didn't attack Aunt Agatha."

"She was your client, and you never believed her?" Sanana asked.

"She is still my client, but her case is complicated. The evidence against her is overwhelming," explained Lawyer Tom.

"That's right, sir," Sanana agreed. "It was a text message. People may think I don't know what's happening in that house, but I do. She's innocent; I can feel it." Sanana fidgeted with his hands in his lap.

Lawyer Tom briefly glanced at the children, considering their words. Sanana waited, hoping Erica or the lawyer would say something, but they remained silent.

"We can leave, Erica," Sanana finally said.

"No," Erica disagreed, shaking her head. "He believes us. He's just shy."

Lawyer Tom smiled, taking a few seconds to gather his thoughts. "I like you guys. You think like adults. This case has already been closed, and many new cases are on my plate. Thank you for coming."

"So, can we go?" Erica asked.

"Go home," Lawyer Tom said. "Take a dollar and buy some sweets."

Once they left the lawyer's office, Sanana began playing with the dollar he had received. Erica snatched it from the air and examined it.

"I remember my social studies teacher in grade 7," Erica said. "Did you know that our currency is not used in South Africa, but the South African rand is accepted as legal tender in our country?"

"Why?" Sanana asked.

"Why do you always ask why?" Erica teased.

"I just want to know," Sanana explained.

"I don't know; we should ask our teacher."

Sanana and Erica treated themselves to some street ice cream. The cold winter air and the ice cream made them rush into a taxi. Jessica and Nadia were watching television when Sanana returned home. He dropped his school bag on the floor, greeted his sister and stepmother, and then walked into Agatha's room.

"Can I talk to you?" Sanana asked, sitting down beside her.

"Why are you coming home from school now? You know the city isn't safe," Agatha said.

"Aunt Lisa didn't do it. She's innocent."

Agatha pulled open a drawer and pushed it shut again.

"I read it," Sanana said.

Agatha leaned towards her brother and touched his cheeks. "Now, tell me, what makes you believe that Lisa is innocent?"

"I don't know... it's a feeling in my heart."

"My heart tells me the same thing, but who could be responsible then?"

"Aunt Mary."

"What could Mary gain from causing all this trouble?"

"She's the new principal now."

Agatha glanced behind her, as if expecting someone to enter the room. "Who else knows about this?" she whispered.

"My friend Erica."

"It's alright. You can go to the kitchen and have some lunch. I'll visit Lisa as soon as I find the time."

"Who is Lawyer Amahle? I've never heard of her."

"I've never met her either."

Reward or Caution?

Agatha met Lisa to tell her about Mary who was promoted to principal by Jessica. Lisa nodded thoughtfully. "She's supposed to be my friend," Lisa said.

"Don't rush into doing anything foolish. Continue your friendship until we devise a better plan."

Amahle arrived. She demanded to be left alone with her client, but Lisa insisted Agatha be present.

"If you insist," Amahle said. "It's confirmed Mr Jeremy and your late husband's lawyer altered the will. They have paid me my share."

"I don't understand," Agatha said. "You mean Uncle Jeremy altered the will?"

"Yes, he did."

Later that evening, Jessica offered Sanana the seat at the head of the table. Jessica recognised Sanana as the heir and leader of the Lingani family, stepping into his late father's shoes.

"This family will live in peace," Jessica declared.

"Thank you, Aunt," Sanana said.

"You can call me mother. Agatha, when will you start work? It seems you have recovered."

"Should I also call you mother?" Agatha asked.

"You are all my children, my two beautiful girls and the man of the house."

"I heard that Mary is now the principal," Agatha said.

"Yes, I was waiting for the right time to inform you."

"What happened to Miss O'Hara? I thought she was your favourite and more qualified for the position."

"Keep your friends close and your enemies closer. It's not wise to disregard your enemies. It's better to be friendly with them but remain vigilant."

"Do you consider Mary as your enemy?"

"She is Lisa's best friend, which makes her an enemy of this family. Appointing her as principal allows me to keep a close eye on her. It's important not to overlook what your enemies are up to. This vigilance gives me the advantage to counter any strategies they might be planning against our family."

"To me, it sounds like a reward. Besides, Lisa is no longer in the picture."

"You're so innocent. Now that you're a wealthy woman, everyone in our society is targeting you from every direction. Have you forgotten so quickly? You almost went home."

"Home?" Nadia asked.

"That's heaven, right?" Sanana said.

"Exactly... heaven underground."

Sanana and Nadia cleared the plates to wash them.

"I haven't seen Uncle Jeremy today," Jessica asked.

"Uncle Jeremy is in prison."

"Why? What happened to him?"

"The will was a fraud, but not everything, just the part where Uncle Jeremy changed Lisa's name to his."

"How did he manage that? Jeremy isn't smart enough to think that way. He can't even read the alphabet."

"He did it with Lawyer Albert. He's in jail too, and Amahle is ensuring Lisa gets her money."

After everyone had gone to bed, Jessica took a phone from her bag. Mary was in bed when her phone rang, and they talked about the Old Driver and the arrested Lawyer. Mary laughed about it.

"Today, I'll sleep peacefully, though," Mary giggled. "All this time, I thought I was terrible, not knowing Mr Jeremy was a silent criminal."

"We're all criminals, little girl," Jessica said.

"Well," Mary yawned, "at least our crime was successful."

"You know what? Tomorrow morning, I'm visiting my best friend for the last time, then I'll abandon her to rot in prison, and then I'll come back home and never sin again."

"Abandon is such a beautiful adjective."

"It's a verb."

"After tomorrow, it will be an adjective."

"I have to sleep now; tomorrow morning, I'm going to prison."

Mary brought home-cooked food to Lisa. Many family members had come to visit their loved ones. She appeared calm, which seemed to bother Mary, who expected to find her friend beaten down.

"I don't understand," Mary said. "You are so calm."

"Congratulations on your promotion," Lisa said.

"How did you know about that?"

"I'm in prison, Mary, not in a coma. How did you do it?"

"It was a surprise... that old witch is up to something."

"Be very careful."

"I will come and visit as soon as I get time. I never knew being principal is hectic."

"Have you heard from John?"

"John travelled as soon as he heard you're arrested. I don't believe John was the reason your husband died."

"If only I could have been a good wife, my husband could still be alive."

"And you wouldn't have ended up in prison. See, my friend, I have decorated my new office, it is now wonderful. I even installed aircon and got myself a new secretary and a driver. Teachers there fear me. Anyway, be strong and take care of yourself. You can enrol in some karate lessons for protection. Life is not safe in prison."

Lisa fell silent, pondering that the devil will soon get his dues. Clever people say a fast horse doesn't run long.

Mary called Jessica's number in the prison hallways, and after a few rings, Nadia answered the phone...

"Mrs Lingani," Mary said over the phone. "Lisa is getting suspicious. We need to be careful. Let's get rid of her."

"Mother is taking a bath."

There was sudden silence before Mary ended the call. Jessica was still in the bathroom, giving Nadia a few minutes to think about what she had heard.

"You seem worried, princess," Jessica said, getting dressed.

"Aunt Mary called."

"Which Mary?"

"Principal Mary. Aunt Lisa's friend."

"Did she leave a message?"

"She said that Aunt Lisa is suspecting something, and you should kill her."

"Did you hear that?"

Nadia stood up and turned to face her mother. Jessica held her daughter's arms and sat her down.

"I did it for you. That little boy came out of nowhere, and he's taking everything that your late father worked hard for you and me."

"But why Aunt Lisa?"

"Lisa wasn't my first target; Agatha was, but she survived because she's a witch. We had to frame someone."

"Why Agatha?"

"When she dies... you and I can do whatever we want with that dwarf's inheritance."

"Sanana is my brother, and I love him."

"Sanana and his sister are thieves. They are stealing from you. Now listen, don't tell anyone about this. Do you understand me?"

Nadia only needed a little time to decide. Her little smile showed that she agreed with her mother's ideas.

Meanwhile, Miss O'Hara's laughter filled the living room as she sipped her tea. She was in the middle of a conversation with Raven. Sophia and Raven had just arrived from the USA. Suddenly, there was a knock on the door, and Miss O'Hara went to receive it.

"Mukenani! Tiwe! You both have grown into such beautiful women," she said.

Sophia and Raven, curious about the commotion, hurried to the door...

"Oh, my goodness, look at you two!" Sophia exclaimed, wrapping her arms around Mukenani and Tiwe. Raven joined in, laughing happily as they hugged each other.

"I can't believe we're finally meeting after four years, Tina!" said Raven. "It feels like forever."

"How is your TV show in the States?"

"It's amazing," Raven said. "We have many followers, and people are starting to recognise us on the streets."

"How is Lisa?" Mukenani asked.

"I worry about your friend, Lisa," Miss O'Hara said.

"I wish she rots in prison," said Sophia.

"Don't speak like that, honey," Miss O'Hara said. "She is an ambitious girl who veered off course. The Lisa I knew as a child is a good person."

"Miss O'Hara," Raven said, "now that Lisa is no longer around, will they reinstate you in your position?"

"They gave it to Mary, Lisa's best friend."

"I don't get it," Raven said. "Why her?"

"Mary is more of a snake in the grass. She is dangerous," Miss O'Hara said.

"Mary knows what is going on with her friend," Raven said. "She betrayed her best friend."

"I completely agree," Tiwe added. "I think Lisa is innocent."

"That's what I think too," Mukenani said. "Based on what I have heard, Mary is concealing something. I need to speak with this character they call Mary."

"Meet me at school tomorrow morning," Miss O'Hara said. "I'll take you to her."

It was the beginning of the first lesson. Mary was in her office as Jessica stormed in, clearly upset. She slammed her handbag on the table and stood with her hands on her hips, ready to confront Mary.

"I hope your daughter didn't figure out the answer to a simple math problem," Mary sarcastically remarked.

Jessica glared at Mary, clearly holding back her anger.

"I know I have to be careful," Mary sighed, "but how was I supposed to know she would pick up your phone?"

"You could have started the conversation with a simple greeting, like hello or good afternoon," Jessica said. "My daughter is now involved in this heavy secret at a young age."

"She'll keep it, right?"

Jessica's lips curled into a wicked grin. "I paid you a fortune for this job, and you failed. Now you're failing again."

"Should we direct our fury on Lisa or Agatha?"

"No one should lay a finger on Agatha... at least not yet. Your little friend should die in prison sooner."

Immediately after Jessica left, Mukenani and Tiwe entered the principal's office. Mary was enjoying her milk when she welcomed her visitors. "This milk tastes off," Mary said as she smiled at Mukenani and Tiwe as if they had known each other for years. "I always liked people with vitiligo. They look beautiful on you as if they were drawn there?"

Mary's boldness surprised Tiwe, who sat quietly. They have just met, and she is already giving comment on Mukenani's skin condition.

"I noticed these changes on my skin at a community school," Mukenani explained. "It was hard to accept initially, but my friend Lisa has always supported me. She taught me to accept what I can't change. When you accept what you can't change, you save energy and time, focusing on better things."

"You look gorgeous! It's like those marks on your skin are tattoos."

"Thank you," Mukenani said. "These marks are my natural tattoos, a gift from God." Mukenani caught sight of Lisa's picture on the wall. "That is her. Lisa and I went to school together, and she used to be the principal here before she went to prison."

"Oh, I remember she mentioned you and your sister. You both are studying law in SA, aren't you?"

"Yes," Mukenani said. "Do you think she is guilty?"

"No way... The Lisa I know wouldn't harm a fly. She's just unlucky," Mary said.

"I think so, too, but that's how life is. We'll let you do your job."

They left to Miss O'Hara's class...

"She is so loud and bossy," Tiwe said.

"I think she's hiding something. She knows what happened to Lisa."

"Of course. She took over her job, but how did she manage it?" Tiwe asked.

"There's someone more dangerous supporting her."

During Miss O'Hara's lesson, she allowed Mukenani and Tiwe to share a seat at her table. She introduced them to her class, stating they were former learners and aspiring lawyers. After they left, Miss O'Hara's daughter and Raven met the twins in town. They spent the rest of the afternoon together.

That same day, Erica, Sanana and Agatha paid Lisa a visit.

"Mary and Jessica are in cahoots," Agatha said. "Erica caught them arguing in the office."

"I'm sorry for everything," Lisa said, holding Sanana's hands. "I don't deserve your forgiveness."

"I forgive you, Aunt Lisa," Sanana said.

"You're the brightest boy I've ever met. You'll become a great man."

Later, Agatha took Mukenani and Tiwe to the Lingani mansion. They bumped into Jessica who was driving out. Agatha ushered Tiwe and Mukenani to her bedroom.

"I don't get it," Mukenani said. "How did you live in this huge, beautiful house?"

"Yeah," Tiwe added. "I remember Aunt Angela used to own a small shebeen in the village. I had no idea you had wealthy relatives."

"It was my brother's father. He died last semester," Agatha said. "The woman we met earlier, Is Jessica, the widow."

"Lisa married a man who was already married?" Tiwe asked.

"He wasn't married; Jessica left her husband and daughter twelve years ago. She only reappeared when the old man passed away."

"So, Lisa and that woman lived together in this house?" Tiwe asked.

"Yes. It was a constant game of cat and mouse."

"She must know what's going on with Lisa," Mukenani added.

In Mary's apartment, Jessica took a seat on a chair facing the screen. Mary was tidying her kitchen when she joined Jessica, complaining...

"I'll betray anyone for money," Mary stated. "Now that your enemy is gone, I want my share so I can move out of this place."

"Do you even get paid at your job?" Jessica asked.

"I was thinking, what if I move in with you? I've always dreamed of living in a house like yours."

"And what will people say?" Jessica pulled out a cheque from her handbag. "Make good use of this money."

Mary took her time smiling to the cheque.

"I've never held such a large amount before. I never realised my help meant so much to deserve this reward."

"Use the money wisely because this will be the last you receive from me."

"With this money, do you think I'll ever ask for more?" Mary surveyed her apartment. "I'll mount a huge television on this wall. Right there, I'll hang a large painting of myself." Mary glanced out the window. "And right there, my car will be parked. I'm tired of driving the school car. I'm thinking of buying a small sedan for myself. How about a Cressida?"

"Make good use of it, and don't call me again."

Another week has ended, yet no evidence proves Lisa's innocence. Jessica and Mary haven't seen each other since their last encounter. Agatha recently started teaching, and Mary has been very kind to her.

One day, while Miss O'Hara was in class, Agatha approached her to talk about Lisa's well-being in prison.

"You should pay her a visit," said Agatha. "She asked about you."

Miss O'Hara couldn't forget how ungrateful Lisa had been towards her. She remembered the young schoolgirl she had met years ago, who was so humble and dedicated to her studies.

"Lisa is no longer that girl," Miss O'Hara remarked sadly.

"You will always be her teacher. She will always need your guidance."

"Life was never fair growing up," Miss O'Hara said, rising from her seat and holding Agatha's hands. She looked deep into Agatha's eyes and continued, "You have the heart of a virtuous woman. You know what? I will make time to visit her."

"Thank you so much, Miss O'Hara. How are Sophia and Raven?"

"I left them sleeping. Those two are becoming quite lazy. But I'm used to it, as they have always been lazy."

It was evening at Miss O'Hara's house, and Mukenani and Tiwe had come for dinner. Sophia and Raven were busy preparing the food. Agatha and her brother arrived a little later, and they all gathered around the table for their meal.

"By the way, Miss O'Hara, Lisa asked if you could visit her. My sister and I are going there tomorrow," said Mukenani.

"You can't visit that ungrateful girl, Mom," said Sophia. "You can't."

"It's alright, sweetheart. I was planning to visit her anyway," Miss O'Hara said.

The next day in prison, Sophia and Raven leaned against the wall, their legs crossed. Sophia's anger burned like lava as she remembered what Lisa had done to her mother.

"Your mother's kindness is truly amazing," Raven said.

"I'm so furious right now," Sophia vented. "Mom gave her food when she was hungry, and this is how she repays her? By taking her job?" Sophia's irritation flared up, and her anger intensified as she stared at Miss O'Hara standing up from her seat as Lisa arrived.

"Control your anger," Raven said, "kids these days can have heart attacks."

"I don't like her," Sophia said.

"Girls," Miss O'Hara called, "come and say hello to Lisa. Remember Lisa?"

"We already know Lisa, Mom," Sophia said as she walked away, followed by Raven.

"Miss O'Hara," Lisa wiped away tears. "I've done so many things wrong."

"It's okay, sweetheart," Miss O'Hara said. "Focus on getting out of this place."

"I didn't do it."

"I believe you, and we are all praying for you. Many people are supporting you. You will leave this place and have a bright future."

It was in the morning; Nadia found a note on her mother's bed. She read it and went on to show the letter to her mother, who was packing up her lunch box. Nadia placed the letter on the counter with a simple message: *I'm in desperate need of money. I need it now. Mary.*

In Mary's office, Jessica slammed the letter on her desk.

"Mary, you're crossing too many red lines."

"Are you threatening me?"

"I'm giving you friendly advice."

"That sounds like a threat to me, and you know I don't handle threats well."

"I didn't write that letter."

"This will be the last time I give you money... next time, don't say I didn't warn you," Jessica said as she left.

A few moments later, Mary got the notification for a large sum. She set her phone on the table and grabbed a stick to drive the kids into class. Walking around the school, she ensured all the latecomers were held accountable. She had employed someone to carry Mr Smith around.

Sanana and Erica snack into her office with Mary's phone on the table.

"Do you still remember the password Aunt Lisa gave us? I hope it works?" Erica asked.

"1979."

Erica stood by the door to watch out for Mary.

"Hurry up," said Erica.

"Just a second," Sanana whispered as he hit send; Jessica received another notification...

I need money; my bed is sagging and needs to be replaced soon.

After reading the message, Jessica slammed the steering wheel, "This woman is getting on my nerves. I'll do something she won't like."

Back in her office, Mary chuckled as she saw another deposit in her account. She said, "Thank you." After a beep, Jessica frowned at her phone and deleted the message without responding.

Sanana kept to himself, with no one suspecting a thing, not even Nadia or Jessica. Nadia and her mother had secrets, and Sanana and his sister Agatha had theirs.

The School Studio: A Stage for Truth

Sanana and Erica revelled in the chaos they had caused between Mary and Jessica, but Agatha didn't share their excitement. Amahle, Mukenani, and others cautioned the children to be careful. The kids were determined to uncover the truth soon, convinced that someone wanted Lisa gone, with suspicions pointing towards Jessica and Mary as the masterminds.

Visiting time at the prison arrived, and Sanana and Erica appeared thrilled, as though they had cracked a complex puzzle.

"Be very careful," Mukenani said. "What if Jessica and Mary end up harming each other?"

"We're almost there," Amahle replied. "Life itself is a gamble."

"You're the lawyer here, and you're using the kids," Agatha interjected.

"They've got a better shot than all of us combined," Amahle retorted.

"From the evidence we've gathered so far, the case is closed. One final push, and the truth will come out."

"What's the big secret you two are hiding?" Agatha asked.

"Do you have the spare keys to the school studio?" Erica asked Miss O'Hara, seated with Sophia and Mukenani.

"I kept an extra one somewhere. Why?" Miss O'Hara replied.

"We're planning to set a trap for them," Erica said.

"How do you plan to do that?" Raven asked.

"You'll find out tomorrow," Erica replied.

It was evening in Blacksville. Jessica combed Nadia's hair as they sat on her bed, Shangaan disco music playing softly in the background. The rest of the family had already retired for the night, and the city's streetlights cast a soft glow over the quiet neighbourhood.

"Mother," Nadia began tentatively, "did you give Aunt Mary money again?"

"Yes, and it's the last time she'll ever ask for money, princess."

"Are you sure, mother?"

Jessica playfully tickled Nadia, causing her to giggle and almost fall off the bed. Just then, Jessica's phone beeped.

It's me, again, Mary. My new number. Meet me tomorrow morning in the school studio. Eight-thirty don't be late.

Meanwhile, Agatha folded some clothes into a laundry basket. Sanana discarded a SIM card into the dustbin near the door before flopping onto his bed. Agatha nudged him gently and asked, "Who were you talking to, sweetie?"

"Erica. Can I sleep here tonight?"

"Is someone afraid to go to his room?"

"I'm not scared."

"This is your room too, honey, but please don't snore like Aunt Angela."

"I will snore a little."

At school, Sanana and Erica sat on a bench across from the studio when Mary walked in. A few minutes later, Jessica entered. Sanana and Erica hurried off to their classes, already in session. An audible noise through the speakers hanging above the chalkboard, was heard in every classroom, and offices.

"Why did you want to meet here?" Jessica asked.

"You're the one who called this meeting," Mary retorted.

"I'm tired of your childish games, Mary. What do you want?"

"What games are you talking about?"

"Stop trying to act clever with me, Mary. If you want more money, you won't get it by being greedy."

"Your constant complaining is starting to annoy me, old lady. I didn't call this meeting, but if it makes you feel better, I'm figuring out how to deal with that fool Lisa."

"You're greedy, and you've got no plans."

"For now, I'll take that as a compliment. But next time you say that, I won't be so kind."

"We're running out of time. Get rid of her before the end of this month."

"Let's just kill them both. You live with that woman, so it can't be that hard."

"Don't worry, the little one in my house won't live to see Christmas. Neither will his sister."

Just then, Miss O'Hara, Sanana, Erica, and others walked into the studio.

"I called this meeting," Sanana said.

"Are you spying on our conversation, little man?" Jessica snapped.

"Everyone in the school is listening!"

Learners turned their heads, curiosity etched on their faces as they tried to catch a glimpse of what was happening. Jessica pushed Sanana aside and rushed towards the door. As she swung it open, a scene unfolded before her eyes that sent a shiver down her spine. Several teachers and learners had gathered outside, their hushed whispers adding to the growing tension. Instinctively, Jessica checked the monitor light. It was on; their secret had been exposed.

The school watched as Jessica and Mary were escorted away by the police. Whispers and murmurs filled the hallways as learners tried to piece together what had transpired.

"We did it!" Erica exclaimed. "Aunt Lisa will be so happy."

A few days later, Lisa was released from prison. Family, friends, and staff gathered at the Lingani mansion to celebrate Lisa's freedom.

"I'm sorry," Lisa said to Nadia, who sat alone on the sofa. "I'm sorry, Nadia. I know I've put you through a lot, and I want to make things right."

Nadia turned to face Lisa, her eyes filled with sadness and understanding. "I know you didn't mean to hurt me," Nadia said softly.

Sanana caught everyone's attention by blowing a whistle, and laughter filled the room. Sophia and Raven, having consumed a bit too much alcohol, continued to dance and sing loudly, demanding to hear the same song over and over, TLC' *No Scrubs*," the latest hit from the big cities of America.

"What kind of silly song is that?" *bana*Monde said, seated as a part of the group with Angela, *ba*Eliza, and *ba*Dorothy. "Play some Afro-Jazz. I want to hear Oliver Mtukudzi now."

"Let the kids enjoy their music," *ba*Eliza said.

"But I want Oliver. And I want him now."

"Oliver can wait."

The DJ paused the music, allowing Sanana to make a speech.

"Let me introduce our new principal, Mrs Lingani Lisa," Sanana said, and the room erupted with cheers.

"Congratulations!"

"I can't accept this," Lisa said. "Miss O'Hara deserves this position."

The room fell silent as Lisa's words sank in, turning the cheers into a mix of surprise and admiration. Miss O'Hara placed a hand on Lisa's shoulder. "Thank you, Lisa," she said warmly. "But I've seen your dedication and leadership first-hand."

"No, Miss O'Hara," Lisa insisted. "I'm not ready for this role. I will wait my turn; besides, I still have much to learn from you."

...Sensing the shift in atmosphere, the DJ started playing a soft, uplifting melody. Lisa and Miss O'Hara embraced warmly.

"Thank you all for your kind words and support," Lisa said. "I am honoured to be considered for the position of principal, but Miss O'Hara has worked tirelessly for this school and deserves the opportunity to lead."

They began to hug each other....

"Oh, and one more thing," Lisa added with a laugh. "I've started writing a book. Prison life can inspire new beginnings."

Part III

Lisa is now principal

The year 2013, and it was Wednesday in South Bauleni. It was Grandma Eliza's turn to empty the bin. The lawn rippled under her sheepskin slippers as she walked back to the house where her granddaughter, Lala Ndafenongo was sipping from a glass full of milk. She reached out to remove a milk stain from her granddaughter's blue school shirt.

"You know, child, I used to be just like you. Full of dreams and hopes. Life can change us, but it's important to hold on to those dreams, no matter what."

"What do you mean, Grandma Eliza?"

"When I was your age, back in 1943, I loved going to school." Grandma Eliza glanced around the room; a habit she had when telling a harmless little lie to convey a message.

"Do you really remember all that, Grandma? 1943 was such a long time ago. Even Mother wasn't born yet!"

"1943 may have been a long time ago, but some memories stay with us forever. I enjoyed school, though I wasn't very bright. I was the fastest on the track and field team. When I got pregnant with your mother, I had to give up my dream of being an Olympian."

Lala looked down, trying to piece together the fragments of family history. "I don't remember much about things that happened."

"One day, you will remember, and it will become a special memory for you," Grandma Eliza said, her voice gentle yet firm.

"Grandma Eliza, do you miss Grandpa?"

"What I remember most about him was his kindness. He didn't say much. Now go on to school. Your mother will be down soon, and you've noticed she's been acting tough lately."

"I hate school, Grandma. I hate Beth and Victoria."

Grandma Eliza held Lala's hands and gazed into her eyes. "If only I had some little magic, I would transport myself back to your age. Even though things were different back then, I miss the things I used to do—like going to school, seeing all my friends, and arguing over nothing with Josephat and Godfrey."

"Who are Josephat and Godfrey, Grandma?"

Grandma Eliza smiled, but her eyes held a hint of sorrow as Lala peered into them. She could have sworn she saw a flood of tears that were blocked by something she couldn't explain. The smile meant to comfort her carried pain, sadness, and a broken soul.

"Who are Josephat and Godfrey, Grandma?" She asked again.

"My older brothers. They died a long time ago. The world may have forgotten them, but I still remember them every day." Grandma Eliza sighed. "That was a long time ago, when I was this sweet little girl—not fat like I am now!"

Lala hugged her grandma from behind. "It's OK to be sad, Grandma."

"Time has a strange way of turning us old. I was quite beautiful in my younger years. No wrinkles, hardly any pimples, and I had very long legs like a little cute giraffe."

Lala grinned and glanced at her grandma's fat short, dark legs. Grandma Eliza rose from her chair, refilled her milk cup, took a sip, and sat back down.

"You're my favourite teacher, Grandma."

"I learn so much from you, too. We never stop learning, even with grey hair. Now, off to school. Enjoy every moment. Your time to be called 'grandma' will come. I thank God as I watched my hair turning grey over the years. Be happy. School is beautiful. One day, you won't be allowed within those walls anymore. So, go to school and show Beth and Victoria how smart and beautiful you are."

Lala grabbed an orange from the fridge and shoved it into her school bag. Grandma Eliza helped her zip it up.

"Have a nice day, my little mouse. Remember, school is supposed to be beautiful."

Lala strolled into the living room. The monster television on the wall was on and the host announced the 2012 World Continental Gospel

Contest. The whole stage and arena filled up with confetti drifting from the sky. Fireworks raptured in the heavens in sprays of colour. The winner, a young White girl, held her trophy high. Countless pictures were snapped. Lala blinked and tilted her eyes towards the ceiling, traces of a smile turning up the corner of her mouth. ONE DAY, THAT WILL BE ME.

'Drop that heavy yolk,' said Lisa – her mother. Her heavy but feminine voice spoke with much authority. In her early thirties, she was in an official-looking tailored dress and was coming down the stairs. She was the principal at South Bauleni Secondary School, known as Principal Ndafenongo. Her friends called her Lisa.

"Sweet child, I understand your passion for the gospel contest, but school is important too. It's where you learn the skills and knowledge you need to succeed in life." Lisa wiped her glasses with her sleeve and glanced at Grandma Eliza in the kitchen, finishing yet another cup of milk. "Oh, Mother, your milk drinking is getting on my nerves."

"Child!" Grandma Eliza shouted from the kitchen. "It's a precaution. Milk keeps the doctor away."

Lisa and her daughter backed the car out of the yard and onto the road. For a little while, nobody said anything.

"Stop wasting your energy with that frown on your face," said Lisa. "As long as you live in my house, you'll go to school every morning."

"I won't learn anything," said Lala as she looked at the busy streets. "I hate school."

Lisa pulled over, tapping the steering wheel with both hands. Lala knew she had said something she wasn't supposed to. Lisa and Grandma Eliza had talked about it, too. School was supposed to be beautiful.

"You'll love it, young lady. You don't have a choice."

"Let me join the music class. Please, Mother."

Lisa looked up at the rear-view mirror before driving away. Lala sat stiffly, uninterested, with her school bag on her lap.

"There's no future in music. You'll go to school, stay in your Aunt Ima's class, and when you're older, you'll thank her."

"Grandma let you sing."

"Africans don't win things!"

"Have you ever heard of the Springboks?" said Lala.

"The antelope?"

"No, the South African rugby team. They've won the World Cup multiple times, even in their first appearance."

"Why are you talking about rugby?"

"In 1992, Namibia won Miss Universe in Thailand. Have you heard of Michelle McLean? She was only nineteen."

"We're talking about singing, not some silly beauty pageant. Any beautiful fool can win Miss World."

"I'm not talking about Miss World."

"So, now you think you're smarter than me? And where did you read all that nonsense?"

'I will sing in the best countries of the world. I will sing in Switzerland, Canada, Japan, Germany, Austria, the UK, USA, and Sweden. They will know me, and they will love me a lot.' Lala let out a grin.

'Wipe that silly grin off your face. The only country you are going to sing in is my bathroom.'

'Very soon, Mother, Germany will be your bathroom.'

Back at the house, Grandma Horn was coming out of the kitchen. The sound of the neighbour's door made her trot back to the window. She turned the tap on, but her eyes left the running tap and settled on a young woman in the next yard, which was always unkempt. Francesca stood leaning against the gutter. She was crunching into her cereal.

"Do you have to eat standing up, child?"

Francesca, the only child of a single mother, had turned nineteen. She was a fresh-faced young girl, beautiful, dubious and of questionable character – and she feared no one. She looked up. Her gorgeous face broke into a serious frown. Young Francesca does not seem to be fond of the old lady. She said to herself that Grandma Horn was a neighbourhood nuisance and that she should mind her own business. Grandma Horn had vowed to herself to bring Francesca to righteousness.

"Good morning, Francesca!" she shouted, holding onto the burglar bar with her left hand.

Francesca pursed her lips. She didn't have anything nice to say to the old lady, but she managed to mutter, "You're lucky you're very old." She got up from the stoop and sat on the steps with her legs crossed. The morning breeze tousled her hair.

"Francesca, my dear. Good morning, sweet child."

Francesca scowled and glanced at Grandma Eliza, but she knew it wasn't worth wasting more time on the old lady. She tied her robe and slammed the door shut.

"I want to be your friend!" Grandma Eliza called after her.

Somewhere in a country farmhouse lay an old man still fast asleep. He was a retired music teacher and an active choirmaster at the local church. A Toyota sedan was parked under the shade alongside three tractors and an old black pickup truck. The area was sloping, with lush greenery all around. There was a chicken coop next to the house. Behind the house, a maize field was starting to grow.

Grandpa Sylvester lived with his daughter, Eva, and granddaughter, Pulelo. Eva worked as a teacher at Riverweed, while Pulelo attended South Bauleni and was best friends with Lala Ndafenongo. Pulelo was ready for school, sitting in front of the turned-off television. Eva came from her room, buttoning up her white formal shirt and tucking it into her skirt.

"Where is your grandfather?" she asked, squinting at the white wall clock.

"He hasn't woken up yet. I will be late for school, Mum!"

Eva went into her father's open room.

"You are still sleeping, Father. She will be late!"

"Why do these born-frees need to be dropped at school? During our younger years, we walked to school, even when it was scorching hot."

"Because you grew up in the village. Grandpa never had a car, and he was poor."

"All right, OK, give me a second."

"Please, Father, hurry up. She will be late for school, and drive slowly."

Grandpa Sylvester began dressing as Eva left the house. He then went to his bedroom window and peered out at his daughter's car driving onto the dusty gravel road.

"Let me make up for the last five minutes I wasted last night watching TV," he said as he exhaled and curled back into bed.

Pulelo glanced at the clock on the wall. It read 06:33. She ambled to her grandfather's room and threw herself on the bed. Grandpa Sylvester lay on his back, wide awake, listening to an old disco tune.

"Grandpa, I will be late for school," Pulelo said.

Pulelo stepped aside. She loved watching his huge jackets from behind. They were twice his size, and Pulelo laughed about it with her friends at school. She said her grandfather's jackets looked funny from the back.

The cold morning wind swayed the fields as they made their way along the gravel road connecting their house to the tarmac road. It was a fifteen-minute drive, and when they reached the T-junction, he turned left, heading into town.

"Tell me about the book you're writing?" Grandpa Sylvester asked.

"You're going to love it," Pulelo replied.

"I can't wait for everyone to talk about your book. I'll be the proudest grandpa."

A big sign saying "South Bauleni Secondary School" stood near the entrance. The school had large trees and a big lawn. The building was painted in grey and yellow. The school grounds were clean, and the paving stones were arranged in black and yellow patterns.

"I remember when I went to school here," Grandpa Sylvester reminisced. "It was in bad shape back then. There was graffiti all over the walls and broken windows. It used to be called South Bauleni Community School."

"Riverweed is prettier," Pulelo commented.

"But Riverweed is for rich kids. Private schools are expensive," Grandpa said.

"I like it here. We have everything we need, and our teachers are nice," Pulelo said happily.

"We should be grateful to the learners who attended school in the 90s. They helped make this school what it is today. Even your principal was part of that group, along with two white kids from Riverweed," Grandpa said, ending the conversation.

In the classroom, Teacher Ima was busy marking her learners' workbooks. Ima and Lisa were blood sisters, with Ima being the younger sister. The classroom was spacious and decorated in yellow and green colours. The eighth graders greeted Teacher Ima as they entered and took their seats. From how Ima was marking the workbooks, it was clear that she loved her job. With some soulful music playing from her phone, she worked with real passion for education.

"Good morning," Ima greeted. "Let's mark the register. Pulelo Banda."

"Present!" Pulelo shouted from the front row.

"Lala Ndafenongo."

"Coming," the class captain, Dominic Chika, replied. Dominic, a boy with a very, very big head, sat near the door and took his duties seriously. Lala arrived at the door. "Come in," Dominic said after a knock.

"Good morning, Chika," Lala said, facing the class captain as was the school tradition to greet the class captain first.

"Please take your seat," he instructed, holding his head high. This was one reason he volunteered to be the class captain.

"Good morning, Aunt Ima," Lala said, her pink school bag hanging from her shoulders.

"I would prefer if you address me as Teacher Ima and next time, don't be late for my class. Go to your seat and put away those headphones."

Lala placed her bag on the table and stashed her earphones inside. Her bag was painted in skunk drawings. Despite her grandmother's warnings about skunks being terrible animals, Lala admired their bravery and persistence.

Ima stood up from her chair and walked among the desks of the well-behaved children.

"Lala!" She placed the test paper face down on the table. "I'm worried about you. You got a U in the last test and now a simple G. What's going on, child?"

"I'm sorry."

"How can I help you if you're not meeting me halfway? If I don't see any improvement in your grades, I'll have no choice but to send you to Mr Derek."

All the learners, even the ones who thought the teacher was kind, went silent. Mr Derek was in charge of keeping the school clean, so learners who returned from there had to see things differently.

"Please, Teacher Ima, I promise. I'll work on my grades and never be late to class."

"I can't keep teaching someone who doesn't show improvement. That would make me a bad teacher."

When it was breaktime, Lala and Pulelo walked to the back of their classroom near the school hall. It was the time of year when the mango trees had ripe fruit.

"Why are you always late?" Pulelo asked Lala. "You come to school with your mother."

"I'm never late, Pulelo. I like it when everyone looks at me when I walk in."

"How does it feel?"

Pulelo patted Lala's shoulder. Two little girls, Beth and Victoria, stood facing them. They wore blue netball uniforms and white sneakers. Victoria was white, and Beth had albinism. They were one grade ahead. The music class was the only class where learners from different grades could be together.

"Look at the principal's daughter, the so-called singer, and this other little one who seems to have skipped a grade," Victoria said.

"I never skipped a grade," Pulelo argued.

"Did you hear that, Beth? Pulelo never skipped a grade."

Victoria laughed, which always sounded like a sneeze through her nostrils. The two netball stars started smiling at each other. They brought many awards to the school and were good at playing netball. They travelled around the country. They played in Cameroon the previous year and never stopped bragging about it.

Plan for Global Fame

Under the open sky, the school day began with the usual assembly. Learners lined up in an orderly manner in front of Lisa and her staff. The principal's approving smile was directed at the netball team, silently recognising their hard work. Victoria, the captain, stood in front, with Beth and the rest of the team behind her, all putting on matching pink Nike sneakers.

"This year, there's so much happening," the principal's voice echoed through the open space. "We're going to have a netball match against Riverweed. I know our girls will do just fine."

The netball team stood tall among the nods and agreements, feeling even more determined thanks to the principal's belief in them. Pulelo couldn't help but stare at the netball stars, especially Beth and Victoria.

"I don't like them," Pulelo said.

"They're pretty," Lala replied.

"We're pretty too, but we don't act like that."

There was a quiet pause, interrupted by the distant sounds of their schoolmates. Then Lala spoke again, "Everyone knows them, and Mother likes them."

"One day, I'll be the most famous writer in the whole world," Pulelo declared.

"And I'll be the most famous gospel singer ever," Lala added.

Lala and Pulelo might not have been netball stars, but they were destined for greatness in their own unique ways.

"We will also have Miss South Bauleni and our National Gospel Contest," the principal continued.

The mention of the gospel contest provoked a ripple of anticipation among the assembled learners. It was an important occasion that promised local recognition and the opportunity to compete on more prominent stages.

"This contest is very, very important," the principal emphasised, "because it leads to the African Gospel Contest and then the World Continental Gospel Contest. Be prepared and join."

After the school assembly, the learners crowded the corridor as they returned to their first class. In class, Lala searched through her school bag without finding what she was looking for. She asked Pulelo, "Hey, Pulelo, how many chapters have you written so far?"

"One," Pulelo replied.

"Since last year! How many pages?"

"Only seven, but I want to stop there and start chapter two."

"When will I get to read it?"

"One day, you'll get to read it. Not even my mum has read it yet."

When school ended, it started raining. Beth and Victoria hurried back to their classroom. Many learners had already gone home. Lala and Pulelo discussed the upcoming netball game between their schools. They walked past the classroom where Beth and Victoria were playing catch. Beth threw the ball to Victoria and then blocked Pulelo's path. Beth poked her middle finger on Pulelo's forehead, itching for a fight. Beth grabbed Pulelo's hair and threw her to the ground. Mr Derek, the strict caretaker who never tolerated nonsense like littering, appeared in the doorway like a hero. He pushed through the crowd of learners and led them to the principal's office.

Lisa was locking the office when Mr Derek arrived with the fighters. She noticed two of Lala's missing buttons and awaited Mr Derek's explanation of the situation – the kids were in a fight and fighting at South Bauleni meant serious punishment.

She was about to unlock her office when she decided to keep the keys in her handbag. "Let them mop the school."

"But Mum!" Lala protested. "Beth and Victoria started it!"

"She started it!" Beth retorted.

"Yes, Principal Ndafenongo," Victoria added, "Pulelo and Lala started it."

"Your punishment begins now. Take them away, Mr Derek."

Mr Derek led them to the laundry room and handed them a mop. Beth and Lala cleaned the school hall, while Pulelo and Victoria cleaned the hallway.

Grandma Eliza was preparing lunch around three when Lisa arrived. Grandma Eliza glanced around, looking for her granddaughter.

"She's been involved in a fight at school. She's facing punishment," said Lisa.

"When did my granddaughter start fighting?"

Lisa grabbed a cold drink from the fridge and went to her room. There, she lay on the bed and turned on the TV. Grandma Eliza followed and sat across from her.

"She's been talking about how unhappy she is at school because of Beth and Victoria. You need to do something. Your daughter is not happy."

"In every school, there are bullies. It's something we must deal with in our lives. Why are you making lunch now?"

Grandma Eliza didn't answer as she went to do her chores. Lisa's phone rang...

"Fighting at school?" asked Pulelo's mother.

"Can you believe it, Eva? It was my duty to set an example."

"You did the right thing. We are losing authority over our children."

"I will pick them up later and drop Pulelo off."

The streets were crowded with traffic. Pulelo and Lala sat on a bench outside the school gate. Beth and Victoria sat on the other side, not speaking to each other. Mr Derek and two security men were conversing at a distance. Beth and Victoria were still angry, their silence hinting at a desire for another fight.

When Lisa's car parked, Pulelo got up. Lala stayed seated. She wasn't mad at Beth and Victoria anymore, but at her mother – for not giving her a chance to explain and making her wait for two hours. Lala grabbed her school bag and went to join her mother in the car. Beth and Victoria remained seated.

"Get in," Lisa said to Beth and Victoria.

"Their parents will pick them up!" Lala protested.

"Get in."

Beth swung her school bag onto her shoulder and gripped the door handle. "Can we go in, Principal Ndafenongo?" Beth asked.

"Get in, now!"

The streets in the nearby neighbourhoods were silent. Lisa dropped off Beth and Victoria, who lived in Riverweed. She couldn't respond to the children, even when they thanked her. She continued down the gravel road that led to the farmhouse. Grandpa Sylvester was feeding the pigs when Lisa arrived with Pulelo. He always fed them at five o'clock before letting them sleep. Eva hadn't returned from work yet. Lisa was about to leave when Grandpa Sylvester asked her to wait. He ran to the chicken house and returned with a white rooster.

"Please accept it. At least for the trouble," he said. "Eva asked me to give it to you."

"Tell Eva I said thank you."

"How is Eliza?"

"My mum is fine. Can I go now?"

They watched Lisa and Lala drive away. Lala sat stiffly.

"Stop sitting like a driver in my car and move your elbow from my space!"

"They started it, Mother."

"No child of mine should use violence to solve a problem. God gave you that big head. Use it!"

"Please, Mother, why are you so mean to me? Everything I do these days annoys you."

"You're my only child, and I love you so much. Everything I do is for you and your future."

"I don't like the way you talk to me sometimes."

Lisa looked around but was too proud to admit her daughter was right.

It wasn't completely dark yet. Grandma Eliza was waiting at the front door, knitting. Young Francesca sat on the steps of the house next door. Grandma Eliza had tried to start a conversation, but Francesca didn't seem interested.

"I was thinking, Francesca, my dear," Grandma Eliza said warmly. "I was thinking..."

"Old woman," Francesca interrupted, "leave me alone!"

"I just want to be your friend..."

"Find someone your age!" Francesca yelled as she slammed the door.

"I just want to be your friend..."

Grandma Eliza sighed and turned towards the gate as Lisa pulled in with her car, parking in its usual spot. She turned off the engine and opened the door, giving her daughter a stern look. "Are you stuck on that seat?"

"Did you put something on it?"

"Ha!" She laughed. "Get out of my car and bring that silly chicken." She walked towards the door and passed by her mother. "Talk to your granddaughter. Talk some sense into her."

Grandma Eliza started shaking her legs, with her hands resting on her knees. She looked down and began humming a local tune. Lala stood still a few steps away from the car, wearing a smirk and holding a chicken in her left hand. Lisa's mind started racing, unsure what to say to her beloved mother.

"Okay," Lisa hissed as she entered the house. "We shall see."

"Yes, we shall see," Grandma Eliza said.

Once she was gone, Grandma Eliza turned to her granddaughter and pulled her close. Lala sat on her lap, but Grandma Eliza stood her up. "You're getting heavier each day. What have you been eating that I don't know about?"

"Grandma," Lala said, "I'm hungry."

"Wait a minute! Is that chicken from Sly?"

"Yes, Grandma. Grandpa Sylvester gave it to us."

"What do you think? Should I boil it or let the oven take care of it?"

Lala smiled. "I'm hungry, Grandma."

"I cooked rice and beans."

Later that night, Grandma Eliza and the rest of the family got ready for bed. She wore her favourite nightgown while Lala lay in bed, scrolling through her phone.

"Beth and Victoria," Grandma Eliza began. "Back in my younger days, I would've dealt with pests like them by squashing them with my foot. Christina and I would crush them. Tell me, how have you dealt with those two troublemakers?" She threw punches in the air and kicked. "Will it last long?"

"What do you mean, Grandma? What will last long?"

"The beating you gave them."

"They are strong, Grandma, especially Beth."

"So, you didn't win?"

"Pulelo is not strong."

"You lost, but don't worry, their time will come. Between us, I am very proud of you. Don't let anyone bully you. I never did when I was your age. Now go to your room and have a peaceful night."

Lisa peeked into the room. Lala blew a kiss to her grandma. "Good night, Grandma."

Once Lala was out of sight, Lisa sat next to her mother, who turned to face the other side of the bed, looking at herself in the mirror.

"Good night, Mother." Lisa went to her room and lay back on the bed. She pulled out her phone...

"Thank you, Eva," Lisa said. "The chicken is so big!"

"What chicken?"

"When I brought your daughter home, your father gave me a chicken. It was a way of saying thank you."

"You're so lucky. We both know it's meant for your mother," Eva giggled.

"Did you know she planned to cook it as soon as we arrived? She even asked my daughter if she should boil it or put it in the microwave!" Lisa laughed.

Back at the farmhouse, Grandpa Sylvester was watching boxing on TV. Pulelo lay on the other side when Eva came from her room and stood behind her father.

"Why did you lie about the chicken, Father?"

"That mean lady wouldn't have taken it for my Eliza."

"So, it wasn't meant for Lisa?"

"No, child, it was meant for Eliza, not your mean friend."

Grandma Eliza's Lively Reggae Party

Grandma Eliza was in high spirits, a smile lighting up her face as she opened the milk carton and took a sip. She playfully pulled the kitchen curtain halfway, her eyes twinkling with mischief. Outside, Francesca went to throw away the rubbish. They made eye contact, but Francesca, lost in her own world, went back inside without acknowledging Grandma Eliza's wave. The old lady then danced into the living room, where her favourite reggae song by Lucky Dube, "Remember Me," was playing at full blast. Grandpa Sylvester, always ready for a dance, joined in from the other side of the room.

"Get us some more drinks, my old clock," Grandpa Sylvester whispered to Grandma Eliza, his hips swaying to the reggae beat. She went to the kitchen and returned with two cartons of fresh milk. She handed one to Grandpa Sylvester and turned up the volume. Their unspoken understanding and shared love for reggae were evident in their actions.

"This reggae song is so catchy, my old cloak," Grandpa Sylvester said, sipping his milk and dancing in place, shaking his head like a mad man. He sang along with the music in his tenor voice, his eyes twinkling joyfully. Grandma Eliza joined him, belting out the lyrics.

They didn't hear Lisa's car pull up. The loud music from inside the house excited Lala, and she joined in the singing and dancing. Lisa turned off the radio, but her phone rang before she could say anything. That made Grandma Eliza to gently push Grandpa Sylvester towards the door. He got into his old truck and drove away. Lisa had always been vocal about how Grandpa Sylvester was a bad influence on Grandma Eliza.

Later that evening at the farmhouse, Grandpa Sylvester sat next to his granddaughter, who was typing on her mother's laptop. He peered at the laptop screen.

"How is your book coming along, princess?"

"Guess what, Grandpa. I have started with chapter two!" Pulelo said, her voice filled with so much excitement.

"You will grow into a great writer. Now, where is your mother?"

"She's preparing supper. Do you want to read what I have written?"

"This should be your work, honey. I will only read it once it's complete," Grandpa Sylvester said.

"Once you finish that book, ask me anything," said Eva, bringing in food.

"Thank you, Mother. I will ask you a..."

"Not now, only once you finish the first draft. How many words do you plan to write?"

"I was thinking of 17,000 words."

"Wow, that's quite a lot, but I'm proud of you." Eva kept smiling as if she was thinking of something more important to say. "Now tell me, what is your book about?"

"It's about a son who goes all the way to save his dying father."

"He may have been a good father," said Grandpa Sylvester.

"He was not."

"He may have been a good son?" said Grandpa Sylvester.

"He was not."

"Why is he doing all that then?" asked Eva.

"I have not yet figured that out, Mother." Pulelo skipped off to her room.

"Did he save him?" Grandpa Sylvester shouted.

"I don't know, Grandpa. I have not even reached the end yet," Pulelo shouted from her room. "But I have a better idea for a new story. This one is not working out so well."

"Well, you can always change it, honey!" Eva shouted.

Grandpa Sylvester chuckled, his deep laughter filling the room. "I can't believe how ridiculous this book is! The characters keep returning to life after dying; it's like a never-ending cycle of resurrection."

"Maybe they're ghosts."

The next day at school, Lala and Pulelo worked on their Life Science project in the library. Children sat with their friends in groups, but Pulelo and Lala sat near the door, their backs against the wall. Mrs Anushka, a happy librarian who knew the library in and out, was busy doing her nails. She always had a smile on her face. The last time Pulelo asked for a specific novel, Mrs Anushka shouted, "Number 107."

Mrs Anushka was a Japanese middle-aged lady with pictures of her family all over her table. There were pictures of her, her husband, two sons, and what looked like her mother. She was always busy doing her hair or nails or calling out numbers.

A boy shouted from the shelves, "Mrs Anushka, I need a book about crop farming!"

Without missing a beat, Mrs Anushka replied, "Number 22!"

The noise at the library entrance could only mean one thing – the netball team, the South Bauleni Girls (known as THE GIRLS), were causing trouble again. They were all wearing yellow and black sneakers, and they looked adorable. They greeted Mrs Anushka, who didn't like The Girls. She made it clear – she didn't want them in the library because they were loud and never read anything. Lala and Pulelo became quiet. The Girls surrounded them.

"I'll go first," said Beth. "Now tell me, Pulelo, where is your father? Oh, I heard he left."

"Stop it, Beth," Lala snapped. "Her father died."

The girls giggled as if being dead was funny. Pulelo started crying.

"Now tell me, Victoria," said Beth. "What do you call a child without a father?"

"A bastard, Beth. A simple bastard," Victoria replied. The rest of the gang chuckled.

"Girls, stop it," Mrs Anushka said as she stood at the door and looked at The Girls. Beth pushed Pulelo's book aside.

After they left, The Girls discussed strategies to beat the tough Riverweed Girls' netball team in front of the library. They heard rumours that Lilian might join their school before the match, giving them hope for victory. Beth was determined to have Lala join their team despite previous failed attempts.

The next day after the break, Lisa was in her office when Grandma Eliza walked in. She brought some homemade food and placed it on the table.

Lisa's silence made it clear that she wasn't happy about her mother coming to school.

"What do you want, Mother?" Lisa asked.

"You're getting too skinny. Look at your sister, Ima; she's a real African woman."

Lala sensed her grandma's presence and rushed into the office, hugging her from behind. She then sat on the principal's table, facing her grandmother.

"Get off my table, Lala. Go back to class," Lisa scolded.

"Go ahead," Grandma Eliza said.

A few minutes later, Grandma Eliza went to Ima's class to share the food. All the learners stood up except for Lala.

"I'll take care of this," Grandma Eliza said, pushing Ima aside. She took the chalk from Ima and went to the chalkboard. Lala seemed to enjoy her grandma's presence.

"Teacher!" called a boy from the middle row.

"Call me Grandma Eliza."

"Grandma Eliza," he said, "tell us a story."

"Let me tell you a story about my youngest daughter, your teacher."

Ima stood up from her seat and pleaded with her mother not to share embarrassing and exaggerated stories. The last time she talked about it; she spoke about her oldest daughter and their childhood poverty.

"Please, Mother, these are children."

Grandma Eliza whispered in her daughter's ear. "There's one condition."

"More milk?" Ima asked.

"I need two boxes. Today, Ima!"

"Okay, Mother. Now go home."

Grandma Eliza glanced at her wristwatch. "I'll wait in the parking area. It is almost lunchtime."

After school, Grandma Eliza, Ima, Lisa, Lala, and Pulelo watched Grandpa Sylvester parks the car and step out with even more style.

"Wow, your grandpa dresses so cool," Lala said to Pulelo.

"Yeah, but sometimes his jackets are too big," Pulelo said.

Lisa looked at Grandpa Sylvester disapprovingly before heading to her car. Grandpa Sylvester shook Ima's hand but didn't pay much attention to the kids. Instead, he went to stand before Grandma Eliza and gave her a long hug.

"Now, my old clock," he said, "do you still remember your solo part? We're going to sing that song again this Sunday."

"Oh, Syl, you're so sweet," Grandma Eliza said with a big smile, making Lisa shout angrily.

"Let's go, Mother!"

"Go ahead, my old clock," he said. "Your daughter will love me someday."

"I love you, Grandpa Sylvester," Lala said. He knelt and pinched Lala's cheeks, saying, "Keep practising! You have a powerful voice. One day, you'll be a superstar."

"Thank you, Grandpa Sylvester."

The next day after school, Grandma Eliza sat knitting while the large TV on the wall remained off. She hummed to the music playing from a massive sound system next to the TV. A half-empty jar of milk was on the table, with a long pink straw she used to sip the liquid every few seconds. Lala dropped her school bag on the sofa beside her grandmother and plopped down.

"How was school, my little mouse?"

"I hate school, Grandma."

Grandma Eliza took a long sip from her straw, pausing their conversation for several seconds.

"Take it easy, Grandma."

Grandma Eliza placed the jar on the table with a soft thud and let out a burp. Lala laid her head on her grandma's lap, and who stroked her grandchild's hair.

"Grandma, I want to sing."

"School should always come first in a child's life, and everything else will follow," Grandma Eliza said.

Lisa tossed her black handbag onto the table. Stood behind her mother. "Hello, Mother."

"Hello, my fearless sheep leaf."

"That sounds sweet, but don't you think I'm too old for that?"

"You are still my little Lisa."

Lisa sat down, keeping a closer look at her mother and daughter.

"Grandma, tell me something. What did you want to say about Aunt Ima in class?"

"To see her face," said Grandma Eliza. "I wanted to punish her. Did you know that your stingy Aunt Ima refused to give me money? Me, her mother!"

Lisa remembered when she refused to give her mother money for the new milk on TV.

"Mother," Lisa said, "did you do that to me because I refused to give you money, too? You talked about our poverty in front of the learners because I refused to give you money for your obsession with milk. Do you want to taste every new milk product on the market?"

"I did that because you don't like my friend, Syl. He is a good man, and he fought for this country."

"Mr Sylvester is a bad influence. Mr Sylvester still needs time to grow."

"You don't understand, my child. Syl is the nicest and funniest man I have ever met. Do you want me to die young?"

"Come on, Mother," Lisa said. "Die young?"

"I love Grandpa Sylvester," said Lala.

"He's not your grandpa."

Later that day, Grandpa Sylvester was doing push-ups. Pulelo stood by the dog, counting to six. Eva sat under the tree, reading the newspaper. Suddenly, the dog started barking.

"Grandpa," said Pulelo, "you ended up in the hospital last time you did that. Please stop!"

"You're right, my princess. Six push-ups are quite an accomplishment." He kissed his weak biceps and pretended to be a boxer, throwing a few punches. "Now go change. We're going to South Bauleni. I'm in great shape to see your grandmother."

Pulelo didn't bother asking because she knew they would see Grandma Eliza. She would also get to see her friend. Grandma Eliza came out of her room wearing a fancy, old-fashioned dress. She looked at herself in the hand mirror and made some final touches before opening the door.

Grandpa Sylvester wore a formal white suit and a black cowboy hat. He held a single rose, which he gave to Grandma Eliza, who sniffed it like they do in romance movies.

"I'll leave you here as collateral," he said to Pulelo. "Now go inside and join your friend."

"She's sleeping in her mother's room," Grandma Eliza said. "But don't worry, sweetheart. Go to the sitting room and watch whatever you want. Your friend will join you soon."

"Can you wake her up, Grandma Eliza?" Pulelo asked.

"No, sweetheart, but I know she'll come down soon. Now go, there's some boiled milk on the stove."

They couldn't allow Pulelo to complain further, so they held hands and quietly walked to the car. Pulelo poured herself a glass of milk and turned on the television. It didn't take long for Lala, who was still half asleep, to join her.

"They've gone out," Pulelo said.

"Let me guess. He left you here as collateral," Lala laughed.

"What does he mean by that? He always says that when he leaves me here."

"I wish I knew, but I understand. Mother will be furious. I can't wait."

Grandma Eliza and Grandpa Sylvester parked their car at an abandoned warehouse. The warehouse used to produce block salt for livestock.

"Why here, Syl? I thought you were taking me somewhere expensive," Grandma Eliza said.

"This is much better," he said, leading her into the building. "You'll love it here. Do you know where I get my inspiration from? I write amazing lyrics here."

"No wonder you're such an amazing choirmaster. You find inspiration here?"

"Yes, my old clock."

Two unlit candles sat on a table in the small room next to the entrance. In the centre of the room, there was a set of tables. Two silver plates, a bottle of wine, and two wine glasses.

"You did all this for me, Syl!" Grandma Eliza said, "Oh, Syl, I love it."

The busy old man took a portable radio from his suit pocket, and Dolly Parton's voice soon filled the room.

"Silver and Gold," Grandma Eliza said. "This song brings back so many beautiful memories. It's a classic."

"I love this song," he said dutifully. "You always bring out the best in me."

Meanwhile, Lala and Pulelo were in the backyard. Francesca was sitting on a mat, browsing on her phone.

"Francesca," Lala called out, "Good afternoon!"

"Are you people crazy coming from that annoying yard?" Francesca scowled at Lala and Pulelo.

"Why is she so mad?" Pulelo whispered.

Before Lala could respond, Lisa arrived with a chair and some corn she was eating.

"Where is she?"

"Grandma Eliza is with Grandpa Sylvester," Lala said.

"He's not your grandfather!"

The last time they went out, Grandma Eliza returned with a throbbing headache. She couldn't say it, but Sly made her drink snifters. Three months ago, she came back close to midnight. It was more reason for Lisa to ban the choirmaster from sneaking out with her mother. She said that when he and Grandma Eliza were together, they attracted too much trouble.

Lisa's phone rang, and the police officer asked her to rush to the station. The officer said a warehouse had caught fire. Eva came, too. Grandma Eliza and Grandpa Sylvester acted like it was no big deal and wanted to leave.

"Please take them home," the officer said.

"I'm sorry," Eva said to Lisa. "I don't know what I'm going to do with this old man."

Miss South Bauleni

It was a good Saturday morning. The school hall was filled with excitement as the contestants—Catherine, Joana, Marita, Suzie, Katie, Evia, Patricia, and Foibe—happily took their seats. Their parents, who had dedicated countless hours to their preparation, sat so proudly. The hall, decorated with colourful posters, was a testament to the event's grandeur. On the stage, a big pink poster proudly proclaimed, MISS SOUTH BAULENI 2013.

At the stroke of eight, the hall doors swung open, and the learners began to fill the space in an orderly manner. Pulelo, the host, took to the stage, and spoke to the microphone.

"The most beautiful day is here! Good morning, parents, teachers, and fellow learners. We have all been awaiting this day. Who among these beautiful girls do you think will be our next Miss South Bauleni 2013? Our next queen!"

Pulelo looked around to make sure everything was going well. The hall seemed to resonate with her excitement. She then smiled at her mother, Eva Banda, seated next to Lisa in the crowd. Eva smiled back.

"Now, my dear learners, let me introduce our contestants for Miss South Bauleni 2013. But before that, let me welcome the sweetest voice, my best friend, our very own Lala Ndafenongo, for a special dedication to the contestants and all of us here."

Lala strolled up to the microphone. Like everyone else, she was dressed in pink shorts and a T-shirt written the event. She tapped the microphone and said, "Hello, everyone, say hi to my grandmother. Grandma Eliza!"

Grandma Eliza waved to the audience, blowing kisses all the way to the microphone. Lisa, who was busy on her phone, dropped it into her lap and whispered to Ima at the back, "How did she even get on the program?"

"I called you yesterday. You didn't answer," Ima replied.

Lisa was about to yell at her sister, but the crowd's cheers drew her attention back to the stage. Grandma Eliza rested her elbow on her granddaughter's head, who appeared to be carrying a heavy load, eliciting more laughter from the crowd.

"Let me say a few words," Grandma Eliza said, holding the microphone with both hands.

This gave Lala the chance to create some distance between them. The crowd noticed and chuckled. Grandma Eliza unplugged the microphone and held it with her left hand. She was going to lean on her granddaughter, but by then, Lala had moved a metre away.

"My family doesn't know this," Grandma Eliza began, "but as a teenager, I almost won a pageant. I would have won if it hadn't been for that judge who disliked me. I walked incredibly slowly, like a lion stalking its prey."

"Incredibly slow!" Lisa muttered. "What does that even mean?"

Lala leaned in and whispered, "Grandma, can we just sing?"

"Hold on, my little mouse," she whispered into the microphone.

Lisa glanced at her sister and muttered, "Do something, Ima. This is all your fault!"

"Leave Mother alone," Ima replied.

"It's not a duet, dear," Grandma Eliza said. "It's a vocal trio. Get up here, my choirmaster!"

Grandpa Sylvester strutted onto the stage with a long red orchestral baton, looking sharp in his black suit. The audience burst into laughter.

"Oh no, this is so embarrassing," Eva groaned.

On the other hand, Ima was having a blast, laughing and clapping. Lisa shot her a glare. "Why are you so happy?"

"Chill, sis. Mother is a natural entertainer," Ima said.

"Ima, get those two clowns off the stage," Lisa ordered.

"Leave them alone. It'll be even more embarrassing if we try to stop them," Eva said.

Grandpa Sylvester nudged Lala aside and stood so close to Grandma Eliza, while Lala moved to stand the other side.

"Hold on a second," Grandpa Sylvester said to Grandma Eliza. "We're not singing our planned song. We're doing 'Amazing Grace.'"

"Why 'Amazing Grace'?" Lala asked. "Isn't that a funeral song, Grandma?"

"I love Amazing Grace," Grandma Eliza said. "Syl, your taste in music has no limit."

Grandpa Sylvester took charge, turning his back to the audience. He was so good as a choirmaster. He could lead the choir to greatness.

"Lala, you're going to sing the second verse all by yourself, like we did at church when the apostle visited," he said.

He flicked his baton and led them through the song. Grandma Eliza, Lala, and he sang beautifully. After the song, they took a bow, and the crowd showed their appreciation. The host then took the stage.

"That song was amazing," she said.

"Well, what do you expect? It was Amazing Grace after all," Beth said, sitting next to Victoria and her friends in the front row.

"Let's give a round of applause to the three singers for that beautiful performance," the host announced.

The applause was warm, allowing the host to continue.

"Now, let me invite the nine contestants to the stage. They need to introduce themselves, right?"

The boys at the back shouted in agreement. The contestants made their way from backstage, walking across the stage and back again before lining up in a row. The audience erupted into a standing ovation.

Grandma Eliza, Lala, and Grandpa Sylvester had taken their seats in the far-left front row. The contestants began introducing themselves one by one.

"My name is Catherine Kani," the first contestant said.

Catherine's parents sat in the middle row; her mother wore a fake white crown she had bought from a Chinese shop. From the proud grin on her face, she seemed to be the proudest mother on Earth. She wrapped her left arm around her husband's shoulders and whispered with a kiss, "Catty is the next Michelle."

"Certainly," said the husband.

Catherine continued, "I'm fourteen and in grade 9 at South Bauleni. I decided to join Miss South Bauleni because I want to make many changes for myself and my fellow learners. I hope to achieve great things through this platform, discover my true calling, and give it my all. I enjoy watching netball and soccer, attending church, and meeting friends. Thank you."

Catherine moved to the edge of the stage, greeted by cheers from the crowd. She posed for everyone and then returned to join the other contestants. Joana, the next participant, took three steps and struck a fantastic pose – she couldn't stop smiling.

"My name is Joana. I'm thirteen years old and in grade 8 at South Bauleni. I live in South Bauleni with my mum, dad, and our cat, Winnie. My mum, dad, and Winnie are all right there," Joana said, blowing a kiss to a couple who could be her grandparents. A shiny Persian cat, Winnie, watched from Joana's mum's lap. "We go to church every Sunday, and I sing in the school and church choir. I'm happy to be here."

The next contestant stepped forward.

"My name is Marita Bonita. I turned thirteen last week, and my mother gave me a huge bear for my birthday. I named him Mark. I love swimming. Our backyard has a swimming pool, and my brother and I swim every weekend. I've always dreamed of being swimmer."

"My name is Suzie Henry. I live in Riverweed with my mum and dad. I'm an only child," Suzie said, smiling at her parents, who looked young enough to be in secondary school. "I'll be turning thirteen this August. My favourite big pageant is Miss Earth. One day, I want to be Miss Earth Water because water is life."

"My name is Katie Jacobs. I like to think I'm Kate Winslet. She's my favourite actress, and I love her so much. My mum says I have a beautiful smile and will become a great queen one day. Every year, we watch Miss Namibia as a family. I love how beautiful the girls look. My mum told me I'd make a great queen; I believe her because she's my best friend. I joined Miss South Bauleni because I want to make a difference. A very, very big difference."

"I'm Evia Tumelo! Tumelo means 'faith.' I'm fifteen and live with my dad and Grandma Cecilia. I joined Miss South Bauleni because I love competing, and my goal is to become Miss Namibia!"

"My name is Florence Billy. I live with my grandparents. They always give me good food and encourage me to do well in school. My grandma even reads me bedtime stories every night. I joined Miss South Bauleni to inspire other kids to believe in themselves and reach for their dreams."

"My name is Patricia LM. I'm thirteen years old and in grade eight at South Bauleni. I live with my parents and my two brothers. My brothers go to Riverweed. My mum thinks I look like Michelle McLean. She says I have her smile, her height, and her eyes. That's cool because Michelle is an amazing woman. I have four pictures of her in my room and a photo album dedicated to her. One day, I want to be a great queen just like her. That's why I joined Miss South Bauleni, so I can improve myself and win Miss University."

"She meant to say Miss Universe," said Beth to Victoria.

"Why?" Victoria asked.

"She is talking about Michelle. My common sense tells me she meant to say Miss Universe."

"My name is Foibe Sheehama. I live in Riverweed with my dad, two brothers, and sister. My mum died three years ago, and Dad misses her a lot. We miss her, but we know she's in heaven with God. When not studying or doing homework, I enjoy singing in front of the mirror or watching my favourite TV show, *Seventh Heaven*. I decided to join Miss South Bauleni because I want to show the world who I am."

The contestants made their way back, receiving quiet applause and music.

"This round is my favourite," the host announced. "Each contestant will wear their favourite sports uniform."

The contestants showcased their sporty looks. The crowd cheered for each contestant, finding it hard to pick a favourite. Joana impressed the audience with her white karate outfit and poses. Katie strutted in dark wrestling attire, complemented by golden boots with her initials, KJ. Catherine, Suzie, Evia, and Foibe followed in their respective sports uniforms...

The sportswear round was a hit for Florence and Patricia LM. Florence rocked a stylish white Nike tennis dress with relaxed mesh pleats on the side of the skirt, a trendy V-neck, and a ribbed waistband. The dress featured crisscross stripes on the front of the skirt, sleeves, and sides, making it stand out. To complete her look, she held a bright yellow tennis ball and a vintage MacGregor paddle racket in one hand.

Patricia LM opted for a fierce boxing costume called Dreamgirl. She wore a black satin robe with gold accents and hems, a gold and black crop top with a lace-up neckline, and red boxing gloves. Her matching black mini skirt had loops, gold striping, star detailing, and an elastic waistband with "UNDEFEATED" printed in the centre.

"The next round is the final round," announced the host. "This round is important to me. People often say anyone can win beauty contests, but that's not true. Only beauty with brains can win. Let's see if these beauties have brains. Please welcome the contestants back on stage."

Foibe led the contestants back on stage, still dressed in their sportswear.

"This is my favourite part!" said Grandma Eliza.

"If you could change one thing about your life, what would it be, Foibe?" asked the host.

"I would change my looks," said Foibe, and the audience cheered.

"Why do you come to school, Catherine?"

"School is meant to change my life," Catherine said.

"What clubs are you part of at school, Evia?"

"None."

"If you could bring back any family member from the dead, who would it be, Florence?"

"My Grandpa. I heard he was a great man and wish to meet him."

"What are you hoping to achieve by participating in Miss South Bauleni, Patricia?"

"The crown."

"What role do beauty pageants play in today's society, Katie?"

"Women are beautiful."

"If you could travel anywhere in the world, where would you go, Suzie?"

"Home."

"If you don't win, who would you like to win, Joana?"

"We all put in a lot of effort. We all deserve to win."

The host announced, "We have four awards to give out. Contestants have been evaluated on their grace, beauty, speaking skills, personality, talent, and attire. The winners have been chosen based on these criteria, but before we reveal them, let's welcome our current Miss South Bauleni, Alicia, for her farewell speech."

The crowd erupted in applause, filling the hall with excitement. Alicia, a fourteen-year-old student at Riverweed was elegantly dressed.

"In the past few months at Riverweed, I have grown greatly. Thank you for providing a platform like this. This platform allowed me to discover a side of myself that I never knew existed. I have met wonderful people and spoken words I never thought I could. I am grateful to my former school, South Bauleni, teachers, parents, and fellow learners. To whoever takes over the crown from me, may God guide you as He guided me. It's your time now. Embrace it because you all deserve to be here. To my role model, Principal Ndafenongo, thank you for supporting me during my reign. Your invaluable advice and kind words have made me a better person. Thanks, Mum and Dad, and everyone at South Bauleni, for everything!"

The host's voice echoed through the packed hall. "Let's give a big round of applause to Suzie for winning the Best Outfit award."

The crowd cheered, all eyes on Suzie as she stood out in her dazzling outfit under the bright stage lights.

"Next up," the host announced, "we have Marita winning the second award for her infectious smile that has won our hearts. Marita, come on up and enjoy your well-deserved recognition."

Marita's smile grew wider as she cat-walked to the stage, her happiness shining through her eyes and the dimples on her cheeks.

"And now," Pulelo declared with excitement, "the moment we've all been waiting for, my dear learners."

The room fell silent as everyone waited in anticipation of the big announcement.

"Introducing our new queen," the host declared dramatically, building up the suspense. Our new queen will also get scholarship to continue her education at Riverweed came next year. Isn't that beautiful?

The crowed cheered...tension rose.

"Miss South Bauleni 2013 is none other than... Patricia LM."

Elegant and composed, Alicia approached Patricia with the crown in her hands, a symbol of honour. She gently placed it on Patricia's head, marking her as the new queen.

"Goodbye, everyone, see you all next year!"

A Unique Welcome

Victoria stood facing Beth, a partner in mischief.

"Patricia wasn't supposed to win. Catherine and Florence walked a bit well," Beth said.

Beth and Victoria sat on a weathered wooden bench, positioned to face the hallway entrance. As learners started to arrive, Victoria was about to say something mean when she saw Pulelo and Lala, causing her to frown. Beth once asked Victoria why she hated Lala and Pulelo, to which Victoria boldly claimed it was just natural and there was no explanation for it.

"In that case, I'll hate them even more," Beth said.

"I have to admit," Victoria said, "I never expected that from little Pulelo. She's such a cry-baby, but she did a great job. I'm jealous."

"Everyone will have forgotten about her lucky performance by next week."

"I don't think it's luck. People call it talent. What do you think?"

Beth leaned back on the bench. The corridors whispered with the energy of the arriving students. "Talent or not, it won't matter much. We know how things work around here," Beth said.

"True. But sometimes, people like Pulelo surprise you. I mean, who would have thought she had it in her?"

"Maybe she had a good day. Everyone gets lucky once in a while."

Learners hurried past them, filling the corridor with a rush of movement and noise.

"Come on, let's get to class. We can figure out how to deal with Pulelo later."

Victoria nodded, but her mind was elsewhere. She knew Beth was right—they always found a way. But this time, something felt different. And that uncertainty gnawed at her as they made their way to the classroom.

Meanwhile, Pulelo and Lala walked together...

"Do you think they noticed?" Pulelo asked Lala.

"Of course, they did! You were amazing on Saturday," Lala replied, smiling at her friend. "Don't let them get to you. Just keep doing what you're doing."

Pulelo glanced back at Victoria and Beth, who were now disappearing into their classroom.

The first-morning bell had not rung yet. Lala and Pulelo were about to enter their classroom when a noise from the corridor entrance stopped them. Patricia was dressed in a pink sash that read MISS SOUTH BAULENI 2013. She wore white trousers and yellow pistols and had shaved her hair very close. She said she liked Principal Ndafenongo's appearance and was a big fan.

Lisa looked out of her office window and heard the first-morning bell ring. In a few seconds, the hallway became empty as the learners took their seats in their different classes. Ima leaned on Pulelo's table, a gesture she always made when she wanted to congratulate a student.

"You'll be a great TV presenter," Ima said.

"No, Teacher Ima, I want to be a great writer."

"You can be both, honey. I'm glad you have a dream. When I was your age, I wanted to be a banker, but things changed along the way." Ima returned to her table, opened and closed a drawer, and then picked up a textbook but put it back down. "Let's do something different! Let's all talk about our future careers. Benjamin, what do you want to be when you grow up?"

"I want to work in a shop that sells medicine."

"So, you want to be a pharmacist, right?" Ima asked. "Well, Lala, what about you?"

"I want to be a singer," Lala said.

The children continued sharing their dreams. Many wanted to be doctors. Little Kelly, unsure yet, held a world of possibilities in her heart.

Meanwhile, Lisa was sitting in her office, typing away on her laptop. The room looked fancy, with shiny trophies and plaques showing the school's greatness. A big family picture was hanging behind the principal's desk, showing Lisa with her husband, Grandma Eliza, Ima, and baby Lala. The door opened, and a man came in...

"I'm Mr Setiawan," he said with a friendly smile. "I'm a volunteer teacher from Indonesia."

"We were expecting you yesterday," she said jokingly, "but I guess it's not your fault."

"Thank you," he said.

"Let's get straight to the point. You're not the first volunteer teacher from Asia. Let me tell you something important, Mr Setiawan. In Namibia, we have thirty different spoken languages, with English being the official." Lisa allowed herself a grin and continued. "Did you know that we rank 100th in the global education system and tenth in Africa?" She pushed her glasses down to the edge of her nose and tilted her head towards Mr Setiawan. He did the same, except he wasn't wearing glasses.

The sound of a drawer opening interrupted their conversation. Lisa took out a novel and placed it in front of him.

"This is my first masterpiece and hopefully not my last. Do you know who inspired me, Mr Setiawan?"

Mr Setiawan gazed at the principal, wondering why he was getting such a strange welcome. Mr Setiawan didn't respond to that question.

"Toni Morris."

"I've never heard of him, Principal."

"Who said it's a man? Do you read, Mr Setiawan?"

"Not much."

"Toni Morrison," said Ima, who walked in.

"Morris or Morrison, what difference does it make?" said Lisa.

Lisa always welcomed new teachers with her novel. The second question she asked was how great her book cover was. The teachers always said the cover was outstanding. It was blue, with her own face and an earthworm eating a leaf, entitled "Raven and the Earthworm."

Mr Setiawan got up from his chair and bowed in greeting to Ima. Ima returned the same courtesy.

Lisa threw her anger on Ima, whom she felt showed great disrespect. She entered without knocking and offered corrections in front of a new colleague.

"You are supposed to knock," said Lisa as she shoved the novel back into the drawer. "And who asked for your opinion?"

"Sister, I have three important issues I have to discuss with you."

"Here I am, Principal Ndafenongo."

Lisa dialled her phone. Minutes later, the music teacher, close to retirement, came in. He carried his violin.

"Mr Sabata, do you ever leave that thing alone?" said Lisa in her usual severe and drawn-out tone.

"Music is good to..."

"Yes, yes, to your soul. Please, show Mr Setiawan to the music class."

Lisa sat playing with a pencil she kept biting when they had gone.

"Your daughter's grades need improvement."

"It's your responsibility as her teacher to help her succeed, right, Ima?"

"You should talk with your daughter to understand her interests."

"Her father's profession as a biologist shows that her academic struggles are not genetic. It's the learning environment that needs attention."

"Are you blaming me, Sister?"

"Pull up your socks Ima."

"I understand, but she's always late for my first class."

"Ima, you must step up and ensure my daughter is on time for lessons. What's the next topic? Let's keep it brief."

"Can my niece stay over at my place next week?"

"Why?"

"Do I need a reason?"

"Bring her back by six. Six, Ima."

"Why six? That's too early, and she needs rest."

"Six, Ima. I take my time seriously."

In the music class, musical instruments were all over the room, and kids teased each other. It was complete chaos because of their old and sickly teacher, Mr Sabata, who was retiring that day. Before leaving, he had come to introduce their new teacher, Mr Setiawan. Beth and Victoria sat in the back row, glaring at everyone. Mr Setiawan wrote his name on the blackboard.

"Let's begin with the basics of music - do-re-mi-fa-so-la-ti-do," Mr Setiawan said.

"Do-re-mi-fa-so-la-ti-do!" the children shouted.

"These silly words help musicians create many songs. You can make different melodies by mixing them up."

"Teacher," Victoria called out, "are you a musician? Anyone who sings is a musician."

"Not everyone who sings is a musician," Patricia replied.

"Shut up, Miss Crown," Beth protested. "What do you know?"

Lala, who had asked permission to use the restroom, peered through the classroom window. Unbeknownst to her, Principal Lisa was approaching from the other end of the corridor. The principal tapped Lala's shoulder, startling her and causing her to almost hit her head against the glass.

"What are you doing spying on Mr Setiawan's class? You should be in your own class, working on your grades."

"Please, let me join the music class, mother," Lala said.

"Stop it! You're not going to any other class. You will stay in your aunt's class, and I don't want to hear any more about you coming late! Go to your class and work on your grades. Go now and stop begging! You look ridiculous when you beg."

"I just want to join the music class!" Lala insisted.

Lisa called Ima, who was in her class, and summoned her to the principal's office. Ima left for the office before Lala could return.

"Ima..." Lisa began.

"Please, address me as Teacher Ima."

"You're not doing your job well. Your learners are wandering around the school during class. Are you unable to control little children?"

"Oh, come on, Sister, I can't say no. I let your daughter go because she needed to use the restroom!"

"She lied, Ima! She lied because you are too nice. She was walking around the corridor and even peeking into the music room. You need to be stricter, Ima."

"Is there anything else?"

"This can't happen again. Oh, and make sure to see our mother. She's so annoying, especially when that old fool is there."

Ima knew who the old fool was. She started smiling.

"Stop smiling, Ima. Why do you always smile when we talk about serious stuff?"

"You're going to have wrinkles soon. You stress too much."

"Now listen, Ima. How about Mother comes over this weekend?"

"I don't have a lot of space, and I live with other teachers. Mum would want to greet everyone."

"Just come tomorrow."

"Can't, I have plans to see my friend Jennifer. Remember Jenny?"

"Who's more important, Jennifer or Mother?"

"Can I come the day after?"

"Choosing a friend over family? That's not right. Just go!"

Ima glanced at her sister's novel, which was on top of a stack of other books. When she reached the door, she said something.

"Your book isn't selling because you're not promoting it."

"I heard that, Ima."

"Pay someone to help you out."

Ima closed the door but then opened it again, sticking her head back in. "Here's some sisterly advice. Trim down some pages. That Oxford dictionary of yours will scare away readers. Remember, we're all reluctant readers in this country, including you. And, please, change the title, for God's sake."

Ima's comment made her sister think. It had been years since she listed her book on Amazon, and the only copies sold were the one on her table and the five she donated to the school library. Lisa flipped through the novel and closed it with a sigh.

"Raven and the Earthworm," she read. "I think Ima is right."

Lisa sat at her desk, turned on her laptop, and gazed at the screen. She scrolled through the manuscript, her eyes scanning the long paragraphs and wordy descriptions. She thought about all the time she spent writing each sentence, but now it all seemed like too much.

"Why did I write this?" she said quietly to herself.

She started to highlight parts, deleting whole paragraphs and simplifying sentences. The story started to come alive, the pace picked up, and the characters' personalities shone through.

Later at home, she continued to work on her manuscript. She looked at the clock. Many hours had gone by, but she was so focused that she didn't even notice. Lisa took a deep breath and reread the first few chapters. The story felt more solid, more interesting. She nodded in satisfaction and created a new document to brainstorm potential titles. "Behind Bars," "Prison Life," "Locked in Life." None of them felt quite right. She had seen too many books with similar titles. She needed something that captured her journey without being too dramatic or childish. Or whatever.

She leaned back in her chair, closed her eyes, and thought about her time in prison. The challenges. The personal growth. The moments of unexpected hope. Suddenly, it came to her.

"MY DAYS INSIDE," she whispered, a smile appearing on her face. It was perfect. Maybe this was the fresh start her book needed.

Days later, she uploaded the updated manuscript to Amazon. She told her friends – Mukenani, Tiwe, Raven, Sophia and even Miss O'Hara. She told everyone who loves to read, hoping that this time, her story would find its audience. Weeks later, she got an email notification. Her book had a new review.

I couldn't put this book down. My Life Inside is a raw and powerful memoir. Lisa's story is compelling and unforgettable. Highly recommended!

She smiled. Ima had been right; a few changes had made all the difference. She couldn't wait to share the news with her sister. She called Ima immediately.

"Ima, you were right! I got my first positive review with the new title and edits,"

"I knew you could do it, sis," Ima replied. "I'm so proud of you."

The Aftermath of Competition

Grandma Eliza sat watching TV. There was a big jar of milk on the table. She wore a basketball T-shirt for Chicago Bulls. She got up and hurried to the kitchen, where a turkey was roasting. She returned to her seat, peeping through the window. She rushed to her room and grabbed the hand mirror to ensure she looked so good. Then, she walked back to open the front door, where Grandpa Sylvester was standing with a bottle of wine.

"I haven't tried this wine before," he said. "I found it in my daughter's bedroom. It must be special. Do you have any old-school disco?"

"Oh, Syl, you sure know your ancient music!"

Grandma Eliza twirled back to her room, singing and dancing. She returned with a CD, and soon they were dancing together. He stopped and sniffed the air. She could tell he was putting his good nose to good use.

"I knew you'd like it, Sly. I took it from my daughter's purse. She buys me cheap perfume thinking I don't notice," Grandma Eliza said.

"Something's burning!" Grandpa Sylvester said.

Grandma Eliza hurried to the kitchen and allowed him to take the turkey out of the oven. "It was for Thanksgiving. My daughter will be so upset."

The clock alarm had gone off long ago, reminding them of the few minutes left before Lisa came home from school. Grandpa Sylvester always left fifteen minutes early. Lisa watched from the kitchen door as they tried to figure out what to do with the ruined turkey. They only noticed her when she spoke up. "Go pick up your granddaughter, sir," Lisa said.

Grandpa Sylvester checked his watch before rushing out. Grandma Eliza ran to her room while Lala stood by, laughing.

"Get rid of that turkey and open the windows," said Lisa to Lala before she strode to her room.

The next day in class, it was during break when Lala was singing on top of the table. Ima was just there, waiting for the excitement to subside.

"Four years ago," said Ima. "I made it to the semi-finals of the national singing competition. My sister, Lisa, had gone even further, almost earning a spot to represent Namibia in the African Gospel Contest held in Zambia."

"That's no secret, Aunt Ima. She lost to that Indian lady," said Lala.

After school, Grandma Eliza was curled on the sofa, her face etched with deep sadness. The front door was half open, but she hurried to hold it for Lisa and her daughter.

"Lunch is on the counter," said Grandma Eliza, her voice lowered.

Lala gave her grandmother a rushed hug, while Lisa, couldn't help but smirk, knowing her mother's flair for the dramatic. With a hint of mischief in her eyes, Lisa retreated to her room, and Lala, her voice barely a whisper, asked, "Is it working, Grandma?"

"My daughter is made of steel," Grandma Eliza chuckled.

"She forgot about the turkey, Grandma."

"I know but I feel so bad. I think I'm making a lot of mistakes these days. Do you think Sly is a bad influence?"

Lala laughed, and before she could say anything, Lisa shouted, "Get a new friend mother, that old man is sick in the head."

Lisa was about to return to the living room when she saw Grandma Eliza's slightly open door. Her favourite nightdress was laid out on the bed. Lisa had often said that if given the opportunity, she would dump that dress so quickly into the bin. When she saw her daughter's reflection in the window, Grandma Eliza hurried there to catch a whiff of the dress. "Not this dress, child. I know you hate Syl, but he gave this one to me with love."

Later that evening, Pulelo told Lala about her favourite TV show, THE WORLD CONTINENTAL GOSPEL CONTEST. Lala turned on the TV and started singing along with Grandma Eliza.

"You've been watching this show since last November. Don't you get bored?" Lisa said, coming from her room.

"She misses her husband," Grandma Eliza said.

"I talk to my husband every day."

"You get angry at everything. You are rude to everyone. Ima called and said you want me out of your house. Soon, you will send me to an old age home."

"I never thought about that, Mother, but come to think of it, that sounds like a great idea. Please reduce the volume and stop singing."

At school, during assembly, Lisa invited Miss South Bauleni to the stage. Patricia received applause from her peers as she waved to the crowd. Lisa also announced the upcoming annual gospel music contest and encouraged learners to participate. She mentioned the opportunity to represent Namibia at the African Gospel Contest and potentially the World Continental Gospel Contest in November. Learners were urged to sign up with Mr Setiawan if interested.

When the assembly was over, Lisa went with Patricia to her classroom, holding hands along the way, much to the dismay of The Girls, who were unhappy about Patricia stealing their spotlight. The last time Lisa held someone's hand was after The Girls won a netball game against a team from the capital. Now, all the attention was on Patricia.

"Principal Ndafenongo," Patricia said, "what about the other winners like Miss Best Outfit?"

"Don't worry about them. Go to your class. The school is proud of you. Next year, you'll be attending Riverweed."

"Thank you, Principal Ndafenongo," Patricia said.

Lisa walked down the hallway; her mind already focused on the work she had to do in her office.

"Lisa!" Eva called from the doorway.

When they were in her office, Eva dropped Pulelo's manuscript on the table...

"Look at what my daughter wrote," Eva said with pride, her voice motherly.

Lisa flipped through the pages, her expression changing from curiosity to admiration as she immersed herself in the world created by Pulelo.

"My daughter is obsessed with something inappropriate for her age," Eva said.

"I understand. Lala is obsessed with the gospel contest. I wouldn't let her participate at her age," Lisa said.

"You wrote a book. Can you give me your opinion on it?"

"I'm surprised. This is quite interesting."

"Do you think so?"

"Yeah. I love it."

Eva placed the manuscript back into her handbag, and they walked together down the corridor, chatting.

"How is your father?"

"What has he done this time?"

"Can you believe it? He sneaks off to my house when I'm at school. I know he's there right now."

"You should get to know him. He's a very sweet old man."

"I know that, but sometimes he puts my mother's life at risk."

"Did you know he has your mother's picture in our living room?"

"I've seen it several times, like on your birthday."

"They're old, Lisa. Let them keep each other company."

At home, Lisa kicked off her shoes at the door and dropped her handbag on the table. Grandma Eliza was watching TV, and the volume was loud.

"Mother! You're ruining what little sight and sound you have left! Can't you read a book or something?"

"Who made my fearless sheep leaf angry?"

"My daughter is spending the night at Ima's."

"We need to talk."

"Can it wait?"

"Right now!"

Grandma Eliza had put on a video recording of the 2009 National Gospel Contest, where Lisa had reached the finals. The host announced the winner, and Lisa came in second place. She couldn't hold back her tears.

"I'm proud of you!" said her mother.

"I didn't win."

"And you stayed locked in your room all day."

"I wanted to win."

"There are so many people in our country, and you came in second place. My child, you shouldn't feel like you lost."

"I don't want my daughter to go through all that. I know she wants to sing."

"Sweetheart, your daughter has talent."

"She has to go to school. Basic education is a basic human right in our country. You know that Mother."

"Yes, and she will never stop going to school."

"She can't handle all those emotions."

"Going through challenges made you stronger. Let her experience it, too. You won't always be there for her. You're not God, who lives forever."

"I'm scared, Mother..."

"Let us all help you raise her."

Lisa lowered her head onto her mother's lap. In that sweet moment, Lisa couldn't help but chuckle - a rare expression of joy.

The next day was Saturday. Ima was still snoozing in her bed when her phone started ringing. She didn't want to answer it because she knew it was her sister calling. Lisa slumped into her car, tapping her forehead against the steering wheel. She pulled out her keys from her purse and struggled to start the vehicle.

Meanwhile, Ima and Lala were enjoying their breakfast...

"Auntie," called Lala, "Teacher Setiawan is so funny! I like him a lot."

Before Ima could say anything, someone started banging on the front door.

"Who knocks like that?" Lala placed a slice of bread back onto her plate.

"Who else? There's only one person who knocks like that."

Ima rushed across the room to open the door. Lisa was panting as if she had run a mile.

"Calm down, Sister. Lala is having breakfast," Ima said.

"For once, Ima, learn to keep your promise. I said six in the morning. Six, Ima, six! Six means six! Just once, be reliable."

"The issue isn't the time, sis. It's Saturday. Can't she stay the whole weekend?"

"Where is she?"

"Relax and come inside."

"Let her come meet me in the car. Now!"

Mr Setiawan came from his apartment to take out the rubbish. Lisa glanced at him from head to his hairy chest. Another local teacher, who was the same age as Mr Setiawan, came out.

"Good morning, Principal Ndafenongo," Mr Setiawan said.

"Mr Setiawan, go get dressed!" She walked to her car, muttering words that she could only hear.

"Good morning, Teacher Setiawan, and good morning, Teacher Martin," Lala said as she walked over to her mother. Lisa drummed her fingers on the steering wheel, the engine's soft purr interrupted by the occasional roar as she stepped on the gas pedal.

"Morning, Mother," Lala greeted, fastening her seatbelt.

With a sudden jolt, the car surged forward as Lisa pressed down on the accelerator. It disappeared, leaving behind a trail of dust suspended in the air.

Grandma Eliza was lounging on the sofa, watching her favourite morning show. She either couldn't hear or didn't care about the commotion caused by her daughter and granddaughter returning from Ima's house. Lala burst through the door and hurried to her room. She threw herself onto the bed, but her gaze remained fixed on the picture of her father in the blue frame. He was handsome, bold, and of medium build, a black man. Then, she slid her mother's picture under the bed. Lisa, who had entered the room, sat next to her daughter and surveyed the entire room. The only pictures she saw were of her husband. A giant monkey puppet sat on the bed. In the corner, there was a desktop computer that was turned off.

"Do you want to talk to your dad?" Lisa asked.

"He called," Lala replied, facing the other way.

"I spoke to him last night. He's coming back soon."

"I know..."

"Do you remember the day he took us to the coast? It was the first time you saw a ship. It was huge! Do you remember, honey?"

"Yes..."

Lisa looked around the room, hoping for a different topic of conversation. The ship story wasn't working.

"How about we go shopping?"

"How about I join the music class?"

Grandma Eliza was still absorbed in her show. Lisa walked past her and went to the kitchen. Grandma Eliza adjusted her glasses and glanced at her daughter. She knew the milk had run out. She turned around and stood behind her mother who kept herself busy by humming a tune out of nowhere.

"You drink milk just like a little calf. I should bring a cow right into your room!" Her eyes flashed with annoyance as she grabbed her car keys from the table. Without saying anything else, she swiftly turned on her heel and forcefully shut the door behind her, the sound of her quick footsteps gradually fading away.

"That would be amazing... having a dairy cow in my room. I'll have so much fresh milk!" Grandma Eliza chuckled, gazed intently through the lace curtains; her eyes fixed on the disappearing taillights of the car as it rounded the bend. With a swift, she pressed the buttons on the phone. After a few rings, Lala answered. "Hello?"

"The coast is clear, my little mouse," Grandma Eliza said.

Lala ran downstairs and sat next to Grandma Eliza.

"Did it work?"

"What, Grandma?"

"The blackmail, pretending to sleep and curling up..."

"I don't think so, but I'll be sad all day."

"And refuse to eat."

"Ha! I can't do that! I love food, and you know it!"

"You eat when she's not around," Grandma Eliza said as she bent down to check under the table. She pulled out a yellow box hidden underneath. Inside the box was a single CD, which she gave to Lala.

"The 2009 National Gospel Contest. Your mother made it to the finals with this song."

"I remember this song, Grandma, and I want to learn it. But why she doesn't want me to sing?"

"Your mother was heartbroken."

"Anyone can lose."

"Expressing grief is normal, tender-heart. Your mother doesn't want to see you suffer. She loves you so much."

"Can you teach me Mother's song, Grandma?"

Grandma and Lala's voices blended harmoniously, their laughter filling the room as they sang together. The front door creaked open, and their song abruptly stopped. Lisa walked in, bags rustling, and set a carton of milk on the table with a thud. Her eyes narrowed as she looked at her mother. Grandma Eliza poured the milk into her bowl.

"Mother!" Lisa shouted.

"Are you monitoring me? I raised you and gave you the little I could get."

"The economy is bad right now."

"It was bad when I had you too."

"Can I go to choir practice with Grandma?" Lala asked.

Lisa knew her daughter wanted to go. She couldn't come up with any more excuses, especially since Lala was using all the tricks she learned from her grandmother.

"Don't you think it's time to stop singing in the church choir, Mother?" Lisa said, trying to avoid her daughter's plea.

"I'm a good singer and love it," Grandma Eliza replied. "Plus, my choirmaster loves my voice."

"Come on, Mother, I know why you never miss choir practice. It's because of that old man they call the 'choirmaster.'"

"Because I had you when I was young, it doesn't mean I'm ancient history. I still have style."

"Grandma, please take me to choir practice."

"You're not going anywhere!" said Lisa.

"Give your daughter a break. It's a church, for goodness's sake!"

"She's not going, and that's my final decision, and my decision is final."

"Semi-final. I'm the only one in this house with the final decision, and she's coming with me."

Lisa's angry stare at her mother could only mean one thing – My mother is deflating my power, and I'm losing control over my daughter. For a moment, they ate without saying a word.

"Sweetheart," said Lisa to Lala, "your grades aren't improving. You have all the books in the world. If you promise me one thing, I will let you sing."

Lala should have acknowledged the idea. It wasn't the first time she had made a deal with her mother, and she had broken it countless times.

"Let me offer you a piece of advice that might sound like a warning," said Grandma Eliza to Lisa. "Get a book on parenting. Your parenting style is like a dictator. You're a bully."

"Please, let me do things my way. She's my baby, and I want what's best for her."

"Your daughter is like a caged bird. She needs room to enjoy her early years."

"You are a negative influence on my daughter. You need to go and live with Ima."

"Are you kicking me out of your house?"

"I'm suggesting you allow me to raise my child my way. If you can't accept that, I must send you to your other daughter. I know you don't like my style."

Lisa turned to her daughter and said, "Make me one promise. Promise that you'll improve your grades."

"I promise." Lala then slipped quietly into her bedroom, her steps almost soundless on the floor. She reached under the bed and pulled out a frame. Gently, she wiped it clean, revealing a picture of her mother. With a soft sigh, she placed it beside her dad's photo on the nightstand, the two pictures now standing together.

The next day, as part of her morning routine, Lisa entered her mother's and daughter's rooms. When she saw the picture in her daughter's room, she couldn't help but stifle a laugh. She knew it wasn't there the day before. Lisa closed the door, not wanting to wake her daughter. Then, she went to the kitchen to make breakfast and do her other morning chores. The morning sun was rising higher in the sky.

Lala and her grandma were getting ready for church. They drove through the wet, muddy roads leading to their tiny white church. The choirmaster led his choir while Grandma Eliza sang. The choirmaster, Sylvester, conducted with energy and smiled at Grandma Eliza, who sang louder than anyone else. Grandpa Sylvester used a baton to direct the choir, waving the stick to the song's content. In the last part, he signalled to the choir to sing in staccato. It was a joyful chorus of "Hallelujah."

"This old man must be crazy," Lisa thought to herself. "All that hard work, just for Mother."

After church, Lisa and her family went to visit Ima who never liked church. Ima was stretched on the sofa reading a magazine. Lala was the first one to go in since the door was half-open. She sat down next to her aunt. Grandma Eliza sat down with her daughter.

"I came here to talk to you, Ima," Lisa said.

"Mother," Ima said, "tell your daughter I have nothing to say to her."

Grandma Eliza started knitting, showing she didn't want to get involved in their silly arguments.

"I'm sorry about yesterday morning," Lisa said.

Ima had to sit up. She remembered having a similar outburst three months ago when Lala didn't return by six. Lisa said they always wake up at 06:30 for their bike exercise.

"You've changed a lot, and it's not funny anymore," Ima said.

"You and your mother always do the opposite. I want to raise my baby my way."

"No one is stopping you, but remember, I'm her aunt. I should also play a role in her upbringing."

"I know, and I'm sorry."

"What do you want to talk to me about?"

"If you help my daughter with her grades, I'll let her join the school choir and classes."

"It's not up to me; besides, I'm doing my best as her teacher."

"I'll let her join Mr Setiawan's class if her grades improve."

"It's all up to your daughter, not me."

"I promise, Aunt. I'll study hard," Lala said.

Grandma Eliza kept herself busy knitting and listening to her daughter's conversation and said, "Don't forget my birthday, whatever you do. Seventy-two is not a silly joke!"

"Should we invite Grandpa Syl again this year?" asked Ima.

"This year, it's a family affair. My two beautiful daughters and my lovely granddaughter."

"Is that all you want, Mother?" asked Lisa.

"I have all I need in life right here."

"I almost forgot," said Ima, "I need money, sister."

"Ima, you have a salary," said Lisa. "Money doesn't grow on trees."

"I know, but you are a rich woman, and I'm your only sister. You inherited a lot of money from your late first husband."

"I bought a car for you, Ima, when you came back from Zambia, and I even gave you a job at this school, and I'm building a house for you in Riverweed. How ungrateful can you be."

"Just a little money, sister, just to buy an alternator for my car."

"I will think about it...but tomorrow, escort me to town so we can book our mother's cake."

The family of four spent the whole Sunday afternoon at Ima's house.

The next day after school, Lisa, Ima, and Lala went into town. The streets swarmed with vendors shouting about their goods on sale. They walked through the crowd and reached the bakery, a well-lit little place with shelves brimming with cakes. The beautiful smell of freshly baked bread and sugary treats welcomed them as they walked in the store. Mr Kavetuna, a cheerful baker they had known for so many good years, stood smiling behind the counter as he normally did to all his customers.

"Beautiful Ladies!" Mr Kavetuna said. "What can I help you with?"

"We need a cake for our mother's birthday," Ima said.

"Seventy-two years is a big deal! What kind of cake does she like this year?"

"Chocolate and lots of chocolate," Lala said, trotting on the spot.

"Add some berries on top?" said Lisa.

"Great choice, Mrs Ndafenongo," Mr Kavetuna said, writing down their order.

"Could you also include a special message? Something like, 'Happy 72nd Birthday, Mother'?"

"No, Mother," Lala said. "Happy 72nd Birthday, Grandma Eliza?"

"As you wish," Lisa agreed.

"I'll make sure it looks beautiful. When do you need it?" Mr Kavetuna asked.

"We'll pick it up tomorrorw the same time," Ima said.

"I will have it all set for you. Happy birthday to her."

The Birthday I Never enjoyed

In Lisa's living room, Ima and Lala danced to the music, making the room feel alive with colourful decorations showing Grandma Eliza's birthday excitement. Grandma Eliza sat calmly, occasionally glancing towards the door. Lala grabbed her mother's hand and pulled her to the centre of the room. Lisa hesitated but eventually joined the dance, moving gracefully and effortlessly to the music. They gathered to sing the birthday song when Ima had to leave to answer a knock at the door. Grandpa Sylvester stood there, holding a single rose. Ima remembered, Grandma Eliza said this year's celebration would only be for the family.

"I invited him," Grandma Eliza said. "Sorry, kids but I was bored."

Grandma Eliza and Grandpa Sylvester strolled to the back of the house, sat under the sprawling branches of a mango tree. Grandpa Sylvester dug into his pocket and took out a rolled cigarette.

"Ganja?" Grandma Eliza asked, "I don't smoke that. I don't smoke at all."

"If you smoke this, you'll have a birthday to remember," he said, lighting it up.

"Do you think so?"

"Four pulls. That's all it takes," he took a few puffs and exhaled clouds of smoke with evident pride.

Reluctantly, Grandma Eliza took the cigarette and inhaled deeply, coughing it out, but the old man didn't stop there. He kept pushing and pushing. At the end, Grandma Eliza felt an unexpected sense of lightness. She shook herself and gazed up at the mangoes as smoke curled from her nostrils. Suddenly, her eyes widened. "Is that gold? Gold is growing on my tree! We're rich, Syl!"

"Those are just ripe mangoes, my old cloak."

Grandma Eliza's excitement grew as she prepared to climb the tree, convinced she had found treasure. When he realized she was out of control,

Grandpa Sylvester decided it was time to make a quiet exit. He tiptoed past the window. Lisa caught a glimpse of him and hurried outside, but by the time she arrived, Grandpa Sylvester was already gone. She looked up to see Grandma Eliza halfway up the tree, reaching for the gold. Lisa pulled her mother back down...

"Grandma is going mad," Lala said, leaning on her aunt.

Ima picked up the cigarette butt. "Our mother has been smoking!"

"Yes, with that old fool?" Lisa snapped.

It took three hours before Grandma Eliza regained her composure. She quietly curled up on her bed...

"Mother," Lisa said, "do you smoke too?"

She turned to the other side and grumbled, "Leave me alone."

Lisa hurried to her car. Through the bedroom window, Ima and Lala watched her drive off. They knew she was off to find the old man. Grandpa Sylvester had a small gym behind the chicken coop. He had a 365-day challenge for his abdominal muscles, which he often skipped. He attempted one sit-up, crunches, leg raises, and plank exercises. Jumping squats and weightlifting were abandoned the same day he made his list, which was posted on the door.

He wore a tight camouflage military vest and sat drinking water, leaning against a tree. The sight of Lisa's car speeding through the fields made him anxious. He grabbed a white towel to wipe his face. He thought about hiding, but he decided to face her with exaggerated obedience.

"Listen to me, Mr Sylvester! I don't want to see you near my mother again." She swiftly turned around, went back to her car, and drove off...

The next morning it was school, Pulelo, Lala, and the other learners sat on the pavilion, cheering the netball players swiftly manoeuvring across the court in preparation for their upcoming match against Riverweed. Every point scored or missed opportunity elicited cheers or groans from the group. Occasionally, words of encouragement or playful teasing reached the players on the court. Pulelo's anger was more on Victoria and Beth...

"Why do you want to join the music class?" said Pulelo. "Beth and Victoria are there, and they don't like you!"

"They want me on their netball team," replied Lala.

"But why not play with them? You were good last year, I remember."

"I hurt my ankle, and the doctor said I should take it easy. Plus, my mother would freak out," she packed up her lunch and taking out some homemade juice to sip. "Did you see the new girl?"

"Her name is Lilian, and she's so tiny," Pulelo chuckled at the same time as the final whistle of practice. Victoria skipped from the field with Beth, and stood before Lala and Pulelo...

"Do you guys like our team uniforms?" Victoria asked.

Lala shook her head...

"But Lala, if you join the team, you'll have so much fun! We travelled to Cameroon last year, and it was amazing," Beth said.

"Yes, you'll see so many new places with us," added Victoria.

Lala grabbed her bag and walked off, with Pulelo following closely behind. Beth turned to Victoria, "What should we do now? We need Lala on our team."

"Lilian plays well."

"You're right. Let's find Lilian instead. She's a great shooter."

Lilian sat alone in the parking area. She was the new girl known for her temper and questionable arrogance, which had led her to switch schools from Riverweed to South Bauleni. Despite her temper, she had excelled as the star of the netball team at Riverweed. Even though she was diminutive, she was unstoppable on the netball court.

"Lilian, would you like to join the netball team?" Beth asked.

"Where I come from, I don't warm the bench."

"You'll play," said Victoria.

"But why me? Patricia is a good player."

"Patricia? Our own Miss Crown?" Beth scoffed.

"Yes, she's so good. I saw her play at our school where her mother teaches."

"We want you," said Beth.

"All right, then," said Lilian. "Where I came from, we practice every day," said Beth.

Days have passed, and Lala's grades have been improving, but when Ima gave the principal the latest test results, Lisa didn't like them.

"C is a useless grade," said Lisa.

"But the rest are As and Bs," said Ima.

"But she got a C now," said Lisa.

Lisa's hesitation to keep her promise made things tense. Beyond school grades, there was a more significant issue.

When Lisa was little, she remembered her dreams that had never come true. She had wanted to win a big music contest but only made it to a smaller one. This unfulfilled dream left behind a mix of feelings and unfinished goals. Because of her own unmet dreams, she promised herself that if she couldn't win the big music contest, someone in her family would. Now, with Lala showing talent in music, Lisa struggled with her emotions. Was Lisa holding back from supporting Lala's passion for music because she was scared of her own past failures? Were there old memories influencing her decisions now?

"She will sing, but not now," Lisa said. "I just want to protect my daughter from disappointment at this age. When she turns twenty-one, she will join the gospel contest."

The next day, Lisa was in her office. Mr Setiawan had the daily newspaper, THE NAMIBIAN. He read about the National Gospel Music Contest, where anyone from Namibia could participate, regardless of age. Last year, the oldest contestant was seventy years old, and the youngest was nine years old. In 2009, a lady from Maldives named Adolfa was the oldest participant in the World Continental Gospel Contest. She made it to the quarterfinals. It had been forty-nine years, and no one from Africa had ever reached round two. Will this year be different?

"Yes, Mr Setiawan?" Lisa asked as the door to her office creaked open.

"Principal Ndafenongo," Mr Setiawan began, "I wanted to discuss starting the selection for the National Gospel Contest. May I proceed?"

"Of course, Mr Setiawan. Please go ahead and let me know if you need any help."

Mr Setiawan was about to leave when Ima and Lala walked in, catching his attention.

"I wanted to show you Lala's recent grades," Ima said to Lisa. "She's been working hard to improve them, and I thought you should see her progress. Hopefully, this will reassure you and clear up any concerns about her participating in the contest."

"Can I join Mr Setiawan's class now, Mother?" Lala asked.

"Only after I see your end-of-semester result. Until then, focus on your studies," Lisa replied.

"But Mother..."

"Anything else, Ima?"

Lala stormed out of the office. Mr Setiawan caught up with her as he offered comfort with his gentle words and a reassuring hand on her shoulder. "Some parents can be tough on their kids," Mr Setiawan said. "Did you know my mother didn't want me to come to Namibia? But here I am, and I've made good friends."

Lala continued to cry and held onto Mr Setiawan's arm. "Teacher, please talk to my mother. I want to sing in the National Gospel Contest."

Throughout the school day, Lala didn't stop lamenting to anyone who would listen. Pulelo had heard enough and finally snapped, "Enough, Lala. I have my own problems." She turned away, crossing her arms.

"I'm sorry, Pulelo," Lala said. "I'm sorry for thinking you didn't have any problems."

"We all have problems. Everyone has something going on."

"I know, and I'm sorry."

Two other learners walked past them on their way to the sports field.

"How is your grandpa?"

"Your mother was mean to him. He's sad. His heart is broken, Lala. It was his fault, but your mother was hard on him."

"He shouldn't have made Grandma smoke that thing. Grandma went crazy."

"Grandpa can be irresponsible sometimes, but he's a good man."

"I know he's a good man. Grandma is happy when he's around. He makes her laugh."

"What can we do to help them?"

"We don't do anything, Pulelo. Focus on your book."

"Last week, I added four thousand words. Mom and Grandpa read it. They say they haven't read it, but I know they did and don't like it. They keep saying they're proud of me, but I can tell from their eyes. They don't want to hurt my feelings."

"It's your book, Pulelo. What matters is that you believe in yourself. You're smart, and your book will turn out great. Now lets go and watch The Girls play netball."

On the other side of the netball court, Beth and Victoria sat with the rest of The Girls. Patricia was there too, even though she wasn't a member yet.

"Hold on a second, Patricia. Lilian said you play netball," said Beth.

"I don't like netball. And who is Lilian?"

"The new girl from Riverweed," said Victoria.

"The new girl lied."

"Who are you calling a new girl?" Lilian said, walking over from the goal ring.

Patricia backed away because she had heard rumours that Lilian had a short temper."I'm sorry, Lilian."

"Call me Huge Lilian."

"Why?"

"Because I say so."

It wasn't until after break that the sun's rays finally managed to break through the clouds. In Ima's class, Lisa introduced a new student. He was of average build and dressed well. "Everyone; meet Vivian," Lisa said.

"I'm Vivaan, which means 'the first rays of the sun,'" the boy said with business-like confidence and spoke with an Indian accent.

"What a beautiful name, Vivaan. Please take a seat behind Lala," Ima said.

"Who is Lala?" Vivaan asked, still standing and holding a red file.

"There's only one chair available here, little man. Go ahead and take your seat," Lisa said as she left the room.

Vivaan carried a blue school bag and placed the red file on the table. The file had green labels that read *Tenants And Pay Dates*.

"Vivaan, please introduce yourself to the class. Is that alright with you?" Ima asked.

Vivaan adjusted his bow tie before beginning. The other learners watched him in complete silence.

"My dad owns *Garlic and Chips*."

"You're Mr Amey's son," Lala said.

"Yes, I am, and the one and only."

"Teacher," Lala said, "Mr Amey donated books and money to our school last year."

"He has many businesses all around the country, especially in the capital," said Ima.

"He owns Vivaan Court. My parents rent there," a girl from the middle row added. "I know you! You're the one who collects rent every month."

"Vivaan Court is my business. I will provide you with a place to live, and you will give me rent money on time. We are all super happy."

"Let's welcome Vivaan once again."

"Welcome, Vivaan!" The learners shouted, except for Lina.

"Tomorrow let's bring lots of food. We will visit Lake Lyambezi and learn how to fish."

After school, Lala went to Mr Setiawan's class to meet him. He was playing the piano, and they started making beautiful music together. Vivaan, who was wandering the corridor, listened at the door.

"Teacher," said Lala, "Did you take the list?"

"I'm sorry, but your mother is against it."

"It's okay. Maybe next year," Lala said.

"Your time will come, and it will come soon. With your deep, sweet voice, you are destined to be a superstar."

"Do you think so, teacher?"

"Those wings of yours will let you fly over the deepest seas, oceans, mountains, and stormy weather. Remember, I will be by your side when that time comes."

Lala smiled as she left to wait for her mother in the school parking area. She had been delayed by a board meeting. Vivaan sat down next to her, threw his file on the lawn, and took two chocolate bars from his bag. He gave one to Lala. He took out his phone, switched it on, dialled a number, and spoke with authority. "Mr Matengu, you have until this Saturday. You are the only one who hasn't paid rent yet."

"Collecting rent. They will hate you!" said Lala.

"They hate me already."

"You don't care?"

"Father said there is no sentiment in business."

"That's why every rich man is an evil man."

"I heard that too," said Vivaan. "When you take what is yours, people think you are mean."

Vivaan switched off his phone and made eye contact with Lala. "You sing well. You and that music teacher are close."

"Mr Setiawan. He's also Asian. I like him a lot. He's so kind. I wish I could be in his class."

"I know you are the principal's child."

"How did you know that?"

"I know you want to sing in the National Gospel Contest."

"Yes, even to represent Africa during the World Continental Gospel Contest, but..."

"...but your mother will not allow it."

"Yes, and it's too late. The name list is gone."

"The contest closes tomorrow. Until then, don't be so sure. Your dad, for example?"

"If my dad could be around, he would have signed the consent form. I know."

"He can still sign."

"My dad works at the Atlantic Ocean. He can't sign."

"He will sign. Give me his number."

Lala stared at the phone Vivaan held, feeling her heartbeat faster and faster with each ring. The phone continued to go unanswered, and eventually, the call went to voicemail. All she was left with was disappointment ringing in her ears.

"We can copy your dad's signature. What do you think about that?"

"I'll do it," Ima said, coming from her class. "But I can't be your manager, sweetie."

"Don't worry, teacher, I'll handle it," Vivaan said.

"I'm done with this crime," Ima declared after signing the consent form.

Lisa came from her office. All the learners had already left. Lala rose and gathered her belonging. "Mother's here," said Lala to Vivaan. "Mother can give you a lift."

"My driver is already waiting."

"You have a driver?"

"Even my nanny has a driver."

"You have a nanny?"

"You'll meet her someday. She's cool."

"Is she White?"

"No, Black." Vivaan packed up his things and brushed off his shorts. "Don't bring anything. I'll ask the nanny to make lots of food for our trip to that lake."

"Lyambezi."

"Yes, Lyambezi. She cooks well."

The next day, Ima's learners skipped with so much excitement as they got into the sixteen-seater VW minivans. The bright yellow markings on the side said SOUTH BAULENI SECONDARY SCHOOL, standing out against the white body of the vehicle. The boys had on black earflap hats that covered their heads, only showing their faces. The girls laughed and teased the boys. On the other hand, the girls and their teacher wore cheerful yellow berets that added a playful touch to their faces.

Mr Setiawan sat in the driver's seat; his hands steady on the wheel as the minivan started up. With a quick honk of the horn, they drove out of the driveway, past the school gates. The children pressed their faces against the windows, waving to those they left behind. Ima walked down the aisle, checking each seatbelt carefully, her eyes softening as she made sure every child was safe.

"Lala, have you ever been to Lyambezi before?" Vivaan asked.

"I haven't," replied Lala.

"Teacher Ima," Pulelo called, "have you ever caught a fish?"

"Well, I grew up in a village with lots of water. One day, my friends and I went fishing in the Zambezi River, and guess what? I caught this big, red-breasted bream! Have you seen one before?"

"Um, is it like a type of tilapia?" a boy sitting in the back asked.

"That's the one fish I remember catching."

"I'm going to catch so many fish today!" Pulelo said.

Pulelo was the smallest in the class, but everyone knew she was also the smartest. She loved wearing her red and pink glasses and her blue scarf. Even though her voice was always off key, Pulelo enjoyed singing a lot.

The minivan turned onto a bumpy gravel road, and the children started complaining to the driver, who slowed down. The road trip started losing excitement as the little ones kept asking how long it would be until they reached the lake. To distract them, the driver turned on some music. Even those dozing off woke up to join Pulelo's singing along with the tunes on the radio. They continued singing as they turned left onto a narrow road that sloped downwards. Their voices became even more joyful as they caught sight of the water stretching out everywhere.

Finally, Mr Setiawan parked the minivan under a big tree. The children hopped off one by one, carrying their bags and fishing lines as they went towards a wooden bridge that extended a few meters into the lake. They sat along the edge of the pier, ready for some fishing and singing.

"There's something nibbling on the bait!" Pulelo shouted.

Lala rushed over to help her friend. They hoisted the line up, pulling out a little fish. Lala scooped it up and placed it into a transparent container. The fish darted around in the water.

"I'm naming him Silas. He's my pet," Pulelo said.

"How do you know it's a boy?" Lala asked.

"Because I want him to be a boy."

"Come and meet Silas," Ima shouted.

The children gathered around the little tilapia.

"Are you going to eat him when he grows up?" Vivaan asked.

"I don't eat fish," Pulelo said.

It was lunchtime, and the children sat in a half-circle facing the lake with their teachers. They could see wetland birds like Cape gannets, white pelicans, and African fish eagles. Cows were grazing all around, and fishermen were in their wooden canoes.

"Teacher Ima," Pulelo said, "what's the difference between a lake and a river?"

"In a river, the water flows from one place to another. Lakes are surrounded by land," Ima explained.

"Teacher, what about a sea and an ocean?" Vivaan asked.

"That is your homework."

Making it to the Nationals

"**N**EXT!"

Vivaan entered the government office, pushing open the squeaky door. The room was filled with the smell of musty air coming from old papers and furniture, and seated behind the desk, a young woman typed on a computer. She briefly looked up as the person in front of Vivaan left, leaving him next in line. Vivaan placed Lala's consent form on the desk. The young woman continued typing, not paying much attention to him.

"Where are your parents?" she asked without lifting her gaze from the screen.

"I'm here for my friend, Lala. She's a great singer," Vivaan replied.

The lady raised her eyes slightly, keeping her head down. "Where is she?"

"She's not feeling well."

"You have to register in person."

"Why?"

"Why not?"

Vivaan's fingers reached into his wallet. The lady's eyes, flicked to the empty cup on her desk. He dropped a twenty-dollar note into the cup.

"More," she demanded, her voice slicing through the silence.

"Why?"

"Clearly, your father is rich, and mine is dead and poor," she retorted, her smirk cruel and mocking.

Vivaan pulled out two hundred-dollar notes and let them fall into the cup. The lady's face remained stony, her eyes cold. She didn't even acknowledge his gesture.

"Are you from the Middle East, Mohamed?" she asked, her tone dismissive as she prepared his ticket.

"Vivaan, not Mohamed."

"Tomorrow at the community hall, from 6am to 8pm. Next!"

Vivaan went home from there where an elderly Black maid was busy in the kitchen, caring for Vivaan like a mother.

"Nanny, why hasn't any African country won the World Continental Gospel Contest?"

"I guess we're not preparing enough," his Nanny replied.

"Africa is the second-largest continent. There must be someone."

"I don't know about that, but I trust you. One day, you'll be a successful businessman, like your father." She ruffled Vivaan's hair.

"Thanks, Nanny," he said with a proud grin. "I'll be like Dad."

"Go to your room and change; then we can discuss why you asked that question."

Vivaan's room was spacious, with photos of his parents, neatly packed clothes, and a bed made by the hard-working maid. She was well-paid compared to others in the neighbourhood, earning a salary equivalent to that of a graduate worker and taking care of the mansion after Vivaan's mother died.

For more than thirty minutes, the boy sat at his desk. He printed out a file of documents and placed them in his school bag. Nanny finished her chores and sat next to him in the living room. Since Vivaan's mother's death, she had become the mother figure he loved. That's why Vivaan's dad never thought about remarrying. He could travel abroad for days or weeks on business, knowing that she was there to care for Vivaan.

"Now, how was your first day at your new school? Did you like your teachers?"

"The school is amazing, Nanny," Vivaan said.

"Did you make any friends?"

"Nanny," Vivaan said, leaning towards her with a smile. "She is so beautiful."

"What's her name?"

"Lala. She's the principal's daughter, and she sings well."

"Just like her name, in Zulu, Lala means to sing."

"Yes, Nanny. I signed her up for the NGC-13."

"What does NGC-13 stand for?"

"It stands for National Gospel Contest."

"And what about the 13?"

"It's the year, Nanny, 2013."

"Is she good at singing?"

"Yes, and she's going for an audition. I know she'll win like Mother did four years ago."

"You miss your mother, right?"

"Yes, but I have you."

It was still early in the morning. Vivaan put on his best black suit and clowned to the mirror. Nanny walked in.

"How do I look, Nanny?" He straightened his black bowtie.

"Is that your new school uniform, sweetie?"

"I'm not going to school today. I have a meeting with a client." He gave his nanny some money. "Buy groceries and send some to your family."

"Take care of yourself, my little V, but remember, school comes first."

He hopped on his bicycle and rode through the busy street. Lala woke up earlier than usual and returned to bed after a bath. Her mother came to check on her, as she always did.

"I have a meeting with the school board this morning, and you're still sleeping?"

"I'm not feeling well." She let out a series of coughs.

"Get up. I'll take you to the hospital."

"I'll be fine, Mother. Grandma will take care of me."

Lisa glanced at her wristwatch, hurried to her room, and returned with medicine, which she placed next to her daughter.

"Make sure you take your medicine and get plenty of rest."

After Lisa left, Lala gave Vivaan directions to her house. They both got on their bicycles and rode through the city to the community hall where the audition took place. The hall was filled with people of all ages and races, but most were learners and young people.

The contestants took turns stepping into the spotlight, feeling as nervous as a bowstring pulled tight. Four judges sat in front of them, their expressions impossible to read. Lady Gloria, the toughest judge of them all, watched with a cold stare. Even though she wasn't a singer, her opinion held the most weight.

The other three judges were from Windhoek. One of them was a famous gospel singer, whose presence brought warmth to the room. Her praise was genuine, and even when she rejected someone, she did it kindly, making it feel like guidance instead of a dismissal. If she said no, it meant singing wasn't their path.

As the auditions progressed, the local contestants struggled. One by one, they left the stage, their dreams crushed by harsh reality. The last girl stood out, dressed nicely but visibly trembling. She stumbled through the lyrics, her voice shaking.

"Was that English?" Lady Gloria asked.

"Yes!" The girl desperately sought validation in her reply.

"I like your spirit. With all the rubbish you're doing, you are very confident."

"Is that a compliment or an insult?" she asked, this time with more confidence.

The gospel singer leaned forward, her smile softening the tense moment. "You're beautiful. Besides singing, what else can you do?"

"I design clothes..."

"Do you want to know how you did?" another judge asked, his voice neutral.

The girl hesitated, her answer a whisper torn between fear and anticipation. "Yes, I mean no."

After lunch, the room grew quiet as Lala walked up to the microphone, her steps making soft echoes on the dark floor. She looked nervous but determined as she grabbed the mic stand, her fingers wrapping around it for support. She began to sing the Christian song *"My Jesus is my dearest Friend,"* her deep voice filling the room with its beautiful sound. Each note flowed smoothly from her mouth, carrying a lot of emotion that caught the judges' attention.

The judges were focused entirely on Lala as she sang, her voice matching the silence perfectly. Every word she sang felt like she was getting closer to her dreams, and her passion shone through in every lyric. They clapped loudly when she finished her song, bouncing off the walls in a big wave of noise. Lala stood there, her eyes sparkling with pride and achievement. She had put her heart and soul into her performance and waited anxiously for the judge's decision.

"You, my little singer, are going to perform at the national," Lady Gloria said. "Now, call your manager. Congratulations!"

Lala couldn't contain her excitement and skipped outside to find Vivaan. He had a file tucked under his arm and walked with his hand in his pocket, looking like someone significant.

"Hello, ladies and gentlemen! My name is Vivaan, and I am the person behind her incredible talent," he said.

The judges laughed, except for Lady Gloria, who stared at him. Lala stood, fidgeting with her hands but keeping her gaze on the judges. She was worried about what was going to happen next. She knew she needed a responsible adult, like a teacher or a parent, to be present. She thought about her aunt and her teacher.

"Lala," Lady Gloria said, "Congratulations and see you at the national."

After they left, Beth and Victoria from Mr Setiawan's class auditioned. Both did not make it through. Beth was even in tears.

The final contestant was a middle-aged man. The judges deliberated on his talent and appearance. He wore two loose boots on each foot, an oversized T-shirt, and a bandana on his bald head. He bounced around the stage while rapping a gospel song.

"You're almost there, but your looks don't match the gospel vibe. You can't speak to God looking like that! Try a rougher style of music," Lady Gloria said.

"Go to hell, lady," the man said as he began to walk out, swaying his body from side to side as if walking in the mud. His left hand held to his loose jeans, preventing them from dropping.

"Get a belt, Makaveli," said Lady Gloria.

A few days later, Grandma Eliza was in a perfect mood; a jar of cold milk sat on the table as she sipped from another glass, knitting and singing. Lisa returned from school, angry because Lala and Vivaan had left earlier. She stared at the milk jar and let out an annoyed breath. Grandma Eliza continued singing. Lisa went upstairs and found a note on her daughter's bed:

I have gone to Windhoek for the nationals. I promise Vivaan and I will be back after three days. I'm sorry for disobeying you, mother. Please forgive me and bless me.

"She's daring me," Lisa said as she plopped down on a sofa across from her mother, jiggling her legs.

She hurried back to her room, preparing to leave for the city. Despite Grandma Eliza's pleas, she was determined to bring her daughter home immediately. She hadn't given her consent in the first place. Lala had been very disobedient, and Lisa didn't like that at all.

Lisa was now in her car. Grandma Eliza continued to plead. When she realized it wouldn't make a difference, she fell to the ground, jerking as if in a seizure.

"Just get up, Mother."

Grandma Eliza slowly opened one eye and saw that her daughter wasn't budging. She started groaning and jingling her right foot, lying so still that she looked dead. It was clear she wasn't joking. Young Francesca sat on the porch, and with her help, they carried Grandma Eliza into the car.

"Your mother's condition is serious," said a small Englishman, Doctor Jameson. "Luckily, you brought her in on time. We will observe her, and tomorrow, we will be able to answer all your questions. For now, you can go and see her."

"What happened, Sis?" asked Ima as they walked to Grandma Eliza's room.

"Let's wait for the doctor to tell us what's happening."

Grandma Eliza lay on her hospital bed, looking almost dead.

"I shouldn't have insisted, Ima," Lisa said, wiping her tears with a tissue.

"What happened? How is it your fault?"

"I shouldn't have insisted!"

"It's not your fault, Sis. Our mother is so health."

Doctor Jameson returned and asked the two sisters to leave so that he could attend to his patient...

"You can open your eyes now," the doctor said to Grandma Eliza. Grandma Eliza began opening her eyes one after another.

"You should be on TV!" the doctor joked.

"Yes, both of us."

In the waiting room, Lisa kept blaming herself for everything. "Our mother doesn't look good, Ima. The last time was three years ago. Her heart almost stopped."

"Mother will be okay, Sis. Doctor Jameson is a good doctor. Let's go home now."

The next morning in Lisa's house, Ima was sipping her tea and flipping through a magazine at the kitchen table when Lisa walked in. She pulled out the chair across from Ima and slumped into it.

"Sis!" Ima said, looking up from her magazine, noticing the tension in Lisa's body language.

"Can you believe it?" Lisa said. "That disobedient girl went to Windhoek with that boy for the contest! I will go there and bundle her back myself."

"We're going to the hospital today, not Windhoek. Lala will be okay. She's very, very safe."

"You don't understand, Ima. Windhoek is a big city, and anything can happen, and they're just kids."

"I know you're concerned; I am too. But Lala is a very, very smart child, and if she wants to sing, let's support her."

"It's all that boy's fault, he is the one putting ideas in her head."

"I understand, Sis, but you have to trust your own daughter. Lala is growing up so fast and needs to make her own decisions sometimes."

"You're so calm about this," Lisa said.

"And you're so overprotective," Ima chuckled softly. "But we must focus on our mother. She needs us."

"You're right. I'll deal with her when she comes back."

"That's my big sis. Now finish your breakfast," said Ima as she went on to throw her arms around her sister's shoulder.

In Windhoek, Lala and Vivaan shared a room. Vivaan sat on the bed, checking his list of tenants who hadn't paid rent. He sighed and hit the pillow.

"How much money do you collect every month?" Lala asked.

"Thirty-eight," he said.

"Thirty-eight what?"

"Thirty-eight thousand. But that man is causing me trouble. He always comes up with excuses and waits for me to remind him."

"Do you mean Lina's father? Where does he work?"

"He has a good job. I heard he drives for some important person."

"Do you mean our governor?" Lala asked.

"When I go back home, I will kick him out."

"Lina will be angry with you. You know she was already mad at you."

"There is no room for emotions in business, Father said."

"Maybe this year is not going well for them,"

Vivaan had to shake himself a little before he agreed. He gathered his papers, put them in his bag, and admitted, "You're right. I've never experienced that before."

Grandma Eliza was awake and watching TV. It was the first day of the competition, and she could see her granddaughter on the big screen. All the contestants lined up on stage, and Lala was the smallest among them. The audience's applause was loud.

"The contestants from all fourteen regions of the country gathered at the Windhoek Country Club," said the host, a man. "Only two will represent Namibia in Tanzania for the African Gospel Contest. For the next three days, these fantastic singers will compete against each other for a chance to go to the WORLD CONTINENTAL GOSPEL CONTEST in Germany this November 2013."

Grandma Eliza lay on the bed, feeling very happy. She was sipping milk through a straw, eating a piece of chicken, and drinking a glass of Coke. Doctor Jameson was sitting, staring at the screen.

"Doctor, look at my grandchild over there in the pink dress. She's the cutest one, like she came from heaven," Grandma Eliza pointed.

"I know Lala. What I didn't know is that she can sing."

"Oh, doctor, she sings like my favourite singer, Rebecca Malope."

"I have to go check on some real patients. Good luck with your grandchild."

When the host's voice echoed in the venue, calling out her name to the excited audience, Lala was in the Green Room. Even though she heard her name being announced, she looked visibly nervous, tapping her fingers anxiously on her thigh. Vivaan walked in with an official. His presence made her feel more at ease, but her nerves lingered beneath her skin like jittery butterflies.

"I really need some water," Lala whispered urgently, her voice showing how parched she felt as she scanned the room for relief from the dryness that seemed to be choking her.

The host then turned to face the next contestant on his list, a man with dreadlocks named PJ.

"Let me guess. Reggae, right?" he asked.

"Kwaito," PJ replied as he walked up to the stage. He sang a gospel song that the audience enjoyed.

"You have the potential to win this competition," remarked one of the judges.

Meanwhile, Lala's hands shook a little as she brought the bottle to her mouth, the cool water giving her a moment of relief. Vivaan stood by her side, but even that couldn't calm the butterflies fluttering in her chest.

"We didn't come this far to let fear take over." Vivaan tightened his fist, as if holding onto all the memories of their hard work and the sacrifices they made. "We fought for this. You fought for this."

"I didn't expect so many people."

"Those aren't just people. They're your fans, Lala. They're here for you."

"But they don't even know me. How can they be my fans?" A slight frown appeared on Lala's face.

Vivaan smiled softly, though his eyes held a deeper understanding. "They know your voice. They feel your heart. And they love you for that."

Lala gulped, her throat feeling dry despite the water, "Can I call Grandma?"

Grandma Eliza was on her bed, laughing to the TV screen. She cheered for the man with dreadlocks, her voice raspy from excitement. Ima entered the room, and Grandma Eliza flopped back onto the bed, tossing and turning.

"You're not sick, are you?" she asked, pulling the covers off.

"Don't tell your sister. Can you believe she was going to the city to get my Lala back? This is our secret. You must keep it. Now, move. You are not transparent, and you know that."

"Did I ever mention that I love you, Mother?" Ima said with a proud grin.

"You don't need to say it, my cute slippers. I know you love me, and I love you too."

"Slippers? You mean shoes?"

"My special slippers. Now, come sit next to me. She needs all our support."

When Grandma Eliza's phone rang, she picked it up right away, her footsteps quiet in the room as she walked back and forth.

"Grandma," Lala's voice was soft, faint. "Grandma, they are so many people here."

"You can do this, my little mouse. Now go out there and sing for Grandma. Show them who you are."

The line fell silent, but the words stayed. Lala took a deep breath, feeling her grandmother's faith in her, and straightened her posture. It was time.

The phone slipped from Lala's hand, landing gently on the chair. Lala could still hear Grandma Eliza's voice, calm and resolute, resonating in her mind. It grounded her, preventing her from being overwhelmed by the doubts that threatened to consume her. The sound of the crowd outside seemed to grow louder. Vivaan stared at her, his gaze waiting for any indication that she was ready.

"I'm afraid," she said, the words barely audible.

It wasn't a confession; it was a release, a way to acknowledge the burden she carried. Vivaan kneeled in front of her, his hands warm on her knees. "I believe in you," he whispered softly, his words soothing her nerves. "Just remember why you're here. It's not just about you, Lala. It's about every step that brought you here, every person who supported you, every note you sang when no one was around. It's all led to this moment."

"But what if I fail? What if I can't do it?"

"You've already succeeded. The moment you entered this room, you succeeded. Now, it's about showing the world what you've always known."

Lala's heart raced in her chest, matching the beat of the crowd outside. With a deep breath, she stood up, her legs slightly shaky but steady. Vivaan stood up with her...

"For Grandma," she murmured to herself.

"For yourself," Vivaan said.

Lala nodded and turned towards the door. The crowd awaited beyond it, and so did she. Despite the lingering fear, a fierce determination was rising inside her, propelling her forward. She reached for the door handle, pausing briefly as the crowd's cheers grew louder. Then, with a final breath, she pushed the door open and stepped into the spotlight. The brightness overwhelmed her at first, but she quickly adjusted. These were not strangers; they were her supporters, here to cheer her on. The fear that had consumed her began to fade away.

Lala took a deep breath, absorbing the room's energy, blending it with her own. The microphone felt cool and sturdy in her hand. She was dressed in jeans, a pink blouse, and glasses, she took a step forward. The crowd hushed...

"Can I sing?" Lala asked.

"Of course, sweetie," a judge replied.

"You mean now?"

Laughter erupted from the audience; judges included.

"Yes, my dear, right now."

Lala tapped the microphone twice, and the spotlight shone on her. The piano began to play, and the song title appeared on the screen behind her. This was a song she knew well; one she had sung many times in her room with Grandma Eliza but this time, it felt different. This time, she was sharing it with the rest of Namibia and even the whole world. Her voice started softly, unsure, but as she sang, she poured her heart into every word, feeling the energy of the audience fuelling her. The fear she once felt was replaced by pure joy, overflowing with each note she sang. This time, she wasn't just singing for Grandma; she was singing for herself, for Vivaan, for everyone who believed in her, and even for those who doubted her.

After the song, Lala stood there, breathless and smiling, feeling the rush of excitement. She turned a bit, met Vivaan's gaze, and saw the pride in his grin. With the audience standing, the lights shining down, and their cheers filling the hall, Lala knew she belonged. She had stepped into the spotlight, and she wasn't turning back. The applause grew louder, like crashing waves, echoing through Lala's chest like a powerful drumbeat. Grandma Eliza was also cheering, taking a sip from a straw, but she curled back to bed when the doctor and Lisa came in.

"How are you feeling, Mother?" Lisa asked.

"I'm not going to die now. My grandchild is on stage and brought me back to life."

"This young girl, like her mother four years ago, will achieve great things," said the host. "The crowd loves her, the judges love her, and I love her,"

"You will come back. I'm waiting for you," said Lisa.

"Aren't you proud, Sis?" Ima asked.

"She will come back," Lisa said as she went into the corridor to call Mr Setiawan.

"Did you know two of your learners travelled to Windhoek for the contest?"

"I saw them," he said. "And your daughter is doing well!"

"Did you know about that, Mr Setiawan?"

"None of my learners made it through the audition. I don't know how, but I'm glad she did."

"Now you have to travel to the city. Use one of the school minivans."

In Windhoek, the six finalists stood in front of the judges and the crowd. In South Bauleni, Pulelo had gathered Lala's supporters in the school hall, where they watched on a screen mounted next to the entrance. They cheered loudly and passionately.

Grandma Eliza, Lisa, and Ima sat in the hospital; their eyes on the screen. The audience chanted PJ, and the applause was deafening. Lala's heart raced as she stared at the floor. Soon, it would all be over, and she would face her mother. Was it all worth it? The lies and the preparation.

"Say it Mr Host," Lisa whispered.

Two will be declared the winners and represent Namibia on the African stage in Tanzania. Lala desperately needed that, or all her hard work would be for nothing.

"Say it now," Lisa said as she was caught up in the suspense. Her whispered prayers barely filled the room, desperate for good luck to come their way.

"First place goes to Lala, and second place goes to PJ!"

The crowd erupted in cheers. Vivaan, somewhere in the crowd, raised his fists in the air and rushed onto the stage. A shower of confetti in all rainbow colours fell from the ceiling. Mr Setiawan, who had arrived, joined them, and the three embraced. The trophy they received, the cheque worth N$1,000,000, and the golden ticket for the African Gospel Contest in Tanzania were all worth the lies.

Lala, Vivaan, and Mr Setiawan held their victory prizes while the media captured the moment on camera.

"We did it, Grandma," she said to the camera, her voice fading amid the jubilant crowd.

Overwhelmed with joy and forgetting that she had pretended to be sick, Grandma Eliza jumped out of bed and screamed for a hug from Ima, which she never had the chance to give. When she realized she was about to reveal her little secret, she leapt back into bed and gently threw herself down.

"Just get up from the bed, Mother," Ima said, pulling away the sheet.

"You're not sick?" Lisa rose from the seat.

Grandma Eliza remained silent for a moment before stretching out her arms, swinging her legs off the bed, and slipping into her slippers. She stood close to Lisa and looked into her eyes. "Do I look sick to you?"

"Where is that lying doctor!" Lisa shouted.

"Leave the good doctor alone."

When the doctor entered the room, Lisa blocked his path. "Start talking," she demanded.

"It was her idea, but I discharged your mother a long time ago," Doctor Jameson said. "Come to think of it, your daughter won."

"Let's go home, Mother," Ima said. "Your mission was a success..."

The school entrance was packed with learners, teachers, and the local media. Lisa stood by the side of other school managers. The car came to a stop. Vivaan bowed dramatically and gestured towards the new celebrity singer. Lala's fans cheered for her, waving and chanting her name.

"How do you feel about winning the contest?" the reporter asked.

Her smile showed how excited she was. Vivaan started goofing around for the camera. He leaned towards the microphone. "We're off to Tanzania!"

"And who might you be, sir?" the reporter asked.

"Vivaan, her manager."

Lisa locked eyes with her daughter. Lala looked down.

"Don't hang your head," Lisa said. "This is your moment."

"I'm sorry for disobeying you, Mother."

"After your trip to Tanzania, you'll face your punishment."

"I love you, Mother," Lala said.

"I love you too, Principal Ndafenongo," Vivaan said with a silly chortle.

Lisa didn't respond to the young Indian as she hurried to her office. Ima and Lala embraced while Lisa watched from her office window. Her daughter took pictures with other learners. Pulelo stood next to Ima, ready to hug Lala, when Vivaan pulled her away. Pulelo's smile faded, her arms falling to her sides as she looked confused. She glanced at Ima, hoping for an answer or some comfort.

Ima saw it all, and kneeled next to Pulelo, gently touching her cheek.

"It wasn't on purpose, sweetie," she whispered, glancing at Vivaan before returning her gaze to Pulelo.

Pulelo clenched her fists. Meanwhile, the Girls—Huge Lilian, Beth, and Victoria—watched from their vantage point, their eyes narrowed, and their lips pressed into tight lines. They were feeling really frustrated, even though everyone else around them was having a great time with Lala.

The netball game

Grandma Eliza had gathered her family to celebrate her granddaughter's win, and Lisa sat eating, oblivious to the others around her. Ima, meanwhile, couldn't stop showering praises on Lala and once in a while running her fingers through Lala's hair.

"You know, Grandma," Lala said between bites, "when they said I was next, I got so, so nervous."

"They call it 'first time' for a reason," Grandma Eliza replied.

"When it happened to me," Ima said, "I took it one note at a time."

"One note at a time," Lala said with a smile.

"Sis," Ima turned to Lisa.

"Hush, Ima. Can you eat quietly for once?" said Lisa.

"You know what?" Grandma Eliza exclaimed happily. "People will start respecting me more at church and in the market. My granddaughter is a singer."

"So am I," Ima laughed.

Just then, Lisa rose from her chair, preparing to leave to her room, when two shadows appeared at the door. She sat back. Lala skipped to the door. As it swung open, Vivaan and his nanny entered, carrying trays of food and drinks. "Good afternoon, Mrs Lisa," greeted Vivaan's nanny.

"Hello, *ba*Jane," Lisa replied, looking at Vivaan and then turning to his nanny. "Don't tell me this boy is Anita's son?"

"Yes, Mrs Lisa."

"You know my mother?" Vivaan asked.

"Anita and I were friends."

"Sweetheart," Grandma Eliza said, "your mother was a beautiful soul. You and Lala were born on the same day."

"Yes," Ima added, "and she was a good singer."

"Anita won the 2009 National Gospel Contest. Is that Vivaan's mother?" Lala asked.

"Yes, sweetheart," Ima said.

"Mrs Lisa," Vivaan's nanny said, "Vivaan's grandfather is not well in India, and he wants to see his grandson."

"Hey, Mr Businessman!" Lisa said joyously, extending her arms wide to give Vivaan a hug. "You've got your mother's nose and eyes. And those big ears of hers, too!"

Vivaan looked slightly pained by Lisa's tight hug and only Ima seemed to notice how uncomfortable the boy was.

"Loosen up the boy, Sis!" Ima said.

Lisa's phone rang, and she answered it. The room could hear her shouting with delight. Lisa turned to her family, whispering, "It's Mrs O'Hara."

"Put it on speaker, honey," Mrs O'Hara's voice said through the phone. "I'm so happy for our superstar,"

Everyone gathered around as Mrs O'Hara expressed her excitement, promising to be in Tanzania to support Lala and her family. Immediately after, the phone rang again. Agatha, Nadia, and Sanana congratulated Lala and pledged their support.

"I miss then all," said Lisa to her family after the call. "Life has drifted us far and wide. After retiring, Mrs O'Hara returned to the States, where she live with her daughter Sophia, Sophia's husband, and their two boys. Agatha is now headmistress of Sunpride, while Sanana and Nadia had used their inheritance to build an empire. And, criminals like Jessica and Mary are still rotting in prison, and the Old Driver died seven years ago, some say from old age and others from a beating. Mukenani and Tiwe are now owners of a prestigious law firm in Windhoek. Angela still ran a shebeen. Aunt Dorothy had retired and is very free from alcohol."

"Death took away my sister and her husband," *ba*Eliza said, remembering *bana*Monde and her husband.

"Its life mother,' said Ima. "The only constant thing in life is change."

The day drifted into good memories and the next day at school, Lala was listening to music near the school netball field while the team prepared for a Saturday game. Pulelo, with a novel she was reading, came from the tennis courts and sat next to Lala.

"You read a lot," Lala said. "Who's your favourite author?"

"I don't really have one," Pulelo replied, stowing away her book. "Beth and Victoria were talking. They said you won't win and that you can't sing. They're just jealous. Don't pay attention to them."

"I know I can sing."

As Pulelo and Lala began to head back to class, the girls from the team blocked their path. They stood before them, almost identical except for Huge Lilian, Beth, and Victoria.

"The little diva," Beth sneered. "How was Windhoek? Last time I checked, your city was flooded."

"Please move," Lala said calmly.

"We all want to be your friend now that you're famous," Victoria added, her team laughing in agreement.

Pulelo stepped forward, but Victoria shoved her aside, causing her to stumble. "Go to the library and pick up one of those novels for from liars like you," Victoria taunted. "Let me recommend..."

"Wait, Victoria," Beth interrupted. "How about Aladdin and that stupid genie? That might inspire you to write some silly stories one day."

"Yeah, maybe you'll write your own stories someday," Victoria added sarcastically.

"One day, you'll read my stories," Pulelo said firmly.

Lala took Pulelo's hand and pushed past Beth to leave.

"The writer and the singer," Victoria shouted after them.

"Do you think she can write a story?" Huge Lilian asked.

"What do you think, Lilian?" Beth asked.

"I'm not Lilian. I'm Huge Lilian," turning around to reveal the words "HUGE LILIAN" on her uniform and shoes. Everywhere."

"Here's the plan," Victoria, the team captain, said. "Tomorrow, we play as a team and win. Huge Lilian, you'll be our shooter, and I know you're good at that."

At the assembly, Lisa made it clear that attendance at the game was compulsory. The Riverweed Girls were the cream of the region, and South Bauleni had never defeated them. Lisa's voice carried loudly across the assembly grounds, capturing everyone's attention.

"Riverweed might think they're better than us," Lisa began, "but let me make something clear. That doesn't mean we're any less valuable as a school. Our girls have worked hard, and I truly believe we can win tomorrow."

The girls stood resolute, with Huge Lilian leading, though she seemed less enthusiastic, perhaps thinking, "Forget it; we can't beat Riverweed."

"Let me tell you a little story. Back in 1992, when I was a student in these very classrooms, we formed a girls' soccer team in grade 9. And you know what? We defeated Riverweed's girls' soccer team. That victory alone helped shape our school's reputation. So, my dear students, remember the strength of those who came before you as you step onto that field. Believe in yourselves, and let's show them what we're made of. Good luck to each one of you."

"Those arrogant girls think they can beat the Riverweed team," said Pulelo to Lala.

"I want our girls to win. It's our school. You must support them, Pulelo. They need us," said Lala.

"I will never support them. I hate them."

"When you support them, you support our school. Forget about their attitude. I'll wait for you in front of the library, and we'll go and cheer for them. Say yes now. You're my friend!"

"Do I have any choice?"

"You know what? Why don't you come over to my house?"

"And where's Vivaan? You should invite him."

"He's travelled to India."

"I see. So, I'm just a placeholder then," Pulelo muttered.

Lala placed her school bag on her lap and pulled out two lollipops. "Pink or black?"

"It's up to you. They're yours. Besides, it's the flavour that matters, not the colour," Pulelo replied.

"Cheer up, Pulelo. You are my best friend."

"I'll take black," Pulelo said, unwrapping the black lollipop.

"I love pink!"

"I know."

"How do you know that?"

"Your socks, Lala, and your school bag."

Lala checked her time, and she whispered to her friend, "I will see you tomorrow."

Ima was still in her work attire, seated in her living room sipping a cold drink while facing the turned-off TV.

"Good afternoon, Aunt Ima!" greeted Lala.

"Your meal is on the table."

Lala skipped happily to her aunt's room, singing along the way. This was her usual routine whenever she stayed with her aunt. She returned wearing pyjamas and ate while turning on a music channel.

"My favourite show is about to start," said Ima.

Lala smiled, knowing all her aunt's favourite shows because she enjoyed them too. "They begin at four and end at nine," Lala said.

Meanwhile, Lisa massaged her mother's feet. Grandma Eliza glanced at the wall clock; it was five minutes to four.

"Your daughter is going to Tanzania. Are all the arrangements going well?"

"I have a bad feeling about this, Mother. That girl isn't emotionally ready."

"You worry too much about life. Take it one step at a time! Can I come with you tomorrow? I love watching netball."

"Who told you about the netball?"

"People talk, child. They're not like you, who keeps things hidden."

"Well, you're not going. You can watch netball on TV."

"I need to get out. I need some fresh air. Are you taking me, or should I call Ima?"

"You're not going, and you're not calling Ima!"

At school, Lala wore pink leggings and a white blouse as she marched to the netball field with her fellow students. The scent of petrichor filled the air, enhancing the beauty of the morning. Clouds shielded the sun, making the fields appear even greener. The Girls trooped onto the court; each wore a bib featuring a two-letter abbreviation. Dressed in yellow and black, players like Huge Lilian were marked as HL, Victoria as VJ, and Beth as BH.

Lisa sat next to Ima, Mr Setiawan, and other teachers. A man in a suit, two others, and Eva from Riverweed were seated on Lisa's left. A white school bus with red markings pulled up, carrying the Riverweed Girls who shouted from the windows. Lala and Pulelo sat at the bottom of the pavilion, with Pulelo flipping through a novel.

"The netball team has their own bus!" Lala said.

The students on the pavilion talked about the big white bus, a rare sight in South Bauleni where only minivans were common. Thanks to Mr Setiawan's efforts, two new VW minivans had recently been donated. Grandma Eliza and Grandpa Sylvester arrived, jogging to the pavilion. Lisa watched them from a distance.

"Look at those two clowns," she said.

"Leave them alone, Sis. Mother needs some fresh air," Ima replied.

"What fresh air? Mother is old. She should stay home and watch TV," Lisa snapped.

Ima waved at their mother, who waved back. Lisa looked down at Grandma Eliza, who was receiving attention from passing students.

"I hope your mother doesn't do something silly."

Ima looked up at the sky and squinted. "Will it rain today?"

"Yes, Ima, it will rain. Go home and place buckets under the gutters of your roof. You'll have plenty of water to use."

"I don't collect water from the roof," Ima said, her gaze shifting towards the Riverweed bus. "That bus looks amazing. Don't you think our school needs one like that?"

"I'll buy it tonight when I go to sleep," Lisa replied dryly. "Are you happy now?"

"We do need a bus like that, Lisa."

"This is a government school; we don't have fancy things like that here."

"Stop talking about bureaucracy. Some things are up to us."

Beth, tying her shoelaces next to Huge Lilian and Victoria, watched the Riverweed girls in white and blue uniforms walking down the bus stairs. "Isn't that Julia?" Beth asked.

Julia's confidence clearly marked her as the best on her team. Their uniforms had only their names, like soccer players.

"What?" Beth said again, sounding discouraged. "Violetta! Who could score against her in defence?"

"I can," Huge Lilian replied. "If you're not ready, Cindy can take your place."

The court cheered with so much excitement as the two teams, dressed in bright uniforms, gathered on the rectangular court. Seven players on each side stood poised to make their moves. In one corner, Huge Lilian and Beth positioned themselves in the attacker's shooting circle. Across from them, a tall girl focused on defending against the two attackers. The referee, a woman from the nearby primary school, wore a red tracksuit and took charge. With a sharp blow of her whistle, the game began, and players dashed across the court, each striving for victory. Cheers erupted from the sidelines, filling the air with support. The visitors' cheers stood out among the crowd, blending into a chorus of encouragement.

Beth passed the ball to Huge Lilian, sparking excitement and a vital energy pulsating through the court. Huge Lilian's determined look revealed her focus as she prepared for the shot. Just as she was about to release the ball, Violetta, a powerful force on defence, swiftly moved forward like a guardian angel, blocking Huge Lilian's attempt with a resounding thud. The ball bounced off Violetta's hands, spinning into the chaotic centre of the court before landing in Julia's waiting hands.

Amidst the frenzy, Julia remained composed, displaying great poise. With one decisive move, Julia threw the ball towards the waiting hoop, showcasing her skill and finesse as it sailed with pinpoint accuracy. The net momentarily shook before yielding to the force of the ball, earning the team another point.

"Who coaches our netball team?" Lisa turned to face Ima.

"We still have time," Ima replied.

The final quarter commenced, Riverweed, buoyed by their earlier success, stood poised to claim victory, their confidence evident as they readied themselves to seal their triumph.

As the game progressed, Beth passed the ball to Huge Lilian, who was prepared and waiting. South Bauleni's hope dimmed like a flickering flame in encroaching darkness. With only six minutes left on the clock, the daunting reality of their situation cast doubt over their spirits. Yet Beth refused to be deterred by the mounting pressure. Once more, she orchestrated the play, delivering the ball to Huge Lilian. They pressed forward, their sights set on the prize that seemed just out of reach. However, as they approached the goal, Violetta stood tall as an imposing obstacle, casting a shadow over their hopes and dreams. With each attempt, she defended with unwavering strength, causing the once bright hope in the hearts of South Bauleni to flicker and fade under Riverweed's dominance.

Riverweed surged forward, their movements swift and decisive. With each pass and manoeuvre, they edged closer to victory, their cheers echoing through the field. Among all the players, Julia's every move was met with applause from the crowd.

As the crowd's cheers peaked, Grandma Eliza said, "That little girl plays well," her eyes following Julia's every move with great interest. "How does she do it?"

The final moments of the game unfolded; tension filled. All eyes on the ball as it soared high above the court. Violetta and Huge Lilian leapt with purpose, stretching their arms towards the ball. In a twist of fate, Huge Lilian caught the ball in her waiting hands. She initiated the final sequence of events, the ball bouncing across the court like a playful spirit. The crowd watched. And then, with a satisfying thud, it found its mark, passing through the hoop and into the net. South Bauleni Girls scored but the game concluded instantly, declaring Riverweed as the winners and igniting a wave of cheers from their supporters.

Pulelo laughed amidst the joyful noise...

"I can't wait to see Beth and Victoria's faces on Monday," she said.

"Are you happy?" Lala asked.

"I never wanted them to win. Those girls can be so mean."

The next day, Lala and Pulelo had breakfast in the school cafeteria. The Girls - Beth, Victoria, Huge Lilian, and the others - entered. Pulelo said, "Fifty-two to one! What a defeat!"

Huge Lilian halted and glared at Pulelo and Lala. "It's just a game, you idiots," Huge Lilian said. Despite being petite, Huge Lilian possessed a fiery temper.

"I was thinking," Pulelo began, "let's form our own gang. I'm thinking of Fenni, Judy, and that Herero girl."

"What can those three do? No one likes them," Lala said, glancing over at the girls.

"I haven't been to Tanzania, but I hear it's beautiful."

"You'll travel too, Pulelo. One day, you'll write great books and see the world."

In Lisa's office, she sat across from Mr Martin. "I'll be travelling to Dar es Salaam. I'll leave you in charge."

Trip to Dar es Salaam

The flight to Tanzania was exhilarating! Lala had her music teacher, Mr Setiawan, and her family with her, including Lisa, Grandma Eliza, and Ima. And Vivaan, her self-proclaimed manager.

Namibia's other second-prize winner also had her family and friends with him. Each of the fifty-five African countries sent two participants. The top singers from each country in all five geographical regions competed for the coveted spot. The winner would represent Africa at the World Continental Gospel Contest in Germany. Six contestants, one from each continent, would vie for the grand prize. However, Lala, still lacking experience, faced formidable singers from across Africa. Were the odds in her favour?

Last year, seventeen-year-old Hanneleen from Dar es Salaam made it to the finals. Her extraordinary soprano vocal range had impressed everyone. Andriaan, a boy also from Dar es Salaam, was a finalist with his polished tenor range. Both returned this season, determined to win.

The Namibian team breathed a sigh of relief as the plane landed at Julius Nyerere International Airport. It was Lala's maiden flight.

Lala and her family were chauffeured to Coral Beach Hotel in a white Toyota SUV. The commissionaire, a genial man in his late forties, greeted them with a smile. Porters ushered them to their suite, number 43. Mr Setiawan and Vivaan occupied the adjacent room.

Later that evening, they gathered in room 43, where Mr Setiawan imparted some last-minute coaching.

"Tomorrow is a big day! Remember why you're here. You're competing against the finest singers from this entire continent. Some boast extensive experience and excellent mentors. But guess what? You, my dear friend, possess the potential to win! Always remember that you are your greatest supporter, and no matter what, believe in yourself. Your voice is unique with a rare contralto range spanning three octaves and two notes. It exudes warmth, softness, and an ethereal quality. And don't forget to engage the audience and enjoy yourself!"

After dinner, Lala and Vivaan strolled through the hotel corridors. They met Hanneleen, accompanied by her two Caucasian friends, Catherine and Gladness. The twins sported matching outfits. Lala recalled Hanneleen from last year's competition.

"What's your name, young girl?" Hanneleen asked.

"Lala."

"Did you come with your parents to watch the live show?"

"She's competing," Vivaan said.

"Wow!" said Catherine.

"Which country are you from?" Gladness asked.

"Namibia."

"Where is Namibia?" Catherine wondered aloud.

Hanneleen and her friends continued exploring before returning to their room. Hanneleen settled into a plush armchair, while the twins embarked on a quick bicycle ride. Moments later, Hanneleen answered a knock at the door to find Andriaan standing there.

"If I can't win this year, you must. Tanzania must represent Africa," Andriaan declared. "This is for Tanzania."

"For Tanzania!" Hanneleen said.

"For Tanzania!" the twins shouted in unison.

The moon bathed the streets of Dar es Salaam in its gentle light. Everyone flocked at the arena, eager for the event. The stage was adorned with dazzling spotlights, casting vibrant hues onto the crowd. The audience erupted in cheers and applause. Colourful fireworks illuminated the sky. A spotlight picked on Dlamini; the charismatic host dressed in a stylish blue suit. He danced, eliciting thunderous applause from the audience.

"Good evening, ladies and gentlemen," Dlamini said to the crowd through the microphone, his popularity evident. "Now, let's welcome our esteemed judges. From Seychelles, we have Judge Fillip Roy!"

The crowd rose to its feet, welcoming Judge Fillip Roy. The crowd cheering and dancing as he made his entrance, leaning on his walking stick.

"He's quite ancient!" Catherine whispered to Gladness.

"In Africa, wisdom comes with age," someone in the audience responded.

Judge Fillip Roy took his time reaching his seat, a leisurely stroll across the stage taking over a minute.

"And our final judge, Judge Maria Jacqueline," Dlamini announced.

The music of the celebrity judge began playing, a shadowy figure of a Brazilian wig visible to the crowd.

"Where did they find these judges!" Grandma Eliza laughed.

"It's not about speed, Grandma. It's about moving forward," Vivaan said.

"This is Africa, mother!" Lisa said. "We respect and value the wisdom of our elders more than the young. They believe that young people have nothing to offer."

The audience erupted into thunderous applause as the two judges took their seats.

"Welcome to the National Gospel Contest, drawing participants from diverse African nations. The winners from all fifty-five African nations will compete here at Coral Beach in Dar es Salaam. To compete for the chance to represent Africa at the World Continental Gospel Contest in Germany. Six contestants from the six continents of the world will compete for the grand title. As you can see, this journey means everything to all of us. Africa should send the best of the best."

The applause filled the air.

"The theme for this year's competition is 'CELEBRATING GOD THROUGH GOSPEL MUSIC'," the host announced. "Now, let's introduce Atshumao from Botswana, performing her winning song."

The crowd erupted as the talented singer, enjoying a four-octave vocal range, took to the stage. She sang with confidence in her native language, leaving the audience and judges alike in awe. Everyone rose to their feet following her performance.

Next up was Hanneleen, a crowd favourite. She strode onto the stage with a serious expression and launched into a song immediately. Her powerful soprano voice mesmerised both the masses and the judges, prompting spontaneous singing and dancing, particularly from the twins.

"You're going to Germany! Believe it!" Judge Roy declared.

The night went on and on. When Lala finally took the stage, Grandma Eliza stood up. Lala held a silver microphone close to her chest with both hands. This was the largest crowd she had ever performed in front of. She recalled her teacher's sage advice: " Be your own cheerleader. Remember, you possess a rare contralto vocal range spanning three octaves and two notes. Your voice is warm, gentle, and airy, a natural gift."

A hush fell over the crowd. Grandma Eliza, Lala's staunchest supporter, let out a loud whistle. Ima and Vivaan clasped their hands in prayer. Catherine and Gladness couldn't contain their laughter.

"The little girl is scared," Catherine chuckled.

Lala glanced at Mr Setiawan, who offered an encouraging nod. She tapped the microphone twice, prompting excitement throughout the arena. Grandma Eliza surrendered a shrill whistle, giving her granddaughter her courage back. She began to sing. Lala's voice reverberated through the arena as she sang the opening notes into the microphone.

"Wow!" Catherine said. "She sings like an angel."

"Quiet, Catherine!" Gladness scolded. "We're here to support Hanneleen and Andriaan only."

One by one, the spectators rose to their feet, hands raised in unified applause, except for Gladness and her sister who watched with reserved interest. Amidst the sea of cheers and waving banners, the diminutive figure of the Namibian girl, Lala, gracefully traversed the stage in gentle circles. The crowd, still on their feet, joined in singing along to the song, creating a harmonious chorus that resonated throughout the arena to the very end.

"In Namibia, they call her 'The Biggest Little Singer,'" announced Dlamini, his voice carrying over the enthusiastic cheers of the crowd.

Once again, applause thundered through the arena as Lala stood proudly on stage next to the host, her arm draped casually around his waist.

"The Biggest Little Singer!" shouted Judge Fillip Roy with admiration.

"Ladies and gentlemen, that concludes our session for today. The show will resume this evening at the same time," declared Dlamini.

In the softly lit Green Room, the contestants gathered after the show, their shared joy and camaraderie filling the space with warmth and excitement. Amidst the friendly chatter and laughter, Lala couldn't help but notice Hanneleen, who appeared more serious and distant than the others. Lala stole glances at her, wondering about the enigmatic contestant. However, Hanneleen's stern gaze warned Lala to keep her distance.

Just then, Latifah entered the room, showing warmth and charm that instantly brightened the atmosphere, drawing Lala's attention away from Hanneleen. Latifah sat next to Lala, extending her hand in greeting. "Hello there! You sing beautifully," Latifah said.

"Thank you. You're so kind and refined. Is that what Latifah means?" Lala asked.

"You're not only talented but smart too!"

As their conversation flowed, Lala felt a sense of connection with Latifah, as if they were more than mere competitors. The Green Room gradually emptied as Lisa entered with another woman.

"Mother, meet my friend Latifah," said Lala.

"You sing beautifully," Lisa said. "You're from Nigeria, right?"

"Yes, auntie. And you have a remarkable daughter," Latifah responded graciously.

"Good luck, Latifah. Now, everyone needs to get some rest."

Later that morning, Grandma Eliza and Ima were already fast asleep when Lisa and Lala returned to their suite. Grandma Eliza lay sprawled on the sofa, snoring softly, while Ima dozed on the other couch. Later, they all gathered for breakfast. Lala basked in the praise and encouragement showered upon her, accepting each compliment with a sense of pride.

"You've overcome the first hurdle beautifully. You're doing well, my dear," Mr Setiawan said.

"Teacher, I think Hanneleen will win," Lala admitted candidly. "Mother!"

"I know what you're thinking, young lady. Let me save you the trouble. Yes, Hanneleen will win. She will crush your soul and you will never defy me again."

Lala exchanged a knowing smile with Mr Setiawan as if her mother's words where encouraging.

"Once this is all over, we'll go home tomorrow," Lisa continued. "I don't like disobedient children." Lisa shifted her attention to Vivaan, eating his breakfast. "And you, where is your father?"

"He travelled," Vivaan replied casually.

Africa's Hope for Global Glory

The contestants stepped onto the stage, sparking a surge of excitement throughout the arena. The host ripped open the envelope.

"For some contestants, their journey ends here. However, the six singers who advance to the quarterfinals will also earn a chance to participate in the World Continental Gospel Contest in Germany, alongside the winner. If Africa secures first or second place, they will perform as a group on stage. Ladies and gentlemen, as they say, the referee's decision is final; here, the judge's decision is final!"

After a brief interlude, the host returned, unfolding the envelope to reveal the first qualifier.

"Congratulations, Latifah from Nigeria!"

Latifah, a gifted mezzo-soprano with an impressive vocal range of 3.6 octaves, dropped to her knees in gratitude, thanking the Lord. The audience, including ecstatic Nigerian fans, rose to their feet, filling the arena with exuberant cheers.

"Next up, we have Lala from Namibia."

The crowd erupted in jubilation. Grandma Eliza and her family sported blue T-shirts with Lala's image, while Lisa celebrated uniquely, her eyes sparkling with joy.

"Cheer up, Lisa," Ima said. "No matter what happens next, we're going to Germany. You should be proud of your daughter. As for me, I'm off to Europe, whether you like it or not."

"You're talking nonsense, Ima! Of course, I'm excited!"

Catherine and Gladness sat with furrowed brows. Among all the announcements, the mention of the Namibian contestant seemed to affect them deeply.

"Bassel from Egypt."

"Andriaan from Tanzania."

Catherine and Gladness leapt up like a volcano, causing a commotion that turned all eyes towards them. They wore bright orange outfits featuring a large picture of Hanneleen's face on their shirts, chanting Andriaan's name with fervour.

Moments later, the five quarter-finalists took their seats on stage, leaving one chair empty. Led by Catherine and Gladness, the crowd began chanting Hanneleen's name. Hanneleen appeared visibly nervous, standing there with other contestants. One of them will join the five quarter finalists. Host Dlamini's manner did little to assuage her nerves.

"HANNELEEN!"

Hanneleen made a few steps to join the host. She didn't smile or acknowledge the audience's applause, a characteristic that seemed to earn her their respect.

"There we have it folks. Our six quarterfinalists."

The other contestants left the stage, their journey in the competition has come to an end. Perhaps next year would bring them another chance. God willing.

The judges and audience accorded the six quarterfinalists a standing ovation. Among them stood Latifah, Nigeria's superstar; Lala from Namibia; Bassel from Egypt; Gatimu from Kenya; and Andriaan and Hanneleen from Tanzania, the host nation. Hanneleen, clad in traditional attire, stood with her thumbs hooked in her pockets.

"This is the moment, everyone!" Dlamini proclaimed. "The judges have done their part, and now it's your turn, the audience and viewers, to vote for your favourite. Who do you want to see proceed to the semi-finals?"

Cheers erupted, names were shouted, and Hanneleen emerged as the clear favourite.

"Ladies and gentlemen, tonight these contestants will compete for a spot in the semi-finals. Don't let your favourite's journey end here. Voting begins now!" The host turned to the judges, he asked, "What are your thoughts, judges?"

"It was a tough decision," replied Judge Maria Jacqueline. "All of them are talented singers. But decisions must be made; that's part of the competition."

"You're right, it's never easy," added Judge Fillip Roy. "This is a contest, and not everyone can win."

The crowd continued to cheer, blowing their noise makers in excitement.

"Each quarterfinalist will now perform a song composed in the last five years by an artist from their country," the host declared. "Please welcome Lala, the promising talent from Namibia."

Spotlights picked Lala as she took the stage, delivering her song with confidence and ease. In the Green Room, the other contestants watched her performance on screen. Hanneleen sat impassively, while the effervescent Latifah couldn't resist showering Lala with praise. Lala captivated the audience with her rendition. Her grandmother raised her arms in excitement, Ima danced and sang along, Lisa clapped to the rhythm, and Vivaan couldn't resist tapping his feet. Mr Setiawan joined in the dancing as well.

"You're my favourite," Judge Fillip Roy said.

"You know what?" Judge Maria Jacqueline said. "Where have you been hiding all these years?"

"In her cradle, sucking on her left foot," quipped Catherine.

Next on stage, Latifah charmed everyone, sparking a dance frenzy. Bassel's performance garnered little reaction from the audience. Gatimu, however, won hearts with a touching Christmas song. Andriaan moved everyone to tears with a funeral song, he dedicated to his late uncle who, his family believed, had succumbed to sorcery and high-level witchcraft on Christmas day.

Finally, Hanneleen, everyone's favourite, stirred the audience with a repentant song sung with deep emotion, though she remained aloof towards the ecstatic crowd.

As the performances concluded, the contestants retreated to the Green Room to rest. Hanneleen chose solitude, while Latifah struck up a lively conversation with Lala, enjoying their camaraderie. Andriaan was on the phone with his mother, exaggerating the praise he had received from both audience and judges.

"I'm so proud of you! I'll tell your dad and all your uncles about your amazing success."

"Please don't let Uncle Vaino know. He's not a nice man."

"Okay, I'll just tell his wife."

"Don't tell his wife. She'll tell him, and she's as mean as her husband."

"But sweetheart, you're on TV. Aunt Dorcus loves TV."

Dlamini entered the room, followed by the two judges. Andriaan kissed his mom goodbye over the phone before joining the judges in front of the contestants.

"Congratulations to all of you," said Judge Maria Jacqueline. "Africa is watching, and we're all immensely proud."

"Yes," added Judge Roy. "Regardless of the outcome, you're all superstars. We can all now rest. The competition continues tonight. Good luck!"

Lala was among the last to leave the Green Room. Hanneleen shot her a frustrated glare, reaching for her phone, only for the door to burst open before she could dial. Catherine and Gladness rushed in, embracing Hanneleen.

"We must celebrate this," Gladness declared.

Hanneleen made her way to her room. Catherine and Gladness followed...making noise all the way. They didn't care.

The next day, the results were announced. Bassel and Gatimu didn't make it to the semi-finals. Hanneleen, Andriaan, Lala, and Latifah captivated the audience with their outstanding performances, creating an electrifying atmosphere. With only three spots available for the finals, the tension soared as the host announced the names. Andriaan, Hanneleen, and Lala emerged as the finalists, securing the crowd's votes. The question now remained: Who would represent Africa—Hanneleen, Andriaan, or Lala? One final performance to decide.

The spotlight fell on the host as he stepped onto the stage.

"Welcome to the grand finale of the African Gospel Contest. Let's give a warm welcome to our judges!"

The crowd erupted in cheers and applause.

"First up, performing a song from her favourite artist, please welcome the people's choice, Hanneleen!"

The audience rose to their feet, chanting her name. Banners and pictures of Hanneleen held high by her dedicated fans. Meanwhile, Lala and Andriaan watched from a separate room. Grandma Eliza, Lisa, and the others sat silently in the audience, acknowledging Hanneleen's undeniable talent.

"I don't like this Afrikaner girl," Grandma Eliza muttered.

"Me too, Grandma," Vivaan said.

Hanneleen sang her heart out while the crowd cheered.

"The voting lines are now open. If you want Hanneleen to represent Africa, vote now," Dlamini announced. "Next up is Lala!"

Namibian fans, including Grandma Eliza and her family, demonstrated their unwavering support and love.

"My mother sang this song at the national finals in Windhoek four years ago," Lala said, taking a moment as the audience welcomed her warmly. "This is for you, Mother!"

Lisa wiped away her tears as the crowd sang along with Lala, lyrics displayed on a large screen. Judge Fillip Roy stood with raised hands in applause. Lala bowed before the judges as the host draped an arm around her.

"You're a diva. A superstar," Judge Fillip Roy praised. "What's your mother's name?"

"Lisa Ndafenongo. She's with Grandma Eliza, Aunt Ima, Teacher Setiawan, and my manager, Vivaan."

Judge Fillip Roy invited Lisa and her family onstage. Grandma Eliza was the first to step forward, amusing the crowd and judges with her agility.

"I remember you. You were the runner-up in the nationals in Namibia four years ago," Judge Fillip Roy recalled.

"She must be your grandmother, right?" the other judge asked.

"Yes, and my aunt."

"And where's your manager?"

Vivaan, dressed sharply in a suit, raised his left hand as if in a classroom, ready to answer a question. The crowd erupted in delight.

"You have a strong team," Judge Maria Jacqueline acknowledged.

The following evening arrived, imbuing the arena with tension. The three finalists, their nerves taut, stood frozen under the bright lights, facing an audience eagerly anticipating something extraordinary, while judges scrutinised their every move. When the results were announced, a heavy silence descended upon the room. Andriaan's disappointment was evident as he was eliminated, leaving just two contenders in the spotlight.

When the host declared "Hanneleen" as the winner, time seemed to stand still. For Lala, hearing "Hanneleen's" name felt like a deafening crash, shattering her hopes and dreams. The world blurred as tears welled up, her heart feeling defeated. She made no attempt to conceal her sorrow, letting her emotions silently spill out.

Hanneleen noticed Lala's tears and, without hesitation, knelt in front of her with open arms. In that embrace, there was no winner or loser—just two souls who understood each other. The once raucous arena fell silent as the crowd watched. Confetti fell like shattered dreams, enveloping Hanneleen and Lala, united in a moment of profound emotion transcending competition.

"Congratulations to Hanneleen, and congratulations to all the contestants. Goodnight!"

Hanneleen raised her trophy of victory, cameras capturing the moment. Her dream of representing Africa had finally come true. Her commanding voice held the promise of breaking Africa's long-standing poor performance at the global stage. For nearly fifty years, Africa had typically been eliminated in the initial rounds.

Catherine and Gladness joined Hanneleen on stage, playfully vying to hold the trophy. Lala collapsed. Lisa and the others hurried back to assist, but paramedics blocked their path. When Lala regained consciousness, she murmured, "Grandma!"

"You frightened me, my little mouse," Grandma Eliza said.

"We're leaving today," Lisa grumbled. "This shouldn't have happened in the first place."

Thirty minutes later, Ima burst into the room with Lala, Grandma Eliza, Vivaan, and Mr Setiawan trailing behind her. They stumbled upon scattered luggage bags near the dining table. Lala's small suitcase sat atop the table.

Lisa stood in Mr Setiawan's way and said, "We're leaving this place. We'll talk when we get home." She then crouched down to Vivaan's eye level, pushing her glasses to the edge of her nose, and added, "Little man, this message applies to you too." She slammed the door shut behind them and was about to say something unkind to her sister when a soft knock interrupted her. Ima answered the door, and there stood Hanneleen, Catherine, and Gladness.

"Lala, sweetheart, look who's here to see you," Ima said.

Catherine reached for some groundnuts from Lisa's plate, but Lisa slapped her hand away sharply. Lala leaned against her grandmother while Ima offered Hanneleen and her friends, seats. Catherine was the first to sit, choosing to perch next to Grandma Eliza.

"We're having a party at my old school. I came to invite all of you," Hanneleen said.

"Child," Lisa said, "can't you see our bags are packed?"

"It would mean a lot to my little sister, who's the same age as your daughter. She asked me to invite Lala," Hanneleen said.

"We're going home. The fame you gained in Africa will only embarrass and humiliate you in Europe," Lisa stated bluntly.

"Please, Sister," Ima said. "That's not fair!"

"It's the harsh reality," Lisa replied, moving from her chair to stand behind her sister and poking her head with her middle finger. "This little girl will return in tears and might even contemplate suicide. We're talking about professionals who study music, not this little girl who still sings nursery rhymes."

Catherine seemed to relish Lisa's outburst, smiling and staring at her intently, which began to grate on Lisa's nerves. Lisa tried to ignore it, but Catherine's persistent gaze wore her patience thin.

"You," Lisa pointed at Gladness, "tell your little clone to keep her painted lips sealed."

"What's a clone?" Gladness asked innocently.

"These children are even more empty than I thought," Lisa said. "Do they even attend school?"

"Please, Mother," Lala said, "can we go?"

"Yes, we're going, but we're going home!"

Mr Setiawan and Vivaan joined. Lisa examined them from head to toe. "Why haven't you packed your bags?"

"I apologise, Mrs Ndafenongo," Mr Setiawan replied. "We can only leave tomorrow afternoon."

"Why not today?" Lisa snapped. "We were supposed to leave today. I have a school to run!"

"We can't just wrap up the competition and leave," Ima said.

Lisa hastened to her room. Ima sat on the bed. Lisa should have been the proudest mother alive. Her daughter, young with a promising future, had performed exceptionally well in the competition. Despite being a newcomer, she had held her own admirably. Lala had achieved what her mother couldn't four years ago. Any parent would be thrilled to have a daughter like her—beautiful, confident, and talented.

"Sister, please," Ima pleaded. "Don't ruin this for her. If you agree, we can all go and return as soon as you say so."

"You know Mother enjoys such events. She'd want to go. She hasn't slept well in days."

"She'll have time to rest. The party is in the late afternoon."

"You still don't understand, Ima. You always need things spelled out! People sleep at night, not during the day. What kind of sleep is that?"

"You're being unfair!"

Victory Party for Hanneleen

It had been three hours since they last discussed Hanneleen's invitation. Grandma Eliza was in a foul mood. She said something about dreaming about the invitation, though everyone knew Grandma Eliza always listened, even in her sleep.

"Is it true?" she asked.

"Whatever you heard, yes, it's true," Lisa replied.

"I'm going for a bath now, and Ima, get everyone ready," Grandma Eliza instructed.

She went to her room for a bubble bath. Lala joined her, combing her grandma's short grey hair. They played and sang while bathing.

"Do you hear that?" Lisa asked.

"I like it," Ima said.

Lisa growled at her sister, who smirked and looked away, struggling to maintain her smile until finally relenting and leaving for the kitchen. Ima followed and sat at the table.

"Are you still single?" Lisa asked.

Ima nearly choked on her rice. She composed herself with a gulp of water.

"If you're not with a man, Ima, you won't get pregnant—unless you're Mary! And if you don't get pregnant, you won't have kids. You're nearly thirty, one foot in the grave."

"You're thirty-four..." Ima said.

"Yes, Ima, I've got one foot in the grave already."

"I'm not single."

Vivaan and Mr Setiawan entered, dressed smartly. Lisa smiled at Mr Setiawan, then back at Ima. "He may be short, but he's fine."

In Dar es Salaam, on Mindu Street, Hanneleen hosted a grand celebration at Muhimbili Primary School. The hall brimmed with primary school children clad in blue and green, waving banners emblazoned with

Hanneleen's name. Seated next to a man and woman, presumably her parents, was a slender, fair-skinned girl—her sister. Suddenly, a stout man stepped onto the stage and addressed the crowd through a microphone.

"I'm Principal Kalenga. I acknowledge all the children and parents who've organised this event for our former student and the winner of the African Gospel Contest, Hanneleen. I also extend my gratitude to the organising committee." Principal Kalenga turned to acknowledge a group of students seated to his left, looking particularly dignified.

The crowd erupted in cheers, further lifting the children's spirits, who beamed at each other.

"Our teachers, students, community, and country stand behind you. We pray for your success in the upcoming competition in Germany. You possess remarkable singing talent. May God continue to bless you." The principal paused momentarily.

In a bid to curtail his extended speech, the crowd attempted louder cheers, though this only seemed to embolden him further.

"I know..."

Before he finishes whatever, he knows, children and committee members clamoured around Lala as she entered, showering her with adulation and causing quite a commotion. They jostled for autographs, thrusting pens and paper at her.

"What should I do with this, Grandma?" Lala asked.

"Sign it, dear. That's what all famous people do."

"Committee members, please return to your seats!" Principal Kalenga called out.

Little Emily, the head of the committee, was the most fervent in chanting Lala's name; she even had it scrawled on her palm. Hanneleen seemed unperturbed by the attention on Lala. She took the microphone and beckoned Lala onto the stage, with Emily guiding her through the excited throng. Catherine and Gladness sat together on the stage.

"Do you want Lala and Hanneleen to sing for us?" the principal asked.

The crowd exploded, particularly Grandma Eliza.

"Go on, my little mouse!" Grandma Eliza said. "Grandma loves you so much."

Hanneleen nodded, and Lala stepped up to the microphone. Together with the audience, they sang.

Later, when they returned from the evening party, Lisa was watching the news, barely acknowledging their greetings.

"Everyone should get to bed. We need to leave early," Lisa said.

The following morning, Lisa rose early. "The plane departs at two," she said. "Get up, Mother!"

Numerous pictures were taken at Mpacha Airport in Katima Mulilo as Lala arrived in Namibia with her second-place victory. They all waited to celebrate with her. She featured prominently in every newspaper, much to Grandma Eliza's delight, who read them repeatedly. Regardless of whether Africa wins or progresses to the World Continental Gospel Contest finals, Lala will perform the celebratory song with Hanneleen, Bassel, Gatimu, Andriaan, and Latifah. But what are Hanneleen's chances?

She was up against five exceptional singers worldwide. Ingrid from Suriname in South America is among the competitors. Luciana from Canada in North America boasts an incredible vocal range spanning five octaves and can reach seven octaves. Hanah from the Maldives in Asia delivers deep, soulful tones with a unique vocal range. From Sydney, Australia, Drew showcases an impressive vocal range of ten octaves and effortlessly hits the lowest note, G7. Alexei, representing Europe from Russia, possesses a rare high tenor and a piercing voice spanning four octaves. The question now is: Is Africa prepared enough this time?

During the first week in South Bauleni, Lala showed off her newfound fame to everyone, particularly Beth, Victoria, and even the newcomer, Huge Lilian. Lala brought along several tops with her picture on them and waited for Pulelo behind the school library benches. Passersby couldn't help but show their affection for Lala. She handed out T-shirts to those she favoured and insisted they wear them.

Just then, Mrs Anushka, the librarian, arrived and parked her car. Lala and Pulelo rushed over to greet her. Pulelo offered to carry her handbag, and Lala gave her a white T-shirt. Mrs Anushka examined the T-shirt, saying, "This is lovely! People wore these at the finals."

"Yes, Mrs Anushka. I saved one for you."

"I'm a huge fan of yours. You've made everyone so proud."

"Thank you, Mrs Anushka."

They walked together briefly until they reached the library door. Mrs Anushka then turned to Pulelo. "How's your book coming along, my dear?"

"I've finished the first draft," Pulelo replied.

"Oh, I envy you," Mrs Anushka said. "I've always wanted to write my memoir, but my life sucks. No one would want to read it."

"Mrs Anushka," Pulelo said, "would you read my book?"

"I'd love to. Thank you for trusting me with it." Mrs Anushka took the manuscript and flicked through its seventy pages. "I'll review this book, and once I'm done, you'll have the best book. Trust me."

As they left the school library, twenty students came to Lala. They all wore the T-shirts she had given to them. Patricia stood hidden at a tree with her outdated sash. A new celebrity singer had emerged at school, and her name was Lala Ndafenongo. Lala led her fans through the corridors.

Meanwhile, Vivaan was in class presenting his business proposal to Teacher Ima. He planned to sell hot dogs, drinks, and other items.

"This is impressive," Ima said. "Present it to the principal. The tuck shop's been closed since last April."

"Would you come with me, Teacher Ima?"

"You're an excellent businessman. You don't need my help."

The bell for the first lesson had yet to ring. Lisa was in her office when Vivaan came in and hesitated before placing the file on her desk.

"I haven't got time to read papers now."

"The school ran the tuck shop, but things kept disappearing, so it closed six months ago. Miss Matengu, the street vendor, managed it for two months before giving up because the rent was too high. I'm prepared to pay double that amount. Let me rent it, Principal Ndafenongo."

"If you pay that much, you won't make a profit."

"I will, Principal Ndafenongo. My business plan says so."

"You're the businessman. Who am I to deny the school's development? The tuck shop is yours now, and you won't pay double. You'll pay the standard fee."

As Vivaan returned to Teacher Ima, the first lesson began. She whispered, "How did it go, my young businessman?"

Vivaan was too excited to reply, jingling the keys before taking his seat.

"I have a gift for all of you. This gift isn't from me but from our singer," Ima said.

"But before that, let's show our love to her. They called her the 'Biggest Little Singer.' I loved the sound of that, and I wished it was me. Don't get me wrong - I'm not jealous!"

The children giggled.

"Lala, Pulelo, and Vivaan, can you help me distribute these T-shirts to my soldiers? Don't worry; I know your sizes."

The children received their T-shirts—a symbol of unity.

"Now," the teacher said, as she took out a camera from her drawer, "shall we take a family photo?"

The children posed for the picture. Ima scanned the corridors for someone to take the photo. Lisa was on the phone. Initially, she intended to decline, but Ima handed her the camera and dragged her into the classroom.

"You need to be in the picture too."

Day later, Mrs Anushka came looking for Pulelo after the rain had stopped while Ima was already in the middle of her lesson. Mrs Anushka stood at the door, but she didn't have anything with her. She wanted Pulelo and Lala to meet her after school. Pulelo was waiting to hear Mrs Anushka's thoughts on her book, but she had been feeling quite nervous lately. Lala tapped Pulelo on the shoulder to reassure her that everything would be all right. Although it was comforting, Pulelo found it hard to concentrate.

Mrs Anushka sat there, busy doing her nails. Since the library was empty, she had enough time to review Pulelo's novel.

"Read my comments. Just remember, they're only my opinions," she said.

Pulelo held onto the envelope and thanked Mrs Anushka.

"No, thank you for trusting me. I enjoyed it. Once it's polished, it will be a great book."

"Are you sure, Mrs Anushka?"

"Once your book is ready, I'd like to introduce it to a friend of my husband's. He owns a publishing company in my country. I'm sure he'll love your book."

Pulelo shoved her envelope into her bag and left.

"You should read it," Lala said without looking at Pulelo. "Mrs Anushka is always kind."

"I can't."

"What do you mean you can't?"

"I'll read it when I get home."

Grandpa Sylvester came to pick up Pulelo, and they drove back to the farmhouse. Ever since the incident with Lisa, who warned him never to go close to her mother for allowing Grandma Eliza to smoke, he hasn't been the same. Eva said that she liked the new version of him. He spent most of his time watching boxing on TV or caring for his animals.

"Grandpa," Pulelo said as they made the final turn towards their farmhouse, "what would you do if someone said that what you did didn't make sense?"

"I would keep working on it until it does make sense."

"Do you think it will make sense?"

"Are you talking about your book?" he asked, parking in his usual shady spot. "Your book will turn out great. Whoever took the time to read it and give you their opinion is a wonderful person."

"Mrs Anushka gave me her feedback. I'm worried she might say something bad about my book. I know she's kind, but I'm scared, Grandpa."

"I don't know who Mrs Anushka is, but my granddaughter will become an amazing writer. Always remember, not everyone will like your book. People will always have something to say. That's what makes life interesting. I've heard people call me an old fool. I ignore them. I know who I am."

Pulelo hugged him before she skipped to her room. Grandpa Sylvester had been keeping the house clean and not burning the food like he did before. Sometimes, when bored, he would sneak a peek at Pulelo's laptop and read her stories. The last time, he almost got caught.

Grandpa Sylvester went to the fridge and poured a glass of milk for the cat. He petted its soft fur as it drank, then turned on the TV. An African Gospel Contest was on, but he turned it off. Pulelo grabbed the remote and turned it back on. The host announced the winner, Hanneleen, who held up the trophy.

"My friend Lala sings better," Pulelo said.

"Let's give credit where it's due," Grandpa Sylvester said from behind her. "Your friend Lala is talented, but Hanneleen deserved her win."

"I know, Grandpa. I'm jealous."

"Envy can push us to work harder. Focus on your writing, and you'll achieve great things, too."

Grandma Eliza was busy knitting a bright yellow pullover for her granddaughter. Lala wasn't a fan of the clothes her grandmother made for her. They were too big, and she didn't like wearing them, but Grandma Eliza assured her she would eventually grow into them. She showed Lala a photo of two little girls, around ten years old, and said, "Look what I've made for you, my little mouse. I copied it from this photo." She pointed to herself in the picture, wearing a sweater and wristwatch.

"This sweater is like mine, except I made it green instead of blue. It wouldn't be unique if I made it the same colour. Try it on," she threw the sweater to Lala.

Lisa, watching them, snatched the photo and scoffed at it.

"Mother," she said with a sneer, "who would wear something like this nowadays? That was from the 1940s! Do you pay attention? Everything you make ends up on top of the wardrobe. Do you know why I buy threads for you?"

"I know, child. It's to keep me busy. Who's the fool now?" She stood next to her daughter, playfully sticking out her tongue. "You all think I'm foolish, but those sweaters you believe are hidden away in your bags and on top of the wardrobe are all sold!"

During dinner, the family of three gathered around the table. Grandma Eliza had finished her meal and was now patting her stomach.

"I'm sorry, Grandma. I should have told you that I don't like your sweaters. I didn't want to hurt your feelings," Lala said.

Grandma Eliza let out a burp and replied, "One day, you will wear them. Keep them safe for when that day comes. You won't have to search for them."

"What do you mean, Grandma?"

"You will wear them when I'm no longer here."

"Grandma, where do you sell them? Do you take them to the market?"

"I lied. They belong to you. I won't sell them. I made those sweaters with love. I wouldn't sell them."

"Grandma Eliza," Lala said, "I'm sorry I never wore them."

"Don't be sorry my little mouse, one day you will understand their sentimental value. Now, go brush your teeth and go to bed."

Grandma Eliza woke up so early and checked on her granddaughter, as she always did. Lala was fast asleep wearing her new sweater. She closed the door and went to her daughter's room. Lisa wore a red pullover her mother had made fifteen years ago. Back in her room, Grandma Eliza pulled a chest from under her bed and took out a well-preserved picture of herself, Him, and their two daughters – Lisa and Ima.

"Your children have grown," she chuckled. "I wish you could have met your granddaughter. She's an amazing singer. She won a national competition and came in second in an African event. She's so beautiful." Grandma Eliza wiped away her tears and continued, "Our daughter is married now, but I'm worried about our little one, Ima. Ima is still single." She scanned the room as if expecting a response, placed the photo back in its spot, pushed the chest under the bed, and left for her morning chores.

Three days passed slowly, like aimless clouds drifting in the sky. Pulelo still couldn't find the courage to open the envelope. Grandpa Sylvester sat next to her, becoming her rock in a sea of doubts. His gentle words brought a sense of calmness to her granddaughter's swirling thoughts.

"You should open it," he said.

"I'm scared, Grandpa."

"I read it, and it is amazing," he gently patted her head before heading out to the fields, leaving Pulelo to face her fears alone.

As the door closed behind him, Pulelo took a deep breath and tore open the envelope. She turned to the first page, steeled herself, and began to read.

Finding a Liver for Grandma Eliza

Lala was in her room when her phone rang. Pulelo called, just as she had expected, and wasted no time in sharing Mrs Anushka's comments.

"Who wouldn't be nervous when being judged?" said Lala.

Pulelo was excited, and with the support from her best friend, her mother, and Grandpa, she felt ready to make her book great. She stayed up late that night working on it.

At school, Lala and her mother had yet to arrive; Lisa had never been late, so Ima knew something was wrong. She searched through her bag to find her phone, and as she did, it started ringing. Lala was on the other end, informing her that Grandma Eliza was not well and they were at the hospital.

Doctor Jameson invited Lisa and Ima into his office and shared the news that Grandma Eliza had experienced acute liver failure and needed an urgent liver transplant.

"Mother always comes for check-ups. How did you not catch this?" asked Lisa.

"We ran several tests this morning, and they all pointed to the same thing. It's strange because her tests came back fine last month," said the doctor.

"How soon can we find a liver, doctor?"

"The chances of finding a liver in our country are slim. People here are not organ donors. Even our blood comes from South Africa, along with coffins and vegetables. We always encourage our citizens to become donors, but unfortunately..."

"Doctor Jameson, you don't need to lecture us. We will find a liver somewhere else. Get one online from America or China. Money is not a problem."

"I will prescribe medicine, but surgery or a liver transplant would be the best options. What does her diet consist of?" the doctor asked.

"She eats regular food, but she drinks a lot of milk. Could that be causing her illness?" Ima asked.

"Having too much of anything can harm our bodies," Doctor Jameson said.

"You have to make our mother well," Ima pleaded.

"There is another option," the doctor suggested. "We can perform surgery."

"Isn't a liver transplant a type of surgery?" Lisa asked.

"I mean, we can take a piece of a healthy person's liver and transplant it. We can test all three of you to see a match."

"My sister and I are ready to do it," Lisa said.

Ima didn't say anything. She knew Lisa had removed Lala from the donor list. Plus, even if Lala was a match, Lisa wouldn't allow the doctor to take a piece of her daughter's liver.

After midnight, all the medical tests were done. Doctor Jameson informed them that none of them were suitable donors.

"Please redo the test, doctor. She's our mother," Lisa said.

"I suggest your daughter Lala takes the test."

"You can't suggest that! She's a child! How could you, doctor!"

"It's my duty, Mrs Ndafenongo, to consider all available options."

"You shouldn't have suggested something so risky for a child."

Ima sat quietly, feeling the tension between her and her sister. She knew that suggesting her niece donate part of her liver would cause a rift, so she decided to leave it up to fate. Lisa loved her mother dearly, but she also loved her daughter.

"Contact different doctors from other hospitals."

"We will continue to look for other options, Mrs Ndafenongo, but we are running out of time."

"Take Lala home. Let me stay here with Mother, and please, be here tomorrow morning," Lisa said as she left the doctor's office.

Ima and Lala arrived at the hospital early in the morning. Lala began to message her grandmother's feet, and trying to crack a few jokes.

"It's been two days now, and we haven't found a liver donor," Ima said, looking at her mother's swollen legs and ankles. "What should we do, Sister?"

Lisa rested her head against the wall. She kept repeating to herself, "Mother will not die." She then left the room and walked into the hallway. Ima followed her, and they stood facing each other.

"Let your daughter donate part of her liver, a small piece, Sister, that's all our mother needs," Ima said.

"I won't allow it, Ima!"

"Your daughter is our only hope. Let her donate part of her liver to our mother. In a month, the liver will regenerate, and she will recover. Please, don't let Mother die."

"I will do anything for our mother, but not at the cost of my daughter's life."

"She's your mother!"

"Lala is my daughter, my responsibility. I brought her into this world. I can't take her life away," he voice raised.

"What about mother? She gave you life."

"I would spend every penny I have to make sure Mother is well again, but this isn't about money."

"If she dies, it would be your fault."

"Would you let her take such a risk if she was your daughter, Ima? Mother has lived her life. My daughter has her whole life ahead of her. Even if Lala was your daughter, I wouldn't allow it. I love Mother, and I know you do too, but please, don't make me carry the burden if something happens to our mother."

"I'm sorry. I'm sorry, Sister," Ima said. "It was wrong of me to push for that."

It was evening in the farmhouse, and the fields were already dark. The pigs were asleep, and the chickens had been in their coop for hours. Grandpa Sylvester and his family had finished dinner, and Eva cleaned the kitchen. Pulelo patted her belly and let out a burp.

"Yes," Grandpa Sylvester said, "it was delicious! You're the best cooker."

Eva and Pulelo giggled. "She's not a cooker, Grandpa. She's a cook."

"Back in our days, people who cooked were called cookers."

"Grandpa," Pulelo said, "Grandma Eliza is really sick. She got admitted three days ago."

Grandpa Sylvester rose from his chair and grabbed Pulelo's arm. "You've known about this for three days and didn't tell me?"

"I'm sorry, Grandpa," she said. "I thought it was something that would go away."

"Her liver is not doing well," Eva said from the sink.

"You knew, too?"

"I only found out today when Lisa called to tell me her liver is bad."

He patted his pockets, looking for his car keys, and walked outside. He got into his truck and backed into the field before quickly turning into the driveway. Eva and Pulelo watched as the taillights disappeared in a cloud of dust.

"We have to go after Grandpa, Mum," Pulelo said.

"It's late. Tomorrow is a school day. I'll call Lisa."

Lisa was refilling her teacup when Grandpa Sylvester bumped into her. She led him to Grandma Eliza's room. Lisa stood frozen, watching Grandpa Sylvester's emotional display.

"Ima and I were not a good match," Lisa said. "She is very sick, Mr Sylvester."

"I will take the test," he said.

After he had taken the test, the doctor came in with a smile...

"Mr Sylvester," he said. "You are as healthy as an ox. We can start the surgery right away!"

He was an old man in love and had a family. Lisa and Ima knew that Eva would not give her consent for the operation.

"How soon can we schedule the surgery?" he asked.

"As soon as possible, but I want to meet with your daughter to get her consent. This is a risky surgery, and we need approval from an immediate family member. According to your records, that would be Miss Eva Banda."

"I'm a grown man, Doctor Jameson. I have already given my consent!"

"Even grown men still need consent from a family member. Let your daughter know," said the doctor.

"The doctor is right," said Lisa.

"You're right, Sister," said Ima. "Let's call and hear from her."

"My daughter will never allow it," said Grandpa Sylvester. "Let's do it now! Every moment we waste makes her condition worse."

"I'm sorry, Mr Banda," said Doctor Jameson. "This is a risky surgery for you, and I can't authorize it without your daughter's consent. Why don't you call her and hear from her?"

Eva was in bed when she got a mysterious text from the hospital: *Come to the hospital right now, or your father will be dead soon.* Eva smacked her lips and took a deep breath. "Is father mistaking love for foolishness?"

Grandma Eliza's condition had worsened, and her family, along with Grandpa Sylvester, sat silently around her bed. Eva burst into the room and pulled her father towards the door.

"What is all this I'm hearing?" Eva directed her anger at the doctor who had just entered. "What kind of doctor are you?" she demanded. "This man is old. Do you want him to die?"

"He's healthy," the doctor responded calmly. "Your father is in good health, but the hospital won't proceed with the surgery without your permission."

"Healthy!" Eva scoffed. "He's so old. Father, are you just tired of living?"

Grandpa Sylvester sighed quietly and left the room. Eva turned to Lisa, who avoided eye contact. "He's the same man you used to despise. Now you're begging him to save your mother's life. You're so mean, Lisa! What will be left of him after the surgery?" Eva paused, waiting for Lisa to respond, but she remained silent. "I'm sorry about your mother's condition, Lisa. She's a wonderful woman, and if my father weren't so old, I'd let him do whatever he wanted. Look at him, Lisa; he won't survive the surgery."

Lisa stood up and took Eva's hands, speaking gently. "Don't worry about your father, Eva. Please, go and take him with you."

"Father, we need to leave now," Eva said urgently. "Come on, Father!"

Grandpa Sylvester leaned over and kissed Grandma Eliza's forehead tenderly before leaving. Grandma Eliza lay still, her once vibrant presence now subdued, her figure almost ghostly against the hospital sheets. The rise and fall of her chest seemed faint, the sound of her breath barely audible. She appeared almost lifeless, as though trapped in an unbreakable slumber. Lisa leaned against the wall, frustration evident. Ima stood behind her, holding her arms.

"Stay strong, Sister, especially for your daughter," Ima said quietly.

Lisa wiped away her tears. "She can't die, Ima."

"Our mother will live," Ima replied, trying to muster hope.

"Oh, Ima, you say things you don't even believe."

"She will not die. Where is your faith, Sister? It's been four days, and all hope was lost, but when Jesus came, He rose Lazarus from his tomb."

"This is real life, Ima, not a Bible story," Lisa snapped. "She's our mother not Lazarus!"

A faint beeping from Grandma Eliza's monitor interrupted them, causing Lisa's heart to tighten with dread. The room fell into a tense silence, broken only by the steady rhythm of the monitor. Then, with a final, heart-wrenching beep, the monitor displayed a flat line...

Grandma Eliza died....

Nearly an hour had passed since Grandma Eliza died. Lala sat on Ima's lap, Lisa stood against the wall, and Doctor Jameson conversed with a nurse.

"Remove that nurse from the room," Lisa instructed Doctor Jameson sharply. "She's negligent."

"It's alright, Sister," Ima said. "It's God's will."

"It's not God's will," Lisa insisted angrily. "This nurse failed to do her job. She let our mother die."

The nurse remained calm as she covered Grandma Eliza's body. Without a word, she left the room, nearly colliding with Grandpa Sylvester and Eva as they entered. Grandpa Sylvester stood at the doorway, tears streaming down his face as he gazed at Grandma Eliza.

"I'm sorry for your loss," Eva said softly to Lisa.

"Thank you, Eva," Lisa managed to reply through clenched teeth, her voice strained with civility.

"If you need anything, just let me know."

As two nurses entered to take Grandma Eliza's body to the mortuary, the reality of the moment sank in. Lala's composure crumbled, tears flowing freely. She watched silently as they wheeled Grandma Eliza away.

"I'll arrange everything with the funeral home," Eva offered quietly to Lisa. "I have a friend there who can help. Remember the poster they did for the governor? It was huge and lifelike."

"Thank you, Eva," Ima said. "We can all go home now."

Lisa was then driving home when her phone rang, interrupting her thoughts. She answered it hesitantly. "You need to come to the hospital immediately!"

The family hurried into Doctor Jameson's office, and only to find him looking shocked. "It's a miracle, she woke up as she was about to enter-the-," he said. "Your mother is alive!"

"Stop playing games," Lisa said.

"Come with me?"

Grandma Eliza lay on a hospital bed, awake but disoriented. Her children broke down in tears. How much longer could she cling to life? She still needed a transplant.

"The worst isn't over yet," Doctor Jameson said.

"How much time does she have, Doctor?" Ima asked.

"Stop it, Ima," Lisa snapped. "None of us should ever ask that question. Not even God can disclose such information. We'll take it as it comes."

"This is science. We need to know," Ima insisted.

"Enough!" Lisa turned to face the doctor. "What do we do now?"

"Let me talk to you and your sister outside."

Lala stayed by her grandmother's side, gently stroking her hair and humming Amazing Grace. She glanced at her mother and aunt.

"We have three options," the doctor explained. "Lala can still be the donor, or Mr Sylvester. The third option is to continue waiting."

"We almost lost our mother today," Ima said. "If we do nothing, we could lose her next time. Is that what you want, Sister?"

"What do you mean, Ima? Am I God?"

"Let Lala decide for herself," Ima persisted. "I know she's young, but she's also our mother's granddaughter. Let's give her a chance to save her grandmother's life."

"People die on that operating table," Lisa said firmly. "Many of them."

"Don't make a decision you'll regret if Mother dies."

Eva skidded her white Corolla to a halt near the pigsty on the farm's gravel road, parking under a tree. Grandpa Sylvester slammed his truck door shut before hurrying into the house. Eva sat, drumming her fingers on the steering wheel. Her phone beeped: *The old lady isn't dead.*

Grandma Eliza's complexion had paled, blood clots formed at the corners of her mouth, and blood dripped from her nostrils. Lala wiped her face with a cloth, humming softly. Lisa and Ima sat at their mother's bedside. Lisa looked distraught, as though she blamed herself for everything happening.

"What did you say?" Ima asked.

"Not now, Ima. Let me think," Lisa replied.

A bald, middle-aged man in green overalls entered the room—Lala's father, Jonathan Ndafenongo. He had taken time off work. Lala ran to him, throwing herself into his arms. Lisa and Ima stood up, following her. "Grandma is dying, Dad," Lala said as she landed back on her feet and took his hand, leading him to her mother, who remained still.

"Grandma won't die, honey. Grandma will live for a long time," Jonathan said. He turned to Ima. "How are you holding?"

Ima attempted a smile but said nothing. Jonathan moved closer and took his wife's hands. She embraced him tightly.

"My mother is very ill," she said.

"She's a strong woman. What are our options?"

"Oh no, I almost forgot," Lisa said, slapping her forehead. "The doctor wants to see me. We need to go now."

She led Jonathan to the doctor's office, intentionally avoiding mentioning to Lala that her liver could be an option for her grandmother. Jonathan needed no time to consider.

"We have to do it," he said. "We need to let Lala know. She should decide for herself."

"Do you agree with that?" Lisa asked.

"We're family. Families support each other. Your mother is part of our family. Do you want to live the rest of your life knowing you could have done something to save her?"

"Lala is our only child."

"Yes, and she's your mother's only granddaughter. Let me propose something. I'll also take the tests, and if I'm a match, I'll donate part of my liver."

"And if you're not?"

"Then we'll let our daughter decide."

Grandma Eliza's Health Deteriorates

It's been two weeks since the school went on a short holiday. It was supposed to be a peaceful break, but things took a turn for the worse for Lala and her family. At least Pulelo had time to work on her book.

Doctor Jameson gave Jonathan an envelope. He wasn't related to Grandma Eliza by blood; his chances of being a match were slim.

"I'm going to be a donor!" Jonathan said, leaning forward in his seat. "Why me?"

"But you wanted this, Jonathan," Lisa said.

"I'm scared."

Lisa grabbed the envelope and read it. A grin spread across her face as she turned to her husband. He met her gaze.

"When can we schedule the surgery, doctor?" Lisa asked.

"Very soon," the doctor replied, heading towards the door. "Tomorrow morning."

"So soon!" Jonathan said, following the doctor.

"We need to act quickly. Your mother-in-law is in critical condition. And one more thing – no alcohol tonight!"

Ima wiped the sweat off her mother's face. Lisa whispered the good news to her, observing Jonathan's mixed emotions.

"Thank you," Ima said to her brother-in-law, who remained silent as he leaned down to gently kiss Grandma Eliza before leaving. Lisa hurried after her husband, catching up with him in the hallway.

"This will all be over soon," she said to him, maintaining eye contact despite his fearful and confused expression.

"Are you staying with your mother tonight?" he asked.

"Ima will stay with our mother."

After they had left, Mr Setiawan entered...

"She sometimes opens her eyes, but she doesn't talk much. It's good she has this room to herself. Any updates on the World Continental Gospel Contest?" Ima asked.

"The media is buzzing with excitement. People have a lot of faith in her," Mr Setiawan replied.

"I've never been to Germany," Ima said.

"I've heard it's a beautiful country."

"It's supposed to be. It's all over the history books," Ima chuckled.

Mr and Mrs Ndafenongo were in their bedroom. Lala rested her head on her father's lap. He tickled her, causing her to move to the edge of the bed before pulling her back.

"Don't worry, Father," Lala said. "I researched it. The liver regenerates quickly. If mine were a match, I could have donated part of my liver to Grandma Eliza long ago."

"Aren't you scared?" her father asked.

"I'd do anything for Grandma. I know she'd do the same for me."

"It's been a long day," Lisa sighed. "I hope nothing bad happens to our mother."

They arrived at the hospital early in the morning and went through all the necessary procedures. Just when they thought things were progressing, Doctor Jameson received an urgent phone call. He called for a meeting with Lisa, Ima, and Jonathan.

"Mr Ndafenongo can no longer be a donor," Doctor Jameson said.

"But he's a perfect match!" said Ima.

"He is," the doctor said, "but we have a problem. The substance abuse screening showed that Mr Ndafenongo has been using alcohol and illegal drugs."

Jonathan glanced at the doctor, silently pleading for him to stop revealing too much to his wife. He had promised her that he had quit all those things.

"Illegal drugs?" Lisa said. "What kind of drugs are you using, Jonathan?"

"It's just alcohol sometimes," Jonathan said, avoiding eye contact. "I swear, it was during my promotion. They threw a party for me three months ago."

"Three months ago, and it's still in your system? Stop lying, Jonathan!"

"You know it's not easy to quit," Jonathan said.

"Tell me the truth. What kind of illegal drugs are you using?"

"Sometimes marijuana. Everyone smokes there. They even do dangerous things like sniffing substances, even crude oil."

"Crude oil!" said the doctor.

"Is there anything that can be done?" asked Ima.

"We have another problem," the doctor continued.

"There's more?" Lisa asked, her frustration evident.

"Yes, Mrs Ndafenongo. The pulmonary evaluation showed that his blood is unable to carry enough oxygen."

Lisa couldn't contain her anger anymore. "Change your ways before it's too late! You're going to die before your time!" She jabbed her finger towards Jonathan's head, but he remained calm.

"Do you think it's easy?" he muttered.

"We also did a heart check-up. Sadly, he is not a good match. Right now, Mr Ndafenongo cannot donate. There are many issues in his blood. He won't be able to save your mother."

Jonathan seemed relieved, almost happy. Everyone knew Jonathan was weak, but physically, he was a big man. Lisa stared at the doctor without blinking. She had no tears or words left.

"We still have other options, Mr Ndafenongo," Doctor Jameson said. "There's an older man who offered to help. The board almost approved him. His name is Sylvester."

Jonathan laughed. He knew the old man they were talking about. He had sneaked him into the house to see Grandma Eliza several times. They had even smoked together.

"He's too old for that!" Jonathan laughed. "He'll die before he even gets to the operating table. That old man is so brave."

"There are no age limits for organ donation, Mr Ndafenongo. Even newborn babies can donate. There're no age restrictions. Anyone can donate if the organs are healthy and meet medical standards. But you have to be very healthy to be a donor."

"So, what are we waiting for? Let's bring in Uncle Syl and see what happens!" Jonathan said.

"Mr Sylvester isn't the issue. Eva will never allow it," Lisa said. "She took him out of the hospital the other day. He was willing to donate part of his liver."

"I get it," Jonathan said. "Plus, he can't be a donor anyway."

"Why?" the doctor asked.

"Because I smoke with him sometimes."

"No wonder he always wears those sunglasses like blind people do; his eyes are always bloodshot. It's like pure maroon, especially during choir practice."

"Is Sylvester still the choirmaster?" Jonathan asked.

Lisa stood up and glared at her husband. "He is our choirmaster. Do you have a problem with that, Jonathan?"

"I understand," he said.

"What do you understand? You understand that my mother should die. What do you understand?"

"Calm down, sister," Ima said.

"No, he needs to tell me what he understands. He's faking it. He's so happy right now."

"Shut up, woman!" Jonathan snapped. "How selfish can you be? Why won't you let your daughter donate? Eva is doing the same thing you are. I don't blame her because she's not part of this family, but you, that woman on that bed, is your mother! Make your choice now - your daughter or let your mother die."

He stormed out, leaving the door wide open, and drove home. When Lisa arrived home, Jonathan was sitting on an old tyre at the back of the house. She stood behind him, but he acted like she wasn't there.

"When we lost him," Lisa began, "it was so hard for me. He was just a baby, Jonathan, but I let him die. We couldn't even give him a name. He was our son. What if we let Lala donate and something goes wrong?"

He got up, creating a gap between them. Francesca watched the two from the bedroom window of the house next door, munching on an apple.

"Let's leave it to God," he said firmly. "We should accept what God has taken from us. Our son and daughter have different destinies. Our daughter won't die. Let her save her grandmother's life."

Lisa was about to speak when suddenly they faced Lala.

"How long have you been standing there?" Lisa asked.

"You knew all along, and you want grandma to die?" Lala asked.

"I was trying to protect you."

"Grandma won't die. I'll give her a part of my liver."

"You can't do it!"

"It's her decision," Jonathan said. "Let her be."

"She's our only child!"

"I'll do it. Grandma won't die."

"Stop! Stop right now and go inside!"

Lala slammed the door behind her and slumped into a dining chair. Jonathan turned to his wife and softened his voice.

"Let her save her grandmother's life. If your mother dies, she'll blame you for the rest of her life, and besides, your mother will certainly die if she doesn't get a transplant. The statistics show that the chances of dying for a living donor are very low."

"How low is it, Jonathan?"

"It's very low."

"How low exactly?"

"0.4%, and sometimes even lower. What I mean is that our daughter will survive."

Lisa thought about it and seemed ready to have faith in him. Jonathan went back inside the house and wiped tears from Lala's eyes.

"Are you scared?"

"...but I'll do it."

The next day, they had been in the operating room for nearly four hours. Lisa sat next to her husband. Ima with Mr Setiawan. Pulelo and Eva occupied the opposite sofa. Grandpa Sylvester couldn't sit still; Eva had to calm him down, growing increasingly frustrated.

"Relax, Dad!" Eva pulled her father back down as he hit his clenched fist against the wall.

"Take it easy, father; you'll hurt yourself."

"This is taking too long," Grandpa Sylvester said. "I need to find out what's happening."

"Sit down, father," Eva instructed. Turning to Pulelo, she added, "Go get your grandpa some water."

"I don't need water; I need to see her."

Doctor Jameson came from the operating room. Grandpa Sylvester blocked his path, with the entire family behind him.

"It was a success," the doctor announced. "We're moving them to intensive care now. Once they're stable, you'll be able to see them. Please keep praying; they're still in danger." Turning to Lala's parents, he said, "She was brave. She'll be okay."

Grandpa Sylvester started hugging everyone. "Come on, everyone," he called out. "We need to pray together. Jonathan, lead us."

"Stop it, Father," Eva said.

"Let him be," Jonathan said. "Everyone, come close."

Even passing nurses joined the prayer Jonathan led...

The day turned into night, yet Doctor Jameson had not provided a formal update on their condition. It was well past midnight; Lala had been taken off the breathing tube and was stable. This was a relief for the family. Doctor Jameson informed Lala's parents they could see her.

"What about our mother?" Ima asked.

"She won't have visitors now, but she's recovering."

"Are you sure, doctor?" Jonathan asked.

"We've conducted all necessary tests—blood tests, liver enzymes, bilirubin, and more. Everything is fine. A Doppler ultrasound showed normal findings. They're both on clear fluids only."

"Thank you, doctor," Jonathan said.

"I'll do everything to ensure your daughter and mother-in-law recover well. Now, please excuse me."

When Lala woke up around two in the morning, the entire family gathered around her. She managed a few words and appeared to be recovering well. "How's Grandma?" Lala asked.

"Grandma is doing well. Once you're out of this bed, you'll see her."

"I want to see Grandma now."

"Not right now, sweetheart," Jonathan gently said. "Grandma is doing great."

"Guess what?" Ima said. "She asked about you too!"

As the sun rose, Grandma Eliza remained asleep. Ima, waiting with Mr Setiawan, grew increasingly concerned.

"I don't get it?" Ima said to Mr Setiawan. "Mother has been unconscious since surgery. I'm worried!"

By ten o'clock, Lala woke up feeling a sharp pain in her upper right side. She began groaning in pain.

"Doctor," the nurse asked, "is this normal?"

"We'll need another ultrasound to check if something went wrong. Please, no visitors."

The doctor stepped out to update Lala's family.

"Doctor," Lisa began, "why is she in so much pain?"

"She'll be okay. Once we determine the cause, we'll know what to do. For now, please try to stay calm."

In Lala's room, the doctor slammed papers on the table and leaned on his hands.

"What does the ultrasound say, doctor?" the nurse asked.

"Everything looks fine. Her liver is receiving adequate blood flow, and there are no issues with her veins or fluid in her abdomen. Everything looks good."

"But why is she in pain, doctor?"

"For now, she's stable. Let's see how she is when she wakes up."

Lisa and the family waited anxiously in the hallway. Ima approached the doctor regarding her mother.

"Please, doctor, how is our mother? This isn't normal."

Before the doctor could respond, Lisa pushed her sister aside. "How is my daughter, doctor?"

"We've conducted all necessary tests. Everything appears fine. Let's wait a bit longer; the pain may go away soon."

"May?" Lisa asked. "You're uncertain, doctor?"

"I can't explain her pain, but we have all the resources we need. My team and I have performed many successful liver transplants here. We'll do our best to ensure your daughter returns to you soon. Please be patient and keep praying."

"We should transfer her to the city," Jonathan suggested.

"It's unnecessary. This hospital is among the best-specialised hospitals in the country. Patients are referred here, not transferred."

"This is a government hospital," Lisa said. "Look at your nurses standing around, doing nothing."

"They're from different departments. Each member of my team is dedicated to their role." Doctor Jameson received call and went to met her nurse. "How's the elderly woman in the next room?"

"She's recovering well. That old lady is strong as an ox. She even spoke."

"What did she say?"

"She wants to see Mr Sylvester."

"Ah, Mr Sylvester," Doctor Jameson smiled. "He's a lucky man."

"Very lucky, doctor."

"I'll check on her. When I'm done, let him in."

Grandpa Sylvester entered with a single rose, placing it by her pillow. Grandma Eliza was then awake.

"I wanted to give you my liver, but they wouldn't allow it."

"I know, Syl," she said. "How's my granddaughter?"

"She's a brave girl. She keeps asking about you. Your children are worried. Should I let them in?"

"You always know what I want."

Lisa, Ima, and Jonathan entered...

"You frightened us, Mother," Ima said.

"Is my granddaughter alright?"

"Lala will be waiting for you at home."

"Why can't I see her now?"

"She's still recovering, Mother," Ima said. "You'll see her when she's discharged. Maybe they'll let both of you go home together!"

Grandpa Sylvester refused to leave Grandma Eliza's side. Lala's health improved, and they were both discharged after two weeks.

Lala returned to school and everywhere they talked about the World Continental Gospel Contest...

Who Will Replace Hanneleen?

The World Continental Gospel Contest was about to begin, and excitement was everywhere. Hope surged among Africans who yearned for a breakthrough, as their continent had never progressed beyond the first round in the contest—a disheartening trend persisting for too long. Despite their success within their respective nations, African singers often faced similar outcomes. Could 2013 bring change?

Some optimists believed so, while others remained sceptical. In Dar es Salaam, the entire city, along with its ghettos and villages, noise everywhere. The African contest committee spared no expense, engaging top music instructors to train Hanneleen. Her presence dominated billboards, TV screens, newspapers, and social media. Even her twin friends, Gladness and Catherine, garnered recognition, faithfully standing beside her in photos, striking identical poses with right hands raised, palms bent, and left legs slightly bent.

Unfortunately, tragedy struck when Hanneleen was involved in a fatal car accident. The pressure now fell on her to select a replacement from the two finalists—Andriaan, from her homeland, and Lala, from Namibia. What were the odds of Lala being chosen? Could Hanneleen decide in favour of someone from another country over Andriaan, her compatriot? The media speculated while Africa awaited her decision. Tanzanians, however, vehemently urged her to pick Andriaan.

In Dar es Salaam, Hanneleen lay in her hospital bed, surrounded by family and friends, with Catherine and Gladness faithfully by her side. Despite her illness, she managed to say a few words. Andriaan and his affluent parents were also present. Mr Samuel, Andriaan's father, a man of few words who owned many businesses, wielded significant influence, leveraging his wealth to secure favours. He aimed to ensure his son's selection with his money, exploiting Hanneleen's mother's well-known fondness for money.

"The press conference is tomorrow," Mr Samuel reminded Hanneleen. "You haven't assured my son he'll replace you. Apologies for discussing this at such a time."

"It's alright, Mr Samuel. I understand," Hanneleen replied. "The world can't stop because I'm a vegetable on this hospital bed."

"You'll recover and sing again," said Andriaan's mother.

"Have you made your decision?" Andriaan asked, standing next his mother.

"Not yet, Andriaan, but soon. Can I have some time alone with Gladness and Catherine, please?"

Hanneleen sat up in bed, supported by soft pillows, with Gladness and Catherine beside her.

"Hanneleen, will you choose that girl from Namibia?" Gladness asked.

"She can't do that," declared Gladness. "She's going to pick Andriaan. That girl lacks confidence. I wish you'd chosen me," she sighed.

"You can't sing, Gladness," Catherine said.

"Everyone can sing! I used to be a soloist at Sunday school."

"Because our mother was our teacher."

Outside, Hanneleen's father and Andriaan's father conversed in the hospital parking area, while their mothers discussed Andriaan as the ideal candidate a few meters away.

"I'm her mother. I'll decide. Your son will sing for Africa."

"You'll receive the funds right after the press conference. I want to hear her mention my son's name first."

"Tomorrow, at the press conference, she'll choose your son—not because of our friendship, but because he's talented and deserving."

It was well past one o'clock in the afternoon when Hanneleen's mother entered, carrying a large teddy bear, which she placed on her daughter's bed, showering her with kisses. Hanneleen's father sat at the bed's edge, while Gladness and Catherine enjoyed ice cream leaning on each other.

"Sweetheart," Hanneleen's father began, "whatever decision you make tomorrow, your mother and I will support you."

"Thank you, Dad. Thank you, Mum."

"You'll recover and watch the live show."

"I wanted to sing, Mum."

"Whoever you choose tomorrow will sing for you and Africa," her father said.

"Honey," Hanneleen's mother said, "what if we choose Andriaan? They've been family friends for so long. Besides, he's an Afrikander. You should pick him."

"Please, Mum, it's Afrikaner, not Afrikander. Afrikander means 'a breed of cattle.'"

"What's the difference? It's all the same to me."

Hanneleen looked at her mother, sensing the motive behind her insistence. Whenever money came into play, her mother tended to sway decisions.

"How much, Mum? How much will you get if I pick Andriaan?"

"It's a lot. We need it for your university. Don't you want to study in Madagascar?"

"What's in Madagascar, Mum? I want to study here in Tanzania. We have excellent universities here. Wait, why Madagascar?"

"You were born there, dear," her mother replied. "And besides, I like it there." She glanced at her husband, smiling. "Tommy, remember when you almost drowned in that river? You frightened me so."

"It was a swimming pool!" her husband said, though his words were lost as he mouthed them.

"Honey!" Hanneleen's mother caressed her hair. "Are you going to choose Andriaan?"

"Matilda, let her rest."

"But I need to know."

"Not now, Mum. I'll think about it."

"I need to know. Is it Andriaan?"

"Not now, Mum. Please!"

"Alright. Rest up but think about your university. Madagascar is lovely."

It was half-past eight in the morning, and the crowd had gathered at the government palace hall near the Ministry of Home Affairs. People settled into their seats, cameras flashing incessantly. Hanneleen's mother basked in the limelight, acting as though she were the reason for the assembly. Hanneleen's father sat, as usual, rubbing his chin.

"Thank you! Thank you!" Hanneleen's mother kept saying. "You're all so welcome."

"Who do you think your daughter will choose?" a reporter asked.

"Who else but Andriaan?" she confidently replied.

All eyes turned towards the main entrance. Gladness pushing Hanneleen's wheelchair, accompanied by Catherine. They wore trousers with zebra patterns, while Hanneleen wore black.

In Namibia, Lala and her family watched the event on TV. Grandma Eliza didn't want anyone move, she yelled at Ima when she slammed the door.

In her calm voice, Hanneleen began to speak...

"Andriaan," she said, "has consistently proven himself. His experience speaks volumes; his talent is undeniable. While we share a homeland and deep connections, Lala possesses a passion and fire that transcends mere experience. Despite fewer accolades, her triumph in Namibia speaks volumes. Her near victory in the African Gospel Contest underscores her potential to rise. I'm sorry, Andriaan, but for Africa's greater good, I choose Lala."

Andriaan felt his mother's grip tighten on his arm, her acrylic nails pressing into his skin as she steered him towards the exit. She glanced at her husband, whose expression remained inscrutable, before catching the gaze of Hanneleen's mother. She had expected her son to be chosen but hadn't anticipated this outcome.

A day after this special announcement, the doorbell rang, jolting Lisa from her thoughts as she hurried to answer it. She peeked through the peephole and saw Mukenani and Tiwe standing outside.

"Mukenani, Tiwe, it's so good to see you!" Lisa said, stepping aside to welcome them in.

"Lisa!" Mukenani greeted warmly, her vitiligo creating an artistic pattern on her skin.

"How have you been?" Tiwe asked.

"I've been good, just keeping busy." Lisa led them to the living room. "But enough about me, how are you two doing? How's work at the law firm?"

Mukenani's eyes sparkled with pride. "It's going really well, Lisa. We've been handling major cases, and the firm is thriving."

"Yes, we've even secured high-profile clients, including government officials," Tiwe added.

Lala and Grandma Eliza took their seats, and Tiwe turned to Lala. "We've watched every one of your performances, both here and in Tanzania. We're here to cheer you on in Germany."

"Thank you, Aunt Tiwe," said Lala.

The next morning, the sun's rays gently touched Lala's face as she woke up. The upcoming competition, a platform where dreams could come true, occupied her thoughts. She imagined confidently standing before a crowd of cheering fans, feeling their love and encouragement. However, beneath her excitement, a hint of anxiety fluttered. The pressure of what was to come weighed on her. This competition was not just any ordinary occasion; it had the potential to change lives.

Lala sprang out of bed and went to her mother's room, where Lisa lay reading a novel. Lala bounded onto the bed beside her mother. The mattress dipped under her weight, causing the blankets to ripple. Lisa looked up from her book...

"I'm so proud of you," Lisa said. "Travelling to Germany means you're representing all of Africa, which is a huge accomplishment. No matter what happens, your adventure will be remembered by everyone in Africa."

"Tell me, Mother," Lala said, "tell me more about Vivaan's mother."

"Anita? She was beautiful, kind, and everyone liked her a lot."

"How did you meet her, Mother?"

"After my first husband passed away," Lisa said.

"You mean Uncle Sanana and Nadia's dad?"

"Yes," she said with a heavy heart, "things became difficult when his older brother changed the will and left me with nothing at all. The villagers provided little help and insisted that I marry my late husband's brother. I agreed to the marriage, but then my husband's first wife suddenly appeared, causing a major dispute over my rightful inheritance. I was unfairly imprisoned but Sanana and others who believed in my innocence uncovered the truth. Justice prevailed, and I regained what was rightfully mine. I taught at Sunpride for five years before returning to South Bauleni, where I met your father. Through him, I met Anita, Vivaan's mother, and we became good friends."

"No wonder Grandma Eliza said Vivaan and I share a birthday."

"Exactly, sweetie. We gave birth in the same government hospital. It was such a joyous day. Your grandma made clothes and brought toys for both of you. We decided to enter a national gospel contest two years after you were born. We didn't make it past the regional audition. But four years ago, we tried again. We made it to the finals together, and when she won, I was happy for her but also a bit sad because no one likes to be second."

"Mother," Lala said, "what happened at the African contest?"

"She made it to the semi-finals but collapsed on stage and had to be taken to the hospital. Sadly, she passed away two hours later."

"I'm sorry, Mother."

"She's in a better place now."

"So, does that mean Vivaan's mother didn't lose?"

"If it wasn't for that tragic incident, she might have won."

"I'll win for Aunt Anita as well."

"I believe in you. You're my daughter. Now go wash up and meet me in the kitchen. I'll make your favourite soup."

Lala went to the bathroom, singing along the way. Lisa glanced at the time - 06:32. She checked on her visitors. Mukenani was awake but still in bed, reading a magazine. Lisa continued to make her rounds; another surprise awaited at the door. Ima arrived accompanied by Miss O'Hara, Sophia, and Raven.

"We should celebrate," Sophia said as she entered the room.

"No need to cook," Raven added. "Sophia is taking us out."

"No," Mukenani and Tiwe said together, "we're all cooking."

The smell of eggs cooking and Lala's singing voice as she watched the TV made the morning beautiful. Lisa cracked eggs into a bowl, singing along with Lala. Grandma Eliza's voice added to the music, blending in perfectly. The kitchen was filled with cheerful noise, covering up Vivaan's quiet entrance, who sat next to Sophia.

"Hey, everyone," Vivaan said, getting their attention as he took out a memory stick. "I've got videos and pictures of Lala's opponents. Let's go to the living room and check it out."

They all followed Vivaan to the living room, sitting on the sofa as he plugged in the memory stick. The screen lit up...

"Ingrid, right?" Lala asked, pointing on the screen as she learned more about her rivals. "She's from South America, country Suriname."

"Exactly," said Vivaan. "My sources say that both her parents are in the music industry. Ingrid's mother is a music producer, and her father is a recording engineer. She grew up in a musical home and attended the best music school in America. The whole continent is betting on her."

"Go on," Grandma Eliza said, sitting next to Mrs O'Hara.

"Canada, North America, Luciana. She can reach a five-octave vocal range with one note and seven octaves. She grew up in a small village in Harrison Hot Springs, east of Vancouver. Her parents are regular people. Until recently, no one even knew they existed.

"Asia has its own star, Hanah, from the Maldives. She has a unique vocal range and soulful tones. Everyone is talking about her. She comes from a wealthy family and is well-known in the music industry. Her father is a tour manager, and her mother is a session musician. They've both done well for themselves."

"She sings well," said Ima.

"Did she hit that note? Who is that boy?" Grandma Eliza asked.

"That's Drew from Sydney, Australia," Vivaan continued. "Drew has an impressive vocal range of ten octaves. He can successfully and peacefully hit the lowest note, G-7, and even playfully. His father is a music professor, and his mother is a housewife. Drew is currently studying music and is in his final year.

"There's also Alexei, Europe's own Russian. He has a rare high tenor and high pitch, covering four octaves. Alexei's mother is a music publicist, and his father worked as a composer. He has composed some of the best music for many famous singers worldwide."

"Great job, little man. Great work," said Raven.

"I'm just doing my job," he replied as he turned off the TV.

"Where did you get this information?" Lisa asked.

"Information like this is everywhere on the internet. These days, we can find and read everything we want."

"It's very important information for Lala," Mukenani said. "She needs to know who she's dealing with."

"Do you think so, Aunt Mu?"

"Yes, sweetheart," Mukenani replied. "Information is power."

"That's right," Mrs O'Hara said. "We all support you and are with you every step of the way. They may have fancy teachers, connections, and experience, but you, my child, have talent and a loving family. They can bring all their fancy musical instruments to the stage, but you will only bring your voice and win because you're amazing."

"Thank you, Grandma Margaret. People can come from beautiful cities and go to beautiful schools. When this is done, all they will talk about is me."

"One more thing," Vivaan said, "Tomorrow we start with basic music lessons with Mr Setiawan."

Lala, Vivaan, and Mr Setiawan sat around the keyboard. The teacher demonstrated musical techniques to them.

"To have a successful music career, you must know your notes. The letters A, B, C, D, E, F, and G are crucial. The note in the middle of the octave is middle-C, always marked with a ledger line. On the piano, this is middle C."

Using his right thumb, Mr Setiawan pressed the white key to the left of the two black keys in the middle of the piano keyboard.

"What does a ledger line mean, teacher?" Lala asked.

"It is a line above or below the regular musical staves. Now, Vivaan, press middle-C."

Vivaan pressed middle-C with his right thumb, followed by the next four notes. "I know that tune," Lala said. "Do-re-mi-fa...."

"Exactly," Mr Setiawan said. "Do is middle-C. Now, start on C and count eight notes."

Vivaan pressed middle-C and counted the letters C, D, E, F, G, H, I, and J.

"No, no, no," Mr Setiawan said. "Music notes are represented by the letters A-G. After that, you start again from A."

Vivaan played the keyboard melody while counting the letters C, D, E, F, G, A, B, and C.

"Lala will sing along with the piano," Mr Setiawan said.

Do-re-mi-fa-so-la-ti-do.

"Women sing notes on the treble clef, which are higher-pitched notes. On the keyboard, you play them with your right hand. The bass clef is for men and has a lower pitch, usually played with the left hand. White keys represent sharps, denoted by the symbol # after a note when written. Flat notes are indicated by the letter *b* and are played on black keys."

"This is pretty easy!" said Vivaan.

"Remember, timing and notes are important," said Ima, entering the room. Each note tells you how many counts it gets: a whole note is four beats, a half note is two beats, and a quarter note is one beat."

"Eighth, sixteenth, thirty-second, sixty-second," Mr Setiawan continued.

A Chance to Go to Germany

On Monday at school, it was assembly day. The kids liked assembly, especially when the principal wasn't mad at everyone. They enjoyed the choir and announcements that made them happy. Mr Setiawan was chosen to make the announcement.

"I'll get right to it," he said. "Lala Ndafenongo, please come up. Choir, please."

Lala stood next to Mr Setiawan, who continued to say that Lala deserved all the good things coming her way. Huge Lilian, Victoria, and Beth could sense what would happen. From the frowns on their faces, they didn't like it. They knew this day would come.

"I have some good news," said Mr Setiawan. "You all should know our very own Lala is going to Germany."

"I knew it," said Huge Lilian, sounding upset. "Why her?"

"I have more good news," said Mr Setiawan. "Twenty of our learners will go with Lala to Europe. It could be you."

With this announcement, Huge Lilian and the other learners who hadn't previously shown interest suddenly perked up.

"Now tell me," said Mr Setiawan, "isn't that good news? Well, it is! Unfortunately, it's only good news for twenty of you. The list of learners going with Lala will be posted on the notice board next Monday. It's a once-in-a-lifetime opportunity. You'll get a free trip to Germany and watch the live show from start to finish."

Immediately after assembly, The Girls convened. Even though it was difficult to accept, Huge Lilian suggested they should do whatever it takes to befriend Lala.

"I can't do that," Victoria protested.

"Do you want to go to Germany?" Beth asked.

"I want to go, but I don't want to embarrass myself in front of that singer."

"That singer is our only chance for the trip of a lifetime!"

"What's so special about Germany?" Victoria asked. "When I grow up, I'll have money and travel everywhere."

"Don't say that Victoria," Beth said. "Don't ruin this for us because I'll never forgive you."

"Do you think that singer will choose you?" Victoria said. "Stop wasting your time. Lala won't choose us."

"I have to go to Germany, and Lala will choose me," Huge Lilian declared.

In the principal's office, Mr Setiawan, Ima, and Lala discussed how the group of learners accompanying her to Germany would be selected. The school management could make the selection, or Lala herself could choose from any student in the school. The idea of selecting her companions herself made Lala smile.

"What do you think, Mr Setiawan?" Lisa asked.

"The golden girl deserves the opportunity. After all, she is the reason we can go on the trip," Mr Setiawan replied.

"Mr Setiawan is right," Ima added. "We leave everything to Lala."

"Well then," the principal said, "but before that, honey, what do you think?"

"I will choose all my friends?" Lala wondered aloud.

"Choose wisely because these learners will go with you to Germany and support you the most. Think of them as your cheerleaders. I recommend selecting the noisemakers. Noisemaker, and empty vessels," Lisa smiled.

"What do you mean by 'the empty vessels,' Mother?" Lala asked.

"Choose those who don't care about what others think. You know what they say, an empty vessel makes the loudest noise."

As Lala was about to return to class, she met Huge Lilian and Beth. Victoria watched from a distance, refusing to engage in such humiliation.

"Lala!" said Huge Lilian with a big smile as she approached her. "Do we have a chance?"

"Yeah, Lala," added Beth. "Do we stand a chance?"

Huge Lilian stared at Lala, unblinking, needing an immediate answer.

"Please, Lala," said Beth. "I've never been to Germany. God will bless you if you choose us."

"Yes," said Huge Lilian. "Say something, please."

From afar, Victoria watched as Lala again became the centre of everyone's attention, feeling greatly annoyed. It bothered her to see others desperately seeking Lala's approval, mainly when she was used to being in the spotlight and having her desires prioritised.

Just as Lala was about to answer their plea, she saw Mr Setiawan and Ima coming. She shifted her focus and went towards her class. Lala couldn't help but boast about her newfound sense of authority in class.

"I was on fire today," Lala said to Pulelo and Vivaan. "Huge Lilian and others were begging me."

"Hold on there, Lala," said Pulelo. "You won't choose Beth, Victoria, Patricia, or Evia."

"Don't worry, Pulelo," said Lala. "Why would I choose those mean girls?" She covered her mouth to hide a soft chuckle.

"We'll help you make the list," said Vivaan. "Pulelo and I are already on it."

"We're best friends, so we'll make the list together," said Lala, sinking into her chair.

"I'm thinking," said Vivaan, "we should choose one to make the others jealous. They'll end up hating each other."

"We can't do that," Pulelo said. "We will pick from our own class."

"That will not be fair. We should pick from the whole school," said Vivaan.

"How?" Lala asked. "How do you do that? We only need eighteen."

"Eighteen?" Pulelo asked.

"Yes, eighteen, Pulelo. You and Vivaan make twenty."

"Whatever you do, don't make a mistake with Victoria and her friends," said Pulelo. "Write Veronica's name and our class captain."

"Our class captain is so quiet. We must pick noisemakers. Maybe Veronica and Ester."

"Alright, we are four now," said Pulelo.

Vivaan tapped his incisor with a pencil. He was going through his own list. Pulelo seemed to be working harder than her friends.

"Peter and Liswaniso. They're cool, and we go to Sunday school together."

Lala broke out from her thoughts and added them to the list. When she was done, Pulelo thought of Vincent and Charlie.

"You have added enough," said Lala.

"Two more," she said. "Marita and Belinda."

"Who is Belinda?" Lala asked.

"The netball team member," said Pulelo. "She's cool and not like the rest of them."

"That will be the last from your side, Pulelo," said Lala. "Vivaan and I will choose the rest."

Thursday had arrived, accompanied by the rain showers of the season. Lala waited for her friends on the bench near the parking area, listening to the latest popular gospel music from Nigeria. Meanwhile, Huge Lilian, Victoria, and Beth leaned against the school minivan, their interaction limited as Victoria attempted to persuade the others to ignore Lala.

"Why should we apologise to that singer?" Victoria asked.

"Who do you think you are?" said Huge Lilian.

"I'm not talking to you, Lilian," Victoria protested, moving a few steps away to lean on the opposite side of the car.

"What are we waiting for?" Huge Lilian asked, locking eyes with Beth. "Are we going now?"

Beth glanced down at her shoes, then over at Victoria, who avoided making eye contact. Victoria stood nearby with crossed arms, kicking the front wheel of a car. On the other side, Lala had her earphone on, seemingly oblivious to their presence despite Huge Lilian and Beth standing right in front of her.

"Good morning," Huge Lilian said.

"Lala, we're saying hello!" Beth said.

"We all want to go!" Huge Lilian said.

Lala grabbed her bag and met Vivaan at the school gate. Victoria began laughing at her friends.

After school, Huge Lilian searched for Lala with Pulelo, who had just exited the library. Vivaan had already gone home.

"Lala," Huge Lilian shouted, slightly out of breath from walking quickly.

"Just leave us alone. You're not going to Germany, neither are your friends," Pulelo said.

"Please, Lala, think about adding me to the list."

Learners gathered around the notice board during break time, particularly Huge Lilian. She had gone to great lengths to secure a spot, from discussing with school management to seeking help from staff, but to no avail. She tried to remain composed as she stood near the notice board, but the list had yet to be posted. Beth, Victoria, and Patricia rushed over from the back of the classroom.

"Victoria," Beth asked for the fourth time, "do you think we'll be on the list?"

"You won't be on the list," Victoria replied.

"It's your fault she doesn't like us. I told you to be nice to her."

Beth rubbed her chin, trying to recall something important. "Where's Huge Lilian?"

Huge Lilian stood next to the notice board, growing increasingly impatient. "What's taking her so long?" Huge Lilian muttered.

"Do you think we'll be on the list?" Patricia asked, adjusting her sash.

"I'm starting to dislike this girl more and more," Huge Lilian grumbled, kicking the wall with her sneakers. "Where is she?"

"But she said Monday," Beth said. "Isn't today Monday? Or which Monday?"

Lala, Pulelo, and Vivaan came from the other end of the corridor...

"It wasn't me, Pulelo, it was Vivaan who included The Girls on the list," Lala said.

When Lala arrived, everyone gathered around her as she affixed the list to the board. Beth traced her finger down the list, starting from the top and scanning to the bottom. She found herself at number nineteen. She screamed with delight. Patricia was also on the list.

"Let me through!" Huge Lilian said, pushing her way past everyone.

"I'm going to Germany!" A few learners began to celebrate. Beth and Patricia were elated, but Victoria grabbed them from behind.

"Are you on the list, Beth?" Victoria asked.

"Yes, Victoria. Both Patricia and I are," Beth replied.

"And me?"

"I don't know. The list is still on the board."

Huge Lilian hugged nearly everyone, Lala, Vivaan, and Pulelo, though Pulelo did not hug back.

"Thank you, Lala," Huge Lilian said. "You're so kind."

A short while later, Huge Lilian, Beth, Victoria, and Patricia sat at the netball field, enjoying their food.

"Did you notice something about the list?" Huge Lilian asked.

"It ended at nineteen."

"Yes, Huge Lilian," Patricia replied. "One person is missing."

"Well," Victoria stated, "I don't care about that. What matters most is that I'm on the list."

"But why? Mr Setiawan said she would choose twenty," Patricia said.

"I never thought that girl would put us on the list. She's a good girl," Beth said.

"I have to tell Mum about this," said Huge Lilian. "She'll be so happy, and then we can go shopping today!"

Later that afternoon, Huge Lilian was feeding her baby brother with a bottle in the living room. Her four younger siblings, who were all as small as her, were watching TV. Huge Lilian appeared to be the oldest and the only girl among them. Their parents, both short in stature, came from their bedroom. The woman was rubbing her belly.

Huge Lilian stood up abruptly. "Not again, Mum!"

"Yes, my sweet darling, this time you'll have a sister," her mother replied.

"The more of us there are, the better chances we have in life," her father said, dressed in a formal black suit and owning a dairy product company.

"But, Mum," Huge Lilian protested, "this is enough."

"You'll thank me one day, and besides, we still want a sister for you," her mother said. "Now, did you make the list?"

"I'm going to Germany."

"Your father and I will take you shopping tomorrow after school," she said, looking up at her husband, who nodded in agreement.

In South Bauleni, Grandma Eliza was preparing dinner while Lala helped her chop tomatoes. She pulled back the curtain and glanced out the window. Francesca was standing at her door, holding a magazine.

"She is always in a bad mood," Grandma Eliza said.

"I have something for her," Lala said, skipping to her room to meet Francesca. Francesca nearly slammed the door in Lala's face.

"Do you want to go to Germany? I have a spot for you," Lala said.

"Germany? What for, girl?" Francesca asked.

"Don't you know what's happening? I'm going to sing for Africa."

"But you lost to that White girl."

"Yes, I did, but she chose me after her accident. Do you want me to include your name on the list?"

"You are so lucky."

"Yes, and you are too."

From inside the house, Francesca's mother appeared. She bore a striking resemblance to her daughter, with dreadlocks and a nice car despite having no formal job.

"I have a ticket to Germany. Can I go?" Francesca asked.

"You're nineteen, Bettina! Can't you make your own decisions?" her mother gasped.

"I'm not Bettina."

"Yes, you are!" Her mother's tone was filled with anger. "Do you think I don't know that your silly, good-for-nothing fugitive of a father named you after his lover?" She slammed the door.

"Who will pay for it? Germany is very far," Francesca asked Lala.

"Even Grandma is going."

"Your grandma, too?"

"Yes, and my mother, Aunt Ima, my friend Vivaan, Pulelo, and other learners from my school. Grandma Margaret, Aunt Mu, Tiwe, Raven, and Aunt Sophia are all going."

"I see a lot of white people in your house these days. Is the old one you called Grandma Margaret?"

"Yes, she was my mother's teacher when she was little."

"Why me? I'm not from your school."

"You're my neighbour, Francesca."

The next day at school, the principal gathered everyone on Lala's list in the school hall. She discussed what they needed and how the learners should behave in Germany. Huge Lilian kept smiling and nodding at everything the principal said as if she were a grown-up. She raised her hand and got a chance to ask a question.

"The list only has nineteen people. It should be twenty."

"Yes, Lilian, and it will be twenty."

"Who's the other person?" Beth asked.

"A friend of mine," Lala said.

Lala sat between Vivaan and Pulelo. They remained seated when everyone else left.

"Now that we're alone," Lisa said. "Who's number 20?"

"She's not from our school. She's a friend, Mother."

"I need the name, young lady."

"Francesca, our neighbour."

"Why Francesca? When did you become friends?"

"I just wanted to add her to the list, that's all."

"Well, you're the boss."

World Continental Gospel Contest

The World Continental Gospel Contest took place at Hamburg's Elbphilharmonie concert hall in Germany. Each section of the audience waved banners in support of their favourite contestants, blowing out their noise makers. Fireworks ruptured in the heavens...

The hosts, Wilson and Q, changed outfits as if it was a fashion show. The panel of five judges, each from diverse backgrounds, presided over the competition.

"Hello, everyone from around the globe! I'm Wilson, your host for tonight."

"And I'm Q, joining Wilson as your co-host," added Q, whose strong German accent was evident.

The audience erupted in cheers for the hosts, prompting Grandma Eliza, who was visiting Germany for the first time, to comment on the unusual names.

"Q, is that a real name?" Grandma Eliza asked Mrs O'Hara.

"I believe so," replied Mrs O'Hara.

"But it's just a letter!"

"Here in Germany, it's a name, Grandma Eliza," said Vivaan.

The South Bauleni learners and Francesca, all dressed in red attire sat together. Hanneleen, Pulelo, and Vivaan were also part of this enthusiastic group, enjoying the spectacle of the event. Ima, Mr Setiawan, Sophia, Raven, Tiwe, and Mukenani sat behind the learners.

"Hello, everyone from across the globe!" said Wilson.

The six contestants made their entrance. After a brief introduction, they went backstage to prepare for their performances.

"The theme for this year is 'Celebrating God through gospel music,'" announced Q.

"Yes," added Wilson. "The contestants will compete for a spot in the quarterfinals, with only four moving on to the semifinals. Which continent will claim the crown this year? Will it be Africa, Asia, North America, South America, Europe, or Australia?"

"May the best continent emerge victorious," said Q. "Representing Africa, we have the amazing Lala."

The crowd erupted as Lala, dressed in traditional African attire, sauntered to the microphone. African spectators cheered with drums and whistles, rallying behind her.

"Will this year be Africa's year? We shall see," Wilson said. "Judges, over to you."

"How old are you?" A judge asked.

"I am thirteen," replied Lala.

"Which country do you come from?" another judge asked.

"I'm from Namibia, representing Africa," Lala confidently responded.

"Good luck to Africa!"

A moment of silence followed. Lala stood still on the stage, drawing concern from her supporters, especially her family. Lala's father made an entrance into the arena, prompting a smile from her as if she was waiting for him.

"This is for you, Hanneleen. This is for you, Africa."

She blew a kiss to Hanneleen, who raised a peace sign. Lala began her song, captivating the audience with every note. The spotlight occasionally picking on Hanneleen, Lisa, Jonathan, Vivaan, and the other learners, even drawing the judges into the mesmerizing performance. Mukenani and the others danced joyfully to the rhythm.

Next, Hanah, the crowd's favourite, took the stage. She was dressed in black trousers, the young Maldivian declared her passion for music. An orchestra accompanied her, conducted by an enthusiastic choirmaster. Following Hanah, Luciana and Alexei performed, wrapping up their sets by midnight.

It was morning when the first round ended. In their shared suite, Grandma Eliza gathered everyone for a heartfelt reflection, showering Lala with affection. Hanneleen, Catherine, and Gladness joined the gathering, while the schoolchildren where in their room.

"What an incredible night!" Grandma Eliza said. "My granddaughter owned that stage. She's Africa's finest, without a doubt. Every note she sang was earned."

Hanneleen set her cup down, giving Catherine a stern look to signal her to push her back to her room. Lala stood to follow Hanneleen, but Vivaan pulled her back. It was evident to everyone that Hanneleen was upset because Grandma Eliza's speech hadn't gone as planned.

"Did you put alcohol in your milk?" Lisa asked Grandma Eliza, who sat next to Pulelo, Vivaan, and Francesca.

"Why?" Grandma Eliza asked.

"You talk too much, Mother," said Lisa. "This is meant to be a celebration, not a competition. You hurt that little girl's feelings."

"During celebrations, people sometimes say things they don't mean," Grandma Eliza responded calmly.

"Oh, Mother, you're getting old!" said Lisa. "Can we go to bed now?"

"That's a good idea," said Ima. "Lala needs some rest."

After everyone left, Mukenani and their friends decided to visit the hotel bar. Meanwhile, in another suite, Hanneleen's parents were preparing for bed when their daughter and the twins entered.

"The day wasn't so bad," said Hanneleen's mother. "Our daughter made the right choice by choosing that little girl. She'll go far in this competition."

"I shouldn't have chosen her," murmured Hanneleen. "That family doesn't appreciate anything."

"Tell me why you feel that way."

"I may be in a wheelchair, but my voice is still ok. I should have been the one on that stage. Why did this have to happen to me?"

"You're still young, honey. Next year is just around the corner."

"Oh, Mother, singing on that stage isn't a choice. Take me to bed, Catherine."

Once out of earshot, Hanneleen's mother turned to Gladness for an explanation.

"It was that old lady," Catherine said. "She claimed her granddaughter is the best singer in the world."

The clock had struck six in the morning. Huge Lilian was already dressed in the learners' room. Patricia was getting ready while Victoria sat across from her on a chair. Victoria gazed at Huge Lilian, who looked stunning in her new outfit.

"You brought your jealousy to Germany," Huge Lilian said to Victoria.

"I never wanted to come here. I never asked to," Victoria said.

"I know you're many things, but ungrateful shouldn't be one of them."

"I'm not ungrateful," Victoria said. "Must I like her?"

"It's time for you to be quiet," Huge Lilian said. "Out of all the learners at South Bauleni, she chose us, even though we're not always nice to her. She chose you."

"You should try to love her," Beth said.

"Yes, Victoria," added Patricia. "Lala is a good girl with talent. We should all pray for her."

"I'll try, I can't help it."

By ten in the morning, everyone was enjoying breakfast, unaware that Francesca was still asleep. As she walked from her room, yawning, Grandma Eliza prepared to say something, but Lisa nudged her arm. Ima made space for Francesca at the table. After breakfast, Lala went to look for Hanneleen in her room, where Hanneleen and Catherine were watching a rerun of the show.

"I apologise for my grandmother's words," Lala said to Hanneleen.

"I've already moved past it. Let's focus on the competition. It's tough, but we can handle it. Today, you're making history. Tonight, is your big night. The whole world will know you from now on," Hanneleen said.

"I'm sorry I took your place. It should have been you."

"We shouldn't question God's plans. We must trust in Him. He has other plans for me too. You didn't steal my spotlight. God gave it to you and will take care of you during the best time of your life. Promise me you'll do your best!"

"I promise, Hanneleen."

"Hanah sings well," said Gladness.

"Ignore Gladness. Come on, let's explore this fancy hotel."

"I'm nervous, Hanneleen. The first elimination round is tonight."

"Don't worry, you won't be the first one out. You'll make it all the way to the end."

"No one from Africa has ever advanced to the next round," said Gladness.

"That was in the past. Lala will win."

The contestants lined up on the stage, with Lala in the middle, the youngest among them. Each wore a white T-shirt bearing their continent's map on the front. An Asian man in the audience said, "We all know who will go first."

"Don't be so certain, Lee," his wife responded.

Grandma Eliza, seated behind them, overheard their conversation, noticing their son making a mess with popcorn, scattering it everywhere.

"Stop it, little Lee," his mother scolded. "You're wasting food while children in Africa go hungry."

"Shut up, woman!" Grandma Eliza snapped. "Have you ever been to Africa?"

"Why?"

"You've never been to Africa, yet you claim children there are hungry!"

"Everyone knows Africa is a poor continent, and people there are hungry. Do I need to go there to know that you guys eat wild berries?"

"Leave them, mother," said Lisa.

Grandma Eliza turned her attention back to her granddaughter on stage. Lala could feel her strength waning. She thought about Victoria, Beth, and Huge Lilian. What would they say? She also thought about Hanneleen, who would be so disappointed. And what about her family, country, continent, and everyone who prayed for her?

"It's the first round of eliminations for the competition," said Q. "First up, North America."

Luciana returned to the stage amidst cheers from the crowd as she bid farewell. Lala dropped to her knees, taking a deep breath.

"Now, for the first performance of the night," said Q. "South America."

The show continued. The following day saw Drew from Sydney eliminated in the quarterfinals, and South America followed suit in the semifinals. Lala, Alexei, and Hanah went on to the finals. The African section of the audience filled half the Arena, wearing T-shirts featuring

Lala. During Lala's final performance, a solo wind instrument played a high note. The crowd joined in, singing along as lyrics flashed on the screen. Huge Lilian danced, and even Beth and Victoria cheered for Lala, who was adored by the audience.

Hanah performed like a professional, followed by Alexei who took the stage with a song similar to a love ballad, strumming a nylon-string guitar.

"Ladies and gentlemen, this is the moment," announced host Wilson. "Now it's time for the world to vote."

"Could this be Africa's moment?" asked Q. "Africa, you can make it happen. Vote now."

"What are the judges' thoughts?" Wilson asked.

"Let the world decide," answered one of the judges.

After the show, in the hotel suite, Lala and her family discussed the competition when Hanneleen and her friends entered. Hanneleen embraced Lala warmly.

"I'm scared," Lala said, placing her hands on Hanneleen's wheelchair.

"I'm scared too. We all are," Hanneleen said, gently squeezing Lala's cheeks. "You know what, win or lose, I'm glad I chose you."

Francesca, Huge Lilian, Beth, Victoria, and Patricia gathered around Lala. "We all want you to win," Huge Lilian said.

"Yes, Lala," Francesca added, "thank you for this opportunity."

"We all love you so much," Victoria said, embracing Lala as the rest joined in.

As the sun set, the three finalists took their places on stage.

"Hello, everyone," announced Q.

"The moment of truth is here," declared Wilson. "The top two, in no particular order, are..."

The audience fell silent, the suspense....

"Hannah," Q shouted.

Hannah dropped to her knees, hands raised in silent prayer, while Asian supporters cheered.

"Lala!"

Applause, especially from the African section, thundered through the Arena. Grandma Eliza let out a loud whistle. Sadly, it was the end of the road for Alexei, who bowed gracefully before leaving the stage.

After a brief performance by last year's winner, the two finalists stood before the audience.

"And now, ladies and gentlemen, the winner of the 2013 World Continental Gospel Contest," announced Wilson.

Hannah and Lala held hands, hearts racing, tears welling in their eyes, stomachs knotted with tension. At that moment, Lala's dream could become reality, yet Hannah was a gifted singer with a strong following. The judges exchanged knowing glances, their expressions inscrutable.

"The winner of the 2013 World Continental Gospel Contest is..." Wilson repeated, holding a sealed envelope in his hands.

The noise in the Arena crescendoed as the crowd chanted Hannah's name. Grandma Eliza and her family held their breath.

"Now is the time to reveal our winner," Wilson announced again.

"Just say it already," said Lisa.

"Cue the music," Wilson instructed.

Grandma Eliza and Lala's team held hands. Other fans continued to drum fervently. The winner's name lay sealed within the envelope—a secret known only to the envelope itself and those who prepared it.

"Africa!" Wilson shouted and danced around.

The spotlight shifted to Lala, who was then on her knees. Applause thundered through the Arena.

From that moment, Lala became more than a winner. She became the standard, the blueprint. Hannah embraced Lala warmly...

"Congratulations!" said Hannah.

"Thank you, Hannah."

Lala stepped into the spotlight, holding her trophy aloft as confetti rained down from above. The music swelled—The World Continental Gospel Contest winner, celebrated by applause, her name echoing throughout the Arena and across every television screen.

"As per the competition rules, Asia and Africa will perform their winning songs with their finalists," announced Q. "Asia will perform first."

Asia took the stage, the entire audience joining in for a beautiful performance. When Africa followed, Lala, Bassel, Latifah, Gatimu, and Andriaan had a blast. Lala invited Hanneleen to join them on stage, and together they sang.

"Until next year," said host Wilson. "And a big thank you to the A-continents."

"Thank you, Europe. Thank you, Oceania, North America, and South America, and thank you to everyone. Goodnight!"

APPLAUSE, CHEERS, AND TEARS FILLED THE ARENA.

Laughter and Memories

It has been a week since they returned from Germany. Grandma Eliza and Grandma Margaret sat together by the kitchen window, basking in the sun. Grandma Eliza, in a heavy sweater, occasionally glanced towards the neighbour's door. Inside the kitchen, Lisa noticed her mother's restlessness through the window and shook her head. Grandma Eliza stood up upon hearing footsteps from the neighbour's house, then sat back down, only to rise again when the door finally opened.

"Good morning, Ester!"

Francesca's mother never acknowledged Grandma Eliza as she escorted her new man to the taxi rank. Lisa, through the window laughed, "That woman will insult you one day, Mother."

Meanwhile, Mukenani and Tiwe were still in bed while Raven and Sophia had already left for their morning jog. Lisa was cutting vegetables when her husband sneaked up behind her and playfully tickled her neck. She wore casual blue shorts and a white top. Just then, a visibly excited Lala came from her room. "Mother," she panted, "Hanneleen and her parents are coming to visit!"

"That's great news, honey," Jonathan said.

"Thank you, Father," Lala said before darting back into her room.

"I have three weeks off," Lisa's husband said.

"With your daughter's money, we could start a business here in South Bauleni."

A few days later, Lala, Vivaan, Pulelo, Francesca, and Hanneleen sat together on the porch, flipping through photos on Hanneleen's phone and sharing laughs.

"Remember Hanah?" Hanneleen said. "She had such a beautiful voice."

Hanneleen's younger sister, sipping on Coke, stood behind them and draped her arms over their shoulders. "I've got four sisters and a brother," she said. "Next year, I'm entering the contest and will win it."

Hanneleen smirked at her sister, knowing well she was a lousy singer. "You can't sing," Hanneleen bluntly stated.

"I'll learn."

"If you can't sing, you can't sing—no matter how much you learn."

Lala was about to interject when her attention shifted to Hanneleen's charming little white dog trotting out of the house, tail wagging and ears perked up. "Is that your dog?" Lala asked.

"Oh, you mean Chikito? She's so well-behaved. I can't imagine my life without her," Hanneleen said. "Catherine has Star, a playful golden retriever, and Gladness has Moon, a mischievous black cat."

"Do you take them to school?" Pulelo asked.

"No way! The last time Gladness brought Moon to school; Mr Patrick tossed him into the bin."

"He must be quite mean," Lala commented.

"Yeah, he's a real piece of work. We're not fans of him," Gladness added.

"Well, my teachers here are nice. My favourite is my aunt, and Mr Setiawan is incredibly kind," Lala said.

In the house, Grandma Eliza, Grandma Margaret, Grandpa Sylvester, Eva, Hanneleen's parents, Catherine, and Gladness gathered in front of the television. Grandma Eliza poured milk into all the cups, took a long sip, then refilled her own cup.

"Your daughter is something special," Grandma Eliza complimented Hanneleen's parents.

"Thank you," her father replied. "You have a wonderful granddaughter as well."

Mr Setiawan and Ima returned from shopping, laden with bags of groceries. Mukenani and the others sat under the mango tree, watching intently as Mr Setiawan knelt, taking out a ring from his pocket...

"Will you marry me?"

Before Ima could respond, Mukenani, Tiwe, Raven, and Sophia enthusiastically replied on her behalf.

"When's the wedding?" Mukenani eagerly asked.

Before Ima could say anything, Grandma Eliza called out from the window, gathering everyone's attention for an important announcement. The family convened around the brand-new dining table...

"Thank you all so much," Lisa began. "This year has been a testament to our hard work and the blessings we've received. I am grateful for my new family, and I hope Hanneleen gets better soon. It means a lot that all of you travelled here to celebrate with us. Your daughter saw something special in our daughter, and for that, we are grateful. My family has an important announcement to make to yours. Lala, sweetheart!"

Lala gave an envelope to Hanneleen. Catherine reached out for it, but Gladness playfully swatted her hand.

"That's for you, Hanneleen—35%," Lala said.

Hanneleen gazed at the cheque for seven million Namibian dollars, tears of joy threatening to spill. Catherine and Gladness crowded around her.

"But wait, Hanneleen," Lisa continued. "The recording studio here in our country has offered you the same contract as my daughter."

"What does that mean?" Catherine asked.

"It means she'll become a recording artist," Ima explained.

"I don't know what to say, Mr and Mrs Ndafenongo. I've always dreamed of recording my own songs," Hanneleen expressed gratefully.

"You deserve it, sweetheart," Grandma Margaret said.

"To my best friend Pulelo, once your book is ready, I'll help market it for you," said Lala.

Little Pulelo couldn't hold back her tears. "Thank you!"

"To my manager," Lala continued, "What can I do for you? I know you have all the money in the world."

"I have an idea," Vivaan said. "Give me a copy of your album—both yours and Hanneleen's. It could be a duet."

"Before we leave, Lala and I will unleash a single to the world," Hanneleen declared with a smile.

Ima couldn't stop smiling at Mr Setiawan. Lisa dropped her fork onto her plate and exchanged a knowing glance with her sister. "Go ahead, Ima," Lisa said. "Everyone can see your ring."

"Yes, yes, yes," Ima said. "Mr Setiawan and I are getting married."

"When did he propose? Do you really want to marry him? He is on a contract," Grandma Eliza said.

"I know, Mother, but I love him," Ima insisted.

"He's from Asia and very soon, he is going back there," Grandma Eliza said.

"I'm going with him."

"You're thinking like a child. Do you know how they'll treat you there? He'll call you a confused monkey from Savanna. Martha came back from Argentina after six months, depressed and crying. They didn't accept her there."

"Congratulations, Sister," Lisa said. "Mr Setiawan is a good man."

"Wait a minute," Grandma Eliza said to Mr Setiawan. "Let's talk about how many people in your family have been to prison."

"I don't understand," Mr Setiawan said.

"How many of them have been to prison?" she persisted.

"Just my uncle."

"And what about death?"

"What do you mean, Mother?" Ima asked.

"Do they die young?"

"Come on, Mother, we're living in modern times," Lisa said.

"That's even more reason for them to get to know each other."

Vivaan went to answer the door. Mrs Anushka had some excellent news for Pulelo—some publishers had agreed to publish her book.

"Thank you, Mrs Anushka," Pulelo said.

"You deserve it, sweetie," Mrs Anushka replied.

"I also have an announcement," Grandpa Sylvester said. "My old clock and I are getting married."

"This is ridiculous," someone said.

Don't miss out!

Visit the website below and you can sign up to receive emails whenever Tobias Nchindo publishes a new book. There's no charge and no obligation.

https://books2read.com/r/B-A-WSAMC-VVCAF

BOOKS 2 READ

Connecting independent readers to independent writers.